THE DEMON OF REGINHART
Penn Scripter

Unexpected Paranormal Romance

www.trollriverpub.com
The Demon of Reginhart
Copyright © 2021 Penn Scripter
ISBN: 978-1-946454-79-9
Editors: Ravindra Banthia
        Carol McKibben
        Stephanie McKibben
Cover Design: Julia Rohwedder of Julia R. Art

Table of Contents

Glossary

There are some words that are foreign and relate only to this book and therefore we have decided to put the glossary in the front to familiarize readers with these terms.

Black fire – Fire that burns black flames instead of orange or yellow.

Brightside – The human world.

Bright eye – The sun.

Dark Land – The Demon world.

Glacias - Element of ice.

Ignis – Element of fire.

No-eye-night – New moon.

Terra – Element of Earth

Ventus – Element of wind.

Weeling – Very young person/demon. Said as an insult to teenagers.

Prologue

HE ASKED, and the winds came. He asked, and the clouds came. He asked, and the rain came. Then he asked *them*, and *they* refused.

Hungry. Wet. Cold.

Furious, Asmara set on this new path and turned away from his people, the Serenite, ancestors that fell from the sky, and cursed by those they would conquer but failed to do so.

Once more, Asmara asked. And this time . . . a demon came.

Enslavement was not a crime to his people, and therefore he could not name the thing that took over him—*them*. But whether the thing that possessed him had a name or not, Asmara referred to the demon as "It."

But *It* didn't care. Asmara was not his own person anymore—not in mind, or flesh, or will. They were two minds in one body—Asmara and *It*.

The monster was inside him now, eating Asmara from within. Eating things for him. Eating *humans* despite him.

It shouted commands in Asmara's mind. *It* forced Asmara's body where it wanted. Both wrought destruction upon the land during their fight for control.

Asmara's desperation to regain his own motor functions back forced him to use an unknown power. He wielded a spell forming a contract made from blood, bone, skin, and a soul all its own.

This contract was a wall. But it was not supposed to be a living, breathing entity. It was supposed to be brick, stone, and protection against the demon.

The contract's name was Marcus. He was a combination of Asmara and . . . *It.*

Where two had been, now there was a third.

Marcus was alive, a being all his own. Three minds now congregated in one body. But there was a tentative peace.

Only peace had come too late.

Chapter 1

MARCUS WAS NOT the demon.

Yet he bore the claws of the one inside him. He kept his talons hidden in his greatcoat and his iridescent eyes concealed under the brim of his hat so that the people he passed would consider him human—if he did happen to pass anyone at this hour.

Despite his efforts, those in the palace had seen his not-so-human qualities. No one in Benicar had ever seen Tiecus, the demon inside him. Left up to Marcus, no one would.

To further complicate his life, he held another entity within the walls of his own body. A mage. A very salacious, pompous, and arrogant mage. Asmara would test the patience of a drunken monk. Therein resided the reason for Marcus's existence. Without Marcus in the middle, the demon and the mage could not coexist. They needed a buffer, a translator, a referee, and counselor. Together, Asmara the mage and Tiecus the demon had "made" him. Because *It* wasn't a viable name, he took half from both creators. "Mar" came from the mage, and "cus" from the demon forming a name that was as human as possible. Thus, "Marcus."

Oh, look how Marcus, the all-powerful demon keeper, runs to a human's every beck and call. Asmara tutted in thought. The mage's ridicule was in full force this evening.

Against the moonlit illumination, Marcus passed a three-story stone tower. The pillar stood in mockery of Asmara, who claimed it a place for only those who possessed true power.

"Are you still sore about a *magician* occupying the *mage* tower?" Marcus goaded.

Ardin is an undeserving hack. He's not a mage, not worth the light that shines on him.

Asmara went on about the differences between mages and magicians, but Marcus listened only partially. Passing the offending building, he walked toward the palace.

The late hour afforded amenity. Instead of crouching in the cramped space of the damp underground tunnels, Marcus could stand to his full six-foot-five-inch height above ground on the cobblestone roads. He despised traveling during daylight hours, when humans cluttered his path like too many dinner plates on a table made for three.

The demon inside came alive when the humans pressed up against Marcus, making him writhe and whisper thoughts that would break several agreements. Agreements made between him and the two personalities taking residence in Marcus's head.

Sometimes, he liked the demon's whispered thoughts, and that scared him most of all. Once a deed was justified, he couldn't count on his conscience as a measure.

He stayed away from humans the best he could. Thus, he slunk through organized rows of shops and past thatched-roof homes during human sleeping hours. People were safe from him in their beds. They were safe believing him a rumor, something with which to scare their younglings.

Are you even listening? Asmara's voice overpowered Marcus's brain.

"I'm not here to quibble about who has more right to own the tower." Marcus trudged past a set of trebuchets nestled by the inner castle walls. He begrudged their ingenuity; the tools were a reminder of his pact with a human. He'd made the choice by entering an agreement with the king of Benicar.

Humans were food, but they also wielded weapons like crossbows that could kill at a distance. Specifically, they could kill Marcus, a host that held both a demon and a mage inside of himself. He wasn't exactly sure if he was mortal, or what he was, but he didn't want to find out the hard way.

Oh yes, King Eric Valder called for you on "urgent matters." If Asmara were in the forefront, he'd be crossing his arms with his nose in the air. *I suppose that makes you feel important.*

Marcus shook his head. "I *am* important." It wasn't bravado, only fact, in his case. He cut his conversation short with Asmara after passing the tower and carried on to the high arched hallway of Benicar Castle. Making haste between marble pillars, he identified each immobile guard by scent. He didn't know the names of all the Blackened Elite, but he knew their fighting style. Marcus also knew their alpha—or was Cornelius their beta? Humans had too many confusing classifications to remember.

Would you say there were as many demon types as human titles? The mage thought he was funny. He was not.

Marcus sneered at Asmara's inward comment in time for Cornelius, the king's most trusted seneschal, confidant, and personal guard, to respond with his own look of distaste.

"Finally. You make our majesty wait too long." Cornelius was the only one brave enough to stand against Marcus with only a shield of honor for protection. The seneschal was a beast of a man, with his barrel chest, meaty arms, and a fanatic sense of loyalty to a young king just past his teenage years.

"*Your* king can wait until his subjects have cleared the road," Marcus snapped.

Valder had requested discretion, which was fine. Marcus's needs were the requirements of the two inside him—the mage, Asmara, and the demon, Tiecus.

"You know your way around our back tunnels." Cornelius's red-and-white-peppered beard bristled with his words.

Crouching in musty five-foot-tall passageways made Marcus roll his head and pop the vertebrae in his neck for relief.

Cornelius was never intimidated by Marcus. Nor did the seneschal look away from a challenging stare. This was one of the demon's favorite games; whoever blinked first was the loser.

"You make him wait longer." Marcus stared back at Cornelius. "May I enter, or shall we settle our differences now?"

Murky-blue eyes flashed in anger, but the seneschal raked a meaty hand over his bright-red hair. More importantly, his short sword remained in its sheath. The seneschal opened the door to Valder's quarters and waved Marcus through. "Remember, I'll be outside."

The threat was not even worth a scoff.

Marcus entered King Eric Valder's modest sitting room decorated with sparse furniture of wood and bloodred velvet. Designs and knotwork trimmed the walls. Plush chairs carved by a delicate hand depicted Valder's oak tree family emblem. Furniture chiseled or embroidered with small touches hinted at wealth without becoming a beacon of jealousy. Tall, thin windows opened to a myriad of hearth lights in the town of Benicar. Fine muslin drapes cascading from the high ceilings framed the windows and floated in the soft fall breeze.

Two finely crafted seats sat before a hearth. Next to the tall-backed chairs, a fire grate with intricate patterns of entwined roses muted the attention unto themselves but, to the refined eye, were a statement of craftsmanship only wealth could afford. Even with his sophisticated tastes, Asmara defined the room in one word. *Grace.*

Fire crackled, and embers spurted against the iron shield. The greeting from the element Tiecus controlled didn't go unnoticed. Marcus smiled at the hearth where the element of fire, Ignis, hailed him.

Valder positioned his chair to enjoy both the warmth and view of the moon through his veranda. The king wore clothes as modest as his room. Darkened leather pants and an undyed silk tunic adorned Valder's sleek frame. Wisps of short brown hair twitched when sharp blue eyes turned to Marcus. The king was scarcely beyond his youngling stage but had already proven his power worthy to follow.

"Come." Valder waved a hand to the other chair. "Sit."

Asmara remained quiet inside of Marcus as exposure to the king would put the rest of his race in jeopardy. The mage wasn't sure if the king held magic or not.

Marcus sat upon a plush velvet seat next to the fire, as commanded.

After a few pleasantries, Valder dropped all pretense and his boyish smile. "I need you to go to the town of Reginhart."

Marcus stared at his ally. King Valder had a knack for disarming others with his innocent face. "You wish to send me away?"

"The Tier Naug are on the move. If we lose Reginhart, we lose a port. If they gain that port city, the inland road leads straight to Benicar. I have on good authority they will attempt another assault soon." Valder tucked his chin in a conspiratorial air and leaned close to Marcus.

Tier Naug were the bane of Valder's existence. They were roving sailors that came from across the sea to pillage. The king's claim of assault seemed zealous.

Uncomfortable with Valder's proximity but unwilling to acknowledge the invasion of personal space, Marcus looked away. "I have nothing to do with that."

Valder's regal face gave away nothing, but for a king, his words unfolded as close to a plea as they would ever come. "You are one of my strongest allies. Once they hear of a demon roaming the coast, they'll move along."

"I don't want to leave." Benicar had been home for months now, and Marcus had finally gained a hold over the demon. Their bloodlust sated by the enemies of Benicar's king kept Tiecus in check. "An attempt on your life was made just last week." Marcus smiled, exposing his blocky teeth and pointed incisors.

Valder returned his own threatening smile. "Assassins have been coming for me long before you helped yourself to them. I will be fine."

They stared at each other for a time before Valder pulled on one of the terms of their agreement. "Friends help each other."

Marcus slid his thumb claw down the other four talons on his right hand, a *shhhiiink* ringing out with each passing claw. Valder implied unbecoming terminology. "Don't use our agreement as manipulation to do your bidding."

Valder leaned back and sighed. His forlorn eyes tightened at the corners.

Marcus couldn't go back to the way things were. He couldn't bear to hear the dying screams of human victims when Tiecus drained them of their blood. He couldn't allow the demon in him to meander from place to place, leaving every town he left demolished in his wake. Leaving Benicar meant less supervision. Less supervision meant Tiecus, the demon, would tempt him into breaking his agreements with the mage. Since Marcus *was* the agreement, he would be the one to face the consequences.

King Valder had given him a chance to be redeemed when he had offered Marcus to stay in his castle. Marcus had a chance at a new life. One without Tiecus's bloodthirsty attacks. But it seemed his time in sanctuary was coming to an end.

Valder glanced at the square table commissioned to hold his marble chess set, and his charming smile returned. "How about a challenge then?"

Marcus raised an eyebrow.

"If I win, you go to Reginhart." Mischief twinkled in Valder's eyes. "If you win, I'll give you the mage tower."

Marcus's jaw went slack. Valder's temptation was genius, but why? How?

Asmara clamored inside. *Yes, Marcus! Say yes! With my help, you can win.*

I don't like this, Marcus thought as he regained composure.

"You would evacuate Ardin?" Even Marcus heard the eager lilt to his own voice.

"I'm sure he would threaten me with some ailment like an accelerated form of leprosy." King Valder nodded and leaned forward. "But if you win, I'll expect you to protect me from anything he sends my way."

Marcus smiled and knelt toward the hearth fire, gazing into the element he knew best. "Why me?"

Tongues of flame reached beyond the fire-shield to touch him.

"Your skills would be invaluable in Reginhart." Valder smiled, ignoring the flames' sudden burst.

Of course, they would, Asmara scoffed in his head. *He wants you to eat the Tier Naug.*

Branches of fire stretched for his caress, and Marcus raked his talons against the iron barrier.

King Valder sat in his chair seemingly uninterested. "I have discovered Tier Naug agents coming in from the shores of Reginhart. I need you to neutralize them. I suspect they will invade there first, and I want you to be my initial defense. You could be paramount in thwarting their efforts."

"Why not your seneschal?" Marcus glanced at the entrance and imagined Cornelius listening with an ear to the door.

"Marcus . . ." King Valder caught his eyes, the steady gaze was like a physical touch that reached through and brought emphasis to his words. "You are a demon. You've done me a great service, but . . . I'm running out of enemies, and my court grows suspicious."

There it was. A heavy weight crushed him from all sides. They could not blame the king for protecting his subjects. Of course, the demon liked the idea of endless blood, but Marcus did not.

A war with humans brought meaningless destruction. The sea of blood would make Tiecus impossible to control. Even with Asmara's magic, Marcus wasn't sure he could rein in the bloodlust the demon—the real demon—would suffer from. After being allowed to kill without restraint, Tiecus would not understand peace, only blood. Marcus had done everything to avoid conflict with humans for that very reason. But the trust King Valder placed in him confounded him.

Valder was putting the triad back into the same situation that had gotten them to make agreements with humans in the first place.

Why for all the stars in the heavens would a king trust a demon not to break his word? And trust him to be the guard and first defense from invaders? But the three of them valued Valder's trust.

I must have that tower! Asmara pleaded in the background. *It's the principle of the thing.*

Marcus turned his head, brought his hand up to cover his mouth, and whispered, "But if we lose, we lose more than our redemption."

They could not rise to King Valder's challenge. He could not go back to the insanity of imbibing whomever he found. He could lose control over the demon's need for food. Tiecus would force his way to the forefront and hurt the innocent, the young, and the old. The humans would rise against him. *Another* army would form for the sole purpose to stop him. Tiecus would kill them, or worse, turn them into demons.

Asmara took over Marcus's tongue, turned to the king, and answered for them all. "I accept."

Chapter 2

"SHALL WE BEGIN?" King Valder waved a hand at the chess table.

Marcus dug his claws into the palms of his hands. A trickle of blood slid down his fingers. Gritting his teeth, he looked to the window. Mirrors and glass revealed what Marcus tried to hide. The mage and the demon could be exposed by reflection. The window was open, and Marcus bypassed the glass as he strode over to the table.

The king's personal board and pieces were crude and made of unpolished marble, matching some of the furniture in the room. White pieces with swirls of gray posed on one side. Forest-green counterparts sat opposite them. Marcus moved his black waist-long hair to one side and sat before his favored white pieces.

"I've won the past three games." Marcus licked the dripping blood from his hands. "It's only fair that you begin."

"I must warn you . . ." Valder glided across the room to his seat. "The stronghold in Reginhart is currently damaged, but you should be able to stay there." He set two green velvet pouches next to the table. The contents inside rattled with a metallic ring. "Masons have been commissioned to repair it. Otherwise, you can stay at the inn. Ask for Bolden Pillar. I believe he has room for you." The king's first move was his green pawn in the middle of the board forward two squares to e5.

Marcus, tall and lanky, didn't have to lean forward to direct his pieces. With a long arm, he imitated Valder's move manipulating his claws carefully around the individual pieces. Both pawns were now locked at their squares.

"How long does your magician need to get out?" Marcus grated his incisors. "A day?"

The king slid another pawn—the one in front of his bishop nearest the king-figure—up two spaces to f5. A brazen move.

How appropriate, Asmara whispered. *A king's gambit. This time it will cost him more than pride.*

"Do you think you can do better than Ardin?" Valder looked up from sculpted eyebrows.

"Are you looking for a replacement?" Marcus captured the green pawn at f5, accepting the risk his opponent made. A hole to attack the green marble king was now available.

Valder slid the green bishop to c5. Marcus saw something carnal sweep across the king's face. Within a flash, it was gone. "If one proves worthy of the task and can excel much further than the magic user I have, it would be advisable for me to consider the options."

Marcus kept a smile on his face despite the flustered feelings inside. The king wasn't going to "castle" this time. In any other game, Valder would never have left the main piece vulnerable. The king was using a different tactic.

Tiecus began to stir within him. The demon did not often communicate with words. Instead, feelings, emotions, and memories were used as a means to "talk." The gnawing sensation of angst was a familiar one.

You'll be fed soon enough, Marcus admonished. He half closed his eyes and sent images to Tiecus, conveying that what he was doing now was more important than food. Convincing the demon of this was not an easy task. Nothing was more important than blood to the demon.

When Marcus looked down at the board, Asmara had taken control of his arm and moved the queen—diagonally to the center of the board—to h5. Valder's main figure-piece was now in jeopardy. "Check."

Silently, he spoke to Asmara. *Should I bring you to the forefront so you don't have to go through me?*

You were talking to it, Asmara said. *I saw the next move. I said I would help, and I am.*

Marcus looked up.

Valder returned his gaze. A thumb and forefinger cradled his chin. Hunger and pride showed in the king's stare, making Marcus uncomfortable. "A great many things I do not know about you, Marcus." The relief in Marcus was palpable when Valder looked and continued, "Things like where you learned to play." Valder slid his green marble representative of himself one square to his right to f8, where Marcus's bishop had been.

Marcus said nothing and intended to remain quiet. His claws clicked against each other while moving the pawn in front of his knight forward to b4 to threaten the green bishop.

"Should I believe what Ardin tells me about demons?" The green king piece captured the pawn at b4 and slipped beyond losing the green bishop. Another piece lost.

Marcus brought forth his knight to f3. The stone walls seemed to curve in as if they wanted a better view of the game. "What does he say?"

Valder jumped his knight over his own pawn to f6. Marcus saw his queen could be taken by a knight and felt a lurch in his stomach.

"He says not to trust them," Valder said. "Even though they always tell the truth and make unbreakable vows."

Eric has learned something from our sessions. Asmara spoke of Valder as if he had known the king for more than the three months they'd been in Benicar.

Marcus snorted and then quieted, realizing Valder might have thought he was reacting to his statement. "Your magician told the truth." Breathing in relief, he moved his queen back beyond the green knight's reach to h3. "You should not trust a demon."

Valder, ever in control, pushed the pawn in front of his queen forward one square to d6.

Marcus gazed at the face opposite of him. He felt wretched for letting Ardin be Valder's only advisor on demons.

Humans knew precious little about demons. No demon had ever lived among humans. But Ardin was not a warlock. Ardin did not call demons forth and use humans to host them. Nor was Ardin "riddled" with a demon. Ardin was a magician. What would a human who studied illusion know about demons?

Marcus moved his knight to h4, and as he stared down at the figure, he felt a sense that Valder shielded him, from what he couldn't say.

Eyes downcast, Valder gave the board a doleful nod, his disappointment unsuccessfully hidden. He moved his green knight in front of the white knight to h5.

"Unbreakable bonds are exactly that." Marcus decided a tidbit of information was harmless. "But that doesn't mean a demon can't find words that are or aren't there. Even specific agreements will not keep you safe. There is no way to foresee every possible outcome." He slid his queen to g4 threatening Valder's knight. "Although . . ." He considered and picked his words carefully. "Phrasing does matter. There is a difference between always telling the truth and not being able to lie."

Valder's eyes turned from despondent to a proud softness. The expression made Marcus wonder if he was telling the king something he'd already known.

"Ardin also says agreements that demons make are magical bonds." Valder's mischievous smirk returned. "The magic is what makes them unbreakable."

"You could say that." Uncomfortable with how much truth he had revealed, Marcus shifted in his seat but kept his face a mask. "It's more of a compulsion."

Valder moved his threatened knight to f4. "So, our agreement is more of a driving need than a want."

"I rather think of it as learning how to be a friend." Marcus moved the pawn before the bishop—on the queen's side—to c3. He had his eyes on Valder's green bishop and was poised to take it.

Valder moved his pawn from g7 to g5, effectively threatening Marcus's knight. He would not get the green bishop this move. "I've always wondered, my friend, whether you appear to us as the demon or the warlock."

He clenched his jaw. "I am not a warlock."

"So, you are the demon then."

"I am neither."

Asmara stung him with a mental lash. *Enough! Keep your useless gob trap shut.*

Marcus looked down at the board to calculate his options. Valder was taunting him. Not only was the green marble king undefended, but also Marcus's white knight could be taken by a pawn. If he captured the pawn with his queen, she would be in direct line to be captured by Valder's queen. He had been pinned.

Asmara's fury reverberated through Marcus's body. The mage's words in his head were loud and distracting. *That scheming human thinks he can take me!* Asmara hissed.

Marcus calmed his breathing and waited for the mage to finish his wrath. His queen and knight were surrounded, cut off from escape, and at the edge.

Like the stronghold in Reginhart, his chess pieces were up against a cliff with nowhere to go. Remembering how the building stood proudly over the sea protecting the village below, he looked down at the board and imagined his marble queen unamused but holding firm. Then he moved his knight to f3. He looked up for any expression his opponent would give away.

Valder wasn't paying attention to the board. The king was inspecting Marcus. Valder's stare drew Marcus back. This challenge the king presented was uncomfortable.

Tiecus held firm, peeking out through Marcus's eyes. The demon wouldn't let Marcus lose this game of "blink" and held a steadfast stare. Marcus got the sense Valder could see through him, to the other entities inside, and the urge to look away was hard to resist. But Marcus shook the thought from his head. It wasn't possible for the king to see what, or rather whom, he held within the confines of his body. He hadn't allowed either the demon or the mage to come to the forefront. He also had been careful to avoid every reflection and sneak by any window that would give them away. The two inside had not been seen nor would he allow either of them the exposure in Benicar.

Valder watched the board again, pushing his rook closer to his own king to g8.

Relief from the king's penetrating gaze was short lived. In every scenario he played out, he saw Valder capturing his queen. The clothes on his back felt weighed down and damp. If he lost his most powerful piece, he might lose the game.

Through images, Tiecus suggested letting the figure be captured. The demon was asking what the fascination was with the queen anyway.

Asmara mentally pushed the demon aside. More involved in the game, the mage argued with Marcus over the next move. In anger more than logic, he captured Valder's bishop at b4.

With deliberate motion, Valder picked up his pawn from h7 and plunked it down, diagonally from the white queen at h5.

Valder had set him up.

Marcus's white queen could be taken by a mere pawn. He would have to waste more moves to save his cherished piece.

A roar from the mage reverberated in his head, making him squeeze his eyes shut. Marcus clamped down on Asmara before he squirmed to the forefront and blasted Valder with a mage's magic ice arrow. He had no doubt Asmara would do it even with the curse of the Serenite, which would make the mage violently ill.

When mental order was restored, he opened his eyes. His clenched fist was inches away from his face, his nose flared, and a dull ache rang in his mind. A cool and rigid item poked into the middle of his fist. It was his white queen. The soft-sloped edges were very sharp. He was relieved she had not been crushed under his inhuman strength.

Looking at the figure up close, he could see the marble really wasn't white but many shades of gray. The different contrasts swirled together in a spiral motion with black veins that reached upward.

"Are you all right?" Valder looked genuinely concerned. The King's bright-blue eyes gave him a strong but compassionate acknowledgement.

"Yes." He set his queen down gently at g3. The possible moves for him on the checkered board looked grim. All he could do now was run and keep his queen from being captured.

Valder lingered his hand on a piece as if calculating and chased the white queen by pushing his pawn up to h4.

"Why me?" He moved his queen back to g4.

"You can stop them, Marcus. They may have numbers, but you . . ." King Valder hesitated then cleared his throat. "You can stop him." Valder slid his queen to f6.

Marcus pulled his knight back to its home at g1. "Am I the first one you asked?"

"You are the only one I'm going to *ask*." Valder slid his bishop from c8 to f5 capturing the white pawn, threatening the queen yet again.

Marcus moved his queen out of danger to f3. "So, you do wish to send me away."

"Marcus." Valder shook his head and tapped the marble symbol of himself. "Ask me why the king can move only one square at a time even though it is the most important piece."

Marcus said nothing but gave the king his undivided attention.

Valder moved his knight to c6. "It mimics the life of a real king. You may see this regal statue giving orders to all his subjects, but he's also trapped by them. For all the directions a king can go, he can't make a move without advisors clamoring for an audience before a decision is made. A king can't make a statement without his subjects taking every word to heart. A king is surrounded at all times, has precious little secrets, has secrets he doesn't even know he possesses. Did you know I can't even perform husbandly duties without being watched? Even now"—Valder waved a hand in empty air—"we are truly not alone."

Marcus slid his bishop from f1 to c4 and held the piece's top while he said, "Ah, I see. You want me to leave because of human politics." He leaned back and watched Valder's face.

"If only it were that simple, Marcus." Valder moved the same knight to d4. "You can move anywhere. Do anything. If an opponent comes along, you crush him without question. You're not impeded by golden shackles everywhere you go."

Marcus kept his eyes averted and thought how very much in common they had. He slid his queen diagonally down the length of the board and captured a green pawn at b7.

The king moved his bishop to d3 and then looked up as if he had just remembered something important and asked, "What if you make two agreements that conflict?"

Marcus took note of the move Valder made and anticipated a close race to checkmate. He was one move ahead of the king, and that was all the difference he needed. He slid his bishop across the board to g8 and captured Valder's rook.

Think of all the books I can horde in that tower, Asmara chirped.

"I would most likely not agree to conflicting agreements," Marcus sneered.

The hearth fire crackled and blew out sparks. Marcus looked closer at the green marble king. Surveying Valder's face, he looked at the resemblance the dark marble had to the man in front of him. The king's calculating eyes fiercely concentrated on the board. Fire light and the deep shadows on Valder's face gave him the look of creatures of the Atra Solumn, where Tiecus was born. The Atra Solumn, a place of darkness, a place where demons walked and no human ever went. Not unless that human had serious magic abilities and a death wish.

Valder's face relaxed when he slid his pawn one square to e4. "What if they don't conflict directly, but circumstances make it so you have to choose one or the other?"

The complex question *combined* with the trivial move confused him. It astonished him that Valder did not try to save his rook.

He doesn't see we'll have him in check. Asmara relaxed, confident of the outcome. *Or mayhap, he just wanted an excuse to place us in the tower.*

"For me, the agreement that was made first matters more, in most cases." He looked at the board but saw no reason not to take the rook. He moved his queen to a8 and captured the second green rook. "Check." Marcus smiled.

He had the winning moves in his mind. He would have the mage tower. Ardin would be gone, or maybe Valder would let him drain the magician. He wouldn't mind eating the poor excuse of a magic user. Besides these were modern times. Humans employed the use of trebuchets. Magic of old wives' tales was the past.

Valder moved his king to e7. "Ah, so seniority counts for something."

Marcus nodded not taking his eyes off the board. There would be plenty of time to chase the king figure-piece into a corner. But he needed pieces out to do it. He moved his knight to a3, avoiding the middle of the board. It was the fastest piece to aid him.

Valder's knight captured his pawn at g2.

"Check." Valder was gracious and didn't smile.

Marcus grimaced and pushed his king over to d1.

Valder moved his queen to f3. "Check." Valder pointed at the velvet coin bags. "Don't forget the currency. I know you say you don't have want for it, but it comes in handy when you don't want to kill for something you need."

Marcus stared at the board. He swallowed. *No. This isn't over.* He captured Valder's queen-figure with his knight, moving it from e1 to f3.

Valder moved his bishop to c2. "Checkmate."

Marcus's vision was hazy. Could this be true? Had he lost? Forcing his vision to see through the fog, he saw he was cornered by the two green knights and a bishop. An agonizing moment later, he stared into Valder's eyes. There was no pity. No remorse. Only hard blue stone. The king was as cold as a demon's killing blow.

The room was silent except for the fire crackling. Ignis laughed at him through the grate.

In a harsh whisper, Valder said, "Always protect your king, Marcus."

Marcus swallowed. Valder's expression punched a hole through him. "This is my home. I can't—"

"You will honor your agreement." Again, Valder pointed at the green bags.

It had been called a challenge, another word for binding contract. Marcus had agreed to the terms, and the agreement was real. "How long do I need to stay there?" he sneered.

"Until I ask you to return."

Marcus tried to use guilt to get out of his new agreement. "You must not care for the inhabitants there."

"Every war has its price." Valder rose and started to walk away.

"As you wish, *friend.*" Marcus longed for a different outcome, for Asmara to have kept to the background instead of taking over him like a demon and agreeing to this game.

Valder spun around. "Go to Reginhart. Search and destroy the Tier Naug there. Try not to let any of them get past you. Leave. Now."

Marcus shot up from his chair, grabbed the two velvet coin bags, turned, and barreled out of the room.

Chapter 3

EVERYTHING HE HAD worked for, the life he had built, the tenuous mental peace, all faced his backside. The never-ending enemies the king acquired meant Tiecus had never found want of blood when they had lived within the king's capital city. The demon's satiation created a fragile balance between Tiecus and the mage behind the walls of Benicar. Now that they were traveling to this new place, Reginhart, Marcus didn't expect peace between the two inside him, much less balance.

His inferno steed, Selkie, drove onward while Marcus brooded over his situation. *Just another cog in the wheel of a king. Even a demon could learn something about manipulation from Valder.*

Marcus slowed Selkie to a stop at a fork in the road. He squinted at a weathered wooden sign for direction. The trees here grew in an uncultivated manner. Winter rested upon the trees, weighing down limbs with snow. Knotted branches reached out, pointing accusations at Marcus. The crisp air settled in, chilling his bones from the exhaustive pursuit to his new place of rest.

Steam rose from under Selkie's dancing hooves. Snow gave way to patches of dry ground the size of hoof prints. Marcus's steed gnashed his teeth, grunting his annoyance, heaving breaths, sending fog into the air. Selkie's pace shortened a three-rides' distance in half. Still, the inferno steed pranced in anxious patience, willing to run longer, faster, more.

Marcus folded his clawed fingers against his palm and stroked Selkie with his knuckles. Valder had commanded an immediate departure and that compulsion had pushed him to exceed Selkie's limits.

"Walk the rest of the way." After his manic ride to Reginhart, Selkie deserved an easier pace, even though the creature resisted it.

Asmara had wondrously been silent the entire way. The mage had fallen asleep. But even dreams did nothing to break their mental connection. Still, Marcus experienced Asmara's feelings. Anger. Doubt. Resentment.

Humility came and went, but the lessons never retained longevity beyond a memory.

Marcus had not fed Tiecus, and hunger made the demon's influences sharper. Now would be a good time to hunt.

His left forearm tingled, and he pulled his overcoat and tunic sleeve back to relieve the itch. There, etched in his skin, like a brand, written in script, were the exact words last spoken to him.

The scars of every agreement between the mage and the demon were written upon his skin in the mage's cursive handwriting. He was littered with writing all over his body. Words scrawled over his chest, his arms, his legs, his stomach, his back. With exception to his face and hands, sentences crawled over his shoulders, his sides, his thighs, and stretched over elbows, knees, and feet, detailing in writing all the agreements Marcus had ever made. In essence, Marcus was a scroll of promises.

The part inscribed *Go to Reginhart* began burning, embossing itself deeper into his flesh. The words *Leave* and *Now* regained form and etched themselves into his arm.

He let go of his coat sleeve and sneered at the punishment for breaking an agreement. Parchment. As if he were a book to write important notes.

Marcus steered Selkie forward, and within a few steps, the burning ceased. He was inside the boundary of Reginhart.

Selkie swiveled his ears forward and jerked to a halt. The inferno steed held his breath and honed his focus to the distance.

A sudden glimpse of a shadow. An erratic heartbeat. They were not alone. The musky scent of a human teased his nose.

"Soon," he said to Tiecus.

The demon growled his displeasure.

"We hunt big game." Marcus pictured a large moose.

No innocent ones, Asmara snapped.

"Be quiet, he doesn't understand your thoughts or speech."

How hard is it to understand "no"? Asmara huffed.

The image of a half-wolf, half-ram, shaggy-haired nightmare—the vision of Tiecus himself—eating grass flitted through their minds.

It was the dead of winter, and the breeze chased a new day's first light. The only grass to be found was dried twigs. Marcus understood the demon's point. Might as well eat straw if the food did not run on two legs.

Tiecus had made a joke.

Good.

A demon mindless from hunger did not make sarcastic remarks. Or, in this case, sarcastic thoughts.

Billows of steam floated in the air betraying a human gasp from a nearby tree.

He nudged Selkie forward and plodded further down the path revealing a man leaning against a redwood as though he'd run a great distance.

There was no mistaking the man's heritage. The Tier Naug reminded him of Cornelius, Valder's seneschal, with red hair and freckled pale skin. If he could see his eyes up close, they would likely be murky blue.

He stroked Selkie with a closed fist and continued forward. The novelty of a random human standing in his presence threw him for a loop. Usually, humans looking into his eyes were prone to panic.

Selkie nickered.

The Tier Naug heaved himself upright and took a step forward, his face expectant.

Perturbed by the Tier Naug's lack of fear, Marcus peered down at the human. As he suspected, murky-blue eyes with a harsh glint stared back at him. Instead of a look of horror, the man assessed him and waited.

Burning flesh and smoke rose from his sleeve. He was willing to bet the passage tattooed on his right arm stating, *Search and destroy the Tier Naug there*, burned a hole through his skin. The agreements magically appeared as tattoos on his body as soon as he made them. It wasn't the mage or the demon that burned him but the agreements themselves. Marcus was the parchment and glue holding the two entities inside him together. If he broke the agreements or allowed the others to break the agreements, that specific tattoo on Marcus's body would burn.

In disgust and pain, Marcus gave away his intentions and sneered, "Tier Naug."

The man bolted through the thicket.

Selkie leaped forward. Low hanging branches slapped Marcus in the face. The scent of his quarry left a wake wide enough to fit a throng of big-horn demons. Tiecus's euphoric thrill of the chase drowned Marcus's angst. His intentions of keeping Reginhart's population whole evaporated in the surge of pursuit.

The Tier Naug scrambled, darting around trees, trying to shake the hunter.

In accordance to the agreement with Valder, Marcus allowed Tiecus his joy of the chase, but he did not relish hunts.

He bounded behind the human, tiring his prey until finally the freckle-faced man pressed his back up against the bark of an older redwood. Out of the shadows, Marcus dismounted and faced the Tier Naug. The pursuit was over. Time for a swift, honorable death. Marcus readied his talons and walked toward the man.

The Tier Naug lifted a shiny hollow branch, thick as a sapling oak that retained an unnatural straightness, toward Marcus. Something was off, but Tiecus pushed Marcus for the kill.

The shiny branch blew puffs of smoke, then made a sound like thunder, and flashed like lightning.

Marcus landed face-first in mud.

Temporarily blinded, he lay unmoving. Pain stabbed him in the chest. Hooves rushed past. Marcus forced air into his lungs. Fire sliced him at every breath. The world tunneled, and soft light blurred his surroundings. Boulders, attached to his shoulders, weighed him down. His legs denied his commands. With more effort than it was worth, he rolled on his back and greeted the slicing-hot pain akin to knives in his chest. He lay in wait for his strength to return. But the consequences of mending the wound would be paid by blood.

Marcus flung his hand and buried his claws into a trunk. Snow from low hanging branches shook loose and dusted his greatcoat. Winded and waiting a moment, Marcus hoisted his torso upright. His other hand reached out, his claws digging into the tree, and he pulled himself up the trunk. He repeated the steps until he could gain his feet underneath him.

Head pressed against the redwood, Marcus stayed there for what seemed like eternity. The wound ached in his chest but no longer bled. The world spun halfway around and then zipped back into place, only to rotate again and again. Incoherent, he went to walk and stumbled to the ground. This time he remained on all fours until the world straightened out.

Tiecus was pushing his way to the forefront, stretching to come out and pulling Marcus to the background, inside Tiecus's body.

"No . . ." Marcus protested the demon forcing his way out into the physical world.

Marcus was hurt, and the demon didn't want to show weakness, not even in his riddled host.

But for all the shortcomings of his abilities, for all the useless negotiating with a beast, Marcus had control over this.

Tiecus would not come to the forefront.

Marcus would not let the demon roam. Tiecus would remain inside of him. He refused to let the demon out.

Though Marcus was delirious, his determined obligation prevented the catastrophe of letting the demon run roughshod. Shock overwhelmed his sense. He pushed Tiecus back to the background, inside himself, and bent a knee for support. When he rose the second time, he was more balanced, but his body trembled.

Aimless, he tripped over a fallen branch camouflaged by snow and reached out to a tree for support. Hunger motivated his course of direction. The need for blood had never been so dire. Now with Tiecus using all his effort to heal Marcus, the demon needed to be fed.

The musk of human intertwined with a vanilla scent called to him. Marcus used a pine tree as a crutch to stand back up. He pushed off his support and landed on another trunk. Again and again he traveled from tree to tree until he got to a clearing near a stream. The scent led him to a young woman loitering over a patch of snow berries. He didn't wonder if she was a villager, and he didn't care. She was vital. Food.

He breathed in, stood straight, and pushed off the redwood. Grateful his hat remained on during the ordeal, he kept the brim over his eyes. Making every effort not to show weakness, his movements were slow and deliberate.

At first sight of him, the girl startled but settled and spoke in soft tones. He wasn't coherent enough to understand, but she was a gem of her species. Long white-blonde hair down to her waist, eyes large and round, like a gentle doe, she coaxed him toward her. Unaware of his intentions, the little creature walked forward and gestured her willingness to help.

As soon as she was within reach, he grabbed her. Marcus cut a slit across her jugular with his index claw before she could scream. Blood ran off her neck. Like a starved wolf, mindless from hunger, Marcus imbibed her blood. Every gulp was like a gasp of air—one breath in for his life and one breath out for her death.

When her heart stopped squeezing life liquid, he eased her body down, moved her platinum hair out from underneath her backside, and wrapped it down the length of her torso. Seeing the madness done to this frail creature, he caressed her face with a knuckle. She seemed so young and at the start of life.

Tiecus gave no solace to him. Humans were food. But ever since the agreement with Valder, Marcus had formed a different opinion. Humans could be companions. He mourned the little doe. She had been kind. She hadn't run from a stranger.

Reginhart was full of oddities.

He held on to her long after the cold absorbed the little doe's body heat. The stone corpse was still frail and beautiful. Humans called out a name.

The crunch of snow from heavy footsteps brought Marcus back to his original task. He didn't want to leave her, but he set her body down.

"This did not have to happen." He rubbed his knuckle over her cheek. "You will be avenged."

Anger overrode his sadness. He would kill that worthless retch of a Tier Naug for this beautiful human doe's sacrifice. While most people all looked the same to him, this girl was different. Her grace and innocence set her apart.

Marcus uttered apologies to the lifeless body until the callers came close. He climbed a tree trunk, clawing his way to the first branch, and made his way along the tree canopy for his unseen departure. The burning on his arm compelled him to destroy the escaped Tier Naug. He vowed to set off to find Benicar's enemy and tried to forget about the little doe he had left behind.

Chapter 4

SELKIE TOOK ANOTHER hunk of flesh from the dead Tier Naug. Marcus stood a respectful distance away. He bowed his head and honored the fact that the kill belonged to the inferno steed. Even if he himself wanted revenge, his one satisfaction was that Selkie liked to rip the flesh off his food while his victim was still alive.

Tiecus would have bled the Tier Naug to the point of just above consciousness before handing him over to Selkie, but Marcus had arrived at the scene too late.

Selkie severed the forearm with the "lightning stick" still in the grasp of the dead man's hand and flung the offering over to Marcus. It seemed trite compared to the life Marcus took. He squatted down and examined what was left of the weapon.

Now that he could see the item up close, the mutilated wood and metal resembled Selkie's meal. The forearm-length stick was made of unpolished metal perched on a wooden stock. Thick wire bands held both wood and metal together. Teeth marks confessed Selkie had "tasted" the weapon, but since it wasn't devoured, the thing must have been found wanting. The barrel was crushed and tweaked. The middle was bent inward.

The demon steed seemed fine. No open lacerations, no contusions. Marcus held on to his trophy and waited.

After Selkie left no trace of the human behind, they continued to the stronghold in a leisurely pace. As the forest line pulled away, he saw the west-facing towers of the keep had crumbled, like a rock eater had come and had its fill.

Sunlight revealed more damage when they got closer to the only standing tower. When he climbed the hill to the grounds, he was surprised the east tower stood at all. Bricks littered the courtyard. Remains of a crumpled wall faced the sea. Ash and charred wood might have been the great hall. Worst of all, there wasn't a stable.

As he dismounted, he could hear Asmara scoff. *Not much like Benicar, is it?*

Marcus was too angry to retort.

Selkie didn't seem to mind about the integrity of the stronghold. The inferno demon stood poised with his ears and eyes to the ever-beckoning sea.

Marcus couldn't tell whether the demon steed's trance was in longing or in fear. He stood waiting for any sign that Selkie would go charging down the hill into the waves or opposite and into the trees. The tightness in his chest urged him to show dominance over his charger.

"Friend," he said, barely audible. "Don't leave me."

At his plea, Selkie turned his neck, and the glow of his eyes shone. Marcus met the steed's empty, sad eyes. Selkie nickered, and Marcus relaxed. The inferno steed would not abandon him today.

Officially, the mage and Selkie had a history before Marcus had even been created. In Asmara's memories, a half-fish, half-man discarded its skin in favor of a land animal. That land animal was the demon steed in front of Marcus. The mage, knowing the stories of selchies, had stolen the seafaring skin. Imprisoning Selkie had never sat well with Marcus, but Asmara charmed and hid Selkie's skin in favor of the demon steed's service. If Marcus ever found Selkie's outer shell, he'd give it back to its rightful owner.

"He hasn't revealed his hiding place, but I'll find it." Marcus stepped forward and stroked the steed's neck under his long black mane.

The charger nickered. Done with his job, Selkie walked over to the most comfortable looking piece of stone and curled up like demon horses do when tired, worn, and not in the first watch.

Marcus let out a sigh and turned his attention to the carnage of the castle. Valder had said it was damaged, but did he really expect Marcus to stay here? Only one roofless tower stood. Despite Valder's recommendation, he was not going to contact Bolden Pillar.

"No." Marcus collected the materials left to him. "Only Tier Naug. He meant for me to eat the Tier Naug."

He removed his coat and set it over a half-burnt chair lying on its side in the middle of the courtyard. Then Marcus collected slivers of a broken mirror and puzzled them together until the mismatched pieces were large enough to show his face.

Three forms stared back at him in the reflection. His own long face and iridescent, shimmering eyes were most prominent. Behind his own image floated the ghost of a humanlike face with wide eyes, corkscrew-curly short hair, and ears that slanted upward and twisted like a swine's tail at the ends.

Beyond Asmara, a larger creature lurked behind them both. Tiecus was not just a monster, but a nightmare. A creature so ugly, so fierce, so utterly terrifying that he caused paralysis in humans. Tiecus loomed in the background over the two of them. The entirety of the demon's face didn't fit inside the mirror, but a single shimmering eye examined itself. Tiecus was as ugly as ever with a wide snout, shaggy face, and horns that now began a slow curl, bending from the demon's temple to behind his canine-like ears. The demon had grown since the last time Marcus had glanced at his reflection.

Asmara, taking the chance to admire his profile, turned his head left then right. The Serenite paid extra attention to the twists at the tips of his long, sensitive ears.

"You're still old," Marcus smirked.

I'm still handsome, Asmara quipped.

Watching all three of them in the mirror was odd. They possessed the same body, and yet they were free to move within Marcus. He was one, and they were three.

With his index claw, he circled around the mirror clockwise three times. With each circle, he called out Ardin's name and used all his concentration on the magician in *his* mage tower. The mirror inside turned to haze. He waited for the reflection to reveal Ardin's lab before casting his gaze back into what was now a connection to Benicar.

You're getting better at scrying, Asmara purred.

Marcus didn't reply. He looked down, where the mirror no longer was a mirror but a passageway back to the king's palace.

On the other side of the connection, herbs and books littered the room. Feathers, globes, pots, and a general pile of disarray filled the mirror, but no Ardin. He called out the magician's name, but no one answered. He would have to sit and wait. His only other company, besides the two always inside his head, twitched his ears to the incoming surf.

"This inconvenience is your doing," Marcus snarled.

You'd rather have to avoid every single mirror in Benicar? Asmara snarled back.

As a *friend*, the mage, through Marcus, had informed Valder how mirrors could be used by demon spies. His sly deception to conceal Asmara and Tiecus had worked. The king had removed all the mirrors from the castle except the one in the mage tower. If Marcus wanted to talk with anyone in Benicar, he'd have to deal with the magician.

From the other side of the mirror, a door opened and slammed closed. Ardin's voice muttered in a language Marcus did not recognize. A round metal object flew in and out of the mirror's line of sight and then landed with a clang in Ardin's lab. Whatever project the magician had jettisoned across the room had obviously failed.

"Ardin?" he said.

The swearing stopped, and a thin hooded cloaked figure padded over to the mirror. The glint of his eyes reached beyond his hood, but his features were masked in darkness.

"Ah, the great demon, Marcus." Ardin's voice conveyed a hint of smug satisfaction. "Are you in Reginhart yet?"

"Yes." Marcus drawled out his spite.

"I'll tell his majesty you've arrived. Goodnight." Ardin turned his back and started to walk away.

"Ardin, wait." Marcus wanted to climb through the portal and claw the magician's backside. "I have unusual news."

Ardin stopped.

"The stronghold is in great need of repair."

"So, repair it. Or can you not do that? I suppose you wouldn't know anything about creation."

Marcus gritted his teeth and retorted, "Valder said it was damaged, but this is... not a stronghold. It's more like a pile of rocks."

"That's none of my concern." Ardin turned around to face him. "But I will tell him just the same. Goodnight." The magician raised a hand to cut the connection.

"I'm not finished." Marcus lunged for the mirror, stopping before hitting the glass.

Ardin lowered and crossed his arms.

"A Tier Naug had something." Marcus reached for the broken equipment. "A lightning stick of some sort."

"Show me." Ardin walked forward.

He held the destroyed piece in front of the scrying mirror and whispered the words that would transform the two-way connection into an actual portal.

Marcuuuusss . . . Asmara warned.

"I have to show him," Marcus whispered.

This is dangerous. You could lose your hand and the tool.

"He wants to see it," Marcus hissed, pushing the weapon *through* the mirror gateway so that Ardin could examine the lightning stick live instead of trying to show him through a hole the size of a dinner plate.

Slow, the mage warned.

I know. Marcus gritted his teeth, holding the tool as the portal pulled it through, wanting to take everything, including Marcus, and deposit everything to the other side.

Let the connection grab it.

Will you let me concentrate? Marcus snapped.

The weapon, along with Marcus's hand, became enveloped in silver. He felt a tug and let the lightning stick slide into the mirror through the boundaries of the connection.

Good. Breathe. Don't rush.

Marcus huffed like a scolded child.

Scrying was hard enough. Concentrating on keeping the connection open between two places taxed his mind. Asmara's coaching wasn't helping.

As Marcus advanced his arm further, the contraption went beyond the miniature worm hole toward the other side of the mirror in Benicar.

Stop. Anymore and it will pull us in.

Asmara was right. The lightning stick and Marcus's hand hovered in midair inside Ardin's lab.

The magician stepped back, grabbed a nearby dirk, and threatened the protruding mass that had just come through the mirror and into his room.

Marcus gave a wicked smile to the magician. "Still want to petition Valder about bringing mirrors back?"

Ardin hesitated and lowered the dirk. He examined the piece in Marcus's hand. Ardin tried to grab hold of the lightning stick, but his hand went through the silver representation of the weapon and Marcus's hand like through water.

"An optical illusion," Ardin said. "You're more a magician than you think."

How little the man knows.

"I could make it materialize on your end if I wanted," Marcus sneered.

"Useless." Ardin sheathed his dagger. "Can't you do anything right?"

Marcus growled and slowly pulled his hand and the lightning stick back.

"I need an arquebus intact." Ardin waved his hand. "You believe a broken one is going to do me any good?"

"So, it's called an arquebus." Sensing opportunity, Marcus gave a wicked smile. "I can find one in working order." Another agreement was not what he wanted, but he'd do anything if it led him back to Benicar.

"What do you want?" Ardin crossed his arms.

"I will bring you a working arquebus if King Eric Valder asks me to return. If we don't have an agreement, then I will destroy any I find." Marcus held up the broken arquebus and waited.

With a hint of malice, Ardin said, "So, you can come all the way through the mirror?"

Asmara sniffed in disapproval. *Should have anticipated your childish remark would give him more information than we wanted him to have.*

"Do we have a deal?" Marcus strained to smile.

Asmara swore in Serenite, *Why settle for an arquebus when you can transport an army wherever you want?*

Marcus then understood what Ardin really wanted but would never ask for and sighed. "It's only fitting a magician know this trick of the light. Do you want to learn how to carry into the scry?"

"Carry into the scry?" The magician's hood turned as if Ardin were tilting his head.

"It's the ability to carry things from one mirror to another."

"How is that possible?"

"You don't need to know the specifics . . . yet." In truth, it was dangerous to cross from one mirror to another. In addition to a disciplined mind, it required traveling into the Atra Solumn—the place where demons lived.

"How far can you travel?"

"If there is a mirror there, you can go."

"So, I could travel from this mirror in Benicar to that mirror in Reginhart?"

"Technically, if both mirrors are large enough."

"That's over two hundred miles." Ardin sounded skeptical.

"So?"

"And you can use any mirror?"

"Yes, Ardin. Any mirror. If there is a mirror there, you can go."

Silence.

He's waiting for terms, Marcus. We shouldn't teach humans . . .

"If you barter King Eric Valder for my return, then I will teach you how to carry into the scry. Do we have a deal?"

"An arquebus for your return and to teach me this mirror trick."

"Say it," Marcus ground out. "Nothing arbitrary." Loose agreements could leave him in ashes. A demon couldn't be too careful.

"I will convince King Eric to bring you back to Benicar in exchange for a working arquebus and teaching me how to carry through the scry."

Passive agreements couldn't always be proven. It would do nothing even if Eric called him to Benicar. If the king didn't confess that Ardin had convinced him to bring Marcus back, the agreement would be nullified.

"Agreed." Marcus noticed a tingle running along his ribs. Inside, he groaned at yet another tattoo. But this one would not set him on fire for failure.

With three counter-clockwise hand motions over the mirror, Ardin disconnected their communication. The triad graced a reflection once more.

Marcus assessed the repairs needed on the stronghold.

"Let's see if we can't find another arquebus."

Chapter 5

IT WAS A snide comment and a personal affront, Asmara said.

Marcus picked up another stone and hauled the rock over to the east tower. "So, now you're using me as a mule because a magician irked you?"

You're going to prove creation is not beyond your repertoire.

"So far, all I'm doing is moving rocks." Marcus laid the fist-sized boulder on top of the neck- high wall of stones. Small patches of ivy weaved their way in between the rock layers, holding each stone in place, acting as mortar.

Moving rocks is part of the process. Asmara projected his teacher tone. *Now, show me. Just like I showed you. Weave the vine around the stone.*

Marcus stroked the dark leaves, willing the plant to grow.

No, no. The mage fluctuated from the background of Marcus's body. Asmara poured forth, threatening to morph himself into physical form. *Foliage doesn't have consciousness. You must propel the growth from the light inside you. You make it grow. You need to visualize the result and pour your desire into it.*

Marcus stroked the leaves again and visualized as he'd been shown, but the vine didn't grow.

Pull its growing force toward your fingers, Asmara coached. *Remember, think abstract.*

Marcus looked over at the very edge of the crumbled wall. Selkie stood and stared with ears locked toward the sea.

"This is a waste of time." Marcus shifted his feet.

He could feel Asmara purse his lips. *You're still young*, the mage said, as if being in this triad for near two decades didn't feel like a century of hell.

"We should be looking for an arquebus." Marcus ground a talon down his foreclaw, leaving a metal scraping in the air.

Selkie's longing gaze toward the reef never wavered.

"We're just going to leave as soon as I get one. Why bother?"

In a rush to get back to Benicar so you can shove me into the background? Asmara's tone mocked. *I like being able to see the stars at night.*

"It's my sole purpose to keep you safe. Benicar is safe."

A faint nicker slipped from Selkie's muzzle. Every wave and rippling of the water held the inferno steed in rapt attention.

"If we don't get this done today, Selkie's not going to wait for you to give him back his skin." Marcus slid his thumb claw down the length of his middle talon. "He'll rejoin his brethren, burning fire and all."

He wouldn't be that foolish, Asmara hissed. *Don't try to avoid the lesson.*

"We've never been this close to the ocean before. Why don't you just give it back to him?" Marcus sneered. "Or is he another demon for your collection?"

From the background, Marcus felt Asmara's gritting teeth, eyes slit in contempt and his tall, slender ears wiggling in agitation.

Puppis, Asmara said. *If you don't want to learn how to do this, then I won't force you.*

"I didn't say I didn't want to learn." Before Marcus's eyes, the vine grew at an accelerated speed and intertwined around the stone layer. Asmara didn't need to take control over their body to call upon his power, but any unassuming human would believe Marcus was the mage. "I simply think that now is not the appropriate time."

I'm not giving back his skin. Asmara continued to let the vine expand, weaving in and around itself growing into a wall of foliage.

"Hence the demon steed's prison." Marcus couldn't hide his agitation. He stepped back from the stone-and-vine cave they had made. "You have stone walls. What about a gate?"

Selkie clomped inside the stone structure. The defeat in the demon steed's flame-flickering eyes killed Marcus.

Clear water gathered in a puddle around the stone cave opening. Marcus watched the liquid crawl up the sides and freeze within a matter of seconds. The thin ice patch crackled as another layer of water bubbled over the frozen layer as if climbing over a bed sheet. The pattern repeated, defying nature, gravity, and logic, each new layer forming another thicker, wider patch of ice. Layer by layer, water pooled at the top of the growing ice block and froze in sections until the mass created a thick, impenetrable door of ice.

Marcus stepped back from the rugged stone barn. The building was made of rock and ivy while the entrance was made of frozen water. Asmara was making the door to the barn out of his mastered element. Ice. Much like the mage's heart.

"Won't he just melt it?"

It's elemental water, living ice. Asmara's answer droned with the flat resonance of tiredness. *No matter the heat, it won't melt.*

Marcus shrugged. He assumed the vine holding the rocks together wouldn't burn either.

Keep still, Asmara admonished.

Marcus sighed.

Asmara's voice became less monotonic. *Tell me you haven't forgotten how to ward the place.*

The element of wind responded faster to Marcus. He stood imagining a dome around the stronghold. Ventus, known as elemental air, obliged Marcus as naturally as breathing.

An ocean breeze played with his black locks. The air tumbled, swirling clockwise. The breeze caressed the walls in a continual circle. Air flowed around the stronghold high up into the sky. A low whistle moaned as Ventus blew across the crumbling towers and through the courtyard.

"Satisfied?" Marcus sneered.

The mage gave a mental grunt. *You trust too much.*

"Why?" Marcus grinned. "Does the noise irritate your sensitive ears?"

Ventus is a viper. An element that will kill you for laughs. It's a double-edged sword.

"Air is also the element of freedom."

Be wary, Marcus. Ventus is not your friend.

"We should concentrate on finding an arquebus." Marcus felt the weight of anxiety as both the sun and Tiecus awoke. "And I need to find a Tier Naug."

Mmmmm. Asmara hummed.

Marcus admired the new oak door to the roofless tower. He'd fashioned it himself.

Proud of your handiwork?

"I am."

Good. There's an entire roof to make.

Marcus huffed, "Then we feed Tiecus."

He opened the door to a sparse stone tower. To the right was a large empty circular space. Directly in the path of the door, a stairway swept up and connected to a landing where it continued and disappeared through to the second and third stories. The left side of the room branched into a hall where a six-person dining table, a hearth, and a makeshift kitchen lay in tatters. But the roof needed attention, and with each step up the three storied spiral staircase, his stiff joints cried out for mercy. He missed the rope bed in his dank cave under Benicar.

Low hanging clouds darkened the sky, which wasn't a problem. Seeing the coming storm through the third-story ceiling was the issue.

The air around Marcus shifted, and the wind whistled a high-pitched whine. The small hairs on his arms tickled. Ventus was not playing mischief. Someone was climbing up the steep incline to the keep.

Marcus peered through the window to the hill leading up to the castle.

A not-quite-grown man, yet no longer a youngling, eyed the open portcullis. His tawny hair fluttered in the wind. The dark-eyed, pale-faced, slightly built teenager adjusted the flaps of his sheep-lined coat as he strode through the courtyard.

Must be one of the villagers, Asmara said.

"I wonder if he'll be missed." Deliberations such as those were telltale signs Tiecus was influencing his thoughts.

Let's not eat the town, shall we.

"Like you care," Marcus uttered.

Oh, I care. I cared when that mob in Dorslin came to churn us out, Asmara retorted.

Marcus licked his teeth and leaned further over the ledge. This was the first human that would knock on his door. The thought brought a warmth he had never known he'd wanted before. A home was more than brick and wood, but having a place to defend brought out the pride Marcus had never let himself feel before.

He waited and watched to hear a knock and greet his first visitor as the youngling traversed the courtyard to the door. Marcus had a mind this time and could negotiate with the townspeople. They'd leave him alone. He'd leave them alone. Everything would be fine.

That knock never came. The pint-sized youngling checked the latch, opened the door, and stepped into the tower.

Marcus stood aghast. It was as if a weeling had lifted a leg and peed on him. "Did he just . . . ?" But Marcus could not finish his sentence. His jaw had gone slack. The human might as well trample him backward and forward. Entering without invitation was just . . .

Yes, Asmara said. *Humans are rude.*

Tiecus nudged Marcus into movement.

"Hello?" The youngling's voice resounded throughout the cylinder tower. "Lord Reginhart?"

Marcus could not hold Tiecus's fierce growl, and a snarl echoed through the tower. He crossed the third-story room and started to descend the stairs. The fight to control Tiecus was like holding fire. Flames of the demon's instinct flickered hot and danced around capture. Marcus continued to grasp for control.

At the last flight of stairs, Marcus took hold of invisible reins and stood at the top of the first-level landing.

One foot extended, paused, and then struck the stair below. Marcus took each stride in deliberate restraint. He squeezed his claws against his palms so hard he could smell a familiar tangy odor of his own blood.

Frost poured from his sleeves and floated down the stairs. Cold mist drifted over the first floor, pushing a weighted humidity into the air. Sparks crackled at the edges of Marcus's fingertips. Two opposing elements, ice and fire, hissed at each other under his footfalls. As Marcus made his way down the flight of stone stairs, the familiar mantra consisting of the fifth agreement held him back. *No unnecessary violence.*

Marcus wanted to prove Reginhart could be different. That he could keep Tiecus from eating the townspeople. *Only Tier Naug.*

He stood at the bottom of the stairs, towering over the intruder, and acknowledged the youngling with a scowl under his hat. "Why are you in my home?"

"This isn't your home." The pip-squeak of a human stood proud, unyielding to intimidation. Years would pass before he filled out. But the youngling's dark eyes had a fierceness Marcus recognized—determination.

"You should leave while you can," Marcus growled.

"You should leave before the king's men get here."

Marcus chuckled and leaned forward exposing his eyes to the human.

The boy flushed and stomped his left foot. "I'm serious. We have sent a horseman to Benicar. When Lord Reginhart comes back, he'll rip your head off and shove you down a piss hole."

Is everyone in this town insane? Asmara blanched.

Excluding Valder, Cornelius, and Ardin, this was more conversation than Marcus ever had with a human. But those were men of power, confidence, and stature. This youngling's mouth hurled him into a death sentence.

His hold on Tiecus attenuated, and the boy's quick movement accelerated the thinning line of his control.

"King Valder got your message. He sent"—Marcus smiled—"me."

The boy stepped back as his face went from scarlet to white paste.

Marcus felt his smile go from wide to painful.

"No. No, he wouldn't have sent you. You're lying." The boy took another step back. "That's what you monsters do."

"Oh, you're a bona fide warlock." Marcus strained to remain standing. "You should be careful, young one. You're all alone up here."

"Morgan wasn't enough for you?"

The crystal-blue eyes and flaxen hair of the girl flashed through his memory. She had been willing to help him, unafraid. Morgan must have been her name. The flavor of her blood rolled over his tongue, and he licked his teeth while the weight of guilt anchored his feet. "She was a mistake."

The boy's eyes flared. "She? There's more than one?"

"The girl . . ." Marcus's anger waned, allowing him a stranglehold over Tiecus. "Heart-shaped face, waist-long blonde hair, blue eyes with the expression of an angelic doe. She is this Morgan?"

"Oh my god." The boy's face crumpled in rage. "Platt—" The youngling bolted out the open entrance and took hold of the handle as he went.

Marcus slammed against the oak door. The thick barrier saved the human's life. While Marcus thanked the stars at being a claws length too slow, Tiecus roiled in hate and hunger.

The mental strain winded Marcus. He breathed trying to calm the rage hovering over the cusp of control. Reason and pain controlled Tiecus to a point. From here on out, things would get worse. Just as he had feared.

Unless Marcus fed the demon on a regular basis, just as in Benicar, the townspeople would die. He hadn't seen any Tier Naug in two days.

Wrung out and starving, Marcus opened the door, caught the scent of the human, and gave chase.

Chapter 6

BY THE BRIGHT star! Asmara cried. *Where are you going?*

An odd sense of déjà vu enveloped Marcus. He walked aimlessly amongst the ancient cedar trees—his nose the only guide until he came to a familiar stream. Across the babbling creek, he watched a young girl crouched over a snow berry bush picking at the winter fruit. The scene was as it had been two days ago.

Camouflaged by trees, Marcus watched, fascinated.

A strand of her waist-long hair caught on the bush, and she pushed the cord of white-blonde over her shoulder. Delicate fingers claimed berries between leaves and thorns. Her crystal-blue eyes remained intent on the search for more fruit. She wore the same light-blue bodice and cream dress as when he'd laid her down and promised vengeance.

This could not be. He'd killed her. He'd felt her die. Yet there she stood, plain as day, as if he'd never drained her of life.

Another set of feet puttered down the path on the other side of the river toward the doe. Marcus dipped further behind the large cedar trunk as a youngling approached. The boy was barely beyond his weeling years. He had brown eyes and brown hair and a face pudgy with baby fat. His tunic and pants were the color of a potato sack, but his contrasting cream shirt spilled to his thighs as though the cloth was waiting for the boy to grow into its size.

"I'm leaving now." The male youngling approached her with a shillelagh in hand. The stick was as straight as one of the arquebus Marcus needed but didn't have the metal casing. "You'll be all right while I'm gone, right?"

"I'm fine, Tim." The doe sighed in exasperation. "Where are you going?"

"Riley called a roustabout." The youngling puffed his chest out. "Men only."

The doe with clear-blue eyes shook her head and smiled. "Men only, huh?"

"I'm old enough!" Tim cried. "Ma said I could go."

The girl—nearly a woman—continued to pluck berries from between dark-green leaves. "How manly, asking permission from your mother to go to an all-men's meeting."

"That's right." Tim puffed his scrawny chest out. "Only a fool would defy Mom."

The doe scoffed good-naturedly and waved for the youngling to go. "Have fun then."

"I will." Tim strode west carrying a pack, a walking stick, and pride in his step.

After the youngling left, Marcus snuck closer for a more careful assessment of the female. She had no magical residue, so no necromancer had raised her from the dead. She had a heartbeat, so she wasn't a golem. And she was much too serene to be riddled by a demon—plus, no shimmer of incandescent light shone from her eyes. She hummed while she scouted for berries, and it was the same tune she'd sung when they had first met.

A thin scar stretched under her jugular. It was new and angry. Shame hit Marcus as fast as any punch to the gut.

His angst found release in clawing the tree he hid behind. Dust sprinkled the snow, and debris tinkled on the way down.

She turned to the noise, took one look at him, and gave out a mousy squeak. Dropping her possessions, she lurched back. Her basket rustled when it hit compacted snow.

The demon-side instincts surged.

Marcus froze.

In a moment of uncertainty, gauging if she would run or stay, Marcus clamped down on Tiecus's hunger. He'd kill her again if she ran. "Easy . . ." He held up a hand in warning, urging her to understand and remain steady.

She regained herself, standing as still as a lamppost, controlling her breaths. She looked downcast in his direction and remained in place. "Good day, sir." She swallowed and inhaled. "I didn't hear you."

"You are wise, little doe." Marcus relaxed and straightened to his full height. "Most humans run, and it is their last mistake."

Her thin frame shook. She wasn't looking into his eyes, preventing Tiecus from playing his game of blink.

She held her fists at her side. The pungent musk of fear filled his nose. "It's said some suffer a worse fate by looking into your eyes."

The little doe was right. He could grabble with her mind and get information from just one look. But that option left him wary. After an experience with a dead human, he never ever wanted to use his demens, his ability to probe a mind, on anything remotely dead. He still wasn't sure she was fully alive. If he could help it, the option of talking was best.

Marcus inched forward, careful not to frighten her. "You are Platt?"

Her eyes grew wide in recognition. The scent of fear blasted his nose like a tornado. Her calm demeanor shattered. The little doe turned . . .

Before she could escape, Marcus leaped.

Platt collided straight into him before she had taken even two steps. A soundless cry came from her open mouth, and she began to back away. Her arms up as if she could shield herself from what came next.

Talking wasn't going to be an option.

Her eyes met his, and it was all he needed to gain access into her brain. He shoved his will through her eyes, and his consciousness went screaming down a tunnel of blue.

A demens created an omniscient effect of two minds blurring. Her mind and his mirrored each other. He could see through her and through himself. Nausea threatened his equilibrium. Their minds spun, recoiling in the different patterns of thoughts, visions, and memories.

He reached for the core inside her brain controlling her motor functions and took hold and commanded, "Halt."

Platt jerked from his possession.

Her fear became his. Torment chased after Marcus. Death. Blackness. Then life. Weakness. Pain. She didn't want to die, again.

It was cruel torment to make her believe she was walking into death once more.

Marcus stiffened, and like a mirror, Platt did the same, stopping her flight.

Mindful of his sharp claws, he stroked her cheek, touching her like the most exquisite flower he'd ever had the honor to caress. After years of solitude, suffering such extravagance of her warm, soft skin could become addicting.

His hand slipped to the shiny scar on her throat. "How long does it take a human to heal?"

I don't know, Platt replied from the inside of her thoughts. She'd answered him without speaking.

Marcus held her by the shoulders and looked deeper into her eyes. With a mental thrust, he pushed his consciousness through the windows of her soul. His thrust was met with no resistance, and her core, her very being, her naked, unyielding truth was his to observe.

White-hot essence filtered in circles around the calm of her soul. She had three spheres that were in constant motion. They coalesced and then separated, always in a methodic slowness, but never in the same direction. Her soul was as beautiful as three suns passing through each other. When they joined, the color was translucent. When they separated, one swirled colors like a demon's eyes, another remained solid yellow, and the last faded between green and blue, depending on the others' trajectory.

Her will pushed against his, but she did not have the experience to kick him out. No demon lurked in the recess of her body waiting to possess her. No necromancer controlled her like a puppet. She was the only personality, but there was something else . . .

Her soul shone flawlessly.

Nothing short of a miracle and timing must have prevailed to save her life.

He no longer pushed for information and did not make her recall the past. What he'd seen of her was more vulnerable than any memory.

He turned his focus to the way back. Thought sparks of red shimmered among an unfamiliar pattern of blue pinpricks like a universe of stars. The colors were merging. Their thoughts were melding together. He sped down a path that suddenly jerked, separating and then connecting to another road. Marcus didn't have much time before the streets of her thoughts shifted and merged with others. Panic slowly crept into his thoughts. He could get trapped in her mind.

Light washed over him. A belt tightened around his being and tugged.

Snapping back into his own mind was much like allowing Tiecus control of his body. He felt disorientated and took a moment to gather his wits. He was back, alone with his two other companions.

Why the elements did you do that? Asmara's anger bounced off the walls inside his skull.

In childlike curiosity, Marcus responded back to the mage, "I thought they were myth."

He cast his gaze down to Platt crumpled on the ground. Her blonde hair draped around her folded knees.

By the bright star, it hurts! Asmara said. If the mage could wrap his hands against the pressure in his head, he would. *Just look at what you've done. You could have been trapped in there! You were trapped in there! If I hadn't come to get you . . .* Asmara yammered on, but Marcus brought his concentration downward.

Platt had wrapped her arms around her chest. Her face was between her knees.

"She is a gem among bones." Marcus kneeled to pick her up. "A true regenerator can satisfy Tiecus. Killing would cease."

At what price? Asmara said.

"Blood dolls were born for this." He scooped the stunned doe into his arms, folding her to his chest.

What are you doing? Asmara pushed to the forefront, attempting to influence his control of their body.

Marcus stiffened, thwarting the mage's effort to manipulate the situation. "I'll not leave her here."

I will not be party to abduction, Asmara said.

Marcus laughed. "Can't you see?" He cradled her long torso and legs against his tall stature. "She is what we need. You've been demanding reprieve from the killing, and here it is." Holding her in one arm, Marcus used his free hand and delicately picked crushed wet leaves from her long straight hair.

Why, Marcus? Asmara dramatically cried as if all of this was a plot to uncover the secret of the Serenite.

"Her soul is the very thing we are looking for."

You'll destroy her. You'll destroy everything.

"She can teach us the secret to her own inner calm." He might be able to live with this unjust action if he could leave her mind intact and untouched.

Happiness is a farce.

Marcus's head throbbed, but the pain would be worse for her. "I'm sorry, little doe. I had to be sure."

"I would have rather told you," Platt sobbed.

Her words stopped him cold. A whimper slid past his lips. He pulled her closer to his chest and dipped his head lightly against hers. "I'll make an agreement with you. Tell me no lies, and I will never do that to you again."

"What *was* that?"

"Reaching into a mind is called a demens. I . . . did not mean to reach so far inside."

She delicately touched her throat where he had sliced her and nodded her head. "Makes sense. Demons, demens. I agree. I'll tell you what you want to know as long as you don't *demense* me again."

A tingle ran along his scalp from the neck up to his crown. Groaning, he knew he had only himself to blame. *Every new day seems to bring another contract with humans.*

When they reached the edge of the trees, he turned east on the road. They weren't far from the keep, and the road they were travelling on was straight and wide enough to see the stronghold ahead. Ventus once again warned him of impending guests.

Platt lifted her head. "Where are you taking me?"

"Home."

"My home is that way." She pointed behind his shoulder to the west.

He kept walking east.

"Marcus, no." Her eyes begged him. "I want to go to my home."

It seemed he wasn't the only one gathering information from their demens. "Clever little doe." Marcus smiled. "What else did you find out while roaming inside me?"

Let her go! Asmara boomed in his head. *Frigidus!*

Marcus felt his mind go numb from burning cold. The sudden burst of Glacias's magic made him grab for his head. He nearly dropped Platt but managed to wrap his arm around her chest before she fell. Her feet dropped to the ground, and he gripped her shoulders more for support than for keeping her from running away.

"Ardere!" Marcus countered the freezing spell. Ignis obliged his command and thawed his mind.

"You must come with me," Marcus croaked.

She shook her head and avoided his stare. "No."

"You know what you are. You know what you can do."

Her face scrunched together, and her blue eyes darted around, refusing to look him in the eye. "What do you mean, what I can do?" Her ignorance was a lie. He knew that much.

"You are a blood doll, a regenerator. All the blood in your body can be drained, and you will regenerate within minutes. A throng of demons could feed from you without ramification."

"Without ramification?" Tears welled up in her eyes. "I died!"

He loosened his grip a little, and his chest fell toward her. Her cries for mercy made no physical mark, yet he felt the backhand of consequence.

"But you survive. When the blood of your friends is drained, they won't be coming back. Is it worth the life of your fellows?"

Horror washed over her face. She tightened her full lips and looked up but was wise enough to not meet his eyes. She was hiding something.

"It may feel like dying, but you will come back. Platt, a blood doll is precious. I can learn how much is too much. I can learn how to make it not hurt when we feed. My demon won't go insane from starvation. Do you know how many villages have suffered because of his hunger?"

Her face crumbled, and tears welled in her eyes. "But . . ."

The air around Marcus pulled and then pushed like a hundred little needles prickling his arms. Ventus. The sensation was the warning ward letting him know several someones were approaching the keep.

Down the road a lynch mob of thirty men traveled up the hill to the stronghold. He stood in disbelief when they rushed the portcullis. The crack-snap of an axe on oak split the air. His door. His new oak, made from the ground up, front door.

Well, that didn't take long for them to gather and attack, Asmara scoffed. *Not a record but still.*

Tiecus roared a territorial howl, but only Marcus and Asmara heard the demon's rage. The demon was far too much for Marcus to control. Marcus had no other choice but to let go of Platt and dart for the stronghold.

Chapter 7

MARCUS WASN'T RUNNING fast enough. Tiecus pounded against the inner walls of Marcus, the custodian who bottled the demon up in a foreign body.

Cage! Tiecus roared. *Enforcer!* Tiecus spat the word in his mind. *Punisher!* Tiecus accused Marcus.

The demon wanted blood. Specifically, the villagers' blood. They were invading his territory.

Marcus pushed him from surfacing while running as fast as he could. If he allowed Tiecus to dictate his movement, he would kill the villagers. While King Valder didn't seem to mind if Reginhart had any survivors, slaughter was not something Asmara condoned.

Finding out he hadn't killed Platt had given him a renewed sense of hope. He would return to Benicar and prove he was under control. He would *not* massacre a whole town.

The mob had crowded inside the east tower by the time Marcus reached the portcullis. They banged around the first floor like ants dismantling a carcass. Wood creaked and splintered.

My new chairs! My door! Asmara sulked.

Marcus, cautious in his approach, slithered across the courtyard to the chopped oak door now split in half. He made sure the snow wouldn't crunch under his footsteps. He barely breathed as he touched upon Tiecus waiting under the surface. Marcus raked clawed fingers through his straggled hair checking for horns, fur, or any sign of Tiecus peeking through to the forefront.

Asmara burrowed deep within the recesses of his own mind where even Marcus couldn't reach him. Marcus needed to handle this alone. If Marcus wasn't in command of the demon, there was no mage to fall back upon to rein in his bloodlust.

Typical, but he never blamed the mage for disappearing. Asmara, or any Serenite, would never be able to withstand the pain of watching physical violence, which rendered them helpless and in agony and was the curse he kept secret for Asmara and the Serenite.

Before Marcus reached the doorway, a low nicker came from the stable. Glowing yellow eyes the color of fire shone through a peek hole, watching as he crept by. Marcus put a finger to his lips, telling Selkie to be quiet. He didn't know what he was going to do, but adding another demon to the mix didn't seem advantageous for the situation.

Shouting commenced inside the east tower. Marcus slipped through the doorway's shadows unnoticed and pressed himself against the curved wall.

Five men scattered pots and overturned the table within the kitchen, seemingly looting the cabinets. Three other men climbed the stairs with six men clustering at the base hesitating to follow.

Ten paces in front of Marcus, a barrel-chested lumberjack shouted at everyone in the tower. "All of you stop it! Stop it!" The human's booming voice echoed through the stone-and-ivy cylindrical walls. The ox-man ten paces in front of him commanded everyone's attention. This person in front of him wouldn't be able to obfuscate well.

Broad shoulders that had seen hard work accompanied a neck so thick he wondered if the man could turn his head.

The ransackers in the kitchen stopped and turned to the large man built like an ox whose like rivaled Cornelius, the king's seneschal, in size.

Marcus remained frozen in the shadows. None of them had seen him yet.

The ox continued bellowing. "Either Lord Reginhart has returned, or some other lord has taken over! What are you doing?"

"Bolden is right." From the first landing of stairs, the youngling that had so rudely trespassed replied to the ox, "We should wait till the demon appears." The youngling's tone was anything but agreeable despite his words. "You can all decide for yourselves whether you want it to rule you or not."

"Riley, I don't know of a demon that arranges a structure like this." Bolden, the ox, waved his hands around, pointing out the rugs, table, and chairs. "I don't know of many *domestic* demons that have furniture and carpets—and vine walls." Bolden eyed the ivy growing up the tower's insides. "We should all wait outside. Hell, I was born in a barn and have more manners than any of you larks."

"Bolden, it's not Reginhart. I know—" Riley's fierce glare fixed solely on Marcus.

Bolden, the ox who looked like he *was* the door for a barn, whirled around and locked eyes with Marcus.

Failing to blend in, now that Riley had drawn everyone's attention to him, Marcus pushed against the wall and stood. He brushed a thumb claw down the length of his other falcula, which made a distinct bone-on-bone *ssshhhink* sound.

Keeping Tiecus's rage in check, he brought the brim of his hat up for all to see his iridescent eyes. He let the humans gawk for a moment, gloating at the villagers' awe. The wave of fear in the room tasted sweet to his senses, and he deliberately inhaled with relish. "Why are you in my home?"

"Around here, demons have graves." Riley stood above everyone on the stair landing. His snow-covered boots spread in a fighting stance. Both hands readied a hoe for battle.

Tiecus yearned to sink his teeth into pliable skin for the reward of abating his thirst. But Marcus held him back. "I was sent here to kill the Tier Naug. I have no quarrel with any of you."

"Right, sent by King Valder." Riley spat on the ground. "And I'm going to harvest my wheat fields today."

Bolden held up a massive square fist to silence the boy and addressed Marcus. "Do you have a letter of marquee?"

The demon sneered. "A letter of marquee?"

"If you were sent by King Valder"—Bolden's voice was low and thick—"he always sends his troops with a letter of his intentions, or a rite of passage."

Marcus removed his overcoat, letting it drop to the ground, and sized up Bolden with the skill of a hunter. The man was large, from a thick head and neck all the way down to wide feet. Bolden wore tan leather pants that must have come from the hide of two separate cows, one for each pant leg. The long-sleeved shirt Bolden wore was natural cotton. One might expect a man so large to be lacking in intelligence, but when Marcus studied the human's face, he saw the man's eyes shone a keen glint.

Tiecus snarled on the inside. Bolden seemed to challenge the demon's authority just by standing there. Marcus would rather not tangle with the man.

Marcus leaned his coat against the wall, untied his right shirt cuff, pulled up his dirty tunic sleeve, and presented his forearm. "Then this is my letter of marquee."

Bolden examined Marcus's tattooed arm with a wince. "Stillwood, come here."

A wisp of a man approached with the grace of a cat. He held a spade as though it would save his life. Stillwood gave Marcus a once-over glance and then peered down at the embossed writing on his forearm.

"Confirm to me what it says." Bolden pointed to the agreement scrawled down the length of Marcus's skin.

The older man with knotted hands and graying hair craned his neck around to read the words etched in Marcus's skin.

"Amazing." Stillwood held his gnarled fingers above the lettering on Marcus's arm. "One of your kind is . . . more than rare."

"Stillwood," Bolden snapped. "Confirm it's the king's."

The older, graying man nodded. "Yes. Yes, of course." Stillwood looked up at Marcus and gestured with his hands. "May I?"

Thrown off by the audacity of these people toward a demon, Marcus, weary but curious, nodded.

Stillwood took a hold of Marcus's wrist and elbow bringing his nose closer to the lettering. The man peered up meeting Marcus's eyes. "Did he say this exactly?"

"Stillwood!" Bolden's voice cracked like a whip.

The gnarled-fingered man cast an angry glare to the ox. "The writing is in the king's own hand. What he says is true."

"What does it say?" Bolden narrowed his eyes.

Stillwood pursed his lips. "Go to Reginhart. Search and destroy the Tier Naug there. Try not to let any of them get past you."

Bolden relaxed his shoulders and took a steady breath. "That's all?"

"All of it but . . ." Stillwood looked down again and tapped at the white scar that finished Valder's agreement that said *Leave. Now.* "This you completed."

Marcus ripped away from Stillwood's grasp. The shock of a human understanding what he was overshadowed his puzzlement. "You have your letter of marque."

"What is the other language?" Stillwood focused on Marcus's chest, never looking above his shoulders. *He knows about a demens.*

"None of your business." Marcus clutched at his open tunic exposing the first agreement between Asmara and Tiecus.

"It's not demonese." Stillwood peered at Marcus's body like he knew there were more tattoos on his skin.

"There is no such writing."

Stillwood's quirk of smile reached to the intelligence in the man's eyes. He opened his mouth but was cut off.

"Enough. He's been sent by the king." Bolden rubbed the stubble on his chin. "At least, we have a common enemy."

Hope rose in Marcus. This conflict might be abated after all. Tiecus conveyed his disappointment without words.

"Oh no," Riley cried out. "He murdered Morgan. He's not getting away with it." Hoe raised high in his hands, Riley raced down the stairs toward Marcus.

"Riley, no!" Bolden spread out his arms to catch the youngling, but the advantage of youth quickened the youngling's speed. Riley's wiry frame snaked past Bolden. Stillwood slipped backward as quickly as a cat, allowing Riley a clear shot.

Claws up, Marcus prepared to slap the youngling down.

Bolden, tall enough to look at Marcus eye to eye, turned around and managed to grab Riley by the collar. He flung the youngling across the room and, with his other hand, shoved Marcus against the wall.

With his guard lowered, the jostle slipped Marcus's control, and Tiecus seeped through, influencing the enforcer. Marcus raised his arms and slammed his claws into Bolden's shoulders.

Bolden's shout thundered and echoed.

Tiecus wiggled his way up more.

Marcus pulled to the side and rolled them both to the ground. Bone-ripping claws slashed at Bolden's throat. The ox threw up his forearms guarding his jugular.

No! Stop! If Marcus allowed Tiecus the forefront, tomorrow's breakfast would entail strips of human bacon.

A metal hoe careened into Marcus in the ribs. The blow should have hurt, should've sent him sprawling, yet it didn't. Blood rage. No one would be safe, Tiecus in the forefront or not. He was losing control. Cracks in his resolve tore at the promise to keep the villagers alive.

Marcus turned his attention to his attacker. Riley tore the hoe out of Marcus's side. Bolden scrambled, regaining his feet. Marcus too rebounded. Stern faces surrounded him. Every one of them staring in contempt.

A rumble escaped Marcus's throat.

The men charged him at once.

He flung his claws at the man leading the charge. Tiecus clawed one from face to navel and kicked him aside.

Stop! Marcus admonished the demon for the brutality. Nothing fazed Tiecus.

They sent a youth sprawling with an open-hand slap.

Bolden charged from behind, and Marcus slammed his elbow to Bolden's nose before Tiecus could claw his face.

Tiecus lurched to the forefront. Marcus pulled at the thin puppet strings of control. The demon in him spread his claws to rip a man's heart out. At the last moment, Marcus curled his hand into a fist and punched, sparing the human's life. He batted a rake out of the youngling's hands and then palmed a face and shoved as hard as he could.

Tiecus surged forth, using claws to swing and tear at torsos. Humans were everywhere. He couldn't tell one from the other anymore. He ducked as a scythe *swooshed* past his head. Marcus stretched his claws, somersaulted, and bounded for another man. Before Tiecus could gut his opponent, Marcus kicked the villager out of the way.

He turned to a lithe swinger and dove. The blade went past his side in a wide arc. A man on fire ran past him out the tower. Puppis! Had he set flame on the humans? In the chaos, Marcus couldn't remember. He grabbed an iron skillet left on the counter and flung it into the crowd. The pan crashed against a wall, made an awful sound, but did no other damage.

Tiecus laughed at Marcus's attempt at defense. The demon pulled his thick curved talons up in Marcus's sight.

Weapons, Tiecus said.

Bolden sideswiped Marcus off his feet and leaped on top of him. Marcus swore a two-hundred-year-old redwood trunk had pinned him down. He barely felt punches to his gut. Blood was right there. He just had to wrap his jaws around elastic flesh. No matter how big Bolden was, he wouldn't be punching after two gulps.

Marcus kicked at Bolden and fought internally with Tiecus. The demon grappled to the forefront.

Riley stood over him brandishing a hoe high in the air while Bolden punched. Marcus grabbed Riley's leg and bit down through boots and rough wool pants.

The boy screamed but brought the hoe down despite the pain.

Searing-hot agony struck Marcus in the shoulder, and he yelled out with an inhuman cry. Pain brought relief—pain never affected bloodlust, and agony meant clarity.

Riley rolled on the floor, grabbing his bitten leg. "Arggh! No! I don't want to be riddled! Don't let them take me! I don't want to be a demon!"

Tiecus climbed to the forefront from anxiety and panic. Skin started to give way to fur. Marcus internally yanked the demon back, doing whatever it took to forget he had just been plowed.

Bolden held Marcus in a rare naked choke, panting with effort, and barked at Riley. "Shut your trap and finish this."

They were going to detach his head. More than half of the men seemed mortally wounded, but the ones that were still cognizant held undeterred conviction. They would not retreat. These men had grit. If he was to live, they would have to die.

And why should he live? Because he was the agreements? Because Tiecus and Asmara had faith that he would keep their interests in mind? If he died, that meant Asmara died. The mage was insufferable at times but certainly didn't deserve a death sentence for it. If Asmara died, the demon would be sent back to the "Atra Solumn," and Tiecus feared that more than death. Marcus had to live because whatever he was, they had created him. Tiecus, Asmara, and Selkie were his throng.

Riley fumbled back to his feet and raised the hoe over his head.

Marcus slipped his hand under Bolden's arm, turned his head, and made space to take a breath. He brought his head forward and then snapped it back, clocking Bolden in the nose. The ox loosened his grip, allowing Marcus to rip away.

Riley was on the down swing when Marcus grabbed the handle and ripped the hoe out of the youngling's hands. The wood and iron clanked against the stone floor.

Riley lurched forward.

Marcus wrapped a clawed hand around Riley's throat and ran his captive backward, up the stairs to the first landing, and shoved the boy against the wall.

The impact stunned the youngling, giving Marcus a blessed moment to rest.

Pulling the youngling around, using him as a shield, Marcus extended his jaw and, with the speed of a viper, clamped his teeth against human flesh without breaking the skin.

The assailants rushed the stairs, and Marcus clamped down, still not breaking the skin but pinching enough to hurt.

Riley screamed.

Marcus's arms ratcheted down, squeezing the writhing body. One clawed hand gripped the short strands of Riley's hair while he swirled his tongue around his neck. For this to work, Riley needed to stay alive. Marcus saw no other way.

"You're going back to the bowels you came from . . ." Bolden pushed himself up bringing a scythe with him, a blood trail staining his shirt from chin to gut.

"Stop!" A voice, as soft as a breeze, commanded the room's attention.

All eyes flew to a feminine silhouette.

Platt emerged, arms over her stomach, hunched over like she was in pain with every step. "You will let him go." She stared at Marcus. "You will let all of them go."

"What are you doing here?" Bolden sidestepped to Platt and grabbed her elbow. "This is no place for you. Get back."

Platt, her blue eyes penetrating him, remained fixated on Marcus. "Can't you see, Uncle? He wants to bargain. He hasn't punctured Riley's neck."

Riley started to struggle.

Marcus clenched his teeth down again, making Riley scream. He contained the boy's struggle, running a tongue over Riley's neck through his canine hold, tightening the fistful of Riley's hair. The youngling got the message, whimpered, and stilled.

Platt cringed and clinched her stomach tighter.

"No!" Bolden outstretched his hand to Riley but otherwise did not move.

"Please, I offer you me." Platt wore her long hair wrapped around her neck like a scarf. "But I want you to promise you will protect all of us, including the villagers."

"Technically . . ." Stillwood raised a finger. "He has no need to, but if I may interject here?"

She nodded.

Stillwood continued, "He is here to destroy the Tier Naug. There have been plenty around to feed him. We could make an agreement with him."

Marcus groaned. Just what he needed—another tattoo.

"Let him go, please." Platt exuded the innocence and serenity of a forest doe even inside the tower walls. Tiecus's nickname suited her.

Marcus wasn't a fool. Instead, he extended his hand. An invitation and a trade. Her for Riley.

"I think he wants you to . . ." Stillwood said.

But it was apparent Platt understood. She stepped forward.

"No!" Bolden grabbed her by the arm and pulled her back.

A louder growl escaped Marcus's lips.

"Let go, Uncle." She went to pull away from Bolden, but the ox held firm.

"You don't know what you're doing." Bolden glared at her. "You think Riley wouldn't die for you?"

"I've been through the trial." Platt raised her head. She took her free hand and moved her long hair to one side. The scar Marcus had left her shone in anger. "And I survived."

Gasps echoed through the first floor. Without her flaxen mane to cover her neck, the gash glistened in the sunlight. A twinge of guilt rippled down his body.

Bolden took hold of her chin and, after examining her scar, directed a murderous glare to Marcus.

Tugging free, Platt shuffled up the stairs.

No other human besides the king had been so imprudent to undertake a contract with him. It made him skeptical of her offer, yet he extended his arm to her in a gesture of hope more than of good faith. She ascended the stairs and offered her hand.

Riley struggled once more, but with Marcus pinning Riley's arms down, the youngling couldn't fight.

Marcus wrapped his fingers around her elegant palm. His pointed claws seemed borrowed from another time or place where he never dreamed he could ever be. He didn't breathe, waiting for a tingling sensation that never came. Their agreement was not complete. Both parties needed vocal confirmation.

His jaw protested with crunches and pops in releasing Riley from his canine teeth. Like he would a dirty rag, Marcus shoved Riley away. Bolden rushed forward and braced Riley's fall down the stairs.

"Get out," Marcus said.

"Stillwood." Platt cast a soft gaze to her uncle while addressing the old man. "Please stay as witness."

Bolden gathered the boy in his arms. Riley stared off, expression crumbled inward, allowing Bolden to carry him like a colander trying to hold water.

Through a tortured whisper, Riley called her name, "Platt . . ."

"Take care of him, Uncle." She looked doleful and resigned.

Marcus wrapped his arm around her waist. She was his now. "Out," Marcus growled.

Broken, bleeding, and bruised, all but Bolden filtered out of the tower. Marcus might need to guard Platt, but a worthy prize was always worth the effort.

Chapter 8

BOLDEN SHUFFLED RILEY'S limp body into his arms, refusing to step out of the tower. "I don't like this."

Marcus squeezed Platt tighter. The blood doll was his. He wasn't about to let her go.

She pushed against his possessiveness contorting her upper body to make space between them. "This is the only way."

"No, it's not." Bolden's eyes clouded over like the weather before a storm.

Marcus could feel Platt's eyes watching for his reaction, but he didn't look away from Bolden's challenging glare. Humans gathered behind Platt's uncle like a pack waiting for their alpha's command to charge.

The little doe had put herself in the middle of the conflict, but he wondered if her own people would hurt her to get to him.

"This is the only way to stop the bloodshed." Her full lips trembled. "He will kill you. You don't know what he's done."

"An even better reason to take care of him now." Bolden jostled the teenager in his arms, shifting Riley more to one side.

"Uncle," Platt snapped with the force unbecoming of such a tiny thing. "Take Riley away from here. If you let him and the others die, I will *never* forgive you."

If the scene were any less somber, Marcus would have rolled his eyes and laughed. Platt's intimidation tactics seemed weak at best. Bolden could not possibly be swayed or commanded by such a feeble creature.

"Please, Uncle." Platt straightened and laid a hand on Marcus's shoulder. "I'm more valuable to him alive. But you, all of you, he would kill. I can prevent that, but not if you continue to fight. I know what I'm doing. Take Riley home."

Part of him gave way and relaxed under her hand. The other half felt wary of letting his guard down. The warmth of her touch soothed him. This new experience was not unpleasant, but it was unfamiliar, and he didn't trust the softening inside him. The combination was an odd pull of desire and push of apprehension. He wanted her and yet was afraid of her.

Bolden brought his forlorn face down to the youngling in his arms. The large man sighed and nodded. "Out. Everyone out."

Marcus blinked at the surprising turn of events. Examining Platt closer, he searched for clues to the hidden strength she possessed. She was no alpha, and human customs were, for the most part, beyond him, but a female commanding the ox to retreat?

The scent of fear, anger, and excitement evaporated under the thin odor of uncertainty accented with vanilla. The villagers cast worried glances at her as they limped and carried each other shoulder to shoulder.

Resolute, she stood stiff next to Marcus. Her eyes followed her friends and family out. "Please, let me help take the wounded home."

Marcus narrowed his eyes. "Your plan of escape is a feeble one."

Her face jerked as if he had slapped her. "I wouldn't go back on my word."

"Oh, but that's what humans do," he said with a grimace. "No consequence behooves you when you say one thing and do another."

"You've *seen* that I would not." She glared at him.

The reference to his demens of her shamed Marcus, but he stood his ground, at least verbally. "Our contract is not sealed," he hissed. "I will not let you go until it is."

"Fine." She craned her neck toward the main entrance.

Bolden cast a final grief-stricken plea to his niece.

Platt lifted her chin in answer.

Her uncle turned a steely gaze to Marcus. "I'll be checking on her. If I don't like the way she looks, there won't be any deals or talking."

Marcus said nothing. He counted for patience until the last man triggered the wind ward to turn his attention to Platt.

"You're hurting me," she said in a soft murmur.

He loosened his grip but did not release her. "You will not poison yourself or commit any acts of suicide."

She gasped in horror. "What? Why would you think I would—"

"You haven't met him yet," Marcus sneered. Humans ran at the sight of Tiecus. Demens or no, she still would fear the demon.

Platt kept her mouth shut and stared him down. The intensity of her focus made him wonder if she were trying to reach into his mind.

Marcus cleared his throat, disguising a chuckle. "You will not participate in acts that would cause me harm. You will stay with me and allow me to feed from you whenever I ask."

Even with her throng departed, Platt's inner strength remained. "I don't want you to hurt them—the villagers."

"It is not my intention to hurt them." He entwined a strand of her hair between his claws and inhaled the white-blonde cord. "But I have a right to defend myself and my possessions." He squeezed her hip with meaningful intention.

"Then do everything you can to avoid them." She dropped her eyes and wouldn't look at him.

"Not if they come to me such as Riley did."

She brought a hand up to her neck and gazed toward seemingly nothingness, lost in thought.

"Agreed?" He licked his teeth anxious to break skin and drink.

"If I'm to stay here, I want to be able to see my family."

"We shall see, agreed?"

"You said you were sent here to protect the town." Her voice remained soft. "Why won't you agree to protect the town's people? Aren't they part of the town?"

"Indirectly protect them, yes." He placed a knuckle under her chin and lifted her face to his. "Protecting them from Tier Naug is what I've agreed to do. Since you seem naïve in the way of negotiations, I'll explain it." His tongue rolled around behind his clenched jaw.

"If I were to agree to protect the town's people, that would mean they could wage war against me, and I would not be able to retaliate. Hence, I would be protecting them from me. I'll not agree to that. Not with your uncle still ready to lock horns with me. Yes, the town's people are part of the town. They are *not* the town. And as for avoiding the town's people, they are everywhere. Patrolling this village may cause our paths to cross."

Her innocent doe-like expression ramped up the demon's bloodlust. She was prey. And prey was pounced on, not negotiated with. Still, the way her eyes drew him in, the way she held herself steady against her fears made him give her a certain amount of respect. The same way the ocean tides near oblique cliffs deserve respect.

"Just try to avoid them. I don't want another incident happening like Mr. Morgan."

"The only humans I've killed here are Tier Naug." Ventus started to swirl around his throat, constricting his air, aware of his untruth. "And you." At the admittance, the element of wind retreated allowing Marcus to breathe.

Her eyes snapped to his, and she looked like she was going to demense him just to be sure he wasn't lying.

"Is it true wind takes the air from your lungs for spoken lies?" Platt's steady stare bore into him.

Affronted, he narrowed his eyes. She knew the answer. She knew much about him, and it was both a relief and a torment.

"I agree to your terms." Finality depicted in his tone, avoiding her question.

Her words were as despondent as her doe eyes. "Then we are agreed."

Marcus sighed and eased his upper body. He hadn't noticed he was holding his breath. A tingling sensation spread across his left arm. Marcus pulled at his tunic exposing his shoulder and inspected the latest tattooed agreement. The handwriting was his.

He dropped his sleeve and turned to her. "You don't know how to write?"

Her eyebrows drew together. "No."

Oh, we must fix that hiccup, Asmara tittered.

Marcus smirked. The irony. "You can't sign your name on parchment, but you can enter into a binding contract."

Her hand smoothed the cuff of his shirt up and traced the tattooed words on his arm with her finger.

A shudder of excitement tingled down his spine. Platt's touch short-circuited his mind. He felt weird—gooey and weak. Marcus wanted to rub himself all over her with a desire unlike any hunger.

"Can you teach me?"

Her melodic voice sent shivers through his limbs. "What?"

"Can you teach me to write?" She stared up at his with her large doe eyes.

Still in his hold, nose to nose, he bent down. "Y-yes. Yes. Anything," he slurred, rolling his tongue along the scar on her neck.

Platt shuddered and tried to back up. "Wait . . . now? You want to feed now?"

Baring teeth, he growled, "Not even past the moment and already breaking your agreement."

"No, I just . . . wasn't ready," she said, flushing. "Can you give me warning?"

"You should have asked for that during the negotiations."

Her eyes went wide with horror. But she stood firm. Understanding washed over her whole body. She swallowed, gripped his tunic, closed her eyes, and then leaned her head back to expose the part of her neck that had healed from a slit two days ago.

Disbelief stunned him at her offering. This tiny but brave female laid herself out for his consumption when all others fought or ran. Humiliation softened his brash words. "Little doe." He brushed a strand of her hair, whispering a prayer for her selfless action. He wanted to give her time, but his threshold in ignoring his hunger had peaked even before the fight with Bolden, Riley, and their band.

Savoring the moment, he surveyed her pained expression. Her eyes were closed. Soft light from the window cast highlights in her blonde hair. The air was still. No sound disturbed the moment, save her jagged breathing and heartbeat behind a barrier of skin.

Careful with his talons, he cupped the back of her head and lowered his mouth to her jugular. Marcus swirled his tongue against her skin. She tasted of winter berry leaves. Her blood rushed faster underneath its shield.

Teeth against flesh, jaw set, claw in between his lips, Marcus was ready to puncture her skin. He suckled the point of contact to seal the connection between his lips and her neck to prevent even the slightest drop to escape.

Frightened eyes blasted their way into his consciousness hurling down from a vault of fifteen years. In that instant, before he could free the blood from her veins, Marcus relived every agonizing heartbeat of every victim he'd taken.

Overwhelming shame revived anew as memories flashed. It was always the eyes—horror, hate, revenge, spite, panic. He relived laying Platt down, caressing her face, and apologizing for taking her life. Marcus relived eating all the inhabitants of Dreshal, which had caused Valder's army to rise against him.

Asmara hurled more thoughts of children, innocent, scared younglings, and the females that clung to them. Marcus remembered striking down men, who would have otherwise run but held fast to protect their mates. Faces, terrified cries one after the other, came tumbling into his mind. Memories of a time when Marcus did not have any control over the demon tore through his mind. All the years of consequences for failing to conquer Tiecus came one after the other.

Marcus turned away from Platt.

"You fallen star!" he yelled to Asmara. "The most aching blissful moment of my entire miserable existence, and you do this! Can I not have one cherished, beautiful moment?"

No. Smug satisfaction radiated from the mage.

Marcus turned back to Platt.

Her eyes were wild, her arms stiff.

"Don't run," he whispered.

Mouth open, holding herself like a cornered animal, she nodded once.

She'd seen inside him, knew more than she let on about him—them. She understood his battle. But her enlightenment of his *situation* brought terror, not comfort to her features.

Unable to disguise the pain of her rejection, Marcus turned away and choked out, "It's your first day here. I should let you explore your new home before business."

She breathed a stuttered sigh. "Thank you."

Tiecus roared inside his mind. Marcus held his head in pain. The denial of food sent Tiecus into a fit, and he clamored for control.

Spent and exhausted, Marcus held no more reserve to stay at the forefront. Marcus could no long afford to hold the demon back.

He rushed down the stairs ripping his boots, pants, and tunic off along the way. When he stepped outside, his skin was covered in fur and horns grew out from his enlarging head. The demon took control of their body, and Tiecus burst out to the forefront with a howl. If all of Reginhart hadn't known a demon inhabited the village, they certainly knew now.

Chapter 9

I DELIGHT IN mud squishing through my paws. My Four-Hoof Friend they call Selkie tramples cold ground with me. We are free! The mage sleeps.

Stay on course, Marcus, the Enforcer, says.

Living pillars smell of bark. The faint cure of leaves tells me stories of battles, travelers, flame heads, so many pass through. I smell the whole of home Reginhart in one whiff. I see better when I am free.

Pinecone tells me of another—a poacher on my land.

No smell.

The Enforcer confuses me.

"No?" My jaw forms the confusing word. I follow the poacher smell.

Living wood pillars whisper to my nose. Terra hides the poacher smell, but the living pillars show me where to look in other ways. Snow brings sleep, and death, and a trail. The broken fingers of living pillars tell me which way the poacher goes.

The Enforcer shows me blackness. Blackness is the Atra Solumn. The Enforcer says the confusing word again. "No." No must be Atra Solumn.

The Enforcer is frustrated with me. *What have I done wrong now?* I send an image of chasing my fat, stubby tail.

The Enforcer agrees.

Where do your thoughts come from? the Enforcer asks.

He is silly. Thoughts come from thoughts.

The Enforcer attempts to make me understand "no."

He is a bad teacher.

You're a bad student.

Four-Hoof Selkie Friend stops at old human-made den. The kind of den made from living pillars, now dead. But their husks remain strong.

I smell musk and burnt geraniums. Four-Hoof Friend dances. He knows I will kill the poacher, and we will feed. Four-Hoof Friend walks on. I pounce on Friend's tail. We must search first. He is going in blind. Tactics must be formed. It would be best to scout the nature of this den and then attack.

Four-Hoof Friend lays back ears. He has found the enemy. I press my chest against Four-Hoof Friend's back legs and peek to the front.

A smilodon demon sits with his obsidian fangs and burning eyes. The smilodon perches inside the man den as a *conquistador* sits atop a pile of bone trophies.

I raise shields of my mind too late.

Futile fight, the smilodon says. He thinks he's already won.

Tiecus! The Enforcer rushes to help me push this intruder out. *His host is a Tier Naug!*

Together, we push the smilodon away from the core of ourselves. He is clamoring for our name, our power, our knowledge.

Four-Hoof Friend's hooves fly and strike the man den, setting the top on fire. The dancing light and heat consumes a course circling the smilodon.

The smilodon's demens shows me the tortures his host puts demons through. I see his host pulling demons from the

Atra Solumn, forcing a pact with him to serve, and pushing them into hosts. Many demons are willing. Some are new to riddling and are confused. A few hosts are a band of Tier Naug. More are survivors of King Friend Valder. They fought the riddling.

Hate burns in my throat. It matches the burn of the Enforcer's forearm. His agreements are blazing as fierce as the man den.

Four-Hoof Friend is beating his hooves, screeching his defiance, battling walls to strike the smilodon.

The smilodon must die for bringing demons to Shatter Side. They will be free. Their demons will return to Atra Solumn. Shatter Side is only mine. Only Four-Hoof Friend is allowed. I curl my tongue behind my teeth and roar my intent. Sparks of black globules fly out and sizzle in snow. Along with my roar, black flame lashes out. My breath is fire. Black fire. Fire the color of Atra Solumn.

Fear is in the iridescent eyes of the smilodon. Black fire engulfs him and then silence.

The smilodon is gone.

My horns seem too great to bear, and I lay them on the ground to relieve their pressure. I have little strength to waste.

Even sound is still. All are still awaiting my approval to move.

What have you done? the Enforcer asks.

I breathe black fire, I say proudly.

That's burning death is what it is, the Enforcer says.

Somehow, I believed the smilodon lived. He was away from here, but somehow, I knew he was still inside his host and on Shatter Side.

I care more about sleep.

Rest, the Enforcer says.

His was the permission I need to lie lion style and greet my dreams.

Chapter 10

FUR RECEDED. Tiecus's form melted. The demon's wide, tapered nose pulled back, and his chin drew down. The snow muffled crunches, snaps of bones, and the stretching whine of reforming ligaments. The lupine body and curled horns disappeared into a lithe human shape. Tiecus's hind hooves expanded to Asmara's feet. Clawed apelike paws recessed into hands. A white-blonde lock of curly hair spiraled into Asmara's face.

Tiecus's tufted ears lost their extra hair and stretched painfully against the cold. Information about his immediate surroundings filtered in through the long, curled tips. The barometric pressure was currently one atmosphere, telling Asmara the land was flush with the ocean—sea level, the humans called it. Wind speed fluctuated from 0.06 to 0.09 knots, blowing just enough to make him curse the cold. Humidity climbed to thirty-five percent with a temperature of zero. Tonight would host another foot of snow.

Asmara groaned as his body readjusted.

"By the bright star!" Shivering, he hugged his mostly hairless body. Chilled from the elements bearing their harsh welcome, he stood up with the grace of an old man with arthritis.

Breathing in with his entire chest, he meditated on the mantra "The sheer act of shivering brings me closer to the element of my power."

With the end of each repetition, the grip of frigidness loosened until the mage stood with comfort in the biting cold. His hot breath made a wave of steam as he sighed in relief.

Asmara rubbed his eyes adjusting from nonuse. He cast his gaze up, trying to gain his bearings from the sky, but only saw the underside of trees. He found nothing familiar, until Selkie stomped the snow.

"Good to see you, old friend." Asmara reached out and caressed Selkie's velvet-soft muzzle. Despite what Marcus thought, Selkie was a friend. The demon steed remained a constant in a lonely world.

Selkie perked his ears and pawed at the snow in greeting.

Asmara looked up toward the sky again to see if there was a hint of a star. Even squinting, he saw only underbrush. "All right, tell me what happened."

A cougar demon riddled a Tier Naug. Marcus relayed what Tiecus had seen. *He seems to be bringing demons over from the Atra Solumn to here. Tiecus fought it with a demens and breathed black fire.*

"Wait, black fire? Has *It* ever done so before?"

This was the first time, but it exhausted him. The other demon got away, and Tiecus went to sleep.

"Great. Where there is one demon"—Asmara dusted the snow off his back—"there's a throng. Did the cougar have a smell?" Asmara sniffed the air for any trace of other demons.

It has an absence of smell. As if it's masking its scent. Marcus shrugged inside him. *Something's been bothering me.*

"Go on." Asmara fluffed and detangled his spiral curls with fingers as adeptly as a spider weaving a silk trap.

The villagers blame us—

"You, Marcus, they blame you." Asmara spun around looking for tracks or familiar ground.

Fine. The villagers blame me for something happening to one of their own. A Mr. Morgan.

"Morgan is probably dead if you had anything to do with it. Assume that they think you murdered their cohort."

I have not killed anyone since we got here.

Asmara waited for Marcus to amend his statement. He had killed Platt—technically. No addition came to Marcus's last words. Interesting. "Then maybe this riddled human is Morgan."

You think a Tier Naug is this Morgan?

"Cornelius is a Tier Naug." Asmara clamped down on his tongue. "Damn. Don't think you can go rip out the throat of the king's favorite advisor. He specifically said destroy the Tier Naug *here*."

Silence. But he knew Marcus understood the rules.

Asmara searched for a road, a path, or even an animal trail and then threw up his hands. "Typical. I see we've been left to search our way back in the dark, as always."

But he wasn't worried about getting back. Selkie had an amazing sense of direction. A horse always knew the way home. But as home might still be Benicar for the demon steed, Selkie might go west instead of east.

"Time to get pointed in the right direction." Finding the cardinal points of a city, village, or town was easy. But as a Serenite, Asmara had another resource to find his new "mage tower" in Reginhart.

"Watch and learn." Asmara stepped up to a large redwood, placed both palms on the bark of the tree, and visualized its roots.

Preparing for the subliminal shift, he pushed his consciousness into the tree as easily as Marcus had demensed Platt. The connection to the trees' network was instant.

How are you doing that?

"Trees have an underground network. It can be utilized as a sense of direction if one knows how."

The infrastructure of redwoods actively riffled through Asmara's mind while he searched for landmarks. A chorus of voices soft as rain told him, *After a chiliad of us lies a stone pillar*, and pulled on his core. It felt like he was being yanked into a vat of emotional soup.

Asmara snapped his hand back. "Puppis!"

What's wrong? Sensing his panic, Marcus rushed to the forefront poised to take over.

"This redwood conglomerate was made."

What do you mean?

"These trees," he said. Asmara did not fully believe they were only trees. "They have specific thoughts and emotions that are not abstract at all."

Explain.

Asmara sneered, "Oh, you're not going to just pluck it from my head?"

Marcus settled as Asmara backed away from the redwood pillar.

"I'll explain this once." Asmara rubbed his palms, expelling the tingle of the trees' ability for conscious thought. "Wild elements aren't conscious."

Tell that to Ventus.

Asmara smirked, "You're assuming there is no difference between wild elements, called elements, and named elements."

Silence.

Asmara went east and took painful measures around anything with a layer of bark. He ducked under ghostly, layered spider webs. The thin strings whispered secrets along the tops of his long ears. Selkie followed maneuvering around trees, vines, and bushes.

"Wild elements don't know what they are. They have no consciousness. They are less predictable and more tricky to command."

What's the different between wild and called elements?

Asmara snorted. "Wild elements are born from nature. They are the breeze off the ocean, the fire started by lightning, trees grown from untampered seeds. They are not awoken. They live and die without knowing of their own existence. Called elements are made by one who has the will and knowledge of how to call them. Named elements are conscious with their own personality. Ventus, Terra, Glacias, and Ignis are all named."

Marcus, surprisingly, didn't interrupt him.

"Think of taking a fetus out of the womb, with the capability of it still being alive, and by that being able to shape its features. You could tell it to have blue eyes and blond hair or how tall it would grow or the shape of its face."

Marcus mentally nodded. *Or tell it to have claws at the ends of its fingers.*

Asmara lifted a brow. "Yes, you get the idea. You've tried to hold wildfire. You know how well that works."

I can hold Tiecus's fire.

"Ah yes, you can. His fire was made, not born. When you call an element, or make it, you change that element. You tell it to have yellow-white skin. You tell it how high it can blaze. You tell it how hot it can burn. Doing that changes the element. It makes it become aware. Through your will, it knows itself. When you call fire, it realizes it was chosen—

that it has a destiny. Much like a god calling on a subject to do his bidding."

Apparently, I call wind that believes its destiny is to try and push me over high ledges.

Asmara laughed. "What fun is to be had in telling it to stop?"

So, what you're saying is these trees were changed.

"They were made." Asmara stopped. He looked around but shook his head. "They were grown with help."

You think they were made by the Serenite?

"No." Asmara paused. "I would have felt if they were. They knew who I was, not what I was."

They'd both felt the network of emotion. The power within these trees was too vast to calculate. But they'd given him what he asked for—directions. Asmara knew the way to the stronghold. He knew the way to Benicar and the way to the Serenites' enclave, Ziodonia. He knew the location of Platt's house, Riley's house, and Bolden's house. In fact, he knew the location of all the buildings in Reginhart.

Can you make wildfire know itself?

Asmara reached the main road that led to the stronghold. Once Selkie and he stood on the path, Asmara hopped onto Selkie's back.

"First, you have to understand that each separate fire is a different being by itself. When it dies, its potential dies. Same with wind. Once the wind had no more ability to blow and dies, it's the death of another being. One body of water is different from another. Mountains have a different personality from the flat lands."

I understand.

"Do you?" Asmara didn't touch Selkie's fiery mane. He held on with his legs as the steed loped the straight road.

Yes. You are of the Serenite race just as the ocean is water. You stand as one of your race. Your name is not Serenite. You are a Serenite.

"Well done." Asmara blocked a section of his mind before asking the next question. "Knowing all that, can you answer your own question? If an element is born and not made, can it grow into consciousness?"

They rode past the portcullis before Marcus answered.

If others of the same kind have the potential, then yes. Wildfire can know itself.

Asmara gave Selkie a grateful pat, dismounted, and stargazed while he built the ice door with Selkie behind it.

"And now you know the potential danger of waking a wild element."

No. I don't. And why are you locking in Selkie if you don't think he'll return to the ocean?

His eyes wandered to the east tower every so often. "This is for his comfort and the safety of the villagers."

Asmara could feel Marcus rankle at his "thoughtfulness." But Asmara's mood turned melancholy as the ice door formed into the shape of a rose.

Platt's inside, Marcus whispered.

"Yes, well, we have three choices," Asmara said. "Stay outside naked in the cold. Cut my time short and let you take over. Or go inside the warm tower, cloth myself, cure my famine, and after swearing the doe to secrecy"—his lecherous smile stretched wide—"end my loneliness."

At the entrance, a basket lay before the front door. Asmara took the handle of the wicker container before he stepped inside. Air pressure rushed past his ears, indicating Platt was still in the tower or at least someone with same mass and density as her was.

A hearth fire across the room lit the kitchen. The pile of clothes Marcus had ripped off were folded and placed neatly before the stairs. He contemplated whether Platt would consider it rude if he left the pile there. Mayhap, he should acknowledge the gesture and stow the clothes away. How terribly convenient for Marcus.

He set the basket down on the counter next to the hearth, walked past the clothes, and went upstairs.

The doe was curled in a ball on his sleeping chair. She looked cold, wrapped around herself with no blanket. She was not fully asleep. The tempo of her breathing was too fast.

He opened the double doors of his armoire and stood in front of his options, as if he had more than one robe. Over his shoulder, he said softly, "Marcus says thank you for arranging his clothes. I don't think he was planning on telling you about me, but I couldn't resist seeing your beautiful face with my own eyes."

Marcus groaned. *Blame everything on the Enforcer.*

Asmara took the only clothing choice from the cubby hole. He held out the blue felt robe with silver piping for inspection. The mage thumbed a charred spot on the sleeve where *It* once tried to burn the robe.

"If you're hungry, little doe, I'll fix stew," he said pulling the attire over his head.

Even in the dark, her face turned sunset pink.

Without another word, he returned downstairs to the kitchen and set about curing his hunger.

"What shall we make?" he said to the kitchen.

Instantaneously, utensils whirled around in the air. Knives cut fresh vegetables. Brooms swept the floor, the hearth fire stoked, and pitchers of water filled the cooking pot. When the cauldron had enough water, it swung itself onto a hook over the fire. The kitchen was chaotic order, with everything in its place performing a job.

"Celery—" Asmara huffed at the knife methodically chopping away. "Again? What happened to all the carrots?"

A faint whinny could be heard in the distance.

"Never mind." Asmara waved a hand.

The knife scooped the chopped celery and dropped the vegetables in the stew pot. A few other roots were added, and it wasn't long before the water began to bubble.

The scuffling of feet behind him brought a smile to his face. Asmara spun in delight for a proper introduction.

Platt was slack-jawed and staring into his face.

"Greetings!" Asmara bowed with his left hand touching his forehead and then brought his bent elbow down to his waist with his palm open and up. The polite gesture gave him the opportunity to examine her feminine frame with more scrutiny. The sack of a dress she wore didn't hide her curves or her strong arms.

"Please call me Asmara."

The only response he got was a blink.

He smirked and lowered his hand to his side. She wasn't a Serenite, but the slight of a greeting unreturned stung a tad. Still, he was groomed for pleasantries, and it'd been decades since he'd talked to anyone face-to-face. "I must insist that if you plan on using my slope chair, then you should let me be your coverlet."

She did not laugh or retort. Her astonished stare began to make him uncomfortable.

Asmara kept his eyes locked to hers. He didn't want to show disrespect by looking away. He wasn't a demon and couldn't demense her, but she might not know that. Her silence continued, and he shifted his weight, straightening his upper body.

Platt took careful, timid steps as if Asmara would vanish before she could reach him.

He tried acting normal. If he acted normal, she wouldn't think he was one of those trite, abrasive, conceited creatures humans mistook for his people.

"Oh, and before I forget," he said, coaxing any two-way conversation, "I suggest you stay away from the barn no matter the circumstance. Selkie will enchant you and then rip you apart if he gets the chance. I care not to recount how many have fallen prey to the harmless-steed routine."

Platt stopped before him and raised a hand.

He thought she was going to touch him, but she stopped short. Outstretched fingers hung in the air. Her gaze shifted from his face to his ears.

Muscles under his right eye twitched. He was used to being objectified. He was the courtier of the Serenite. But humans didn't understand Serenite customs. Platt didn't know she triggered erotic responses by paying attention to his antenna. Asmara gritted his teeth and reminded himself humans had misconceptions about his kind.

Crazy stories had been told about mythical long-eared creatures in the woods. It infuriated him they were only known for their "peaceful" ways.

Asmara took hold of her outstretched hand. He'd gently set her straight before she presumed what he was.

"You're an elf," she whispered.

Asmara's nose flared, and the kindness he felt soured. "What did you call me?"

Fixated on his ears, she didn't seem to notice his rising temper.

He batted her hand away and reeled back in disgust. "I am not a shoemaker! Nor do I grant wishes. I don't have a stash of shiny, glittering round flat pieces to give you. I don't know where your mythical one-horned horses are, and I am certainly *not* the savior of this mess you have gotten yourself into."

The room turned cold. Frost spread out from the ground under his bare feet.

Shock mingled with awe in Platt's wide eyes.

He pointed a dangerous forefinger at her. "I am not some feeble do-gooder that goes around helping humans and their ridiculous problems. You are brave, little doe. It's apparent in your name calling of me and that small feat of stupidity agreeing to Marcus's terms. What good do you think it will do? You are human after all. And you will *die* much sooner than *It* or Marcus or I for that matter. And when you do, he'll go back to killing. . . probably the villagers you want to protect. So, that makes your contract with Marcus useless now, doesn't it?"

She stood not breathing. All sense of wonder in her expression turned to disbelief. Her lips thinned to a line. Then she said, "What contract did you make with Marcus?"

His chest tightened. She knew. All the way up the curls of his ears, he knew Marcus shouldn't have demensed her. "None of your business." He gritted his teeth, regretting he'd exposed himself.

"Then don't call me stupid."

He liked her. She was both soft and strong. Lively verbal sparring seemed likely in their future. But he needed to appeal for her silence about him. Instead of bantering, Asmara took the high road.

Locking his eyes on hers, he brought his left hand and touched his fingertips to his forehead. He touched his lips and brought his palm over his chest. Finally, he lowered his hand holding air.

"My apologies to you, Platt Ottern. While I find your words rude and offensive, my reaction may have been too harsh. I carry no ill will toward you." Standing before her, waiting to be released from this posture of humility, Asmara waited for her acknowledgement.

Dropping her eyes from his gaze, she fiddled with her fingers. "I'm sorry if I offended you."

Asmara's mouth dropped open. Without eye contact, her apology was a slap in the face. Heat warmed his throat and traveled up. He breathed and reminded himself that she was human. How would a human know what was courteous?

"Don't disrespect me." He grabbed her chin and tugged upward.

"I wasn't trying to." She shoved his hand away.

"Look me in the eye. Recognize my presence. When you look down or at the wall, you belittle me. You think you're better than me?"

"What is your problem?" She stepped back. "I can't even apologize without offending you."

She looked straight in his eyes, and he saw defiance. Asmara closed his eyes, forcing his climbing arousal away. Opening his eyes, he said, "Have the self-respect to say it to mine eye."

"I was trying to show respect by not looking in your eyes," she growled in frustration.

Asmara waited. He admired her courage to look anyone face-to-face after what Marcus had done to her.

Platt kept her eyes trained on his. "I'm sorry if I offended you."

He nodded. The situation was over. Bygones were bygones.

"Are you hungry?" All the resentment he felt was gone. That was the way of the Serenite.

She gave him a weak smile, seeming at a loss for words.

Two bowls presented themselves, one to Platt and one to Asmara. He took the bowl and spoon in front of him and began shoveling soup like this was his last meal.

She reluctantly took hers from the air and looked at the contents inside. When she didn't eat right away, the spoon inside her bowl lifted and brought stew to her mouth. She took the utensil, blew on the food, and began to eat.

"Ventus seems to like you."

She laid the bowl in her lap and looked at him with disgust.

"What?" He scraped the bowl for another mouthful.

She wrinkled her nose. "Nothing."

He stopped eating and frowned. "If you like, I can have Marcus show you some things you can do with the elemental."

Don't promise things on my behalf, Marcus huffed.

The light in her eyes returned. "Oh, is Ventus magic?"

It warmed his ego at having to explain his world to such a pretty figure. "Ah, magic. Calling Ventus magic is like calling the most delicious apple that you've ever tasted food." His ears twitched, and she shot a glance at the movement. "It would be as if I didn't acknowledge your name and called you 'human' to get your attention."

He rose from his chair and tossed the empty bowl. It landed on the chopping block with a soft rattle. "Come. Let me show you how you can see your family."

Platt didn't seem to know what to do with her barely eaten food. She went back to the butcher block and set her bowl down next to his then ran over to him.

He sat down next to the broken mirror staying out of its reflection, staring, and waiting for her to join him. Terra was already weaving vine tendrils on the floor and would soon have the ground layered like the walls. Platt sat next to him and looked at the mirror.

Asmara breathed in and reached out to her chin. "Eyes, please."

She flicked her eyes to him with enthusiastic wonder.

"First, you must visualize where you want to see. Then you circle the mirror three times. On the first ring, call out who you are. The second ring, call out the place you want to see. During the third ring, call out why you are contacting this place."

She nodded.

Asmara brought his attention to the floor. He brought his index finger to the mirror and started moving his hand clockwise. The first circle, he said, "Asmara Grey." During the second circle around, he said, "Ziodonia." The final circle, he said, "I wish to see Alene."

The cracks and imperfections in the mirror fogged over and then revealed a room. The walls were convex and wooden. Stumps grew out from the wall in a spiral staircase. A sloped chair like the one she'd been sleeping on sat against the far wall. A table that grew from the floor like a mushroom occupied the opposite side. The center of the room was clutter-free except for a circular rug on the floor.

"No one is there." Platt peered into the room.

He breathed deep, reminding himself she was not trying to anger him by avoiding his eyes.

Asmara leaned under her gaze in obvious search of her attention. "Except Alene."

"I don't see anyone." Platt raised her head to him.

Asmara laughed. "Alene is my home. She is the tree I grew since I could wield Terra."

A glow of amazement shone in Platt.

"Terra is the magic of earth." He smiled. "Slow and devastating once unleashed, and there is no stopping her. But scrying isn't too dangerous. Just don't visualize the Atra Solumn, and you'll be fine."

Platt pointed at the mirror. "Why is earth magic?"

Asmara waited for her to look back at him. When she did, he replied, "Mirrors are made of glass. Glass is made of sand. Sand is Terra's domain."

"This is how I can see my family?" Platt looked down in awe.

"Yes." He made a show of searching for her eyes again. "If they have a mirror, you can communicate."

Asmara sighed and spoke softly to Alene. The tree didn't have eyes or a consciousness, not like the forest outside, but Alene flowed with energy. "Everything is as the day I left."

Platt faced him, and this time when she met his eyes, he didn't like the pity within them. "Ziodonia is where you lived?"

Lifting an eyebrow, he edged his words with a dangerous lilt. "Looking for elves?"

She gave him a sad smile. "You can't ever go back, can you?"

Deduction and reason could be a wonderful ally and a formidable enemy. Platt was not as dumb as she acted.

"Touché, little doe." The mage pointed his index finger and circled the mirror widdershins three times. The image of Alene disappeared and was replaced by the reflection of three entities that resided in one body.

Platt pulled back with a hand to her mouth. The doe trembled as if Asmara had shot her with an ice arrow.

He didn't blame her. Even asleep, Tiecus was a right ugly cuss. If her fear wasn't from the demon, seeing three beings in the same space was disconcerting enough. He grabbed her free wrist and made his face a mask of calm. "Don't be frightened."

"I thought Marcus was the demon and you the warlock." Platt's eyes remained fixed on him. "By the bright star! What is that!"

"Another assumption." He felt the need to defend his title as mage. "I'm not a warlock, and Marcus is not the demon."

He could feel her shaking and waited until his words sunk in. "I am a mage. A master of the element I choose. Marcus is a barrier between me and *It*."

He could see in her eyes she was working the logic out. Platt swallowed. "The other is the demon."

"Yes." Asmara grinned but not in amusement. "That is what you made your agreement with."

Her body went stiff. "I made my promise to Marcus." She averted her eyes from him and swallowed. Closing her eyes, she shook her head. "I promised Marcus not that—"

"Thing," Asmara finished for her. "Monster. Abhorrent animal."

Platt blinked and then looked at him with new eyes. She scooted toward him. "This explains much." The shakes returned to her body, and her fingers vibrated when she touched the knuckles of his hand.

By the bright star, she was brave. "You have nothing to fear while I'm with you." He patted her hand in reassurance.

"You are all of them?" She tossed a strand of her hair back. "They are both inside you?"

Asmara tilted his head. "I guess you could say we are all in Marcus."

Platt looked up and down the length of his ears.

Keeping calm, he tried to distract her with questions. "Where did you learn that curse?"

Platt scrunched her features up. She looked rather adorable confused. "What curse?"

"You said 'by the bright star.' Where did you learn that term?"

"It's something my mother says. Why?"

"Haven't heard it coming from a human's mouth." He shrugged. "I was curious."

"Tell me something." Her whole body trembled. "Tell me about Ziodonia, since I won't be going there."

He lifted an authoritative finger upward, but the air around him pulled then pushed notifying him that the warning ward had gone off. Someone or something was coming up to the keep.

"Here comes your cavalry." He lowered his hand.

Or, Marcus forewarned, *maybe that demon in the forest.*

She looked quizzically at him.

"Oh please." He rolled his eyes. "Those men aren't going to just give you up. It's probably them coming to try and catch Marcus by surprise. There's going to be at least one more fight for you. The large one—what was his name?— ah, Bolden—thank you, Marcus—that one threatened he'd return."

Platt gave him a guarded stare.

Asmara rose. "Don't worry, I'll just throw a few ice arrows at them, and if they're smart, they'll reconsider."

"Wait!" Platt shot up. "Please don't hurt them."

"As if I could," Asmara uttered, but he wasn't going to be the one to give away the secret of the Serenite curse. He started for the stairs.

Platt raced up behind him. "How do you know they are coming?"

He stopped dead in his ascent and turned to her. Again, she had spoken without meeting his eyes, and it was beginning to really irritate him. He'd rather she grab him or even knock him down to the ground before speaking to him without eye contact.

"Oh, I get it, human humor. I have ears so long I can hear them from the gates, right? Well, maybe I can. How is it that even the timid of your race are so rude?"

Her eyes cowered at his scolding, but her body nearly brushed up against him. She glanced at his ears, and he was flabbergasted with her inappropriate flirting.

Asmara held up his hands. "All right, let's play by these rules. First, look me in the eye before speaking to me when you want a response. Second, glancing at my ears means you want to have sex with me. You've been looking at my ears yet not advancing to the next stage. I'll be direct. Do you want to have sex?"

Platt stammered, looked away, then back at him speechless.

He huffed and stomped up the stairs. Perhaps he was being too harsh. Perhaps he should teach her some of the Serenite ways so she wouldn't tick him off.

Or maybe we should learn human customs, Marcus said. *We are in human territory.*

Asmara went to the third floor, opened one of the heavy double doors, and walked across the highest room in the tower. Platt followed behind where Ignis had yet to burn in the hearth, and the stone floor felt as cold as the moon. Long slits in the walls, barely wide enough as peek holes, allowed Ventus to whip in and out the so-called windows.

"These quarters are yours, by the way." Asmara flipped a wrist to the barren room. Asmara strutted toward the exit. He wiggled his ears in case Platt was looking.

"See, I can flirt at inappropriate times too." It was childish, but he was irked.

"I wasn't trying to flirt."

Asmara whipped around and met her eyes. "First, I wasn't speaking to you. I'd look you in the face if I were. Second, if you're not flirting, then stop looking at my ears."

He turned around and peeked through the window.

Platt grabbed his arm, spun him around, and pinned him with her gaze. "My apologies."

He nodded. She was learning. "Let me know if I can assist in decorating your room." He smiled in sultry satisfaction. "Or if you'd like to use me as a decoration. I make a great *comforter*."

Shouldering out of her grip, he stepped onto the ledge outside the window, powdered in snow. The battalion's catwalk spanned the portcullis side. The path allowed them to see the village, the pathway up to the keep, and the land northwest of the stronghold. Down the path Asmara expected a dozen or so torchbearers, maybe even a demon.

An army of fifty well-organized men with pikes, swords, and horse-drawn carts marched up the steep incline to the stronghold. All of them bore red hair and pale freckled skin.

"Puppis!" he cursed.

Asmara flung his hand. An ice arrow shot out and landed on the ground outside the portcullis gates. Ice spread covering the incline to the stronghold as the Tier Naug climbed. If Asmara's idea worked, slippery ground would slow the approaching battalion and give him time. He retreated to the tower trying to prevent the "plight of the Serenite" before it took hold.

Shouting soldiers, the clang of metal on ice, and clomping hooves triggered his pain. Hearing the mayhem, Asmara clenched his stomach and doubled over.

"I will not spew." Asmara concentrated on getting inside. "I will not spew."

"Are you all right?" Platt took his arm and led him to the room.

He nodded and wrapped a hand around her to support himself. "Tier Naug."

"Can Marcus help?"

"He'll have to do. That purposeless demon is asleep." Once Asmara was inside, the nausea diminished.

Platt's jaw was set in a warrior's stance ready to face off with an enemy.

"Stay here." Asmara was unbuttoning his blue velveteen garment. Marcus was a breath away from taking over control. "Don't get in the way."

Asmara sailed down the stairs while lifting his robe over his head. With the grace of a cougar demon, Asmara put his clothes back in the armoire, closed his eyes, breathed out, and fell into the background.

Chapter 11

THE ONLY CONCESSION Asmara insisted on was to *not* rip his robes. Marcus was taller and wider and double Asmara's size. Marcus usually metamorphosized to the forefront naked for that reason.

He walked across the empty room and cracked open the door. The stairway below was a black void. Marcus dashed naked through the darkness and took careful steps to the landing above the first floor, ducking his head, checking if Platt was there.

Just get down there, idiot! Asmara scoffed.

"I'm—I'm not dressed." His newfound modesty kept Marcus on edge.

You're ridiculous! She doesn't know how to read. She doesn't know what any of the agreements say.

"Yes, but she'll see them as scars." Marcus wanted to retrieve his clothes from downstairs before he could frighten her more. Seeing Tiecus had shocked her.

She saw all your scars when you went traipsing off yesterday.

He'd ripped his clothes off in front of her without a problem, but now he'd rather face an angry Tier Naug mob instead of standing before Platt in the buff. But she wasn't anywhere to be found.

Marcus streaked down the stairs to his folded clothes and fought each piece to get them on as fast as he'd torn them off.

He squared his hat and searched the room with more scrutiny. The air left remnants of her vanilla scent, but she was not here.

"Platt?"

No answer.

Get going. There is no time for modesty or playing hide and seek. You have a battalion to destroy.

Marcus opened the door, crossed the courtyard, and strode through the open portcullis. Down at the bottom of the hill, a pile of Tier Naug collected their bearings. They hadn't caught on that they were under attack. A surprise bout of black flame could wipe them out.

What I want to know is how a mass of Tier Naug can hide from a demon. Marcus mentally poked at Tiecus. The gesture was a vain attempt to wake a demon known to sleep soundly for days. Tiecus's black fire had spent all the energy the demon had left.

One good thing about all this is you don't have to save food for later.

Marcus smiled. "That's right. We have a blood doll."

Asmara nestled deep in his core. Far enough away so the Serenite wouldn't feel, hear, or see the violence to ensue.

Lightning crashed, breaking off into sticky fingers greedy for Terra's touch. New snow crunched under his feet. Selkie nickered with anticipation and clomped to his side.

"He was a fool to think he could keep you locked away." Marcus snickered. "Hungry?"

A toss of fiery mane was answer enough.

Marcus's right arm began to tingle where Valder's agreement was etched. Marcus stepped toward the slick road of ice and tested the downhill-sloped ice chute Asmara had created to send the Tier Naug skating to the bottom of the hill. Marcus howled a territorial warning and jumped on the iced-over path. He slid, gaining speed and using his hands for balance, down the icy slope. But staying on two feet didn't worry him half as much as the wall of soldiers at his destination. Long twelve-foot soldier pikes pointed in his direction. They were more of a concern for him than riding the ice chute on his ass.

Anxiety charged the magic of his inner strength. Sliding down the hill, he pulled on Glacias—elemental ice—as Asmara had shown him, focused on his target, and flung his hand out. Nothing happened.

"That's disconcerting." Without Asmara or Tiecus assisting, the elements paid him no respect. But he had more to offer a worthy adversary than ice arrows. He also wasn't alone.

Selkie galloped past, gnashing teeth together, and leading the fight. The Tier Naugs' line held their stance. Marcus had never seen, only heard from the mage, what the inferno steed could maneuver.

Selkie spun at the last moment, sliding backward toward the pikemen. The demon steed leaped, lashing out with his hind hooves and sweeping an arc across heads, shoulders, and weapons.

The steed's maneuver was called an airs-above-the-ground, and Selkie's execution of the exercise was glorious and effective. The defensive front line now had a hole. Fire erupted. The stench of smoldering flesh permeated the air. Tossed chunks of leather-covered limbs followed the demon steed's progress.

The hole Selkie had made began to close. They may have been unprepared, but the Tier Naug were not untrained. Making sure he wouldn't get the pointy end of a stick, Marcus leaped into the air. His wild acrobatics launched him well over the line, but Marcus had no control. He backflipped into a wood cart.

"Ohmph," Marcus grunted at impact. Unyielding objects jabbed his muscles. Long straight sticks clanked at his thrashing arms and legs.

Below him was a cart full of lightning sticks. Gratification halted his floundering. He was sitting on the Tier Naugs' stash of arquebus.

With a working arquebus in hand, he could return to Benicar if Ardin didn't renege on his agreement. This time, when he got out of his Reginhart agreement, he'd find some distant den to sleep, eat his blood doll at will, and keep to himself.

Tiecus would be happy. Asmara would be happy. He could finally find the "tranquility" he'd yearned to learn. But that was after he killed this batch of Tier Naug soldiers.

An upraised claymore came hurtling above him, ready to split him in half. Marcus grabbed an arquebus from the cart, and it held against the two-handed weapon. The Tier Naug behind the sword glared death and malice. Marcus kicked the soldier in the stomach.

The human stumbled backward. Marcus scooted out of the broken cart. The clatter of a few dozen lightning sticks came along with him. The thwarted soldier swung from the side. Marcus blocked, and the metal stick protested with a ring. He stepped close to the Tier Naug and elbowed his opponent in the nose.

The soldier laughed throwing his head back. It was a hollow sound. A sound reserved for the insane. Marcus hit him hard. What rendered other men unconscious only angered this one.

The Tier Naug raised his sword and planted the butt of his weapon against Marcus's head. Stunned, Marcus fell back. Sword raised in both hands, the Tier Naug exposed his throat. Demon reflexes responded.

Marcus jutted upward. His jaws wrapped around the Tier Naug's throat. Thick, hot liquid poured into his mouth. A metal butt pounded on his back. Marcus let out a grunt.

Pulling back, he brought most of a throat with him. The meat tasted wrong, the blood smelled fetid, and sooner than he had ripped out the Tier Naug's jugular, he spat out the chunk of flesh.

The human with no neck remained standing. Raising his sword to strike again, the Tier Naug stepped forward. Dumbfounded, Marcus gripped the arquebus in his hand. The Tier Naug's resilience faded. Eyes glazed over. Pale death covered his face. The human crumpled to the ground.

Vertigo unbalanced Marcus. The blood in his mouth tasted putrid. Bone-crushing pain tore a screech from his lips. His arquebus disappeared into the powdery snow. The tip end of a broad sword stuck out his left shoulder.

If there was a time to go into blood rage, this was it. But Tiecus didn't stir.

Marcus whirled around. Agony near took him. The sword was lodged in his collar bone. Marcus swung around, but the owner that wielded the weapon didn't come with it. With his good arm, Marcus caught the human by the throat. The man choked and clawed at Marcus's arm. All the enforcer's hate came to focus. Marcus crushed his enemy's windpipe under his claws.

Another sword wielder shouted his approach. Marcus brought his human-shield into place, and side-stepping another sword tip, he pushed his captive into the other man's weapon. The two humans intertwined and tumbled backward.

His stomach churned. The world spun with no end. His mouth turned dry. Disoriented, his thoughts clouded over, and his focus scattered.

Over Selkie's war cries and the shouts of men, the demon steed accosted warrior after warrior. Rearing up on his hind legs, he caught each in the chest with his front hooves, smashing them to the ground and stomping their heads until they exploded like ripe watermelons. Fire spewed from his nostrils after each defeated human. He reminded Marcus of ferocious wolves howling after a kill.

A Tier Naug shouted orders. Their language sounded like hisses and broken coughs.

Marcus used his right arm to take hold of the sword tip in his shoulder. Breathing in preparation only prolonged his anxiety. He yanked up, breaking bone and muscle. He yelled and a sweeping wave of nausea sent him to the ground.

"Wake up!" Marcus swayed to his feet and positioned himself in a fighting stance.

Tiecus remained asleep.

The scenery weaved and bobbed in front of Marcus. Five, or maybe six, pikemen surrounded him, pushing metal spikes against undeniably calculated key points to his body.

"What is in your blood?" He didn't move. Marcus looked down at the pikes. "So, a painful and slow death or painful and quick one." Depending on which soldier pierced him first, there were only two choices for death.

His core, the rage within, and the power of his magic were the only things keeping him vertical. Valder's embroidered contract itched.

Shouts, clangs of metal on metal, and the sounds of a skirmish brought his attention outside the ring of certain destruction.

Bolden wielded a shovel. Or perhaps a pickaxe. Marcus's vision became unreliable. But the ox handled his weapon of choice like the finest sword ever made. Beside him, Riley swung an arquebus as a club. More villagers followed.

Selkie waged war in his own circle-trap of death. The steed bucked and caught a Tier Naug by the stomach. But strength faded from the inferno steed. The Tier Naugs' blood had affected him too.

A surge of angry helplessness created a moment of clarity.

"What do you want with me?"

Beyond the crowd, a different Tier Naug parted soldiers. He wore a loose-fitting robe, and his walked seemed familiar. Glowing iridescent eyes over a sarcastic grin proved to be the commanding officer of this band of over-sea landers. The Tier Naug had a warlock. *No*, he corrected himself, *not a warlock. An infested, riddled warlock.* The cougar demon Tiecus had fought in the woods ambled toward Marcus.

His adversary moved with such sleek, precise movements that Marcus bet the Tier Naug's demon was a smilodon. Marcus sneered at memories of obsidian teeth.

Bolden swung his shovel with accurate force. Riley bolstered with fevered blows. The youngling did not have Bolden's control, but Marcus had felt the force of Riley's blows. Riley had the concept of survival in their two-man circle. The team fought well together. Marcus knew from experience those two were a deadly combination.

But the villagers were outnumbered three to one. Bolden's attempts forward were slowed by an increasing number of soldiers. Marcus and Selkie were contained, allowing the Tier Naugs' focused efforts on the villagers. Standing there, watching the two men fending off the Tier Naug, made the tattoo on Marcus's arm, the agreement he'd made with Platt, burn in agony.

Side by side, Bolden and Riley held together as more soldiers came after them. Here he was, standing in the middle of a sphere of pikemen, doing nothing. Platt's uncle and the man she bargained her body for fought the Tier Naug.

"Bolden, Riley, what are you doing? Run!" It wasn't an act of chivalry. It was a request to stop his damn arm from burning.

In anguish, Bolden roared. One of the Tier Naug landed a blow. The ox-man lowered to one knee. Riley bellowed out and swung his club with even less control.

Their cries sharpened his senses. Little doe would be displeased if her uncle died, especially if Marcus stood by and watched.

The thought of Platt in Tier Naug hands caused a vile reaction. The challenging fire rising in his gut was unexplainable. Defending Platt was something more than protecting property, more than retaining his blood doll. His heart thumped harder with every beat. He took deeper breaths. Marcus embraced his white-hot core.

He grabbed the pole pointed at his heart. The pikemen shoved hard. Marcus had enough control to push the spear down and guide the pointed end under his rib cage.

All the other spears hit their mark. Marcus folded, and the demented attackers laughed. The Tier Naug warlock shouted and began to run toward him. Holding the pole under his ribs, Marcus roared befitting a demon. Rising, he shoved the pole back into the spearman's ribs, cutting the laughter short. Marcus would put these new porcupine quills protruding from his body to use. He spun.

Some held on to their weapon, but others couldn't. Those that let go crashed into their other companions.

The burning in his arm stopped while the rest of him felt the agony of his choice.

Marcus pulled out a free pike and savagely returned it to a stunned foot soldier.

The warlock rushed him and pulled out a pole from Marcus's arm with the vicious mercy of a badger. A snap of air escaped Marcus.

"Alive!" The warlock turned to a downed soldier. "I said keep 'em alive!" The warlock stabbed the soldier with his own weapon in maniacal repetition.

The holes in Marcus's side ached. His head spun. With the ground spinning, he wanted to lie there till everything was over. Even snow looked as favorable as a soft mattress. He reached inside his core.

"Tiecus?" he whispered. "Will I have a body to bury?"

Shut up, Asmara thought back. *If you did, he'd burn it.*

Surprised, Marcus started to fall into the background. Asmara's healing power instilled a sense of relief. "How are you awake?"

Don't give up on me. A flicker of Asmara's terror escaped.

Finally, his spinning head no longer held consciousness.

Chapter 12

FACE DOWN IN the snow, Asmara morphed to the forefront, trying to breathe air and not frozen water. Staying alive meant getting away from the battle ground. If he left them all lying there, they were all dead.

Is living worth all this? The doe flashed in his mind, and a small flicker of hope answered. *Yes.* Asmara willed Platt safe with all his power-commanding elements.

Gurgled cries, sharp orders, and the clash of weapons broke his concentration. Asmara seized with nauseous spasms rippling through his body. The effects of the curse came ramping up and out his throat. The last of his energy went to throwing up his dinner. Celery, turnips, and bile kept company beside him.

The battle surrounded Asmara. He could hear, more than see, the fighting. He clutched his stomach and heaved. Piles of warm stew soaked in the snow. His eye lids squeezed together. It didn't matter. Crushed bone, lacerated arteries, and every dying breath funneled in his ears and through him as it happened. Every blow executed on a sentient being reverberated inside his body.

Sitting in clothes five sizes too large, physical agony drove him to begging. "Stop! Stop! It hurts! I'll go mad," he whispered.

With this many people inflicting harm against each other, Asmara was helpless to the pain. Phantom swords slashed his arms. Invisible maces crushed his legs. While no physical harm came to him, Asmara felt every blow inflicted on everyone else. His forehead rested on the snow, and tears of agony dropped off the bridge of his nose.

"Away," he chanted the one word continuing to rock back and forth. "Away, away, away."

The snow below him complied. Small crystals rolled away at first. Tiny flakes collected onto themselves. Collections of flakes made fist-sized snowballs. It wasn't long before he sank into a hole of wet dirt. The snow took itself *away* until an igloo of spheres surrounded him.

His repeated mantra rolled the white globes further away. Powdered lumps tumbled and grew.

Shouts of anguish, the murder cries of demented, deranged, and maniacal the Tier Naug threatened Asmara's sanity. A stab of lightning passed through his chest. He gagged at the squish of flesh and blood nearby. Asmara forced a breath inward and used the pain to command Glacias.

The snowballs tumbled with purpose. They struck hard against the Tier Naugs' legs. Snow spheres built on each other traveling up the soldiers' feet hardened to ice. The Tier Naug were trapped where they stood.

Confused shrieks deafened Asmara. Their fear echoed inside him. Through a break between seizures, Asmara directed the element of ice to his favor. A small burst of clarity gave him enough concentration to send his snowball troops into battle.

Cold, bony fingers wrapped around his right ear and yanked up. This time, it was his own sensitive appendage under attack. Asmara's high-pitched scream, thick with magic, sent a rippling shock wave through the air.

His attacker let go, but the chance to escape was moot. Violence was everywhere. Asmara was a sponge to the hate, the fear, and the damage inflicted on others.

His body crumpled to the ground. Rough, crude rope tied his hands behind his back. A burlap bag slipped over his head. The scratchy material irritated his long ears. Shaking his head to get the bag off only rubbed his antennae raw.

Someone, he presumed the warlock, moved in close and whispered, "Sleep."

The words were laced with magic, but the Serenite curse was stronger. He couldn't *sleep* even if he wanted to. But he played the game. Asmara stopped struggling. He poured all his will into remaining still and muffling his gags. Breathing slow and deep, he tried to emulate sleep.

Cold hands dragged him feet-first through the hard-packed ice.

Asmara suppressed his scoff. The nerve of the warlock, his brutish, uncivilized manner tweaked Asmara's sense of propriety. *Can't even carry me? Yes, I adore snow up my arse. Use me as a wet soak, go ahead. Shall I lick your boots while I'm down here?*

The battle was getting further away. His queasiness subsided. The urge to expel his guts waned. The pain of battle had exhausted his reserves, and now he wished for sleep.

Not the brightest idea I've had lately, but I'm not going to just lie here and take it, Asmara mused waiting for one of the two to acknowledge his double entendre. Nothing.

Not unless he apologizes for dragging me around and then asks nicely. Still nothing. He inwardly sighed. *Oh, but it'd be too much to hope for, him wanting something to do with my courtesan talents. And, as usual, no one's listening. I'm officially talking to myself. Ah well, here goes.*

He kicked out.

Someone gasped, and his legs were free.

Asmara croaked for air. Even with the price of sparring, a morbid sense of pride washed over him. "Thanks for the new meaning of snow packed."

Cold sweat pasted the oversized clothes to Asmara's skin. The inside of his mouth burned from the raw fibers of the bag over his head. Marcus was dying. The useless demon was still asleep. Asmara was on his own. *Typical.*

"Get up." Asmara coached himself.

The burlap bag was removed and scraped against his ears. He could see. The warlock punched him in the solar plexus. Asmara heaved.

"Ya *b'rk* is m're vicious th'n you're bite." The warlock tied a rope around the gag. "I will remember next time."

You want a bark? I'll give you a bark. Asmara flailed against his restraints. The sack muffled his cries of anger. Tears streaked down his face. His tongue lashed at the itchy material. *I'll develop canker sores from this blasted bag.*

"I've never c'ptured an elf before," the warlock chuckled.

Asmara yelled out, but with the material in his mouth, he was unable to cuss out the Tier Naug warlock.

"Tell me, 'ow did you abscond wit' ta selchies skin? Is t'at w'y 'e is so loyal to you?"

Tier Naug accents were difficult to translate. Even when they spoke a language Asmara knew, the Tier Naug seemed to slur each word together. But a name caught his attention. Selchie.

Selkie. Asmara's burst of energy faded. *I never bothered to learn your real name.*

The warlock leaned down and clasped Asmara's head. Iridescent eyes stared into his. Asmara shut his lids tight. His mind's secrets were too valuable to be given to a demon and his warlock.

"Tell me, 'ow your eyes don't possess a demon's glow?" The Tier Naug warlock shook Asmara.

The voice was familiar. He'd heard this warlock speak recently but couldn't place where or when. But no matter what, he didn't trust this voice. He kept his eyes shut. He refused to be mind-raped.

Sounds of skin curdling back, being reshaped, followed bone-breaking snaps. The warlock's demon was coming to the forefront.

It was time to leave.

Asmara rolled free of the Tier Naug's grip while he morphed into his demon. Every second counted if Tiecus's metamorphosis was any time measure.

Hands tied behind his back, Asmara muscled to his feet. Not looking back, he ran. Asmara held the top of Marcus's pants up, expecting the demon to pounce on him any moment. Calling upon the element of his power, Glacias, he covered his tracks. Behind him, ice patches disguised as snow hid in waiting.

Trees whizzed past. The fog of his breath escaped the gag and trailed behind. His jaw ached. Sweaty fingers. tied behind his back. grasped and fumbled to pull up Marcus's sliding pants. He thought of letting them go and running without clothes, but the cold would shock his system into hypothermia. *This is why I hate pants!*

After a league, he slowed down. The Tier Naug's demon wasn't after him, yet. He hoped it slipped and broke its neck chasing him. Shimmying his hands in front, he untied the ropes and coughed the gag out.

Scanning the trees like a paranoid rabbit, he held his breath. No birds sang. Scurrying noises of critters were unnervingly absent. As his ears had been rubbed to irritation, distorted information filtered through them. The temperature was nine degrees, winds southeast 0.05 knots, air pressure perfect for flying at sea level, and something directly west breathed . . . no . . . panted.

Asmara felt the hairs on the back of his neck lift. A snapping branch brought his attention beyond the redwoods. Closing in, marble-white teeth gleamed. A wolf demon.

The wolves were masters of the hunt, which meant the sound was intentional. No worthy wolf demon allowed his prey to hear him. Their attacks were silent, their prey dead before they knew it. This one wanted to play with his food.

The wolf demon circled. Asmara turned, never exposing his back. The wolf demon began to growl and bite at the air ferociously.

The creature prepared to pounce. Asmara sipped in as much air as he could and waited. The demon leaped.

Asmara expelled a loud yell, and the air rippled with the full force of his strongest defense. A shock-bark. This wasn't violence. It wasn't inflicting pain with tools or body. It was an indirect force disrupting an action. It was the Serenite's quickest defense causing no harm to the attacker.

Stunned, the wolf demon rolled back. The creature lay paralyzed, his paws twitching.

"Nasty bark I do have indeed," Asmara smirked. "Stupid, you'd fall for it . . ."

A crushing weight pushed against his shoulders. The mage collapsed face-first. Bile began to rise in his throat. He lifted his head and spat out a mouth full of snow. Whatever was on top of him hooked his arm and flipped Asmara on his back. Before he could identify his attacker, a paw struck his throat. Claws raked his neck.

Sitting on him like he was a prize, a cougar demon perched on his chest. Pinned and suffocating, he recognized the eyes. The iridescent gaze belonged to the Tier Naug warlock. Asmara snapped his head sideways. Needle-like claws dug into his chest.

Asmara screamed through a gurgling choke. He tried curling into a ball, but he was trapped between hard-packed snow and a snarling cougar demon. In spurts, he called to the elements, crying desperately to get this thing off.

The wind picked up. Sleet blew into their faces but nothing more. His concentration faltered.

"Please, I'll tell you what you want to know." Forced through a raw throat, his words came out as a harsh whisper. "Don't demense it from me."

The cougar demon snarled and kneaded deeper into his chest. Asmara's hoarse scream filled the cold air. Teeth clamped down on his exposed neck. He gagged at the sensation of blood being suctioned from his throat. He moved his arms, trying to push the cougar demon off. It didn't budge. Asmara grew lightheaded at the blood loss. The demon mewled greedy satisfaction. Thoughts of escape drained away.

My hypothesis. Asmara grew delirious. *Maybe, Tiecus will . . .*

Asmara welcomed the respite. Tiecus would return to the Atra Solumn. Marcus would probably die with Asmara. It might be better this way. A dead brain gave limited information. The Serenites' secrets would be safe.

With relief, he embraced his body's weakness and drifted his thoughts to something of no consequence. *Let the Tier Naug have King Valder's secrets, not mine.*

Platt floated through his mind. *Probably captured.*

A vision of the doe being defiled by the Tier Naug angered him. A kernel of will sparked defiance. *No! They will not have her.*

He brought a weak hand up to the cougar demon's forehead. *This is going to be painful.* Asmara dug his thumbs into the demon's eyes. Asmara screamed. The cougar demon howled and jumped off.

True to the Serenite curse, the agony inflicted was mutual. Asmara covered his blind eyes and hauled himself against a tree.

At his touch, the redwood remembered him. As soon as he made contact to the trunk, the consciousness of the clutch entered his mind.

Asmara realized his mistake. These trees weren't just made. They had the power to demense by touch.

Interwoven thoughts rushed over his senses. A chorus of a thousand voices sang to him as one. Their multitude of conversations was foreign to his individuality.

He *felt* hundreds of thoughts. Each thought was connected to another. But thought traveled faster than sound, and all ideas came in a flow of understanding. The power of the multitude before him was primal and ready, but Asmara had no means to manipulate it.

They shared the caress of the wind. They communed with heavy blankets of snow telling them to reserve strength. They consumed the nourishment of the sun and water. They knew fear of death and how fire, for them, was life for their young.

But they didn't understand running or seeing. They couldn't grasp individuality and searched Asmara for his "others." Awed by the vast power, he felt as a weeling in the arms of eternity.

The conglomerate didn't force or prod. They coaxed and asked. They comprehended the damage done to his "moving pillar."

I call it a body. He corrected their terminology.

They weren't offended, only amused.

Warmth pulsated throughout his wounded form. Whispers called him "sibling," "protector," and "soul-burner." He felt whole with the conglomerate cascading in his mind.

The trees began to manipulate the resources they held deep below the surface and used it to fill him with strength. Slow but unstoppable strength revived him. Terra, elemental earth, fed him its willpower.

In a state of otherworldliness, he stood up. On one side, his moving pillar body rose. On the other side, he was the redwood holding him up. The strength of earth rushed to his aid. Asmara released the connection he had with "the multitude." Harsh reality crashed the flow of peace. No welcome sight played before him.

Behind him, the wolf demon locked paws around the cougar demon. Each somersaulted, avoiding jaws and teeth.

Typical demon behavior. Asmara grimaced. *You can't drain him. He's mine.*

Deluded and weak from blood loss, Asmara waved a drunken hand. "Oh, stop, girls; there's enough for everyone." Turning from the scene, he landed on hands and knees. Dizzy and nauseous, Asmara gave yet more stew back to the world.

Platt! He had to get to her.

Asmara dry-heaved at the snarls of violence. Haze touched the edges of his vision. His throat coated with film, slim, and grit. Blood seeped down Marcus's tunic. The trees had not healed him. They had given him strength and a chance to run.

Grabbing a handful of snow, he pressed it against the wound on his neck. He felt too large for his own body. His hands felt swollen. Asmara thought the ice pack would slip out from his bloated fingers.

Sharp, pressing pain brought him back to a world of contrast and hard lines. *How, by the bright star, am I going to do anything?*

A dry-heaved gag reverberated through his sore voice box. Snarling cries from the cougar and howls from wolf affected him. He concentrated on a fur swatch that tumbled along with a gentle breeze. One hand on his throat, two knees on the packed snow, he turned around. A forced cough proved his vocal cords were useless. Another bark blast wouldn't be possible. Still, it was the only thing he had left.

Patches of skin and fur drifted along snow. Splattered blood covered both demons. The fight continued. This was not a territorial spat. This was a life-and-death struggle. Their fight meant something more than just another meal.

The two demons crashed over Asmara, and the mage tumbled backward. Hand still pressed to his neck, Asmara sprawled in wet clothes. The strength loaned to him ebbed.

The snow beneath him felt comfortable. Numb, he reached and touched bark. Once more, the conglomerate obliged him and absorbed his pain. They knew his plight. They lent strength as their help. They were the only hope he had.

Asmara broke from the redwood. He rolled to his feet and stood. A whirl of motion sent him to the ground. Asmara succumbed to the loss of blood with a lifetime of memories and Platt on his mind. In the fading light, huge wings and claws floated straight down, grabbing for him.

Chapter 13

ASMARA WOKE IN his slope chair covered with a quilt. He looked down on himself and found loose soiled bandages draped where Marcus had been impaled. The compress wraps wouldn't do any good for him. Wounds didn't transfer over between the triad.

His neck was sore. Prodding his muscles felt like touching gooey cauliflower.

Relax, Marcus said. *We're healing the slow way.*

Asmara cleared his throat testing his voice. "What good is being riddled by a demon if it doesn't heal you?"

I've been healing us.

Asmara snorted, *You? You can't even get weeds to grow.*

It never occurred to him Marcus might have talent for healing. The boy was half demon. What did *they* do but eat? But Marcus was also half Serenite. That was worth something.

Platt walked into the room, tray in hand, and jerked to a stop. Clay mugs and a pot rattled on her wood plank.

Smiling at the circumstance, Asmara dropped the quilt exposing his bare chest. "I think my bandages need to be tended." He grabbed the back of his chair letting the cloth dressings fall around his waist.

"I just changed them." She moved forward and set the tray next to him on the floor.

I told you not to, Marcus said, as if he were speaking directly to Platt.

"Ah, tea." Asmara adjusted in a sultrier pose. "How wonderful."

"It was for Marcus." She flushed and smiled, pouring hot water into a cup. "But I guess you can have some."

He chuckled, scanning the room. No sign of iridescent eyes for what felt like moments before. "Your uncle, is he all right?"

She furrowed her brow. "He's been hurt worse, but the wound on his leg looks bad."

No one else was in the room. But he got the sense someone besides her had been here. "Why did they get involved in the first place?"

"When the Tier Naug came, I went to my uncle's house." A soft hiss escaped the pot she put down. "I told him they were invading again. He took all the able men and went to help Marcus." Platt stirred the tea with a dowel.

"And look what they got for it." But that still didn't tell him how she got past the warning ward or the Tier Naug.

"We've been defending Reginhart from Tier Naug for a few weeks now." Platt averted her eyes from his nakedness. "They're as much our enemies as yours."

Agitation rose in him that she did not speak to him with her eyes and voice together. "I should go and do what I can to heal them." He scowled.

She dared a glance. Light of realization glowed in her eyes. She set down the dowel and lifted her face to him. "No need. Mother is taking care of them."

A smirk preceded a snort. "Rehan? Hair like a nag's unkempt mane, wild as a mother bear with cubs? Taking care of the injured?" The instant it was out, he wanted to take it back. Not because of what he said, but because of how he'd obtained the knowledge.

Disapproval shot through Platt's face. Jaw set and chin raised, she thumbed her nose at him. "The same mother who told me to keep my promises. The same mother who fought with the men last night. The same mother that taught me how to make a compress for your neck."

He sat up and rested a hand on her shoulder. "Platt, it wasn't right what Marcus did to you."

She lowered her eyes.

He gave a weak smile, squeezed her shoulder, and waited for her acknowledgement. When she met his eyes, he continued, "It wasn't right when he looked into you. I shouldn't have allowed the demens."

"How much do you know about me?" Biting her lip, she pulled back.

Asmara shrugged. "I know you have a courageous heart. I know you have sacrificed much for the good of your kind. Marcus is fortunate to have you as a companion."

"No specifics?"

"Anything you were thinking of at the time." Which was a lot.

She picked up a cup and offered it to him.

"So . . ." Taking the cup he felt all niceties sufficiently dealt with and wanted answers. "How did you find me? How did I get back here?"

Platt avoided his eyes. "He said you'd get angry."

He grabbed her arm irritated at the insult of looking away. Fear turned into a burning pitch of anger. Someone else knew he was here. "Who is he?"

She looked into his eyes but said nothing.

"I can't have people knowing about me." Fire consumed his rational thoughts. Want of violent action pushed to test his endurance of the Serenite curse.

"So, he should have left you to freeze, bleed out, and die?" She blushed and wrenched out of his grasp.

"Give me a name."

"He carried you here and left." Shoulders back in defiance, her body dared him to convert his rage into something physical.

"So, you had one of your boy's bring me here?" Asmara tightened his ears and narrowed his eyes. "You should have left me where I lay."

Being looked down upon by this inferior creature echoed through his body. Need to inflict pain reached the core of his being and overflowed in crevices reserved for Tiecus. He looked Platt up and down.

"He's not my boy." Platt matched his hostile glare. "And you have the most ungrateful way of saying thank you."

"Grateful!" Asmara roared. "I should be grateful some idiot is going to spread a rumor that an elf is in the village to bring their wounded and ill?" He couldn't express into words what this meant. He was trapped here. He'd have to hide in Marcus to keep from being accosted. This was a disaster.

"Dash," she said.

"What?"

"His name is Dash McGrady, and he knew more than I did about you." Her anger was befitting a demon. "He said he felt sorry for you. He said any Serenite that tries to hide the curse by being riddled is short cause to worry for."

Asmara felt the breech. *It* was awake. The demon took hold of Asmara's rage and burrowed through his hate-fueled tunnel.

Immediately, he regretted the loss of control. Anger unleashed the animal within, both Tiecus and a demon all Serenite called heritage. He owed her a warning, an explanation, but it came out a weak sputter. "Platt—run."

"Why?" she spat.

"He comes." Asmara constricted every muscle in his body. The ball of anger radiated outward. The doe's unwillingness to yield for her life frustrated him all the more.

She folded her arms. "I made an agreement with Marcus."

"He will rip you apart!" His own emotion had fueled *It* to circumvent his control.

Doubt crept up in her voice. "Marcus wouldn't hurt me."

"Marcus isn't coming." Asmara folded over trying to give her time.

Tiecus pushed through holes that made a path to the forefront.

Platt stood where she was. "I won't go back on my word."

Marcus roared, *Asmara! You have no right to deny Tiecus the forefront.*

Asmara couldn't argue. Every ounce of concentration slowed the demon. But it wasn't enough.

Tiecus pounded the inner walls of his cage.

Asmara convulsed. A flailing arm knocked a mug Platt had lifted from her hand. Tiecus was no small pup to force down anymore.

"Asmara?" Platt sounded less confident.

"Run, little doe." The mage succumbed.

Black fur exploded over the entire body of Tiecus's host. Asmara's narrow chest jutted out exposing Tiecus's sternum, his nose elongated. His ears grew tuffs at the ends. Tiecus's back sloped down one vertebra at a time, and hind legs formed into what looked like the back of a goat complete with cloven hooves and a stubby tail. His hands darkened and grew wider with talons.

FREEDOM! I LAUGH. Silly mage thinks he controls anger. I am anger. I am also hungry. They speak, the mage, the Enforcer. Instructions after food. Two-legged doe pays me homage. She is afraid.

Gentle, the Enforcer says.

He has the nerve to ask. Let the mage attempt his tricks on me. We will see how far that gets him.

Two-legged doe understands running is futile. She is calm. I am calm. Her skin rips easy. Her blood is flowers and stone. Beautiful strength. A good combination. Her heart stops. The Enforcer says she will live. I will believe when I see.

Full belly, clear mind. This is unfortunate. Now I understand the squabble of the mage and the Enforcer.

"What now have I done?" I rumble.

The mage is livid. The mage is always livid.

The Enforcer is weak. Visions re-enact glorious battle. Enforcer and flame heads. The mage and flame heads! Great battle I have missed!

Feed me more. I am perturbed to miss battle. I sleep less when fed. I nudge two-legged doe. The Enforcer says she will feed me.

You've killed her! The mage wallops my mind.

I seek my revenge. He hits me for the last time.

Shush, the Enforcer says.

I receive satisfaction. The mage is brought to temper by one word. The Enforcer has talent in this.

Thump-thump. This sound is faint. Only I hear.

Thump-thump. I paw at two-legged doe. The others continue their fight.

Thump-thump. Her heart answers.

I sniff her heart. I inquire the doe with a bark.

Their rambling quiets.

Thump-thump. Two-legged doe gasps for air. She rests back down.

The mage retreats. The Enforcer stays.

I pick up two-legged doe.

Mind your claws, the Enforcer says.

I place her on the mage chair. I watch her breathe. She sleeps. I will guard.

She is magic, I say.

Yes, the Enforcer says.

I doubt we mean the same thing.

Chapter 14

TWO-LEGGED DOE stirs. Shatter Side is a strange and wonderful place. Darkness prevails in Atra Solumn. The Atra Solumn itself is a demon. Here light counters darkness. The mate of bright eye rides the skies, but her eye is closed.

It's called a moon, the Enforcer, forever my teacher of Shatter Side, says.

Blinking eye, moon, will grace us another night. I huff. My jowls rest on two-legged doe's chest. Her heart pumps fast. She is awake!

I greet her excited, nose to ear. She happy weeling squeals. Her ear hides in her shoulder. She is two-legged doe. Two-legged *demon* doe. I know what she is. Vanilla scent is strong, but I smell the Atra Solumn upon her. The Enforcer ignores this.

I wait on haunches. Vanilla-fear, I smell. She is still and watching as if she stalks me. I like this game. She blinks first.

Curious fingers reach out.

Still. The Enforcer squelches my urge to snap.

My horns are death. The two-legged-demon-doe touches gentle. My horns give us pleasure. Hers is touch. Mine is feel. Fingers smooth away tension. Her hands glide along my horns' curl. Respect is her scent now.

Two-legged-demon-doe lies back. Her voice croaks a word: "Water?"

I see her request. Pleasure is repaid with pleasure. I will oblige. Bounding as a youngling from first hunt, wood gives way to horns.

Please don't break any more doors, the Enforcer groans.

"What is door?" I leap the crinkled stone. The Enforcer and the mage need it to climb up. I trust flat stone.

The Enforcer grasps his head. It is his way of being frustrated.

Ignis must stay in its place. Growl threats remind my brother I am in charge. He cowers to a smolder. Shiny metals scamper from me. The Glacias vessel knows what I want. This might be a more difficult task than first recognized. But I am a demon. I *can* accomplish this? I ask the Enforcer. They are confusing words. Things are done. But "can" and "cannot" is knowledge that roams away from me.

I take the pitcher in my teeth by its arm. The arm is round and slips down. This renders the vessel useless. Water will spill and two-legged-demon-doe will drink from the floor if I continue. My teeth were made for battle, not service. But I can do this. I am a demon.

Balancing on hind hooves is awkward. I am not meant to walk like the Enforcer or the mage. But if they can do it, I can too. My front paws are more like human hands with claws. They mark me as an abomination from my kind. A deadly abomination for those who dare call me that. Today my paws are useful. I grab the vessel.

Glacias needs to remember her place. A snarl brings the metal contraption over the hole of water to life. The handle raises and lowers. Each time metal contraption lowers, it makes a squeak and water pours out into the vessel between my paws.

Count the squeaks, the Enforcer says. He tries to explain math to me. I am yet to understand what math is or why I need to understand.

Squeak.

One, the Enforcer says.

Squeak.

Two.

Squeak.

Three.

I am confused. How is the squeak all those words?

Why do you bother? the mage says.

The Enforcer ignores him. *There was the first squeak, correct?*

"Correct," I say.

Then another, correct?

"Correct."

Then another squeak after the first is two.

I sit with the vessel and think. "Squeak is one. Squeak, squeak is two. Squeak, squeak, squeak is three. My mind explodes making room for a new thought den. "I understand."

The Enforcer is insufferable when he is smug.

Well done, the mage says, but not to me.

To me the mage says, *Don't just sit there like a trained pet.*

Crumpled stone obstructs my path. I must now hold my prize for the two-legged-demon-doe and learn how to overcome this challenge.

He's not stupid, the Enforcer says to the mage.

Oh? He can't even walk upstairs.

The Atra Solumn doesn't have stairs.

This is painful, the mage says. *Just take over.*

"My present," I say.

The mage barks a laugh. *Water a gift?*

Asmara, shut up.

My first attempt to walk the crinkled stone as two legs brings pain. I wobble and fall forward. The vessel in my paws is whole, and I am closer to my goal as well. But I would rather be free from humiliation.

You would rather not be humiliated, the Enforcer says.

"Enough." I am complete of lessons for now. I must concentrate to get up. I will fall backward if my balance fails.

One leg lifts at a time. I must balance on one leg, lift the other, push and pull as one, shift my balance, pull the other leg up and repeat. My respect for balance by two legs rises. This is a hard task.

Perhaps the bright eye opens by the time I reach the top of crinkled stone. It feels that way. I make way to splintered wood.

That's a door. The Enforcer is angry. *Was a door.*

What have I done now?

It's your own fault, Marcus, the mage says. *You should've opened the door for him. You know he likes to create holes.*

Two-legged-demon-doe sleeps. Eager to give her my gift, I paw for her attention. She startles.

Still. The Enforcer helps dampen the urge to bite. It is easy now with a full stomach.

I show her the vessel. She smiles. Two-legged-demon-doe is the morning sky. Pride makes me want to give her my present. I help her drink water. But she drinks slowly. Glacias overflows.

Two-legged-demon-doe shrieks. She pushes the vessel away. I am confused. Is she denying my gift?

You stupid kur! The mage is angry.

Tiecus, that's enough. The Enforcer is angry as well.

I have done something wrong, again.

She is grateful. The Enforcer sighs.

I believe he is exaggerating.

She likes your gift. There is just too much of it.

The Enforcer pushes me to the cage of his mind. My whines of apology are muffled as he comes forward. My fur recedes. My mass shrinks. Hooves crack, reform, and become feet.

Hocks pop and reverse their hinge to become knees. My pelvis moves up and back bone shortens. Shoulders deflate. Horns disappear. Snout reduces to a flatter nose and jaw.

Black hair grows from his scalp and pools around Marcus's bent-over body.

PLATT COUGHED IN fits.

"You should exchange your gown." Marcus searched her from one end to the other looking for any clues to help her. "You and Asmara are similar in size. He doesn't mind if you borrow something of his."

Her coughing fits lessened, and Marcus lifted her to stand and started undoing the ties to her sleeve.

"I'm all right." She grabbed his arm for support. Platt turned, and her cheeks grew bright red. "What are you doing?" she said through fits of choking.

"You're wet, you're cold, and this gown will chaff you in your sleep." He wasn't getting anywhere with the knots. His claws were getting in the way.

"You're a male and naked." Her eyes drifted to his chest. "That's inappropriate."

"Then sit by the fire to dry."

She gazed at the first agreement along his defined pecks. Fingers traced the tattoo on his chest. Marcus caught his breath and enfolded his hand around hers. Removing the light touch didn't stop the quickening of his blood, and the removal brought a sense of loss.

"What happened to you?" She was so close he could feel her breath.

"It's an agreement," he said hoarsely.

"What does it say?" She stared at the agreement, entranced.

"No killing Serenite."

"Do you have one of these for each agreement?" Her voice cast alluring warmth around his body.

He managed to stutter out, "Yes."

Marcus wasn't used to answering questions so directly. But to keep her next to him, he'd tell her anything.

Resting the crown of her head against his swiftly beating heart, her white-blonde hair tickled down to his knees. Her touch felt wonderful. He stroked the back of her neck absently. He didn't care if she could see all his agreements.

She gasped in surprise and turned too abruptly to keep her balance. He caught her and pulled her in close before she fell.

"You have marks . . . everywhere." Her body no longer pliable, she resisted.

He grunted and breathed in her vanilla scent. Holding her stirred his gut and sent fire down his legs.

"Let me go." She squirmed. The light scent of her panic rose.

He moaned a pitiful sigh and swept her up into his arms.

"Please, no." Her plea desperate. "Put me down."

Marcus set her gently in a chair before the fire, but it was Asmara's smile that pulled the corners of his lips and said through Marcus, "Getting a good look at all his front-side agreements?" Asmara chuckled. "I suspect you've seen the fourth one so aptly placed?" Marcus stroked the tattoo wrapped around his shaft. "That was made specific so don't worry, little one. None of us will force you."

Platt turned her eyes to Marcus. "Asmara?"

The mage smiled through Marcus. The Enforcer brought a finger to her lips. "Shhh . . . I ask you don't reveal him."

He stood and walked toward the armoire and opened the closet door.

Folded and stacked in the bottom drawer were his overcoat, shirt, pants, boots, and hat. After shoving his pants on he carefully folded his claws into his palm and pushed his arms through his shirt as to not rip the fabric. Modesty cured, he grabbed a quilt.

"Is there anything I can get you?" He wrapped the quilt around her.

Platt looked up at him in scorn. "Yes, I want my mother's cooking."

He didn't wince, balk, or hesitate. "Then you shall have it."

Platt's surprised face was worth his stomach's nervous rumblings at meeting Rehan. He'd seen Platt's mother within her memories, and how she saw her mother frightened him. Not because Platt was afraid of her own mother, but because he was desperate to impress his little doe. Marcus hurried out of the room before consequence paralyzed him.

All manner of mess in the kitchen had been righted while they were upstairs, and he crossed to the entryway when he remembered . . .

"Selkie!" Marcus berated himself. He'd been so preoccupied that he'd forgotten the demon steed.

He charged through the front door, tripping over a wicker basket. The snow broke his fall, and a white cotton towel kept the contents inside. But he had no time to worry about it.

Selkie snickered with a sideways glance.

Marcus huffed in relief. The demon steed hadn't tried to venture back into the sea. Nor was he terrorizing the village.

"Oh, thank the bright sun. You are well, friend?"

Selkie nickered and turned back to watch the waves of the ocean.

Calamity averted, he turned to the basket. He hesitated to pick it up. How long had it been there? Did the warning ward go off while he was unconscious?

Pinching the cloth at a corner, he ripped the towel off.

Nuts spilled out and fruit kept a pie in place. Amazing it hadn't folded over or leaked. He didn't know what to make of the food. Before he left, he brought the basket inside and set it on the chopping block and then went back to the enraptured horse longing for the sea.

"Carry me for a chore?"

Ears forward and flaming, eyes that gave no malice or insight, the demon steed faced him and nickered.

He rode Selkie to the Ottern's small cottage on the outskirts of town. Dismounting, he walked five strides and knocked on the door. He shifted from foot to foot as he waited for an answer.

In the version seen in Platt's mind, Rehan was larger and stronger than Bolden. Marcus didn't expect the shrewd face, thin lips, and high cheekbones of a woman that only came to his waist. Platt's memory of her mother was accurate, just not the woman's size.

Unlike her daughter, Rehan possessed eyes that held contempt natural to one who'd seen much and hadn't found life amusing. A face filled with disgust and hatred met him. The sheer violence of her disapproval made him swallow his heart.

"You're not welcome here," she snarled. Rehan slammed the door almost before she finished her sentence.

Marcus growled at the oak entrance, "Your daughter needs you."

A muffled voice said, "Bring her here then."

"She is too weak to move."

The oak entryway swung open. Rehan held an iron hearth poker in warning with one hand and used the door like a shield in the other.

A male youngling burst out from behind Rehan. "A real demon!"

Marcus recognized the face as that of Platt's brother, Tim. Rehan may have hated Marcus, but Tim was awed.

"You're not the imposter; Lord Reginhart is," Tim said.

"Timothy Regalius, in the house now!" Rehan released her shield, grabbed her youngest by the tunic, and pulled him back.

Marcus tapped his index claw against his lips and emphasized the threat. "Timothy—Regalius—Ottern."

Rehan gritted her teeth and raised her weapon.

Marcus inspected his fingers and slid his thumb claw down the length of each talon. "Your daughter has requested you. She is in no capacity to travel. I suggest you come with me to her side."

Rehan trembled, and by the time the scent of her fear and loathing reached his senses, she had slammed the door in his face.

Marcus stared at it for a moment and then turned to the inferno steed. Selkie gave a snort and balked backward, ears perked forward at the door. Holding Selkie from bolting, he mounted and sighed. "I thought for sure she would come. How do I get her to tend to her daughter?" Marcus curled his claws in his palms and stroked Selkie's neck with his knuckles.

Muffled tongue-lashing instructions floated through the door, causing Selkie to shy away from the house. Marcus kept him in place and didn't blame Selkie for his flighty reaction.

"A wonder where Platt gets her spite."

Rehan charged out the door, took one look at Selkie, and pressed her round body against the wall. "Oh no! No horses."

He pushed Selkie toward her and offered a hand. "Selkie isn't a horse."

Clutching her basket, she near ran from the steed. "Oh no. I'll just stay on the ground."

"Mrs. Ottern, the Tier Naug just attacked the stronghold. I'd rather not be away from the keep for any length of time."

"He's half fire," she said walking briskly away. "I'll burn."

"He doesn't burn people he likes." He tried coaxing Selkie near enough to grab Rehan. The inferno steed wasn't getting within ten feet of her. "I can cast a temporary fire ward upon you."

Rehan glared over her shoulder and walked faster.

"Do I need to press the matter?" he hissed.

Rehan turned to face him, unsheathing a knife.

He looked straight into her eyes. "Halt—"

No! Asmara pierced through his concentration with enough magic to break the demens. *You will not do that. No mind tricks.*

Marcus reeled back from the mental slap. "Mrs. Ottern, the stronghold is compromised. More invaders will come. Your daughter is in there, too weak to run. Every moment you waste fearing us is a chance for a freckled, wire-haired berserker to harm her. Time is of the essence."

"And you left her alone."

His jaw grated together. "What do I need to do to get you on this mount?"

Rehan lowered her dagger. "Don't hurt me."

"Agreed." The tingle of another tattoo formed below his left knee. He grimaced at his haste.

While Rehan was still immobile, he pushed Selkie forward. His long arm hoisted her up in front of him.

"Frigidus." He cast the fire ward. Sparks flew like dying stars off Rehan.

Selkie leaped forward and charged like the devil was behind him.

Rehan spurted a cry and clutched his arms. "Oh mother of all, slow down!"

Marcus grasped the demon steed's flickering mane and held Rehan close so she would not fall.

Holding the mother was not as pleasant as holding the daughter. When this was over, Platt would be the one riding with him to Benicar. With detours. At a walk. After he got an arquebus.

"By the bright star, how did we forget the arquebus?" There were so many that he didn't worry about holding on to the one he'd had.

As they came up to the place where they had last seen the cart, he scanned the area. New fallen snow covered all traces of the battle. The field looked smoothed over. No sign of even a skirmish. He'd have to check later.

"What happened to the arquebus?"

"You're talking to me?" Rehan quivered.

"Yes." The taste of fetid blood soured his tongue. "You were here, were you not? Platt said you'd fought with the men."

"We melted them down. Lord Reginhart will need the metal to rebuild the keep. The cart isn't much but for burning though."

"You didn't keep one?"

Rehan shook her head.

He let out a drawn-out sigh. "If you have one, or find one and give it to me, it will permit me to leave. But it must be in working order."

"I'll remember that."

They cantered up the hill through the gates and stopped by the tower door. He dismounted and helped Rehan down. Selkie snorted and sidestepped back to the barn as Marcus led Rehan. Before he entered, he watched Selkie's glowing mane cast light through the stable windows and an equine eye peeking through. If Asmara wanted to keep him prisoner in there, he'd have to do it on his own time.

"This way." He marched inside with Rehan on his heels. He traveled the stairs three at a time, and Rehan followed as fast as she could.

Platt's mother cautiously eyed the splintered door Marcus pushed aside and poked her head into the room. "Platt?"

Little doe jumped from her chair. "Mama?"

Rehan lost her apprehension, ran to her child, and enfolded Platt in her arms.

Marcus slipped to the back of the room and faded into the shadows. Two silhouettes embraced in front of him.

"Oh, Mama, I didn't think he would actually bring you."

"I'm here now, my sweet child." Rehan stroked her child's hair. "It's going to be all right now."

A pang in his own heart made him long to comfort Platt.

"Mama," Platt whispered. "I think I died."

The comment put him in a free fall. She had come back from death. Who knew how many times she would have to endure regenerating? How many times could she keep recovering?

Rehan's voice cracked. "No, honey, you're alive; you're with me now. It's all right." Rehan looked around the room.

"Is this where you've been staying? Do you not even have a bed?"

Rehan's words stomped on his chest. Platt's comfort hadn't reached his concern. Her loyalty might come if her life was happy and worry free. Valder had taught him that.

"Make me something?" Platt said.

It was awhile before Rehan let her child go. "All right, what would you like?"

"There is stew, I think." Platt stroked her mother's hair.

"I'll see you to the kitchen." Marcus stepped out of the shadows and opened the door. "The elements can be temperamental about . . . handlers."

Rehan glared at him when she passed by. Her hands balled in fists. They barely reached the bottom of the stairs when she turned around and verbally attacked him. "What did you do to her?"

"I did not overstep the binds of our agreement." Marcus slid past her and continued down the stairs.

Rehan paced him. "Have you even fed her since she's been here?"

"She has eaten," he replied, reaching the bottom floor.

"Then why is she so thin?"

Marcus scraped his claws together. "She was a bit overtaxed."

"Is she going to be like that all the time?"

"I don't know."

"What are you doing to her?" Rehan's lip began to quiver.

"Her body is under repair," he stated in his best monotone voice. "I'll be sure to feed her properly and make sure she drinks plenty of water. She'll be fine."

"Fine?" Rehan stopped before reaching the last plateau. "That isn't my definition of fine. She's just a piece of meat to you, isn't she? Just another lamb to slaughter! Who cares if she dies, right? What kind of monster are you!"

He turned to Rehan and cast a shadow over the woman half his size. The slight had cut him deeper than he cared to let on. "When you find out, Mrs. Rehan Ottern, let me know."

She blinked but stood firm under threat of his size.

Marcus turned back to the kitchen and flicked his wrist. Ignis responded with a crackle and leaped a greeting of flames. The kitchen was in its usual whirlwind of activity. Pots filled water, spoons skidded across the counter, and towels chased wet cutlery. Knives cut yet more celery.

Rehan was two steps behind him. "You're marring her beautiful neck with scars."

"There may be a remedy for that."

"Her dress was all wet." Mrs. Ottern seemed oblivious to the twirling utensils around her. "She'll catch her death of cold."

"It was an accident—"

"Then be more careful with her or you'll accidentally lose your head." She passed by him and went to the cauldron. "And if you think you're going to get your filthy claws on my boy, too, I'll tell you, you aren't. You so much as speak his first name, I will raise whatever spirit I have to. I will lend myself to whatever dark god will execute my vengeance just so I know you will feel pain before your death."

Rehan finding some fire demon to riddle her sent a shiver down his spine. She'd probably survive the process. He imagined her satisfaction in chasing him with teeth and claws.

Rehan raised a soup-filled spoon to her lips and blew. After taste testing, she plucked a floating bowl happening by and ladled the food inside.

It was curious that Rehan seemed unperturbed by the magic dancing around her. Even Platt had seemed cautious. Yet Rehan ignored the dancing macabre and briskly walked back up the stairs.

Platt, still in the chair, leaned over her knees weeping. Rehan's pace quickened, and she hugged her child again.

"Is this my life now?" Platt said to no one in particular. "Will it be like this for the rest of my life?"

Marcus crossed the room and knelt to her level while Rehan gave him the death glare. "I can't promise you anything. Our deal is not very specific. Your negotiation skills are quite lacking."

"Thanks." Platt took the bowl from her mother. After two bites, she spoke again. "You aren't human." With an odd emotionless lilt in her voice, she said, "You have no idea how my fear will turn into hate, and my hate will turn into revenge."

"Revenge?" Marcus ignored the stab to his heart. He understood her completely. Her words were mirrors of his sentiment after Valder's chess challenge. "You speak to me of revenge?" He shook his head. Deeper than regret, her words killed each of them—the mage, the demon, and Marcus. "Be careful of the vulnerabilities you expose."

Platt cast her eyes to the fire and said nothing.

Indifference was a mask that suited Valder, not his little doe. He couldn't stand to see her raise that wall before his eyes. He would take her hate, fear, or outrage but not her impassionate calculations. Marcus squeezed his eyes shut. He couldn't be here. The blood in his stomach—her blood—churned.

"I will leave you to your childish motives." Marcus rose to his full height.

An arquebus, Marcus thought. *I need to find an arquebus. Where? Tiecus.* A demon's nose could find the Tier Naug and their stash.

The silence prompted Marcus to slink out of the room. He removed his clothes leaving a trail down the staircase.

Tiecus took the forefront, but this time no roar accompanied his dejected manner.

Chapter 15

MORNING SUPPLIED NO arquebus, no Tier Naug, and no idea of how to approach Platt. Marcus hadn't even gone into the tower to retrieve his clothes but remained within sight of the castle, standing guard.

Don't get nostalgic for Benicar, Asmara said. *This is a much better place.*

"We were safe there." Watching the morning rays overtake the ocean, Marcus sat on the ledge of the crumbling walls surrounding the keep. "Responsibility did not claim me in Benicar."

We have a tower. An idea of the perfect mage hideaway thrust into his mind. It looked suspiciously like Ardin's spire. *We can converse with these people. Albeit it's arguing, but they don't seem to be afraid of you.*

Marcus stood and walked the length of the wall and balanced on the edge. The breeze kissed his skin.

You can't tell me you don't feel a certain amount of purpose here. Asmara knew him well and laid out facts with which he couldn't argue.

Rehan stepped out the front door, and Marcus ducked behind a crenellation.

Tiecus growled in displeasure at the cowardice.

Shush. Asmara turned his thoughts to Tiecus. *Our youngling held his own against her last night.*

"I'm naked," Marcus whispered in explanation.

If you don't want her to know you're here—Asmara turned back to Marcus—*you might want to say that on the inside.*

Watching Rehan from above, Marcus remained out of sight. Murder holes used to throw boulders on trapped men in the portcullis below sufficed as peek holes.

Rehan passed the portcullis safely.

Platt's lifeless analogy replayed in his mind, and he wanted badly to take back his words to her. What she'd said made sense. He could keep hurting her. She could continually berate him for it. Or he could invest in what she offered. He could build something with her. But Marcus wasn't ready to leave the lure of Benicar behind.

Forget it. Asmara threw mental hands in the air. *Find an arquebus. Go back to Benicar. We don't need her anyway.*

"Don't give her away like she's nothing," Marcus spat.

Asmara ran hot and cold from impatience. A trait they all had in common.

She's just demon food. The mage's level cadence pierced Marcus's rationale, and a spike of rage hit him in the heart. Anger moved his blood. Every limb vibrated. Muscles tightened and shook. He wanted to take this energy and shove it down the Serenite's throat.

"No." Marcus ramped down his anger. "I will not make your mistake again. I will not give in to the rush of anger. I will not use hate as a shield of protection from hurt."

Tiecus chuckled. *The Enforcer learns. Where the mage fails to control rage, the Enforcer succeeds.*

The prize was confidence.

His boots, pants, shirt, and long coat were folded and waiting for him by the door. After he felt the push and pull of the warning wards telling him Rehan had left, Marcus traveled the courtyard and slid a leg into his pants.

Platt's voice carried down the stairs. "No! I'm not going with you."

"Listen, missy—" Bolden's deep, husky voice echoed.

"You'll all die!" Her protests echoed. "He's a demon! If I leave, he'll eat the town!"

"Puppis!" Marcus cursed under his breath and slipped on his boots. "Worthless warning wards."

Ventus hummed, affirming the wards were still up.

Platt cried out, "Put me down!"

Marcus opened the door and crossed the room to the base of the stairs.

A cane assisted Bolden's measured steps down the staircase.

Riley followed.

Platt flailed over the perch of the youngling's shoulder. It was a wonder Riley hadn't dropped her.

"Put me down!" Platt kicked in the air. A soft-buckle shoe hit her captor in the chest. With every free limb, she beat Riley enough to leave bruises.

"Would you stop it?" Riley spanked her bottom.

Platt's demands to let her go continued.

Marcus ran a thumb claw down each falcula. "Little doe, is he hurting you?"

Bolden stopped dead and spread out like a tree stump refusing to be uprooted.

Riley whirled around and ran back upstairs.

"Marcus!" Platt braced against Riley's lower back. "Please don't hurt them."

"She's not staying here with you." Bolden hunkered down.

"That is not for you to decide."

"This place is too dangerous for her." Bolden held his cane, ready to strike. "Let her go."

Marcus raked his tongue across his teeth and took one step up. "She belongs to me."

Bolden raised his cane like a weapon. "No, she doesn't."

Marcus smiled. He'd waited long enough. Acting as if he were engaging Bolden in battle, he took one step, feigned a swipe at his legs, then turned his back on the ox and ran outside.

He was too late.

A shrill cry from the third story curdled his blood. Human desperation never ceased to amaze him. Riley was trying to escape by jumping down the catwalk. His heart skipped watching Platt sail down the remaining ten feet.

Riley hit the ground first and gasped for air. Platt fell on top of the youngling with an *oomph*.

His doe tried to roll away from her kidnapper, but Riley clutched at her dress.

"You're crazy!" She slapped at Riley's hands. "I think I have a better chance of surviving with a demon than I do with you!"

"Oh please." Riley gasped for breath. "You're not hurt."

Marcus shook in anger. That puny, stupid youngling had put his little doe in jeopardy.

Riley lost his hold on her dress, and Platt fell back, landing on her butt.

Marcus rushed to her, helping her up and giving her a once over before facing Riley. He was mad enough to spit black fire. "If you have injured my little doe, I will eat your organs while you're still alive."

"You couldn't stop a handful of Tier Naug." Riley held his ribs and stood favoring his left ankle. "Some powerful demon you are. If the king really did send you here, it was to die."

The slight stung, and he bared his teeth.

Riley scowled back at him.

Platt grabbed Marcus's arm and yanked. "Don't."

She clung to Marcus, blocking the two from engaging in combat. She craned her head to Riley and said, "I don't think you could have survived without his help."

Platt speaking on his behalf against the youngling flooded him with power.

Demon doe, Tiecus interjected.

Platt *was* acting like a female demon protecting her territory. A female demon guarding her throng could wreak more havoc in an hour than most males given a week's time. But Marcus denied Tiecus's suggestion of her being a demon and prepared to face any enemy with Platt.

"Niece, this is no place for you." Bolden leaned heavy on his cane with a hand on the arch of the doorway. "The Tier Naug might not be the best fighters, but they come in droves. We can't fight like this." He gestured at his own state of injury.

"Marcus and the others will protect us."

Marcus glanced a warning. He'd have to press upon her the importance of keeping quiet about Asmara and Tiecus.

"I can't believe you're defending him and that *band* of his." Riley pointed at Marcus. "He killed Morgan!"

"Band?" Marcus looked to Riley. Now he was worried. Had everyone seen Asmara during the battle?

"I'm not going with you!" She backed into Marcus, and he wrapped an arm around her. The ploy kept Marcus rooted. He wasn't going to move an inch, not while she pressed against him.

"I'd rather take my chances." She clutched her hand around his arm.

"What?" Riley dropped his jaw. "You'd rather die here with *that* than come with me and your family?"

Platt unhooked her arm from Marcus and stepped forward. "He keeps his promises."

"That's what this is about?" The angry gleam in Riley's eyes turned wounded. "Platt, I'm sorry." Riley spread his hands. "The timing was wrong."

"You know what I want?" Platt lifted her chin. "I want you to give me nothing. No promises that take years if ever to fulfill. Not your hearth, not your name. I want nothing from you except the final acknowledgement that you know nothing about me."

Riley stood heaving breaths. His shoulders slumped. Shock overtook his face. Marcus thought the youngling might fall to his knees.

Riley searched her face. "You don't mean that."

"Out!" She pointed toward the portcullis. "No more excuses."

"Platt—" Bolden took a step.

"No!" She swept her outstretched arm across air. "His word is no good to me."

Riley's face crumpled like dried bark. "Fine! You're not worth it anyway."

Platt snapped a breath and clung tighter to Marcus as the youngling turned away and limped out of the courtyard.

As he left, Marcus felt the pull and push sensation of his warning ward. "Now it tells me," he sneered.

Bolden glared at Platt. "You are just as stubborn and unforgiving as your mother."

"Oh, so you think a promise is trite?" Platt turned to her uncle.

Bolden gritted his teeth.

Hands in fists, she and her uncle seemed to be playing the "blinking game" that Tiecus loved so much. But even as the demon appreciated a good game, Tiecus's intense attention to this match confused Marcus.

Tiecus? The inquiry made the Enforcer even more baffled.

The demon weighed foreign options in his mind Marcus didn't comprehend. The winner of this contest was important. That's all Marcus knew.

Bolden broke eye contact and walked with the aid of his cane through the courtyard and down the hill without another word.

Tiecus? Marcus asked again. *What was that?*

Some decision, one that Tiecus didn't explain, had been determined. The demon's whole demeanor toward Platt had changed. The closest word Marcus could interpret was *equal*, yet she was more.

As she turned to face him, Marcus kept still. Raising his own mental shield, he prepared to stand against her anger, her disappointment, and whatever else chased two humans away. But her face was placid.

Then it all came to him in a rush, like a deluge of water. He understood what Tiecus knew and why Asmara wanted to remain.

Marcus wanted her on his side. "Little doe, you fought to stay."

"Of course." She looked away, demure.

He placed an index finger under her chin and lifted her gaze back on him. "I am no longer fooled by your modest behavior."

She was ice so cold it burned, water that could not be directed against its will, an agreement without a tattoo.

Marcus lowered to one knee and looked up into her reddening face. "You are the word, and I am your sword. I am sorry for yesterday. For saying such things to cut your heart. I felt enslaved by our agreement, but I see you for what you are now. You are my Nar Shadar, my near heart. With you holding the reins of consequence, I am free."

Her breaths came in short gulps. The scent of anxiety, regret, and vanilla wafted up.

Marcus stood, concerned, wiped a rolling tear from her cheek, and softly asked, "What is this about?"

Platt gulped sobs and more water cascaded down her face. She buried her head in his chest, and hiccups racked her small frame.

He held her in his arms and endured ache in his heart, unable to wipe away her pain.

"Thank you," she said and pulled back. Platt brushed the tears from her face and smiled.

Marcus waited, but the silence continued. He understood she wasn't going to say anything more. Not about her failed kidnapping or otherwise.

She's hiding something, Asmara whispered.

I will let her have her own secrets, but if she thinks to avoid conflict, that won't happen.

"So . . ." Marcus drawled out the word. "Have you been trading information?"

"What?" Her eyes went wide. "No."

"What about this *band* of mine?"

"The other demons." She swallowed. "Your throng."

Oh, puppis. Asmara pulled back. *The demens. I knew she had gathered more from our mind when you reached into her soul.*

Marcus growled, "My throng?"

"Dash." Platt darted her eyes down. "The one who carried Asmara when he was wounded."

Wait. The gears in Asmara's thoughts turned. *So, if she thinks Dash is part of your throng, that means he's a . . .*

Marcus gritted his teeth. "A demon touched Asmara?"

"I thought you knew them." Platt trembled. "He brought you back from the woods. He knew so much. I thought he was with you . . ."

"They are not friends." He turned and sniffed the air. He wasn't worried. Not for himself. "Stay away from them."

He inspected her with a more critical eye. There wasn't anything he could do about the mage's exposure. "Don't speak about Asmara to anyone."

She nodded rubbing her arms.

Marcus released his agitation and moved her hair off her neck. "How is your wound?"

Black and purple bruises wrapped around her nape. Being careful not to scrape her with his claws, he cupped his hands to her face and rested his forehead to hers.

"It hurts."

In a whisper, he said, "Thank you for not lying."

He looked out beyond the open portcullis. There was nothing he could give as compensation for what she'd been through. No material item was going to replace her hurts.

"Come." He walked toward the east tower. "I have a proposition."

The basket he found outside the door was still on the chopping block. What *weren't* present were the dancing utensils. Something was going on with Ventus. First, the warning wards, and now a kitchen with no breath—no life or magic—swirling around. He rummaged inside the basket for whatever smelled of warm berries. Marcus pulled up a hard fruit. "I found this on the porch."

"It's for you." Platt waved off the offered pomegranate.

He took hold of her hand and put the food in her palm. "Don't rebuff my gifts."

She was transfixed by his claws.

"What is all this?" He tipped the basket and found a light golden crust of snow berry pie sitting at the bottom.

"Some believe you are Reginhart reincarnated and back from his travels." She peeled the outer skin of the pomegranate and laid the rind on the chopping block. "Others think King Valder is a powerful warlock who sent you to help defeat the Tier Naug." She grimaced at the bottom of the basket. "Many revere you. This is their homage to you."

In stunned silence, he stared at her while she took a bite from the fruit.

Save the pie, Asmara quipped. *I want it for breakfast.*

Marcus grinned ear to ear. "Would you like some pie, little doe?"

Platt gave him a queer sideways glance.

He sighed in frustration. "Will I ever understand humans?"

"Some don't like that you're here." She looked at the pie and bent down to smell it. "I wouldn't trust this."

He waved her off. "I want to try something with you."

Platt stilled mid-bite.

"Your ability." He leaned on the butcher block opposite her. "You can make blood out of water. That's how your magic works."

Setting down her treat, she said, "Does it help heal me faster if I drink water before?"

Interesting, Asmara mused. *She doesn't understand her own power.*

Marcus nodded. "That would help. But I have an idea that might be less stressful on your body."

Astonishment softened her eyes. Her understanding was all he could ask for.

"We can see how long I can extend feedings." He searched for answers in her face. "Or I can take a little every day."

Platt set the fruit down and wrapped her wrist over the other and entwined her fingers with palms together. It was her nervous tick. A tell.

"I can dampen the pain and help with your scars." He came forward around the counter.

"No." Her hands fell loose at her sides. "Wait a day or a week, but leave the scars."

"Why?" Marcus could only think of one reason.

Demon mates scar each other, Tiecus supplied. *Shows ownership.*

She looked up at him, her eyes hard, her mouth a thin line.

Unable to pinpoint if she'd given him an insult or if human pride didn't allow her to answer, Marcus stepped back. He didn't push for clarification. He liked Tiecus's reasoning.

She'd be a fine Serenite. Asmara preened. *Must be my influence.*

Marcus tried a different tactic and changed the subject. "How much did this *Dash* know about Asmara?" He leaned a hand against the cutting block and admired her figure.

"He answered most of my questions."

"Which were?"

"When he carried Asmara from the forest after the Tier Naug came to try and take over the castle, he answered anything I wanted to know."

Oh, how Asmara did not like that—at all.

Marcus crossed his arms. He wanted to kick himself for making his first agreement with her. She wasn't telling lies, but she wasn't telling him everything either. It made him crazy, but he loved her sly game. He was part demon. Puzzles sharpened his mind.

"He said Asmara is a Serenite," Platt continued.

"And did he explain what a Serenite is?" Marcus leaned against the chopping block.

"He said they were elemental users."

I've not heard of any Dash in the enclave, Asmara said.

But Marcus picked up on the "they" part of her sentence. "How long were his ears?"

"His ears?" Platt looked confused.

"The length and curl of a Serenite's ears expose his age."

"Oh, he was human."

What? Asmara panicked inside. *Humans know about the Serenite? This is bad. Very bad.*

"So, he was riddled then?" Marcus remained calm.

"Riddled?" She looked at him quizzically.

"Yes, riddled. When a demon inserts itself inside a physical body in this plane of existence, we call it riddling. If the demon is in full control of the vessel, it's called a possession."

They were both quiet for a time until Platt looked at him with poorly hidden wonder and asked, "He did not say what station a courtier of the Serenite commands."

Marcus flared his nose.

Asmara had slipped in his entire name and designation at their first meeting. *I am Asmara Grey, master mage and courtier of the Serenite.* Names were power. If she were magically trained or inclined, and with enough power, she could use their names to control them.

"Asmara," Marcus said, turning his head. "You are incredibly conceited."

Pft, Asmara scoffed. *She can't even read. The only thing she's going to use my name for is when she screams it in bed.*

"A courtier of the Serenite"—Marcus turned to Platt—"is the equivalent of a human courtesan."

Platt's eyes widened, and a blush spread across her cheeks. "Oh."

For the first time in—well, ever, Marcus laughed. It wasn't a chuckle or a guffaw. He laughed with as much joy as a child enamored with a delightful game. "What did you think courtier meant?"

Avoiding him, Platt grabbed a kettle, filled it with water, and set it on the fire.

Blonde strands reflected sparkles of gold. Marcus gathered a handful of hair and lifted it to his nose, inhaling her vanilla scent. Eyes closed, he nibbled on her long strands.

Fine straw hair pulled away from his mouth. Platt finger combed her hair pushing her mane back and muttered, "Sometimes, you're very creepy."

Marcus grimaced at the sight of her hideously swollen neck. "You spoke of others. There is more than Dash?"

"Yes," she said. "He spoke about another."

"How did Riley and Bolden get past my warning ward?" He leaned against the butcher block.

"Warning ward?" Platt walked to the counter, placing two cups between the two of them. "I know very little about magic."

"My warning ward surrounds the walls of this keep." He set his elbows on the counter lowering to her eye level. "I would know if anyone came in or out of those gates whether I was here or not. Somehow Riley and Bolden got in, and I didn't know about it until they nearly had you out the gates."

Platt puckered her lips and scrunched her thin eyebrows together. "This warning ward surrounds the keep?"

"Yes."

"Does it go underground?" The kettle whistled, and Platt grabbed a towel, but the metal pot was already pouring water into two cups. She watched, wide-eyed and open-mouthed as herbs spun in a torrent of steam and water. She regained herself, sighed, and tossed the cloth onto the butcher block.

"Ah, I see. There is a passage, isn't there." Marcus grabbed his cup in agitation.

Platt startled and pulled back. With practiced restraint, he locked himself in place. The urge to chase was strong. Thankfully, her flinch was the only reaction to his quick movements.

"Sorry," he uttered. "I will try to move slow."

While she transfixed her gaze on his hands, he set his cup on the counter. Platt reached for his claws, and Marcus stilled. She lightly examined the extensions of his fingers with her thumb.

His talons were not the most sensitive area of his body, but flashes of hot and cold surged through him. Thick musk filled his nose. Instead of wrestling with his overwhelming urges, he went with them. He stepped in front of her with conscious intent. "Are you driving me mad on purpose?"

She grabbed her cup and turned away.

He was much too warm now to drink hot tea.

"Do you fight with them often?" She blew into her cup.

"Ahhh . . . who?"

"Ummm . . ." She waved a hand at all of him. "The others?"

"Oh. You mean the mage and the demon." He slowly took his tea and watched the steam roll over the lip. "I must look insane. Seemingly talking to myself."

"Believe it or not, we all have conflicting thoughts within us. I mean, it's not the same, but . . ." She looked up at him, her eyes wells of understanding.

Marcus appreciated that she tried to understand him. "We coalesce, but it makes us seem erratic. Regardless of which one of us speaks through me, you know whose words they are, don't you?"

She smiled and ducked her head. Scents of mutual desire mingled together. Her aroma musky inside the kitchen. Marcus closed his eyes and inhaled, deep and slow.

The next moment, he was leaned over Platt. His arms boxing her between him and the butcher block, while she smiled nervously holding a cup of tea as though it would shield her.

"Asmara," Marcus growled and pushed off Platt.

Like you'd ever initiate anything, Asmara huffed. *It's not my fault. I am who I am.*

Marcus sighed knowing the mage would never force anything on anyone.

"You have more agreements than before." Her back was to the block.

Observant little thing. Asmara squirmed.

"Tell me about this passage everyone knows about." Tit for tat. If she wanted to know about his agreements, she could pay for the knowledge with information. He drank his tea but never let his gaze leave her.

"It's a hidden passage, and if everyone knew about it, it wouldn't be secret," she teased. She sipped tea and spoke without a hint of the desire her body professed.

His claws clicked against the cup. "Keep your hidden passage." He smiled. "It is enough I know one exists." He would find it. Find it and prove his cleverness to her.

"I'm going to Morgan's burial." A statement. One she expected him to honor.

"Tier Naug are still out there." He set the cup down.

"I won't be alone." Her tone hinted agitation.

Marcus rose to his full height, jealousy spiking. "I'll go with you."

"It would be better if you stayed here." Her eyes sparkling as firmly as her words, she pressed her hand to his chest.

Clawed fingers tapped on the wooden block clicking against the surface. "I did not kill Morgan."

"I believe you, and you can trust me to come back."

"I do trust you . . ." After her refusal to go with Riley willingly, she deserved that much.

"Please. Let me go. I will return."

Marcus sighed. "And if they attempt another kidnapping?"

Softie, Asmara teased, feeling Marcus relent.

"They won't."

Marcus paused knowing in his heart that she would keep her word. "Go."

Chapter 16

"WHERE IS IT?" Marcus growled at the kitchen fire.

The coals roasted and ignored him. The hidden passage remained a secret.

Agitated, Marcus grabbed the wicker basket as a distraction. It was filled with fruit and nuts and nothing else.

Insultress! Asmara squeaked. *She took the pie! Call the Rawg out, and we'll track the little thief.*

"Rawg?" Marcus snorted at the mage's use of a nickname for Tiecus. "Her scent permeates the air. Why would we need him to track her?"

Track the pie, Asmara said in earnest.

Marcus almost smiled when an idea to find the passageway hit him. Platt had cleaned up, changed her dress, and hadn't triggered the warning wards. Which meant she'd used the secret passageway.

Tiecus possessed tracking abilities and could scent the air, which was always saturated with the smell of those who had passed through it.

Because Riley and Bolden had only been here a handful of times, with Tiecus and Asmara's shared abilities, he could easily waft through Platt's vanilla scent and perhaps find the way they'd entered without warning.

Which leaves an interesting question. Asmara seemed invested in the puzzle of the secret entrance. *Why didn't the villagers ambush us with this hidden passage?*

Marcus went to the landing where drops of Riley's blood had been spilled a few days ago. His scent was burnt-musk spice. Riley's blood had sung of sweet revenge and treachery. Marcus inhaled deeply, the scent coaxed him under the stairwell.

Marcus jammed his nose against the wall opposite the underside. Trace scents of revenge and treachery found their way through the tiniest hole. He didn't know how, but Riley and Bolden had passed under the stairs.

He'd been down hidden walkways before when he lived in Benicar. Their entrances were covered by illusion, a trick of light confusing the eye, causing people to pass over the open entrances. A wall could be a wall, or it could be a recess into the dark cramped passages of Benicar.

He examined the unlit cove where bricks created the faint outline of a door. It wasn't large enough for Bolden to come through unless he walked sideways, but this had to be the passageway.

He pushed against the supposed door built under the stairs, but the wall didn't budge. The small cubbyhole did not reveal a lever, switch, or any other secret opening. Only a torch hung on the wall.

"Tiecus could ram through this door." Marcus pulled down the corners of his mouth. "But his horns might rip apart the passageway."

As useful as the demon could be, Tiecus was a master of destruction without trying. No, he was going to have to figure this out. It was a puzzle. A game of chess.

Marcus traced the outline of the door. A full survey of the area underneath the stairs didn't give him any other clues or any out-of-the-ordinary subtleties to glean secrets.

Just ask Terra how the door works, the mage said.

"Of course," Marcus said dryly. "You'd use the elements and not your intelligence."

Do it your way then. Asmara's irritation was clear.

Marcus traced the door again. "Asmara, your way is just as destructive as sending a demon down the passage. Humans built the stronghold." Marcus paused. When he thought of it, he did notice a faint smell of burning pitch. "Perhaps, I should think like a human to solve this riddle."

Ignis was happy to oblige, and a torch lit up. The thin space under the stairs exploded in light. Marcus shielded his face with the crook of his elbow. Red spots exploded in the back of his eyelids.

A slant underside replaced where the grooves of the stairs should be. On that smooth surface was a mirror. Reflection was the reason for his intensified blindness. Hiding his face in his arm, Marcus stepped out of the tiny room. Acclimating to the light was almost as bad as trying to look at the sun.

The mirror was polished to perfection. It showed no warps or blemishes. The glass was clean, and it reflected the image of Tiecus, Asmara, and Marcus occupying the same space. His second shock aside from bright light was Tiecus. Now that he could see Tiecus's full body, he saw the demon had grown from a clumsy large-pawed youngling to a dangerous, hulking monstrosity. "Rawg," Marcus decided, was the most appropriate term for him.

Marcus hadn't changed much. A longer face littered with lines of weariness. Broader chest, taller frame. At least, his body had abandoned the scraggly immaturity of younglings.

Asmara hadn't changed one bit. The mage noticed neither of them. He tossed his white-blond curls, turning his head this way and that in self-admiration.

Disgusted, Marcus turned back to the door. A tiny keyhole, large enough for a pinky finger, framed the silhouette of a stag. The keyhole was the deer's eye.

He looked back at the mirror, at the placement of the torch, and then back at the hole. Two bricks, odd in their square shape, under his feet caught his attention.

Marcus squatted down, examined the clean spots on the rough floor, and placed his knees on the square stones.

A mechanical *click* rewarded Marcus's inspection. The rock wall separated and slid backward to reveal a tall, slim opening. The scent of Riley and Bolden assaulted Marcus's nose in the draft. Mildew and darkness followed the chill air.

It was odd, being on his knees in submission, but the gesture gave Marcus a sense of relief. The demon stag, for it was a demon the way a soft glow emanated from its eyehole, gave Tiecus the sense this was a depiction of an alpha. A good alpha. The kind of leader that sought the survival and happiness of his throng.

Marcus shook off the desire to become part of an imaginary alpha's throng and went to stand. When he got up, the door began to close. Marcus ducked down and turned sideways to enter the passageway. Vanilla, mud, and the musk of Riley and Bolden were the only scents he could identify. Darkness was his only company.

"Puppis." Marcus cursed his lack of caution. "This could be a trap."

We're in it now, Asmara said. *Let's see where it goes.*

Tiecus agreed.

The contrast of the walls pressed against his shoulders. Uneasy at the vast space ahead, Marcus jogged, sideways, down a slope.

Your warning ward is lacking. Asmara tested for magic around them. *It should have gone off when you passed the stronghold's walls.*

"It was never meant to go underground."

Oh, how little do we know? Asmara's haughty tone rose with more arrogance.

"Then you make it," Marcus scoffed.

Asmara closed off the flow of consciousness they shared. Unfortunately, he kept the communication part open. *Tell me, when you raised the ward, how did you do it?*

Marcus loathed the absence that Asmara's higher knowledge lent him. "As you taught me. I make a dome around the keep."

Yes, and what is a dome?

The questions hinted at some secret code, something Marcus should know and yet without Asmara's aid was as mentally prepared to understand the elements as a weeling. Not only was he a bit helpless answering the question, but also the superiority Asmara washed over him in satisfaction irked him.

"A dome is a dome, half a round shield, a sphere." Marcus twisted his body to the side to travel down the narrow corridor faster.

And a sphere is? Asmara gave a rap on the boundary that separated him from Marcus. The feeling was equivalent to a wooden spoon being smacked against a forehead.

Intolerant of Asmara's ridicule, he answered in haste. "It's a circle."

So, when you think of the ward, you think of a half circle and not a whole one?

Marcus stopped so fast he nearly rode the rest of the way down the corridor on his arse. "Wait, you mean to tell me that if I think of a whole circle, the warning ward can penetrate Terra?"

How clever of you. I think you're beginning to understand the possibilities magic has. Asmara returned the flow of consciousness between them.

"You could have just told me that," Marcus grumbled and continued down the tunnel.

Yes, but then you wouldn't feel clever for figuring it out.

A section of the tunnel widened, and a fork appeared. Riley and Bolden's scent took the far-left fork.

As he continued down the left fork, Marcus reflected on the consequence of using elemental air. Each element had a "requirement" in exchange for lending its power. Ventus required its user to be honest—or "true."

Marcus blurted out his question before thinking. "How does Ventus know what is true?"

Ah, you're wondering about the rhyme "three times a lie and then you die." Asmara collected his thoughts before sending them. *Ventus isn't like the others. It has no fear of its siblings. It shapes Terra and dances with her. It stokes Ignis and encourages Glacias. It also carries thought.* Asmara paused and realization flooded through him. Marcus sensed Asmara's reaction, but the mage didn't share what he had concluded.

"You're saying it knows my thoughts?"

Asmara answered half-heartedly. *Yes.*

"Does that mean that truth is an opinion? If this is so, how does it affect my agreements? If I believe I'm not breaking an agreement or can rationalize it, do my tattoos not burn?"

He didn't get an answer.

Asmara retreated. But the mage took his question seriously and climbed into a space far away from Tiecus and him.

Fresh air replaced the battle between the putrid scent of musty dirt and the sweet scent of burnt-musk human. Filtered light came through hearty winter bushes into the dark tunnel. Marcus pushed the foliage aside and stepped out into an open forest.

The mold had been oppressive, and he welcomed the snow's blinding reflection. Marcus couldn't tell exactly where or in what direction the hidden passage spat him out. He squinted and followed a familiar scent.

Overhead, the wind combed through treetops. Stillness in the air dampened sound. After a mile, he no longer shielded the light with his eyelashes. It took him that long to realize he was following the scent of vanilla, snow berry, and another familiar trail. Her escort retained the scent of bark under a day's worth of hot sun.

Stillwood. The bony-fingered soothsayer and only educated man of the town qualified to approve letters of marque.

Trees dropped off to reveal a clearing. Headstones in sequential placement sat on dark ground, void of snow. Tiecus rushed to the forefront and caused Marcus to halt and reel back.

Marcus sensed it too . . . the ground wasn't covered in dirt or snow. It was the same emptiness of the Atra Solumn. This wasn't ground at all. This burial place was a huge gaping hole, a mirror, a direct line into madness. The Atra Solumn and Shatter Side leaned against each other in a thin veil ready to crack at the slightest pressure.

Puppis! Asmara rushed into their consciousness. *Is that a gateway to hell?*

Marcus shook in reaction to Tiecus's fear. People stood on the barrier of Shatter Side oblivious to the dangers of the Atra Solumn directly below them. It was like watching an upside-down world beyond the grave. Demons on the Atra Solumn side milled around, circling the people on Shatter Side.

A group of thirty humans disbursed from the congregation. Each villager had one or two demons circling, watching, crouching, and following them—paws to feet as if the people walked on a mirror surface showing their reflections as demons. Several pairs of iridescent eyes darted from one human to another in hungry anticipation. An elk demon fidgeted underneath an older lady who conversed with Platt.

Marcus wanted to warn her, protect her, but he was paralyzed. Torn between Tiecus's terror and Asmara's awe, he couldn't move. Platt had her back to him, and his throat was too dry to call out.

Asmara wanted to go forward, study, and observe. The Serenite's curiosity about two worlds meeting was unusually strong. Tiecus was ready to run away from the anomaly but didn't dare. The opposing forces ripped Marcus apart.

"I am in control." Marcus gritted his teeth. He had no idea why Asmara had the need to inspect the strange surface, but he knew exactly why Tiecus wanted to leave. The demon feared his kind. He never trusted them except for his own throng. But they were gone. None of his family was alive.

Marcus closed his eyes and mentally separated himself from the other two.

Nothingness quieted the fear of Tiecus and the strange hunger from Asmara. He pushed the two further away like a father splitting up two siblings fighting over food and then attempted to shove them out of his body in separate halves.

Now he was in control. Calculations of risk versus advantages filtered through his mind. He wouldn't be prone to the antics of those from the Atra Solumn. He could pull a demon through if he wanted, just like any other warlock, but he'd rather pull out his own falcon-curved claws than bring another demon to Shatter Side.

As the people left, the demons that followed disappeared. Only a few humans lingered, surrounding Platt and the old woman. The elk demon on the Atra Solumn side circled below them. A closer look at the old woman accompanying the doe sent a shock of memories back through his mind.

Marcus gasped. Mrs. Morgan was a shadow of a memory.

"Reginhart?" A voice from the right penetrated the silent forest.

A chill washed over Marcus realizing that Reginhart was a name, and the taint of Ventus was spoken behind the word.

Marcus turned to Stillwood's searching eyes. "What?"

The gaunt man squinted as if he could see through him. "No. I didn't think so."

"Didn't think what?"

"You see them, don't you?" Stillwood faced the squared-off section between the Atra Solumn and Shatter Side.

Marcus narrowed his eyes and said nothing.

Stillwood appraised Marcus from a side-long glance. "The demons in the cemetery on the other side." Bony fingers stroked his beardless chin. "You see them."

"Yes." Marcus looked back at the anomaly. "They seem to be able to see the villagers."

"They actually don't, but they feel them. Each family has a signature, and this is the place where both worlds are thinnest."

Marcus recognized Riley, but the youngling was leaving. If he left Platt alone, he had no quarrel with the boy. Although, he wouldn't hesitate to treat him in kind.

"Did you kill Mr. Morgan?" Stillwood crossed his arms.

"I do not know who this person is, but I suspect I had no hand in his demise." Marcus punctuated his agitation with a glance.

Stillwood gave a sigh, but not of relief. "Thought so."

"You believe me?" The hairs lifted off Marcus's neck with pinpoint precision. He didn't feel comfortable near Stillwood, but he wasn't going to set a foot on the graveyard's soulless ground to avoid him.

"I'm the only one in this town that *will* believe you." Stillwood kept his eyes on a proud antlered demon stag approaching the edge of the accursed cemetery. A contemptuous smile spread across the educated man's face. "They've all forgotten the true ways of a demon."

Agitated, Marcus shifted from foot to foot. Platt exchanged more words with the elder woman. The conversation looked unpleasant by the severity of the woman's expression.

Stillwood tightened his shoulders. "Rehan says you're looking for an arquebus."

Platt pushed a flat round dish into the woman's arms.

Is that the pie dish? Asmara broke through.

"She says you can leave if you find one." Stillwood's eyes burned the side of his face.

"If it's intact, I might be able to," Marcus said. Here comes another proposal.

"Well, I don't want you to leave Reginhart."

Marcus blanched before he could school his expression.

"You've been a helpful barrier between them and us."

Platt broke away from the elder woman and walked toward him. When she saw him, she stopped dead in her tracks. Her face grew pale.

Ha! Asmara huffed. *She knows she's in trouble.*

Straightening, Platt resumed walking at a cautious pace.

Itching for a reason to get away from Stillwood, Marcus walked forward.

"Marcus . . ." the soothsayer called out.

He turned back to the bony-fingered man.

Stillwood's voice lowered to a rogue's disclosure. "Take care of her."

It took the skip of a heartbeat for Marcus to expose his back to Stillwood and turn back to Platt.

Platt curtsied and addressed Stillwood. "I greatly appreciate your escort, Firstborn; may I continue with Marcus?"

Marcus could feel the man behind him make a gesture and say "Dominae."

With fists in balls and a hardened expression, Platt glared at Stillwood. "I am not anyone's mistress."

The soothsayer bowed. "It was a term of respect and endearment."

Platt sighed and closed her eyes, and Stillwood slipped away as quietly as he'd come.

"Where's my pie?" Marcus tried to make light of the situation and dislodge any reminisce of Stillwood's conversation. But his question came out more accusatory than intended.

"I'll make you another," Platt snapped and then rubbed her temples with a hand. "Sorry. Trust me, you didn't want that one."

Without another word she turned and walked with purpose toward their stronghold. His long legs easily matched Platt's suddenly fervent pace. "Don't ever come here again."

Platt halted. She closed her eyes and breathed in deep. When she opened them, she looked ready for battle. "I did not agree to obey you."

He couldn't help the smile forming on his face. She was learning. "But staying with me is part of the agreement."

"I haven't left you." She gritted her teeth and stood her ground. "I'm still here in Reginhart, aren't I?"

He held a twinge of sadness for her sake, but the same emotion brought hope for him. The kind of hope he had once had in Valder. Platt deserved to be rewarded, not scrutinized.

"Forgive me." Marcus lifted her chin. "In my delight to find one worthy of banter, I forget all you've left behind. But I must insist that you don't ever go to that place again. I have reason to ask this of you."

"Well, then maybe you should have asked that before you settled our agreement." Her eyes widened as she covered her mouth with a hand. "I'm sorry."

"I deserve that." Claws brushed wisps of her blonde hair away. Marcus took ahold of her face and stared into her darting eyes.

Their eyes met, and it was as if lightning had struck his heart and electrified his whole body. Words danced in his throat but didn't form the way he wanted, and he spoke a gibberish that even he couldn't understand. "Yatak kilim kaplamalari."

Well, Asmara said. *At least, your heart is in the right place. That was as eloquent as two comets colliding. I believe the words you're looking for are—join the covers with me.*

Marcus took a breath—or tried and couldn't. Oxygen was circulating through his lungs, but he became dizzy, happy, and as light as a feather. "What is this feeling?"

A mental illness, Asmara astutely replied. *And don't drag me into it.*

Platt stayed as still as prey wishing to be overlooked.

Marcus let go of her face and with a minimal command of the Benicarian language said, "I meant, I want to give you something."

Eyebrows raised, Platt looked somewhat skeptical.

Marcus didn't understand why the doe was pulling back. He called inward. *Asmara, help me with this.*

Asmara's essence whooshed into place and took control without morphing. Marcus stood up straight, offered her an elbow, and said, "Your room needs rugs, and your bed needs a comforter. Surely, there is a place of business that sells these things in town. If you would so permit me, I'd like to acquire these things for you. Are you agreeable?"

Platt looked at him dubiously and took his arm. She looked around and then got up on her tiptoes and whispered, "Asmara?"

"Maybe." Marcus smiled and shrugged. It was technically both speaking.

She smiled with warmth. "Yes, I'll go with you to town."

Marcus's heart thundered, his head felt stuffed with cotton, and he let his little doe guide him toward the town square of Reginhart.

Chapter 17

WITH PLATT ON his arm, Marcus walked with her through sleeping woods and fresh snow. Marcus was at odds with wanting to say anything to her. Even menial small talk seemed trite. Keeping the easy silence between them felt right. Peaceful.

"I know your secret." Marcus grinned proud of his ingenuity. She'd challenged his prowess by way of a hidden passageway, and he'd succeeded.

She'd kept her pace even with his up until now. As her face paled, she slowed. "What will you do with the knowledge?"

"Nothing." His peace of mind faltered. Did it bother her so much he knew about a passageway? "If anything, I'd block or ward the exit."

A heartbeat later she breathed again. "The hidden entrance. That's what you're talking about."

"Yes."

What was she talking about? Asmara huffed. *Little secret keeper.*

"So, you gave homage to Lord Father Reginhart." It wasn't a question. It was a test.

"If you want to know whether I opened or destroyed the door under the staircase, then my answer is this: the stag with fire in his eyes, once I lit the torch, allowed me entrance." Flaunting his craftiness, Marcus smiled triumphantly.

"You are part of a handful that knows that way." She returned his smile giving Marcus his due. "No one has ever found the back way. It's been tried several times. Even those that know what to look for don't find it."

"Then how did Bolden and Riley find it?"

"Ah." Platt nodded. "Bolden is blessed."

"Blessed?" Marcus turned his eyes to her. "Not cryptic at all."

She laughed. "There's one every generation. One that is blessed by Lord Father Reginhart at birth."

"So, this lord father goes around blessing children? Planting his seal upon a worthy babe?"

Platt laughed. "I suppose that's accurate enough."

He sensed there was more, but as they strolled through the forest, time collided in a surreal world where he and his little doe walked forever in this moment.

In the real world, cottages peeked behind a shield of trees. Too soon, he had a reason to crash their peaceful dream. "Are there many villagers?"

"Yes." Her pace slowed. "You haven't eaten in a while."

Eyeing her bruised throat, loosely covered by a shawl, he kept walking. "I will be fine."

He hadn't thought about agreements or treating villagers in kind. His version of abiding by Platt's agreement was keeping out of sight. Now that Marcus was headed straight into the heart of town, where he might interact with people, there was a chance through his varied agreements that he'd pay the price for his ill-versed ways in human customs and formalities.

Valder had once asked which would Marcus chose if two agreements conflicted with each other. His answer in theory was one in seniority. But practice might not turn out so simple.

His tongue passed over bumpy lettering across his upper gums, across the first agreement ever made. *No feeding from Serenite.* Marcus grunted equivalent to a demon's acceptance. He could do this.

Platt yanked him to a stop. "You agreed."

The vehement, determined, wild face reminded him Platt was Rehan's daughter. Her words were an echo of her mother's threat.

"I will treat them in kind." His voice was soothing, impressing upon her she had no cause for worry.

"That's what I'm afraid of."

Marcus cocked his head and smiled. "I can promise to be on my best behavior during this endeavor, if you grant me a kiss."

Platt stiffened and pulled away. "That's something Asmara would say."

Marcus growled, checking if anyone was near. "Why yes, it is."

In apprehension, Platt studied him. "If he can control you, then that means the demon can too."

Feeling foolish, not knowing what to say to reassure her, Marcus resumed full control of his body. Her eyes widened, and her demeanor grew defensive. Marcus wanted to ask her what she'd just seen. How she could tell if it was him or not.

Life emerged at the edge of town. Raking his tongue along his gums, he offered her his arm. Platt ignored his chivalry, turned toward the row of thatched roof cottages, and walked alone.

The world he imagined living in, his one beautiful moment of peace, was obliterated.

"She's ashamed of me," Marcus whispered.

Why should she be proud of someone who forces her into a contract and then abuses the right. Asmara's words constricted his ribs. Platt was like Ventus taking his oxygen away.

Each step she took pulled at his entrails. She hadn't wanted him to go to the funeral. She didn't want to be seen with him now. Platt worked his gut breathless without landing a single blow.

Tiecus jerked him forward, catching up to her in six strides. Platt's sideways acknowledgement was enough to calm the flutters in his chest but not enough to release the squeeze around his lungs.

The town was like all the others Tiecus had destroyed. Box buildings rooted in perfect lines, ideal for the demon to crush one at a time. Marcus relived the burning houses, scattered human parts, and blood running down crooked paths of least resistance.

"No." He jerked his head to gain control. "Not this time."

"What's the matter?"

He released his clenched jaw and relaxed. Platt searched every muscle in his profile. Settling his shoulders back, he walked in silence.

Tense, poised to fight, Platt *wasn't* inviting any type of weakness. Touching her was out of the question. He didn't want her angry with him. If he could demense her, he could express everything. Doing so was a guaranteed scalp burning, and he'd transfer his pain while doing it without meaning to.

Homes, shops, and a distinguishable road built for mongers' carts came closer. Slowing his pace, matching her stride for stride, he tried guessing her mood.

"You're angry." More of an observation than a question, Marcus sighed.

She stopped in front of him turning her back on the open street. "I'm wary."

His heart ached. Pushing into her mind would be so easy. *Talk to me.* Marcus willed her. *I don't have the words. You must find them for me.*

Platt bit her lip. "I don't understand any *one* of you. I can't tell who's talking to me. I can't tell *if* you're talking to me. You do strange things. Horrible things one moment, and then you turn around as if nothing's happened, then you apologize, and I feel . . ." She looked down seemingly lost.

His heart plummeted. She was afraid of him. He was a monster and that's all he'd ever be to her. But Platt's ardor mingled in his nose. His lust was triggered by hers. She was telling him one thing and her body another. Which signal was he supposed to follow?

Afraid to show his confused hurt, he turned toward the town and walked.

Desire turned into hunger. Hyper aware of every movement, Marcus stifled the demon's need for blood.

A monger shuffled on one lame foot and ambled pushing his cart.

Cull the weak. Tiecus squirmed.

Marcus bolted forward. Searing pain stopped his follow-through. The monger meant him no harm. Marcus was not treating the trader in kind.

A weeling darted after its mother. Marcus cut short of chasing the child. Rock on metal scraped against his ears, irritating his fraying nerves. The source was a man shoveling snow to make a better path. Marcus wanted to kill for the noise alone.

The smell of burnt flesh rose, and a puff of smoke escaped his sleeves. Platt laid a hand on the burning arm. Scratchy material on raw skin incinerated his self-control. Marcus snarled.

Platt grasped his arm tighter, rubbing the scratchy cloth and pressing more pain into already kindling flesh. His skin was burning. Specifically, one of the tattoos on his arm that proclaimed one of the agreements he'd made with her about the villagers.

Infuriated, he realized the full extent of his stupid, mindless haste agreeing to her demands. Treat them in kind when they weren't demons? Such was the agreement that it annulled a resource of food. If the Tier Naug were depleted, if they could be eaten from at all, that meant Tiecus's only sustenance was Platt. How long would she live?

Another reason to get an arquebus and get out of here. Marcus managed to keep the quip inside.

"No." Marcus ripped away from Platt and hurried back toward the uninhabited woods. "I don't want to do this."

"Marcus?" The inflection in her voice implied she didn't know if it was Marcus or another entity to which she spoke.

Irritated at the underlying question, he whirled around baring his teeth. The tattoo on his arm was no longer burning, but the wound stung.

"You're burning." Platt wrinkled her nose and brought a hand to her lips. Blood dripped down the hand that covered her mouth.

Drool pooled down his incisors. Swallowing to rein in his need for life water, he took ahold of her hand. Lifting her fingers with his knuckles, he examined four claw marks on her wrist. When he had turned from her and yanked out of her grasp, he'd filleted her wrist and hand. His claws were razor sharp to the point they left no pain when they slashed through skin.

Platt stared at a trail of thick red blood dripping down her palm as though it wasn't her own. "Did you cut me?"

Marcus lifted his own hand showing blood on four of his claws. Marcus applied his tongue to her wounds and sucked. His heart thundered under her gaze. Blood was bringing his sanity back.

The cuts gushed. He'd have to be more careful. Claws sharp as his could swipe through bone without resistance. Her heart beat faster replacing what she'd lost. A quart, a pint, or maybe a liter later he finished. Marcus swadded his tongue along her cuts, the bleeding stopped, but her hand would scar.

"Your skin burns"—soft fingers traced a line down his arm—"when you disobey."

She glided her hand over his chest. Over the *No killing Serenite* agreement she'd asked about earlier. Her gaze looked past his clothes.

Asmara cut into his thoughts with a sultry tone. *I say take off your clothes and let her fondle those agreements again.*

Marcus squirmed unpleasantly. *This is Reginhart, not the Serenite alcove. Don't assume everyone wants an orgy.*

Happy voyeurs are everywhere.

Asmara's comment brought Marcus to attention. He glanced around.

"Our agreement is on your arm?" Her tone rang firm. "You were thinking about it—not treating them in kind."

He winced. "Yes."

A sheen of acceptance washed over her face. The tension left her body. Within a blink, a shield he never knew she held dropped. He could see into her. Her gaze seemed to wander inside him. It was not a demens per se, but an ethereal communication. Energy pulled them together where souls touched. The wisdom of predilection drew their bodies closer.

Doe eyes filled with wonder and weeling trust, the kind that recognized their lives were dependent upon kindness. Speech never left her lips, but he specifically heard the words "Forgive me."

Unable to look away, Marcus drank in a need he thought he'd eradicated. He surrendered in her receptive pools of acceptance. If she had any power, any command of the art of demens, she could sink into his wide-open consciousness.

No, he thought. *Forgive me. Forgive me for killing you twice. Forgive me for hurting you. For taking you away from all you've known. I have caused this. I lost to Valder. I have taken out the wrath I've felt for him on to you. The only one who has shown me selfless kindness. Why would you sacrifice everything for a bunch of worthless, conniving men?*

Engulfed in her, Marcus had no more words or thoughts. The grip of her gaze clamped around his furiously beating heart.

Platt showed no judgment of his past and no concern for her future. Only the present remained in a clarity that held them and nothing else. It was as if she had made time converge into this one place and stand still.

Tiecus had not been wrong. She was an element unto herself. Whatever she was doing to him, he wanted more. He wanted her to feel it. He had to show her, make her know what she had given to him.

"Take this." He dipped his claws into his pocket. In solemn tribute, he clasped the underside of her hand and laid a heavy gold-laden velvet pouch in her palm. "Buy what you need."

The contents inside clinked as she fondled the bag. Then her eyes flew open, and she shoved the coin bag to his chest.

"No," she rasped. "No, I cannot take this."

A huge gasp sounded a few feet away. Platt whipped around with the bag of coins still in her possession and waved her hands at her brother. "No, he didn't—"

Tim broke out in a broad grin, turned, and raced down the snowy streets happily shouting, "Mom! Marcus gave Platt dowry!"

Platt pushed the bag at Marcus. "Please take this back."

"It's a gift." A twinge of hurt coiled around his chest.

Platt looked back. A few people who'd noticed the demon congregated around a wood-fenced yard. Manic, Platt searched for the pocket he had pulled the bag from.

"Little doe?" Concern reached his voice.

"If you take this back, I'll grant your request of a kiss—in private."

Confused by this turn of circumstance, Marcus nonetheless took the coin bag.

"All right." Anger swirled in his solar plexus. What started as being miffed grew into an outright blazing resentment.

Oh, is that how it's played, Asmara lashed out. *We're going to get her a bed, and when it arrives, I'm going to fuck her on it.*

"Not without her permission," Marcus snapped.

Don't try to use my own agreement against me, Asmara said. *My own charms are enough to get what I want.*

Platt ran after Tim in a blaze rivaling the meals Tiecus had chased and lost.

Marcus locked his knees and closed his eyes knowing anger was a double-edged sword that could defend or cut the handler. Thwarting his aggression, he soaked in Platt's promise of a kiss.

Another consolation . . . this type of agreement didn't form a tattoo on his skin. Promises apparently didn't write themselves on his body.

Agreements and promises are different, Asmara said.

Marcus wasn't sure if that was good or bad, because while there was no formal embossment on his skin, his heart burned in a new kind of way.

"Should she be running right now?" Marcus said. "How much blood did we take?"

Tiecus yawned, stretched, and hunkered down in his usual sleeping area of Marcus's mind. *Enough*, Tiecus answered.

"Rest then." Marcus mentally stroked the demon's head. Sleep lessened Tiecus's instincts, and Marcus needed every advantage going into a village full of walking meals.

Tiecus grumbled about not needing permission for sleep, and Marcus chuckled as the demon left his consciousness.

Believing the villagers safe, he strolled in the direction of three humans with grime on their arms and faces. He classified the group as working men that were hard on their clothes. Their lack of fear made them stand out from Benicarians. They stood erect with the pride of purpose. Marcus wished he could feel that kind of confidence instead of faking it all the same.

When he neared, the three men faced him and bowed like subjects to King Valder. Absence of screams at his presence was a novelty. And he was taken aback by their reverence but recovered with the first question that came to his head.

"Is there one who makes beds here?" He waited for crazed hunger or burning pain, but neither sensation adorned him.

One man snickered. His companion elbowed the laughing man. Marcus never seemed to have any communication problems with Platt, but he wondered if he'd said the words correctly.

Forming the question differently, Marcus said, "Do you have a human that assembles furniture?"

The three men sobered.

"Sir," the third man answered. "Old Man George can make you one, sir." He pointed with his thumb toward the town. "You'll know the house. It's the only one with front stairs, sir."

"I'm not human." Marcus narrowed his eyes. "Don't ever tag me with a human title such as 'sir.'"

"As you say . . . Lord Marcus." The man avoided his eyes.

Marcus sighed.

Lord Asmara has a ring to it.

"Fine." Since they were going to assign whatever title to him they wanted, he'd let it pass. There were worse things to be called.

He left the three men, kept his head down, lowered the brim of his hat, and shoved his claws down the pockets of his coat. Being taller than an average human would draw unwanted attention, but the roads felt unusually quiet. Villagers of Reginhart passed by in handfuls. Strangers bowed before him as he passed.

In Benicar, during daylight hours, humans packed the cobblestone streets, pushing their baskets or carts. Benicarians sold their wares by calling out or screaming verbal barbs at their competitors. When they saw him, they ran in horror.

In Reginhart, he stretched out his arms and didn't touch a single person for paces at a time. It was quiet. Peaceful. Carts carved thin grooves on dirt roads. One monger, not dozens, sold his wares. Best of all, Reginhart's buyers came to the seller. There was no need for screaming duels in the streets. In a way, it was more civilized.

The town's endearing difference was the calm silence. Reginhart was equivalent to the cogs of a watch turning slow and constant that rejoiced in quiet movement behind a blank face. The reprieve from terror-ridden pleas after one look at his face caused Marcus to relax. No one smelled of fear or panic, and he loosened the iron hold on his instincts.

Bobble! Asmara swung Marcus around to a sparkly sphere behind a window. The glitter alone retained Asmara's rapt attention.

"Old Man George's shop is one house away," Marcus said. "Can it wait?"

A tug on the thigh of his boot accompanied by a high-pitched voice reclaimed Marcus's attention. "Are you a demon?"

Marcus scoffed at a brown-haired, brown-eyed weeling not tall enough to reach his thigh. This child's audacity rivaled a warlock's.

The weeling's eyes grew wide, his tiny voice pronounced words as if they were epiphanies. "Are you Reginhart?"

Marcus crouched to the pup. "Who is this Reginhart?"

"Which Reginhart?" The boy shimmied side to side from the waist up and swung his arms. "Lord Reginhart doesn't have glowing eyes," the boy said with awe. "But you're a real demon, aren't you?"

Oblivious to the dangers of a demens, the child stood still in curiosity. "Momma says if that imposter comes back without the real Reginhart, you're gonna bleed him dry." The boy enunciated every syllable.

Marcus cocked his head. He'd never heard such a tone come from a human.

The boy giggled. "You're like a puppy."

Cautious and slow, he lifted the boy's hand with the dull side of his index claw. Tiny fingers wrapped around the top of his thick talons.

Without warning, the boy placed his small palms against Marcus's cheeks and with worry on his weeling face said, "You're gonna save us from the Tier Naug, aren't you?"

A wave of instinct to protect swept Marcus. This town was his to defend. The scent of this tiny creature's uncertainty brought a different type of hunger. The drive to hunt and slay those who would hurt what belonged to him.

"Jacob!" a typical woman of Reginhart with brown hair and brown eyes anxiously called out.

The weeling swung around at his name but returned his questioning look to Marcus.

He nodded to the boy, and the small human ran back into his mother's arms.

The woman walked away with a bow and swift efficiency, holding Jacob who stared back at him.

Concerned about what the weeling asked, Marcus tromped up the stairs of Old Man George's cottage. Jacob had seen the Tier Naug and probably not under the best circumstance. Marcus made a mental note to scout the weeling's house for lurking outsiders.

The door to the bed-maker's cottage was wide open. Wooden frames, tall and wide, short and stout, leaned against the buckled wooden walls. Rows of raw silk and cotton and burlap fabric hung on reels attached to a bowed ceiling. Rope as thick as his talons coiled around termite-ridden spools that doubled as worktables. The shopkeeper, Old Man George, looked as rustic as the building.

Reginhart might be a small village, but it looked like the bed-maker kept busy. Old Man George sat on a stool bent over a coverlet sewing the ends together. Marcus tilted the brim of his hat covering his eyes and stood further away from the human than normal. Circumventing the drive to search for those that terrified Jacob, he didn't want to turn his aggression toward a villager.

"I understand you provide bedding," Marcus said.

The old man didn't look up. His flailing voice gave no indication he would discontinue working. "I make it and sell it, ya."

It was one thing to show no fear to a demon, but the terse, informal attitude of Old Man George didn't suit Marcus. Still, he kept his pride in check and said, "I need one."

"Ya! I suppose you're going to up and carry it too." The shopkeeper sniffed. "There's a tax for delivery, up front."

"Fine." He searched in his coat for two gold coins.

He took the currency between his knuckles and, without revealing his claws, dropped the coins on the table.

The man glanced at the money but never stopped working on his project. "I don't have time to convert your coin." Old Man George snorted out the words. "Go to Druthers and exchange it."

Refreshing as the villagers' acceptance of him was, this lack of prudence uncorked the mildest of the triad. Marcus pulled out a fist full of the king's gold reserve and slammed the gold pieces down on the makeshift table. Dragging his claws and splintering the wood top satisfied a part of his ego. "Keep what's left."

For the first time, Old Man George gazed over his glasses and raised his head up. Staring, the man pressed his lips together. "You poor, soiled soul." Old Man George set his work down, got up, and hobbled over to another table with quills and parchment. "What're your preferences?"

"The best you have." Marcus stepped back. He was in control again. He preferred life that way.

"Where?" Old Man George said.

"The stronghold."

"Lord Marcus, everybody knows where you live. Which room, yours or Ms. Ottern's?"

Marcus was thankful to be too far away to reach out and choke Old Man George. "Platt's."

The keeper scratched down some notes. "I'll have it to you in a few days, sir."

"I'm not a 'sir.'" Marcus turned around and walked out with his long coat chasing behind him. "Soiled soul," Marcus huffed.

But the expression Old Man George had given him wasn't familiar. Platt had had a similar expression the very first time they had met, but he hadn't understood the emotion.

Pity, Asmara said to him. *The look on his face was pity.*

Marcus sank against the wall of the cottage with folded arms.

"What is pity?" Speaking aloud got Marcus a few curious looks. The brim of his hat covered his eyes from villagers' curiosity. As if Asmara were standing beside him, he listened.

It's empathy for another. Platt and that shopkeeper feel sorry for you.

"Why should they feel sorry for me?"

Why should you feel concern for Jacob?

Peeking under the brim of his hat, he shoved his hands into his coat pockets. Across the way, Tim bounced beside Rehan while teasing his sister. Platt strode beside her mother and vehemently professed something to the effect of not receiving gold, coin, or any other currency from anyone.

Paying no mind to her daughter's convictions or her son's teasing gestures to his sister, Rehan waddled along with her children.

He would have a conversation with his little doe later. Whatever his faux pas, Platt was going to have to overlook it.

He spent a moment imagining life coiled around Platt in a dark den. In his imagination, he was larger, fiercer, and more powerful than any other. Able to thwart enemies easily as nuisances, he'd bury Platt under horns harder than steel and keep her safe. From there, his thoughts grew darker.

Marcus was going to have to get an arquebus.

A distant chime far away caught his attention. Marcus cut short his musings. Something in the bell's ring sounded familiar. It called to him and whispered commands with every chime.

Dong. Come.

Dong. Intruders.

Dong. Attack.

Chapter 18

A SCREAM DOWN the path caught Marcus's attention. Ten riddled Tier Naug in two rows of five sauntered down the main road like any other drill making its rounds. Under the commander's hood flashed iridescent eyes.

The Tier Naug warlock looked untouched, at least by the physical sense of the meaning. The smilodon's fight with the wolf demon hadn't made the warlock worse for wear. Even his flowing robes and cloak were seamlessly pressed and crisp.

Marcus threw down his overcoat, mentally jostling Tiecus to wake up. The demon was asleep during a critical time, again. Starting a pile of clothes, Marcus screamed at the demon in his head. "No wonder your whole family was slaughtered!" Marcus hissed. "You were probably asleep during watch."

No response. If the last battle hadn't woken Tiecus, nothing would.

That actually might be a bit harsh, Asmara chimed in.

"Why?" Marcus hissed.

I may or may not have . . . oh, let's say, spiked his punch earlier.

"What?"

He was giving you trouble. It would have never worked going into the town.

"Are you telling me you put him to sleep?"

It won't be waking up in time to help you fight.

"That . . ." Marcus pushed aside the disturbing thought of having to fight ten riddled Tier Naug and one warlock alone. "We'll speak about this later."

One riddled—whatever Marcus was—against ten Tier Naug was not good odds. Valder either had the utmost faith in Marcus, or he really did send him to his death.

It didn't matter. Tier Naug were Tier Naug. Riddled or not, the agreement along his arm provided enough encouragement. Fight and potentially live or burn to death by agreement were his choices. But what made his gut twist was the overbearing fact of other demons trespassing on his land—of them hurting these people.

Villagers ran. Jacob, the little boy that had asked him if he'd protect them from the Tier Naug, was picked up and taken away by his mother. Jacob's fear-soaked eyes scanned the streets until he found Marcus, his plea clear on his face. Marcus lifted his chin and gave a nod to the boy.

Platt was nowhere in sight. Thank all for small mercies.

A second scream came from a female being dragged by her hair. The soldier held her as she scrambled to keep pace with the unit.

The warlock turned back toward his men, waved his hands in a gesture implying "be done with it," and said something in a language that sounded like coughs and gags.

The held woman's captor stood her up, exposed her neck, and savagely bit down on her throat.

Humans screamed, running. The other Tier Naug turned and converged on the villagers. Two of the riddled men grabbed the woman's arms, another latched on an exposed part of her neck, and another pair ripped at each other for her life water.

Instinct as old as the stars took over, and Marcus charged the poachers. In swift fury, he toppled the Tier Naug feeding on the woman's throat. Claws dug into flesh. The soldier shouted in surprise as they tumbled. Shock registered on the Tier Naug's face, and Marcus pinned him to the ground. With a heavy swing of his claws, Marcus severed the riddled human's head.

Nine riddled soldiers turned and converged on Marcus. Hands grabbed and shoved him to his back. The warlock hung back and watched his fellows take Marcus down. He flashed his cougar demon's eyes behind his hood. If the warlock wasn't careful, its demon would take over.

"I will 'ave you." The warlock pointed at him.

Marcus clawed at a Tier Naug at his thigh and was rewarded with the riddled human's howl of pain. Marcus wasn't going down alone.

Hands grabbed for him, but he and his demon had merged, unlike the riddled Tier Naug, and Marcus had the advantage of Tiecus's weapons of choice. Claws. Marcus swiped, and in the wake of his flailing arms, fingers flew off, an elbow was torn to shreds, and a hand plopped on the ground. The middle of the street became a river of blood. The screams of the intruders were just like the pleas of every other human he'd run his talons through.

When a fist landed on his gut, it felt like boulders landing the blows. Gasping for air, he wished the odds were not so much against him or that Tiecus would wake up.

"Keep 'im alive!" the warlock said. "T'at one is valuable, demon and 'ost."

One Tier Naug continually punched him in the stomach. Another lay over Marcus's arm, pinning it down while trying to avoid getting slashed. Two rode his flailing legs. One crushed Marcus's wrist with a knee to keep him still. Of the four Tier Naug standing aside, one howled in pain holding a severed arm. One fellow soldier tried to staunch the bleeding with a shirt. The third and fourth guarded the warlock.

The five riddled Tier Naug on top of Marcus paid a dear price. Their blood covered his torso. Panic rose above the thrill of fighting. Not because he was afraid of losing, but because the warlock wanted him alive and unhurt. He didn't want to find out what was in store for him if he was captured.

He tugged on his right shoulder and then his left. Marcus thrashed his legs. One Tier Naug didn't have a good hold and struggled to control Marcus's foot. He kicked and pulled his leg out from under the Tier Naug's weight and booted the riddled human in the nose with such force the crunch was audible.

Crunched Nose slumped over and didn't move again. A sunken hole replaced the middle of the Tier Naug's face. An iridescent cloud escaped through the new opening and dissipated. Eight remained.

Tingling numbness crawled icy webs up his hands toward his shoulders. Marcus tried to roll, and a shot of ice fire ran up his arms.

Stump Limb and his friend threw their bodies over his legs and held him down. His right hand was being crushed by a knee. He clawed, but the Tier Naug seemed oblivious to the pain. His other arm was twisted in a wrist lock, and he couldn't move it.

The warlock hovered over him, and Marcus jerked his face away. He squirmed to no avail, and the only body parts not pinned down were his hips and neck. He wasn't sure he could fend off a demens from the warlock. Not without Tiecus.

"Don't fig't," the warlock said in a Tier Naug accent. "You're starving. Be mine, and I will take care of you. I want your service. We'll trade, you and me."

"No." Marcus squeezed his eyes shut. His mind was too disorderly to fight a demens.

"But I offer you to be part of us," the warlock said. "You will be the general of my army."

At this moment, Valder's seemingly insignificant question about conflicting agreements during the chess game no longer seemed trivial.

He'd have to fight and win, because if he lost, it was suicide by agreements burning his flesh until he wasn't useful for anything but a cooking fire. If the warlock controlled him through a demens, he'd be forced to do the warlock's bidding, burning flesh or not.

Asmara! Marcus screamed. *Wake him up!*

There was no acknowledgement.

"Open your eyes." The warlock commanded with a tint of strength and magic behind the words.

This was it. He couldn't avoid the warlock forever. Marcus didn't have Tiecus, but he had strength from Platt's blood. He kicked at Tiecus once more to get his help, anything to assist. But if the warlock commanded him to sleep, they were all done for. It was up to him.

Marshaling his thoughts, he remembered his walk with Platt. Scattered trails of emotion corralled into one calm focus. He held still under the weight of five Tier Naug. Prepared to fight, Marcus opened his eyes to push back a demens.

He was in time to see a rock ricochet off the side of the warlock's temple.

"Hey, Nidra. Stop picking on the youngling that's not past his puberty."

The warlock snarled in the direction of the rock thrower.

Marcus felt oddly insulted by Stillwood's comment. "I'm seventeen!" Marcus declared, indignant. He was well into his manhood and no longer the gawky creature that could barely stand when Asmara and Tiecus had first made their agreements.

"Oh, sorry," Stillwood snarled. "I didn't have time to evaluate earlier."

"Stillwood!" the warlock said with an odd combination of respect and resentment.

"You've retained your heavy accent," Stillwood said. "I would think by now you'd have disguised it."

The warlock snapped his fingers. Three of the four riddled Tier Naug moved in front of the warlock Stillwood called Nidra.

"Keep 'im 'ere," Nidra commanded the five riddled Tier Naug remaining to hold Marcus down. "I 'ave a demon to read."

Feigning compliance, Marcus concentrated on Glacias.

No matter how inclined, no one was impervious to freezing. The ground temperature beneath Marcus plummeted while Ignis insulated his core with warmth. Ventus played with the Tier Naug's red hair, bringing a biting chill into the breeze.

Marcus grabbed hold of the two pinning his arms and called upon the water flowing in his captor's veins. Glacias was a sneaky force, taking its time to affect anything, but it was also slow to retreat. Ventus chilled the air, making the Tier Naug shiver and ebb their strength.

But it wasn't the cold winter wind that would kill them.

Ice magic froze liquid—any liquid. Even blood.

The Tier Naug on his right shook uncontrollably. With momentum and speed, Marcus pulled his right hand free and punched the riddled human on his left. The body twisting his wrist slumped to the side. He swung back to the right and knocked down the Tier Naug on the opposite side.

Iridescent mist from the Tier Naug's mouth, nose, and ears poured out. The soul of the demon escaping the red-haired, freckled-faced body was a beautiful but deadly cloud settling into mud-covered slush. Another demon had been set free.

Platt walked up behind one of the riddled men with a frying pan the size of a chair seat. With all the range of her wiry arms, she lifted the iron skillet and smashed it down on her chosen victim's head. The Tier Naug went down, and so did Platt, both out cold.

"Platt!" Marcus cried.

The last Tier Naug holding him was encased in a thin layer of ice. Marcus kicked with his free leg, and the body holding him down broke into shards of ice, breaking the man in half.

One riddled Tier Naug crawled away, and Marcus let him go. He had to get Platt off the ground, or she too would freeze.

Taking great pains to be careful with his claws, Marcus wrapped his arms around his little doe and picked her up off the ice. Glacias was not quick to retreat just as it was slow to gain power.

"Wake up." His words laced with the power of Ventus commanded her.

Moaning acknowledgement, Platt cracked open one eye.

"Little doe, wake up." He couldn't set her down, and he couldn't fight holding her. The battle between the warlock and Stillwood was not the usual scene between soldiers and swords. No one could see the struggle between the two locked in a demens twenty feet apart, but the battle within them was just as real as a tethered knife fight.

They weren't the only ones fighting.

Men from the village began to fight back. The three men Marcus had approached about bedding had their farming implements in hand, fighting off two riddled Tier Naug trying to ambush Stillwood, while another guarded the warlock from behind.

Rehan was there with her brother, Bolden, both holding off one burly Tier Naug. Platt's mother had a knack for defending herself with a dirk while her uncle carried a spiked hammer. Riley shielded Old Man George doing his best to land a blow with a polearm. None of the villagers were stupid enough to look the riddled Tier Naug in the eye or get in front of Stillwood and the warlock lest they get trapped in a demens.

"Get me out of here," Platt whispered.

She clung to him, every muscle in her body rigid as she turned away from the fighting. Two agreements burned on his body, enough for him to smell his own flesh. King Valder's agreement, *Don't let any pass*, and Platt's, *Treat them in kind*, waged their own war on his body.

"I have to fight." His voice was gruff. "I have to honor agreements."

She nodded and pointed at the nearest house. "Put me in there."

In two long strides, he leaped to the door and kicked it in.

"The door was unlocked," she said, exasperated. "Where do you think I got the skillet?"

He grunted, set her in a chair, and unable to deal with his burning flesh any longer, he raced outside to join the fight.

Bolden and Rehan systematically kept one brute busy, working together like they'd done this before. Rehan faked and blocked a side blow at the same time Bolden went for the opposite side. The riddled Tier Naug blocked Bolden's spiked hammer.

Rehan drove her dirk into the Tier Naug's side striking a kidney and pulled back in time to avoid a blow to the face. The riddled host healed fast and didn't tire as quickly as a human. Presumably, their demons were not asleep.

Brother and sister were defending Stillwood's right side well, but the Tier Naug fighting with Riley and Old Man George's group seemed to be getting closer to Stillwood's left.

Stillwood and Nidra were staring at each other. Stillwood didn't look so well. His jaw was set, and his body was drenched in sweat even with the temperature being that of a typical winter's day. The warlock remained still, and because of his cloak, Marcus couldn't tell who was winning. But it wasn't the villagers.

Old Man George, the three men, and a few others were hurt and bleeding. Riley was left on his own. The youngling wasn't a strong fighter, but he was fast and agile. He was two against one now. Nidra was alone, but if Marcus didn't help Riley, he'd become overpowered.

Marcus roared and stalked his way toward Riley. He locked eyes with the guard nearest Nidra and entered into a battle of will. Marcus pushed against the demens with a mental force that crackled the air between them.

The Tier Naug lunged with unsteady footing and no grace. Wobbling like a newborn foal trying to gather his legs, the Tier Naug raised his sword, but Marcus had him.

"No!" Nidra yelled without looking away from Stillwood.

When the Tier Naug lunged, Marcus stepped aside, clamped down on the forearm that held the sword, and bent the hinge of his elbow unnaturally. The snow covered the muffled *thump* when the sword hit the ground.

Marcus raised his other hand, swung, and decapitated the Tier Naug. The essence of the demon inside the dead body gathered and sank into the muddy snow.

A thunderous roar brought Marcus's head up.

The largest Tier Naug Marcus had ever seen came out from two houses swinging a two-handed axe. But this warrior was familiar. They had sparred together behind the walls of Benicar. Cornelius. But when Marcus had last seen him, the king's seneschal had not been demon riddled.

Cornelius Van Hoepen with his red hair, pale skin, and over-abundant freckles looked much like a Tier Naug. But the man was forever King Valder's war commander and self-appointed king's guard. Marcus had never thought of Cornelius as a Tier Naug. He'd always been a Benicarian seneschal since the day they had met. Now Cornelius was demon-riddled, complete with iridescent eyes.

Cornelius joined Riley and fought alongside the town's people. Bolden roared in renewed triumph, sinking his spiked hammer into the opponent in front of him.

The warlock rocked back on his heels now only defended by the three riddled Tier Naug soldiers left standing.

Stillwood went down on his knees, and Nidra stepped forward.

Marcus didn't know how much longer Stillwood could last. The soothsayer was crying blood.

"Give 'im to me," Nidra said. "Why protect 'im. It's mine!"

"No . . ." Stillwood shook as feebly as he looked. Marcus knew the soothsayer was using every ounce of will power to hold his mental wall.

Marcus launched his body into Nidra's hips. The warlock made a *gawk* sound at the impact. They tumbled to the ground spraying mud as they rolled. Reaching up without looking, Marcus raked his claws alongside Nidra's chest.

Nidra screamed. The riddled Tier Naug that had recovered from frostbite wrapped an arm around Marcus's throat and lifted him off the warlock.

"No!" Nidra toppled onto Marcus and grabbed his face. Grim and determined, the warlock forced Marcus's eyelids open with his thumbs.

Marcus couldn't scream—couldn't look away—couldn't resist. His body arched as his mental wall started crumbling.

Tiecus! Marcus flailed, desperate for a lifeline.

A streak of brown, a familiar screech, flash of claws and wings, and Nidra was ripped away from Marcus. A winged demon akin to a human-sized bat tumbled with the warlock. This was the demon that had floated down to Asmara during the last battle with the smilodon demon.

The frostbitten Tier Naug tried again to pin Marcus to the ground. But Marcus wasn't afraid to face this riddled Tier Naug. With free hands, Marcus reached one arm around the warrior's neck, laced his claws together, and ran his talons through the Tier Naug from shoulder to hip. The torso shredded into four slivers.

Blood, strips of flesh, and iridescent powder filtered from the body. As the iridescent haze climbed up toward his head, Marcus growled. The non-corporeal demon flitted down, disappearing in the ground.

Marcus whirled at a whimper behind him. The demon that had attacked Nidra, thus saving Marcus, curled in on himself. Its wings receded. The creature transformed until a naked human curled in a ball, cowering under Nidra's sneering gaze. Marcus's savior had succumbed to Nidra's demens and had reverted to his human form. The warlock tormented the riddled human with mind tricks no doubt from a demens, most likely in retribution for the time the bat-like demon had saved Asmara in the woods after the first Tier Naug attack and now again for helping Marcus.

Marcus wanted to lash out, pour black flame in the warlock's face. All he could do was roar with the conviction of a demon.

Nidra backed away abandoning the satisfied smirk across his mouth. Tiecus was still asleep, but by the stars, if Marcus wasn't going to take his demon's form and annihilate this contaminated freak. When Marcus grabbed his own boot and began pulling it off, Nidra lost all sense of amusement. The warlock surveyed the area. His fury at his dead soldiers was tempered only by his apprehension of what was to come.

"You want my demon?" Marcus grunted at his bare feet on cold ground. "Well, here he is."

Marcus flung off his left boot attempting to bring Tiecus's form to the forefront. If the mage and demon could control his form, he should be able to control theirs.

Nidra turned and ran.

Instinct kicked in, and Marcus went after Nidra before he could morph into Tiecus. Within six steps, something equivalent to a stone wall crashed into Marcus's ankle. He was flipped off his feet, tumbled end over end, and landed on his back next to Stillwood.

Chapter 19

A THUNDEROUS LAUGH, the likes of which Marcus had never heard, could never have been mistaken for coming from anyone but Cornelius.

"Idiot. Falling for a trap like t'at." The seneschal's laughter sent shards of resentment and self-deprecating curses through Marcus. Cornelius had tripped him, using the force of his own momentum to send him flying back. Typical of the king's guard to use underhanded moves to win a fight.

"Ho ho. Have a nice fall?" Cornelius roared harder. "Big, bad demon. Your strategies work in concept, yeah?"

The clip-clop of hooves stopped before his head, and Selkie leaned his muzzle down to blow in Marcus's face. The hairs on his neck tingled. Blood covered Selkie's muzzle, and he hoped the demon steed had a hoof in defending the town, not eating it.

"Why?" Marcus snarled at the seneschal. "Why did you stop me?"

Cornelius snarled back. His iridescent eyes glimmered with sunlight peeking through the high tree grove surrounding the small town. "Because it was a trap."

Marcus huffed. The seneschal was right. The ambush the Tier Naug had used at the stronghold's gates was a favored tactic among demons. Nidra had taken Asmara after his army had pinned Marcus and forced him to the ground. But the other demon had saved him from Nidra. Then Dash had brought him home.

Gravel burns hurt as badly as a broken agreement, and Marcus looked at his arm. He identified Cornelius as a Tier Naug. He not only didn't pronounce the letter "h," but also the seneschal proudly wore all the features of Benicar's enemy. And yet Marcus's arm wasn't burning. Valder's tattoo saying *Don't let them pass* remained passive.

Interesting.

Thank the bright sun for small mercies. He hadn't *let* Nidra escape. The warlock had gotten away—no thanks to Cornelius.

"Get out." Stillwood, moaning in distress, hunched over on his knees.

Marcus sympathized. He knew the soothsayer wasn't speaking to anyone but himself.

The demon steed backed away as Marcus sat up.

"Mirror?" Voice weak, Stillwood focused on the ground.

"There was a mirror in that house." Marcus pointed a thick talon where he'd set Platt inside. Hopefully, she was safe, but right now he needed to find out why the seneschal, riddled by a demon, stood before him. Best she stayed out of sight.

Stillwood held his middle and rose. The soothsayer's eyes remained closed while he turned with the dignity of a politician unwilling to concede any pain in front of the masses and shuffled to the house.

"Chief," whispered the naked, riddled Benicarian soldier curled on his side.

The young soldier's thick black hair pasted a layer of sweat and curls against his tan skin. He wasn't older than a youngling with the slight build and frame familiar to Asmara's kind.

He's Frazzerian.

"Now you're awake." Marcus felt Asmara's noncommittal shrug. "Thanks for the help."

I helped, Asmara pouted.

A few of the villagers surrounding them looked to Marcus and eyed him with suspicion and anticipation as if they were waiting for his command.

The Frazzerian moaned and tossed around the pine-needle ground as if he were in a bad dream and unable to awaken. The unconscious soldier spouted a language and a name that Asmara had not heard in over a decade. "Hayır. Çalıştır.Vansky, biz ağaç kaydedemezsiniz."

Puppis! Asmara shouted. *Shut him up.*

The Frazzerian rolled his head side to side with closed eyes. The youngling reached out trying to grab something in his dream.

It triggered a flash of memory. A face. A tree canopy high above. Asmara being carried. Platt speaking to someone.

That meant he could only be one person. Dash.

The riddled human that had carried Asmara from the forest after the first Tier Naug attack. Dash, the riddled human that Platt spoke to about the Serenite. Dash, the same riddled human that answered her questions about the mage's people. Dash, the same riddled human whose demon had protected both Marcus and Asmara from Nidra, was the same person who now thrashed on the ground. Marcus glared at Dash. "So that's the one . . ."

Who's giving Serenite secrets away, Asmara finished.

Not only had Dash spoken about the Serenite to Platt, but also he was now spouting in Asmara's native language for Stillwood, Cornelius, and all else to hear. Dash was a linguistical nightmare.

Cornelius clamped his hand on the Frazzerian, and Marcus's naked savior, Dash, quieted.

"Stillwood!" Cornelius shouted. "Stillwood, get your translating butt back here!"

The king's seneschal knew the soothsayer.

Curious.

The rumpled soothsayer strolled out from the house. Life's battering wear had drained Stillwood's face, but his eyes were no longer bleeding and had returned to their black depths of infinity. Despite recent abuses against his body, determination radiated out from the soothsayer. He made a straight line to the frantic Frazzerian still spouting nonsensical words—at least they made no sense to the humans and the one riddled seneschal.

"What's happened to Dash?" Cornelius asked. "He's not speaking in Nauger. Do you know what he's saying?"

Stillwood shook his head. "No. That's not a language I know."

Cornelius scoffed, "Boy must know every language there is."

Shut him up, Marcus. Asmara pushed against the shields of his mind. *Shut him up!*

Marcus mentally tallied how many agreements he'd break if he were to get up and snap Dash's neck. Only one, and he could possibly justify it as self-defense. But that wasn't his thought—it was Asmara's. A disturbing one at that.

"That's how you would repay him for saving us?" Marcus uttered to Asmara, taken aback by the Serenite's bloodlust.

Cornelius glimpsed over at Marcus, his accusing eyes narrowing. "Are you trying a demens on 'im?"

Under his brows, Marcus said, "You're a Tier Naug."

Cornelius snorted, "I've not been one since I was gifted to Valder." All the muscles in the seneschal's face dropped. "If you're the one hurting Dash, I will pull your insides out with my bare hands."

Marcus spoke the words in his head to Asmara and pointed his gaze to Dash, forcing the Serenite to watch the youngling's writhing pain. *An eye for an eye.*

Shut up, Asmara snapped.

Is that not the Serenite way?

He has broken a sacred pact.

Will you let your weakness destroy the one who saved you? Marcus hissed to Asmara in his head. *Or will you call it pride?*

Damn you . . . you . . . you're nothing but parchment.

Parchment doesn't lie. It only records what is written.

Asmara screeched like a wild bird within the chamber of their minds, the echo piercing into their skull. Marcus clenched his jaw, squeezed his eyes shut, and waited for the temper tantrum to pass.

Rough hands took hold of Marcus's coat. Steel-blue eyes punched his soul. Hate and rage painted Cornelius's face. Marcus was used to the seneschal's ire. Their long-standing dislike for each other was well known. But something had changed. Cornelius wasn't just spiteful, he vibrated violence.

Under the jabbing remarks lay a madness Marcus hadn't ever seen in the man before. He was beyond angry. Beyond rage. He was out of control. Unpredictable. A human under the influence of a demon's power went mad. Demons started believing they were invincible. It was often their downfall.

Cornelius's voice came out low, threatening, and vibrating in fury. "No king is going to save you now."

"Lee!" Stillwood knelt in a meditative state holding his hands above the Frazzerian.

Cornelius whipped his head around. "What?"

"I need his help." Stillwood brushed the pads of his fingers to Dash's forehead and pulled back like he'd been burned. Stillwood shook his head. "Your friend won't let me help him, but I can tell he's suffering."

"Damn warlocks," Cornelius spat, gripping Marcus's coat even tighter. "Then we'll figure it out."

"Hurry." Stillwood nodded with a grim expression. "Soon, there isn't going to be anything left of him."

Cornelius turned his murderous gaze back to Marcus, gripping his collar tighter. "This one is useless. All he knows to do is kill."

Asmara scoffed at the seneschal. *Don't listen to him. He's projecting.*

Marcus didn't refute his murderous past. It was true.

Stillwood stood and stepped closer to the two, holding a withered hand over Cornelius's knuckles holding Marcus hostage by his lapels.

The seneschal pushed Marcus away with a glare that served as a warning signal and stalked back to Dash. The ball of murder welling inside the seneschal glowed and wrapped its tendrils around his heart, poisoning his mind.

Stillwood cleared his throat to catch his attention. "Tell me, Marcus, did you hear the bells? The bells telling you the town was under attack?"

"What does that have to do with anything?"

"Please, answer the question," Stillwood insisted.

Unsure and feeling trapped, but unable to lie, Marcus nodded.

Stillwood grinned at him with conspiracy in his eyes. "I thought you might have."

"'e's no Regin'art," Cornelius growled at Marcus.

"That's what I've been trying to tell everyone." Riley brought his cocky attitude with him standing beside the seneschal.

"Yet he heard the bells." Stillwood lifted his chin and aimed superior confidence to Riley.

Asmara spoke through Marcus. "What is this nonsense about hearing bells?"

The words were out and everyone focused on Marcus. Stillwood studied him like he was just confronted with a new facet of a diamond. Cornelius narrowed his eyes in suspicion. Riley looked Marcus up and down as if he'd never met him before.

"Puppis," Marcus whispered. *Keep your giant mouth shut.*

Asmara reeled to the background, his heart fluttering like a bird. *Do you think they know . . . know about me?* Asmara peeked to Dash. *Bastard Frazzerian. He told them.*

Dash moaned, breaking the standoff as Stillwood sighed and waved a helpless gesture to the youngling. "At least, pick him up off the ground."

Cornelius scooped the boy up in his massive arms, making the unconscious soldier look younger. Riley took his coat off and draped it over Dash.

Everyone was acting as if Tier Naug attacks and a seneschal of a king visiting the town were everyday occurrences. It unsettled him—them.

Marcus and Asmara put the pieces together. The town's people knew Cornelius. They knew he'd been riddled. The seneschal knew everyone in Reginhart. Intimately. Had they known him all this time? When did Cornelius become riddled?

"Ardin says you can transport from mirror to mirror." Cornelius scowled at Marcus. You're going to help me bring Dash to him."

"Am I?" Marcus smiled showing teeth.

"Help him or die," Cornelius growled.

"Generous options." Marcus's dry voice accompanied a raised brow.

"Father?"

Marcus, Cornelius, Stillwood, and Riley all turned to Platt's soft voice. She approached Cornelius with tentative hopefulness.

"Papa!" Tim shouted from the street side. The youngling squirmed trying to free himself from Rehan's arms to no avail.

Marcus looked from Cornelius to Platt trying to see any family resemblance. He looked at Rehan, Cornelius, Tim, and Platt. His little doe was the only one that had little family resemblance. His mind spun trying to make the pieces of father and daughter fit, but nothing clicked together.

Cornelius turned to his daughter, and the little doe's face plummeted from hope to shock. Platt covered her surprise with a slight smile and took a step to Cornelius.

"No." Cornelius backed away. "I'm not safe."

Her smile faltered, and the doe's thin body swayed.

"Papa!" Tim broke free from his mother and ran toward Cornelius.

Cornelius shied away, holding Dash, and warning, "Stay back."

"Stay away from my son." Rehan leaped to her runaway child and hauled him back, hissing a warning to Cornelius. "Traitor! You promised!"

Cornelius took more steps back as though she'd given him a blow. His presence, indomitable will, and mastery of the indisputable comeback had been crushed by the heel of Platt's mother.

"Why?" Platt stood dazed. "Why didn't you tell us?"

Stillwood cleared his throat and gave an "I told you so" glance over to Cornelius. "There wasn't anything I could do. It was too late, my dear. Something about . . . his kind." Stillwood glanced at Marcus, no doubt weary about mentioning Cornelius's Tier Naug origins. "Demons prefer those born of—" Stillwood waved at the seneschal.

"Tier Naug, Stillwood," Platt snapped. "You're saying demons prefer Tier Naug hosts."

Stillwood gave her a weak smile. "Yes. The bond is almost instant. Tier Naug are superior, even when it comes to being riddled."

Tim, never having given up his struggle, kicked at his mother. "Why does Platt get to live with Marcus, but I can't even go near Papa?"

"What?" Cornelius spun on Platt. "What is this?" The seneschal then pointed his fury to the older man standing among them.

Stillwood grimaced in apology.

So, the seneschal didn't know about . . . their arrangement. Asmara couldn't help himself and once more spoke through Marcus. "Oh dear, soothsayer. You've been hiding family secrets from both sides."

Marcus and Stillwood held fast as everyone else backed away avoiding the wrath of the riddled Benicarian Tier Naug.

"Riley?" The seneschal bore his full iridescent attention to the rude youngling who'd remained unusually silent.

Cornelius shuffled Dash to one arm and lunged for the other youngling.

Riley sputtered, flailed backward, and tried to make space with placating hand gestures.

The seneschal wrapped a huge hand over Riley's throat. "You're letting your wife-to-be live wit' a monster?"

"Lee . . ." Stillwood warned.

Wide-eyed, Riley never had a chance, even if the boy had a mental shield. Marcus felt the demens rolling off Cornelius from ten feet away.

Seconds later, Cornelius let go of a dazed Riley, shuffled Dash in his arms, turned toward Marcus, and stared, placid in his expression.

Experience had taught Marcus the pendulum swing of emotion preceded catastrophes. He didn't want to be near its source.

Riley's body shook, recovering from the demens.

Platt approached the seneschal. "Father?"

Cornelius refused to look at her. As quiet as Ventus, the seneschal's voice rang clear of his contempt. "Get away from me, you disappointing tramp."

The doe gasped, her hand pressed against her heart. Open-mouthed, staring in a daze, and blinking away tears, Platt stumbled back.

In essence, she'd become a victim of Cornelius's wrath. A wrath Marcus expected to take from the seneschal. What he hadn't anticipated was the icy fingers of emotion he had experienced on her behalf. Fiery rage bubbled from the depths of his soul.

Marcus leaped to her, catching his little doe before she crumbled to the ground. She was his, and he wanted to protect her. Enfolding Platt against his chest, careful of his claws, he snarled at Riley, "What did you show him?"

Whatever Cornelius had seen in Riley's mind had to do with her shock.

Riley, keening in pitiful torture, slumped to his knees.

Marcus understood why she'd wrapped herself in the protection of words. She must have endured a lifetime of the seneschal's pride, his curt approval, his biting tongue, and his begrudging acceptance. *Her strength and weakness extend to her family honor.*

Cornelius looked at Rehan, and whatever he saw pushed his gaze down to the dirty snow.

Platt withdrew. Her eyes became flat in self-mockery. Marcus was losing her to contempt. Losing everything he loved about his gentle little doe.

"Don't," Marcus whispered, steady and mild. "Whatever you've done, whatever Riley's done, whatever Cornelius's words mean to you . . . don't."

She didn't hear his words, her expression settled into defiant resentment clawing to lash out. Her face crumpled. "If he thinks I'm a whore, then—"

"Do you believe it?"

She turned in his arms and hid her face in his chest.

Marcus looked at Cornelius through new eyes and understood why Asmara spoke wistfully about the value of torture and vengeance. Hurting the father as much as he'd done to his daughter would not be enough of a retaliation, which gave Marcus a wicked idea. But it would be just as much Platt's revenge for her father's words as it would be with her permission.

"Little doe . . ." Marcus cast his eyes down.

Platt craned her neck and raised her chin. Her eyes held a gleam of insolence. "If I'm accused of being a whore, then I might as well be one."

They understood each other. Much like their walk in the forest he did not sense her in his mind like a demens, but they were of the same mind. For a moment, Marcus felt a pang of regret for tempting Platt into the mire of petty retribution, but then she nodded, closed her eyes, and offered herself like the day they had made their agreement.

"Cornelius." Marcus set Platt on her feet so the riddled seneschal could get a good look at her face. "You do not have permission to enter my stronghold."

Cornelius whipped around. "You will assist Das', or I will ram my boot down your gut and use you like a squirrel slipper."

Marcus smiled.

He's angry, Asmara said. *Good. Strike now.*

Cornelius pointedly scowled at Marcus's hands seductively holding Platt's waist. The curve of her hips molded gently with the arc of his talons. The seneschal's eyes went from an iridescent hue to a solid red.

"You can't even protect your own daughter. You think you can fare better with me?" Warm satisfaction sent an eager smugness within Marcus to push Cornelius further, and Marcus pulled her shawl free. "Is that what you humans do? Cast each other aside the moment you see any weakness?"

The savaging Tiecus had made of her neck a few nights ago was laid bare for everyone to see. Her raw flesh open to the air, tormented by his bite, created a black-and-blue claim on her skin that spanned from jugular to nape of her neck. Marcus didn't like the bruise, but in demon terms, it said to everyone, she's mine. He exposed his trophy of ownership by lifting her chin, all the while watching the play on Cornelius's face.

Iridescent eyes blazed, and the seneschal froze. Horror, disgust, and bloodlust flickered over his face. Marcus watched as the battle for the foreground between the demon and Cornelius began.

He'd never let the seneschal's demon touch her. Still, he huffed a laugh at the riddled human and said, "She's not a whore, but even if she were, she belongs to me."

He brought Platt harder against his chest and kissed her unmarred side.

The thrill of his lips on her ear sparked need, a different need other than blood. "I know what you said," he whispered in her ear. "But I will not make this hurt."

"It doesn't matter." Platt kept her eyes closed, a tear rolling down to her chin.

Whispering so none but Platt could hear, he moved his lips to the line that met her neck and jaw, reveling in her attentions, her body, her luxurious platinum hair. "How far may I take this?"

"Show him how words bleed," she hissed low.

It wasn't a definitive answer, but he understood. Cornelius needed to know the power of his statements. Sentences must be chosen carefully because words were guardians of intent. Words were tools of destruction, of creation, of pain. But they were also born of pleasure, elation, and trust.

Testing the limits of an agreement wrapped around an appendage Marcus thought useless, he slid a hand under her right breast. She flinched, and Marcus's hand retreated. But Platt pinned his hand and lifted it back up. Soft. Comfort. Safety. Warmth.

His heart jumped, and his breath stuttered. Marcus rested his open jaw on her shoulder muffling his cry of desire. Saliva dripped down his pointed teeth and pooled on her blouse.

Platt leaned her head back on his chest. Her permission and the proximity of Platt's body urged him to lean in more. Marcus slathered his tongue liberally along the curve of her neck, his control evaporating.

"So soft," Marcus moaned.

Platt gasped and squirmed. Her heartbeat raced.

"Yes?" He tried to stop, tried holding back this overwhelming need. Marcus was too enthralled with pleasure to stop. He'd stopped noticing anything else but her right after they began. But Platt allowed this. She held the reins of this display. If she'd said *no, enough,* or *stop,* he would have. He might claim her, but she had control.

"Tell me when it's too far," Marcus said because he couldn't stop himself. Not unless Platt said the word.

She lolled her head to the side. He complied, unable to resist, and Marcus slit a short cut with his claws along her neck and wrapped his lips around the dripping blood.

It was only her and him. Hunger for a sustenance— something that was not blood shielded him from reality. He was drinking a substitute of what he desired, but a poor substitute.

Pressure drew up from his loins to his chest. The fervor to keep building upon the pressure lapsed reason. His body was out control. He paid no mind to the crowd around them. Only Platt and her rhythmic breath and steady heartbeat filled his world. In the silence he felt nothing and everything.

Marcus found the quiet he'd searched for since his conception. Utter stillness of mind allowed the core of himself to surface. And his core spoke. *I am not a what, but a who*, it said.

"Oh, my incomparable doe," he moaned in her ear. "Please . . ."

"Stop."

By her word, he snapped back. Marcus erected his back and felt as tall as the surrounding two-hundred-year-old conifers. He wasn't taller or wider, but he straightened to give truth to the affirmation.

That was when sound and vision returned.

Cornelius held his broad sword and an insane gaze. Dash had been laid against a tree. At least, the man had sense enough to lighten his burden.

Stillwood planted himself between the seneschal and Marcus holding his weathered hands out trying to block

Cornelius from coming further. "They made a deal of her free will. I was witness. Bolden was witness."

"He's rightfully claimed the stronghold and his blood doll." Old Man George came forward.

Bolden gritted his teeth, the words hissing out trying to deny the truth. "You interfere, and he'll have the right to kill her, you, and all of us."

The words of the three men kept Cornelius at bay, but only for a moment. Marcus stared, chin raised in defiance. That's all it took to push the seneschal forward.

Marcus moved Platt behind him, crouched, and opened his fingers spreading his claws out like knives.

Cornelius moved—not like a human, but with lightning speed. But Marcus was just as fast. Metal clashed against claws, the steel being held back by the obsidian talons extending beyond Marcus's fingers. For a moment, two pairs of iridescent eyes locked in battle. Both forces of will collided as Cornelius and Marcus tried to demense each other. Neither gained purchase inside the other's mind.

Then the physical dance began.

Five claws raked iron. Cornelius slashed like a madman, bringing the sword down like a hammer. Sparks ignited every time Marcus cast the weapon away with his own daggers.

"Stop!" The air vibrated with the word like a screech and shook both fighters apart. Platt, arms trembling, eyes wild, face pale, running with sweat, said with a voice that carried the same power halting their battle, "Dash needs your help. Neither of you should bother defending the honor of a demon's whore."

Cornelius closed his eyes, expressing the pain of his own words flung back at him, and smiled in cruel self-mockery.

Platt's body relaxed, and the seneschal washed a hand over his face. The insanity dissipated to just anger. He sheathed his sword.

Platt turned to Marcus, her expression a plea for compliance.

"So, the seneschal is your father," Marcus said.

"Adopted father." Platt softened as if she watched days gone past.

Slowly, the quiet world of Reginhart returned. As soon as the fighting stopped, the villagers dissipated in pockets of two and three. The change of attitude among them swung in such a dramatic fashion that Marcus questioned if violence such as this happened here every day. People began taking the dead Tier Naug away. Except for the dead one, Selkie playfully dragged about ripping apart; the quiet work grew eerie.

Cornelius gathered Dash, like nothing had happened, and started walking east to the stronghold. Rehan and Tim were gone. So was Riley. Bolden remained with his hammer in his belt in a relaxed stance helping take away the dead.

Marcus wrapped the shawl around Platt's neck and made a mental note to inspect her bruises further in private.

Calamity evaded, Stillwood held, of all things, a sketch book and charcoal pencil. Where he got the items, Marcus couldn't tell. Glancing from page to demon steed, Stillwood ticked short strokes on the page while comparing the subject to the page.

"You owe Dash." Platt's doe eyes were insistent.

She could have asked him to hand over his heart, and he would've pulled it out of his chest to let her watch the muscle beat before her eyes.

"Doesn't seem like I have the choice," Marcus grumbled. But if family traits like stubbornness were hereditary through osmosis, Platt had gotten that from Cornelius.

The little doe swayed with exhaustion, and Marcus held her fast. Cradling Platt in his arms, Marcus whistled in sharp command, and Selkie finished the hamstring of a dead Tier Naug and trotted over. He would have his ride with his little doe. Unfortunately, they weren't traveling back to Benicar.

Chapter 20

FROM THE BOTTOM of the hill, the west tower looked like a dead branchless tree overtaken by creeping vines. Ivy coated, the crumbled wall gave an impression of privacy and security.

Ventus used its pressurized push-and-pull method to salute Marcus as he approached the gates. Selkie slowed before draped greenery where the portcullis should be or had been. The hair on Marcus's arms and neck stood on end greeting the hum of air charged with elemental influence.

A gust of wind twirled a stray green tendril. The vine wall separated like a curtain exposing the open portcullis, and Selkie continued to the courtyard.

"I'm expecting two riddled." Marcus carefully edged his command with respect. "Please let them in."

The keep answered. A gust of wind played through his hair with the ease of a comb. He took the breeze as compliance. Marcus dismounted with Platt, leaving Selkie to his own agenda.

Vines over the tower door separated, letting Marcus carry Platt over the threshold. He walked across the open foyer to the kitchen and sat her on the chopping block. Again, he took off her wrap and inspected her neck. Wincing at the bruise Tiecus had left, he looked at the other side of her throat.

A floating glass of water presented itself to Platt. She took hold of the mug and drank. Two more cups were offered and drained.

"Did I hurt you?" Marcus smoothed her skin where his talons had cut. She had healed fast.

"No." Platt didn't look at him.

Everything that had been revealed to him—Cornelius being her stepfather, her stepfather being riddled, the town keeping that knowledge from his own family, even Dash being the same person that saved them and betrayed them—all of it was human politics.

Marcus bent down until he could taste vanilla scent. "I'm not human. I'm not going to pretend I understand everything, but—"

Platt put a finger to his lips. So many words danced in her eyes. An entire conversation for him to glean, yet he couldn't understand her silent communication.

"Tell me," he said. "I wish I could demense you, but I can't, not without burning."

She gasped. "Where is it?"

He pulled his brows in confusion.

"Our first agreement." She touched his chest. "Where is it?"

He took her wrist and bent his head. Marcus laid her fingers over his crown.

Platt set the mug down and separated the strands of black hair, following the embossed lettering along his scalp.

Marcus leaned into her touch. This was what he'd been hoping to earn when he took her to town. Her trust. But she had refused his gold—something all humans seemed to value. And had insisted she didn't need gifts. "Why have you refused my attempts of generosity?"

Stroking his head, she let the question die in silence.

"What did Cornelius see in Riley?" He craned his neck directing her touch to places he wanted. "What did he see that made him angry?"

Compliant nails scratched, but they offered no answers.

He lifted his head. "Little doe?"

"The questions you ask are related." She bit her lower lip. "I heard what mother said to you."

Marcus nodded. He had expected as much. The bedroom door wasn't exactly a barrier from sound at the time Rehan had visited, not that the door was fixed now. Rehan had called him a monster. She wasn't wrong. She'd promised a world of terror if he ever hurt Platt.

"Rehan's threat is a dim echo compared to my own guilt," he admitted, hoping for reciprocation.

"Is what that warlock said true?" Platt peeked up. "Are you starving?"

Of all the things Nidra had said, she'd picked up on that jab to his ego.

"Don't listen to him."

"Truth is truth, no matter who says it."

It was his turn for silence.

"Do you know the story of Reginhart?" Platt folded her hands around another mug of water.

"I get the impression there's more than one," he said. "Does this have anything to do with the bells I heard?"

She nodded. "This isn't about Lord Reginhart that lived here." Her hand waved to all the kitchen. "This is about the demon named Reginhart."

If this was her version of an answer, he would oblige. He crossed his arms and let her have some room.

"The real Reginhart, the first Reginhart, was a stag demon who took a human bride. They lived many years ago before my grandmother's time."

Platt told the story with as much emphasis as any wistful maiden telling the romantic tales of another age. "Some say Reginhart riddled her, and they returned to his home. They say after they married, she climbed on his back, gripping his antlers, and he carried her away, both never to be seen again." Her eyes were distant. "Still, many claim they lived here and she gave him many children and the town flourished until war broke out."

She wouldn't look at him, but her body was giving him possessive permission making him press forward and take control.

He lifted her chin with the pressure of his claws. "Is this an explanation of why you entered this agreement with me?"

Her eyes searched tempting him to demense the answer out of her.

Marcus entwined her long strands of gold locks with his claws that spilled over his palm. Touching her hair was like touching her skin in liquid form. He could shape this part of her, but when he let go, it straightened to its original figure. His breath became labored, and his heart beat elevated. Tension built in his body threatening to lose control.

"Don't look at me like that," he said, in defense of his wits.

The push and pull of Ventus warned him three, not two, were coming up the hill.

Marcus pulled away before Cornelius, carrying Dash, came in.

"Call off your vine of terror before Stillwood cuts it to pieces," Cornelius said.

"Vine of terror?" Marcus lifted an eyebrow.

"Yeah." Cornelius jerked his thumb out the door. "Your gate is trying to rip him to the four winds. It's not going well for either of them."

Marcus stepped out the door and saw Stillwood at the portcullis wielding a dagger in each hand. The ivy was alive. Vine limbs thrashed octopus-style at the soothsayer. Stillwood might be old, but he was fast when he wanted to be. The vine lurched for a leg, and Stillwood rolled and cut a tip off the vine.

Amused and impressed, with both entities, Marcus watched as the ivy tested the soothsayer. Green arms converged at the man on all sides. Stillwood twirled in a circle with effortless grace. This was not the decrepit old man the soothsayer projected to the world.

"Marcus!" Stillwood was not amused, and it showed.

"Let him pass," Marcus called out. "Please."

The ivy retracted and draped harmlessly over the wall. Stillwood glared at the vine. The old soothsayer crossed the portcullis mumbling curses. One thin vine strayed in the wind, and Stillwood snarled, a deep demon snarl, at the daring stray. "I am the firstborn." Stillwood gnashed teeth, yelling at the ivy. "You know that. How dare you?"

Confused at the disquiet in Stillwood's voice, Marcus chose not to make the soothsayer's problem his own. "I didn't invite you, Stillwood."

The soothsayer stopped and glared at him. "Nidra has a hold on Dash. If you can't help him, then he needs passage to the king's mage."

Marcus sneered. "Ardin is no mage, and I have little interest in going back to Benicar." Marcus turned and went into the tower, letting Stillwood enter or leave.

When he returned, Cornelius, taking most of the space, stood in the middle of the room. Holding Dash and staring at the ground, the seneschal seemed out of sorts.

Marcus scanned the room. "Where's Platt?"

"Upstairs," Cornelius said. "Your mirror?"

"Take him to the third story," Marcus snarled. "I'll help him."

Gripping Dash like a sack of laundry, Cornelius bounded up the steps taking two and three at a time but stopped at the second floor staring at the broken door.

"Up one floor." Marcus pushed past the seneschal, leaving him behind.

"Where is the mirror?" Cornelius held Dash and didn't move.

"Not in there."

A moment passed before the riddled human continued. His steps deliberate this time.

Marcus opened the door to a fire-lit room. Slashes of light escaped slits for windows. Flames chased shadows. Marcus pointed to Asmara's sleeping chair. The chamber's silence was as tangible as his claws. Cornelius set the Frazzerian in the chair and sat on his knees next to his friend.

"Out." Marcus pointed to the door.

The Benicarian shook his head. "An' if 'e starts flailing?"

"That's fine." Marcus stood firm. "Now, out."

Platt, her eyes hurtful daggers pointing at her stepfather, pushed the door open. Not faltering, she made her way to the hearth. The wake of her presence refreshed stale air as she crossed the stone floor. She made no mention of what Cornelius had said to make her run away and sat in the chair by the fire.

"Do it wit' me 'ere." Cornelius squatted down and held Dash's hand.

"Out or I'm not doing this." Marcus crossed his arms over his chest spreading his legs in an unmovable stance.

"So, you can kill him?" Cornelius's voice was not human anymore. It was a voice peppered with gravel matching the red of his eyes.

"If he wanted to do that"—Platt remained seated forward in her chair—"your friend would already be dead."

"I'm not leaving him," Cornelius said.

Marcus straightened in formal attention. "I will give the utmost sincere effort to rid Dash of the ailment from which he suffers."

Cornelius's voice ratcheted down to human again but was somehow more menacing. "I'd rather take him to Ardin."

"If you decide that"—Marcus lowered his voice in warning—"then you will not be the one to take him there." The demon in Cornelius was barely bonded, unpredictable, and the man didn't seem like he had enough control to wade through a crowd.

"You will show me," Cornelius growled.

"No." Marcus pointed at Dash. "And the more you fight, the less time he has."

Cornelius scanned the door looking for answers in the air.

"I may owe him, but I don't have to help him." Marcus remained steady. "You think working with an element of this kind is easy? That any amateur can do it?"

The Benicarian gazed down at his helpless friend. "You won't kill him?"

Marcus gritted his teeth. He was not giving in. He wasn't going to promise anything to any of them.

"I'll be here." Platt got up and approached the recliner. "I won't let anything happen to him."

Cornelius stared at her as if she was an undeniably stupid child. "And what could you do? Glare him to death?"

With a voice as chilled as night, Platt said, "I could leave this room, and Marcus wouldn't help him."

Cornelius flicked his eyes to Marcus.

Like the enforcer he'd become, Marcus backed her statement up with folded arms.

When the silence stretched on, Marcus turned and extended his hand to Platt. "Shall we continue our discussion? I enjoy your stories of Reginhart lore."

"Fine," Cornelius snarled. "I will hold you to your word."

Marcus moved to let him pass. The door clicked shut leaving Marcus and Platt alone with Dash. The youngling began to toss in the long chair and mumble.

Platt stepped back avoiding flailing limbs.

Marcus moved to his armoire and started undressing. His modesty returned, and he wished for more privacy. Throwing his clothes off as fast as he could, he hoped Platt wouldn't stare at the agreements on his body.

"What are you doing?" Platt said.

"It's not me that's going to be able to heal him." As Marcus stripped out of his blood-soiled pants, the smell of sex hit his nostrils. "That's why I needed Cornelius out. This is not a time for me to practice. I need the master."

Asmara's sleek form was already coming to the forefront, shortening in height, narrowing in build. While Marcus had muscle, Asmara had agility. In trade of long black hair, Asmara's was thick like straw, curled in spirals and void of any color. His ears lengthened and twisted at the tips. He turned around, proud of his body. Asmara was a courtier after all.

Platt made a valiant attempt to look at his face and not anywhere else. Asmara grinned and noted the flush creeping up her neck. Raising his arm and resting a hand on the cabinet door, he gave her his best sultry pose. She spun, and with her back to him she tried to soothe Dash with words.

Asmara rolled his eyes, faced the armoire, and chose a green crushed velvet robe with cream lace trim. The ensemble was simple and unadorned and one of his favorites—and one of the outfits he'd left behind in Ziodonia.

"Great," Asmara whispered. "Father is sending me gifts now?"

The tunic top of the one-piece robe molded around his torso. Long sleeves clung tight around his sinewy arms. The bottom half hung loose, sewn to flow around his form.

He strolled over to Platt and waited until she acknowledged his presence by facing him. She smiled in relief and stared into his eyes as was proper for a Serenite.

"Would you like for me to do anything?" Her glance slid to the sides of his face.

"Oh yes." He gave his best mischievous smile, and his lascivious implications oozed from his sultry voice. "But I don't think we have time for that now."

Her stunned moment brought another mental notch to his victory tally. Delighted that his sexual innuendo was not dismissed, he chirped, "Maybe later."

Platt regained herself and crossed her arms. "I meant . . . would you like for me to help you in healing Dash."

He relished every one of her exasperated words. "Of course!"

He turned, blocking her off from being able to say anything more to him in the polite Serenite way, and examined Dash.

Curled into a ball, as best anyone could in the sleeping chair, Dash twitched and mumbled. The boy had all the traits of a Frazzerian. Black hair, light skin, fierce bone structure, quite striking, if one enjoyed humans.

Asmara prepared himself and touched Dash's wrist. The shock was not pain but a disturbing vision. Asmara pulled back with a yelp.

The next moment he was on the cold stone floor, looking into blue eyes. Platt's lips moved, and he focused on her until he could hear.

Grasping the sanity of her calm words, his own lips repeated, "I'm fine, I'm fine, I'm fine," until he believed it.

Terror oozed out of her pores and concern latched on to her body as stiff as her bodice. He expected her to ask what had happened, but she didn't. He suspected it wasn't from lack of worry or that she was afraid of the answer, but out of respect for his privacy.

"Should we send him to Ardin?" she asked.

"No." He grimaced. "I don't think Ardin has what it takes to get him out. Remind me not to intertwine ears with that warlock," Asmara said in admiration. "He's a genius."

Her incredulous face accompanied a *tsk*.

"Alright, there's only one thing that can effectively battle fear and overcome it." He chuckled at his own inside joke. The "one thing" wasn't bravery in this case but lust. But he wasn't going to tell her that, not in a direct way. Her cooperation was imperative. His plan was not a conventional one, and while she was flirtatious, it might be better to take advantage of her ignorance of the Serenite. Better to ask forgiveness than permission.

Taking her hands in his, he wanted her undivided attention. "I'll do this because you want to help him. This is not going to be pleasant."

She nodded.

"I'm more prepared now that I know what he's facing. But while I'm in his head, I'm going to need you as my guide home." Asmara halted further explanation. If he was going to do this, he needed her full cooperation. Worrying about indecencies could be the difference between life and death to the Frazzerian and possibly him. "So, what I'm going to do is kneel before him, and you will gently, carefully, lightly, with no grabbing involved, stroke my ears."

After his last three words her eager attentiveness turned to suspicion. She broke the long pause by saying, "Stroke your ears?"

He nodded.

"But you said looking at your ears is . . ." She flushed.

"This is important." He squeezed her hands. "I'm going inside his mind. If I don't have a point of reference to come back to, or if I don't have a reason to come back, then Dash and I are going to get lost in that nightmare."

"Can't I just pat you on the back?"

He leaned in closer to her. "If you like, we can take off our clothes, and you can hold your luscious body against mine and stroke—"

"Ears are fine." She pulled away from his light grip. "I'll stroke your ears."

He chuckled.

She then added. "With both our clothes on."

Asmara turned thoughtful and imagined the two of them wrapped together inside a makeshift quilt made by the clothes they wore. Years had passed since the last time he'd been touched. His excitement jittered inside, but training tempered his eagerness.

"Platt." He sobered. "You don't have to do this. I don't want to do this. Honestly, I'm content to leave him as is."

She opened her mouth.

He lifted a finger. "Ah . . . ah . . . no . . . he's dangerous. He knows too much about the Serenite. This could be for the best."

The Frazzerian moaned and rolled in his nightmare.

"You owe him," she said.

"I am a Serenite." He lowered his hand. "I owe him nothing. You forget. I'm not bound by human customs."

She looked down at the Frazzerian.

Asmara continued, "If you do not wish to do as I say, I do not wish to die trying to save him."

"I'll do it," she sighed.

"Let's get started then." He clapped his hands together. "Remember, once you start, don't stop. I'm depending on you." He splashed a smile on his face that felt forced and then sat close to the recliner. Rubbing his hands together in nervous anxiety, he brought his nose down and laced his fingers in a prayerlike stance.

He was entrusting his life and Dash's to someone who didn't comprehend the consequences or the importance of her job.

I must be insane. I must be desperate. No, I can do this. I've mixed pleasure with pain before. This isn't any different. I'm a trained master of the elements and a courtier of the Serenite.

Platt touched the curled tips of his long ears, and he almost exploded with a cry. He bit down on a knuckle avoiding explanation. A sharp intake of air was the only indication he let slip that he was ready to turn around, rip her clothes off, and pump his way to their climax.

Good thing she can't see your face, Marcus said.

Lust built the courage Asmara needed. He gave a silent prayer she would continue as the needed lifeline back to reality. He stifled a moan when her fingers expertly traveled around the spiral down the base of his ears.

Platt had the touch of a sun-kissed dewdrop. Liquid, caressing warmth like hers came from affection. He was one to know. Trained in the art of pleasure, he knew the difference between performing a necessity and enjoying his task. If the situation were different, he'd release the tension of two dry decades right then and there.

Asmara took hold of Dash, and the magic that plagued the Frazzerian collided with the only element that could combat fear and win.

At first, Asmara had to connect back to his lust. Strong tendrils wrapped around his mind. They were ropes connecting him to the hands gliding up and down his ears.

The vision that was so terrifying to Dash crowded Asmara's thoughts. Ignoring the perpetuated fear, the mage clamored through smoke and ash. Dash's nightmare was one Asmara wished he'd never seen.

Ziodonia, home of the Serenite, was not box buildings with thatched roofs. Asmara's home was a grove of live trees the Serenite grew, shaped, hollowed, reshaped, crooned at, designed, and labored over. But much like box buildings, trees could burn.

A Serenite's tree was his identity, his unique touch of tree magic, and his private space for the rest of his life. A Serenite without a tree was worthless. Homeless. Had no place in their society. A Serenite that couldn't grow a home was cast out to die.

Everything about this nightmare was terrifying. Dash had either been to Ziodonia or it had been described to him in perfect detail. Each tree was exactly how and where it was supposed to be, except each tree was burning.

The oddity was the grove was devoid of other life. No other Serenite were trying to protect their homes. No other mages called Glacias to stop this inferno. The fire raged, and there was no one to stop the destruction.

No one except Dash.

The Frazzerian raced with buckets of water desperately trying to put out fires. His attempt was comical. The human couldn't decide which tree to save and kept sprinting from one home to another, all the while screaming familiar names for help.

"Vansky! Where are you? Master Lerwin?" Dash coughed uncontrollably.

Asmara heard a name that almost sent him down to his knees.

"Ignatius!" Dash saw Asmara and ran to him. "Oh, thank the stars! Ignatius!"

Dash came face-to-face with him. The Frazzerian's expression twisted in an odd mix of familiarity and uncertainty. He looked at Asmara as a stranger that was familiar but couldn't be placed. It was understandable to Asmara. He was the spitting image of his father, and at a distance, Asmara had been misconstrued for Ignatius many times. Especially when he wasn't smiling. Dash expected the father, not the son.

"Ignatius?" Dash coughed and bent over.

Asmara offered his hand and lowered his tone in authority. "Dash, we have to get out of here."

It was the wrong thing to say. Dash stood eyes wild and backed away. "No." He held his palms out. "Get away from me. I'm not leaving them."

"Dash, this isn't real." Asmara turned to a burning tree, extended his arm, and flicked his wrist in five successions each sending an ice arrow into the flames.

The fire responded by screaming and throwing a wave of flame shaped in a demonic impression of Nidra.

Asmara launched out of the way and rolled under the flames. The heat was as hot and real as any fire he'd ever felt. He sat up and looked through the smoke at Dash.

The Frazzerian was on his back with his hands over his head.

Soot floated like snow, getting into his mouth, ears, and nose.

"This isn't real," Asmara reminded himself.

But everything from the fire, the ash, and Ziodonia being just as he'd remembered, it felt real. He was losing reality. The only reminiscence of the outside world tingled in his ears, a sensation completely out of place with the scene.

Asmara crawled to Dash. The boy, covered in soot, stayed in the fetal position. He gripped the Frazzerian's arm. The limb, charred to the bone, broke off.

Chapter 21

"NO," ASMARA WHISPERED.

Dash's burnt corpse melted to ash. Soot blackened Asmara's hands as he watched the limb crumble and fade.

"This isn't happening." Asmara only half believed himself. His home was burning.

Alene, the tree that was his home, the tree he had nourished and worried endlessly for in the beginning of his young life, was engulfed in flames twenty yards away. Asmara's books, his collection of mage bobbles, his favorite peacock quill with blue ink inside Alene, all burned.

He was in a dying mind, and he didn't care. His tree . . . Alene, the last connection to his people, was a pillar of smoke. Dash's body seeped in ash, left him alone.

Palms to the ground, he mentally reached out to the roots of his beloved tree. He wanted to tell her she was not alone, that he was there with her. For everything she was to him, Asmara would endure her pain in her last stand.

Through tangled roots, intertwined with the collective, he reached out to one individual tree. He'd never spoken to Alene in this fashion. Never knew it possible until the redwoods near Reginhart helped him survive the warlock's attack.

"Alene," he called out. "I'm here."

He did not feel pain. A sense of homecoming surprised him. Inside her hollowed walls, everything was fine. She was burning, but she did not fear fire. She welcomed it. Not a welcoming of death, but of new life. She knew Asmara would find the saplings germinating from the fire's birthing gift.

To produce offspring, Alene needed fire. It was the only element that could pop the wall separating her children from their Terra-made shells. Her "body" would die, but her saplings would have a chance to be nourished from her ashes. The collective was calm, almost eerily rejoicing in their destruction. Their trees were that of the phoenix. Life would rise from the ashes.

Asmara pulled back gawking at the burning trees. They didn't "feel" in the manner of flesh-covered creatures. The trees felt a certain pleasure from all the elements, even fire, though it meant death. He shook his head and realized while his possessions were precious to him, they were not as precious as Alene. She was in herself a being from which to learn.

While he watched Alene's last moments, Dash, whole and unburned, ran with a bucket of water trying to decide which tree to save.

Stunned, he watched Dash chase the carnage with buckets.

"Vansky! Where are you? Master Lerwin?" Dash coughed.

The boy was in a mind-loop.

Relief was too soft a word. It brought Asmara back, understanding he was in Dash's consciousness. How many times had Dash gone through this scenario? How many times had Dash suffered death?

They still had a chance. The tingling in his loins brought the Serenite to his feet.

"Ignatius! Oh, thank the stars! Ignatius!" Uncharred, Dash ran to him just like the first loop-go-round. The mage studied the hope in the boy's fierce dark eyes. Like Dash's people, his face was handsomely severe. His cheekbones slashed down hardening the curve of his plump lips.

"Dash." Asmara reached out a hand.

The Frazzerian stopped short tightening his strong jaw. "Ignatius?" Dash coughed and bent at the waist.

Getting out of this torture had to be the boy's idea. Forcing him wouldn't work. Even if it did, his mind would be . . . wrong. Forever living this nightmare even in the real world. But he could use deception to get Dash out. Asmara straightened and bore a hard, icy calm under indifferent selfishness. He hoped he was a convincing imitation of his father.

"What have you done, boy?" Asmara stiffened his ears, imitated Ignatius as best he could. "Take my hand, and I will destroy this intrusion on my home."

Dash nodded coughing and retching. Maybe it was because he looked so much like Ignatius or maybe because he was a Serenite, but for whatever reason, Dash trusted the mage and grabbed his hand.

"Think, boy, where were you before this?" Asmara firmly held the Frazzerian. He pulled at Platt's lifeline, cultivating lustful feelings and shared them through physical touch—even though Dash and he were only holding hands in the Frazzerian's mind.

Dash did not immediately respond. The boy's raven hair fluttered from hot wind. A breeze culminated by the Frazzerian's mind. His perfect nose wrinkled, breaking the straight line of his lips. "You're the reason this place is burning."

Ignoring the comment, Asmara delved into the connection and shared Platt's ear-stroking sensations with Dash.

"Where were you before this?" Asmara stared at the contours of the boy's lips.

Dash thought while Asmara injected more of what was happening on the outside into the Frazzerian.

The boy looked up. "What are you doing?"

"Tell me where you were before this," Asmara commanded.

The uncontrollable fear in the boy's mind broke off. Dash could rationalize. The disparity between his fear being combatted by rousing lust allowed Dash to think. "I was fighting. Protecting." Dash pulled Asmara closer, wrapping an arm around him. "Protecting you."

"From?" Asmara stoked the fire of lust and sent the rush into Dash. The boy stuttered in breaths and fluttered his eyes. Ziodonia whooshed into haze, leaving them standing in cold fog. Trees loomed ominous as guardians beyond the gray background.

"Can you stop that?" Dash quavered. "It's disturbing."

Asmara laughed and shaped the trees into naked female and male bodies. Merging into Dash's mind, the mage combated fear with personal sexual experiences.

"Dash, come back. Who were you protecting me from?"

Even now, halfway in their own bodies, they were still connected in mind and enjoyed Platt's caress through the mind-link. Asmara didn't expect an answer. He knew Dash could feel the pads of Platt's fingertips slide down the ridges of his ears to their base. Every one of his nerve endings reached down to his core and built a pleasant tension.

Dash and Asmara slipped their minds away from the nightmare and back into their respective bodies, but the mind-link continued.

Biting his lip, he held a plea for her to caress the back of his ears and allowed the pressure to climb. She glided her hands back up to the curled tips that had stiffened straight. He tilted his head back while she played with the most sensitive area. All five of her fingers, on both hands, tugged at the ends of his pointed ears enough to make the process balanced between pleasure and pain.

As Asmara and Dash teetered on the edge of reality, the mage felt his recliner and leaned his middle to the chair hoping for friction in just the right place.

"I always wondered what the deal was with the ears," Dash said with closed eyes. "Now I can understand why you all enjoy being stroked so much."

Platt's hands jerked away. "Dash! You're awake."

"You diminished Polaris," Asmara groaned at the Frazzerian. "You ruined it." Platt would have kept going if she hadn't been disturbed.

"Hello, beautiful." Dash flashed a smile to Platt.

Asmara squashed a retort and ignored Marcus's palpable jealousy. *Don't get me involved in your mental illness.* Asmara shoved Marcus down a notch to the background.

"Thank you, little doe." Asmara glided the back of his hand against her cheek. "You were perfect."

She flushed and turned as red as the sunset outside. "I was glad to help."

He took her hands and gave a squeeze to emphasize the importance of his words. "If it wasn't for you, we'd be lost."

He paused, separating appreciation from what he had to do now. "But, I must speak to Dash alone. Why don't you see how your father is?"

Platt's shyness vanished, and she gave him a deadpan, accusatory stare.

"What could I do to hurt him?" Asmara pouted.

The color drained from her face until the flush was gone, and she glanced over at the Frazzerian.

"We have private business." Dash nodded.

She got up to her feet and padded to the door. The lock barely clicked when she closed it.

Asmara whirled around and with no gentility said, "What did you tell her?"

Dash, head back in the recliner with eyes closed, breathed deeply.

This was a Serenite's way of stalling. Asmara waited as was the social custom.

Dash rose to his feet, turned to Asmara, and waited until the Serenite gave him the audience of his glare. The Frazzerian touched his fingers to his forehead, moved his fingers down to his lips, then to his heart, and with palm upheld his hand as if in an offering.

Asmara slapped his hand away, grabbed Dash's leather coat, and pulled the taller man toward him until he was forced to see nothing but his eyes. "Have you been telling everyone about us?"

"Since you have saved me from hell"—Dash gritted his teeth—"I will ignore your rudeness."

Asmara let go and stepped back. The only courtesy he could extend was keeping eye contact. "How am I to let you live knowing what you know?"

At that, Dash laughed.

The mage twisted his lips as if in on the joke. "Oh, you think because I'm Serenite, I won't lay a hand on you?"

"You have the curse, like them all. You crumble at the sight of violence."

Dash's implication of the curse, the physical and emotional helplessness while observing brutality, twisted in the mage's gut. He wanted to wipe that superior grin off the boy's handsome face. Whether Dash were riddled or not, Asmara would rip the smug right out of this pissant.

"Oh, I won't be the one to kill you." Asmara crossed his arms. "But I am the one allowing you to stand here and answer my questions."

All expression dropped from Dash's face. His black iridescent eyes flickered orange, then back to iridescent. "Let me introduce myself."

"Please." Asmara raised his hand to his forehead and flourished a salute.

"I am Dash McGrady of Frazzer, the envoy of the Serenite."

The title startled Asmara, and the mage thought about its implications. "The Serenite no longer have an envoy." Having someone go around being a diplomat representing his people was not only dangerous but also insane. A whole civilization that had succumbed to physical violence could be enslaved, easily targeted, losing any freedom they had.

Stone faced, Dash said, "They have re-instated the honor, and I am the first since then."

Asmara paused. The blood ran out of his face. His natural language was so deeply ingrained he hadn't noticed until now that Dash was speaking to him in Serenite. "Who taught you our language?"

"Everyone had a hand in that," Dash smirked.

The air began to thicken. Ventus flowed through the window and wrapped a snake-like body around Dash's throat and squeezed.

The Frazzerian's smile faded. The element claiming Dash's lie was much like watching a boa constrict with prey in its clutches.

"You're riddled now. You have to be careful about what you say." Asmara snorted and crossed his arms. "Amend that last sentence, or you'll suffocate."

"Most . . ." Dash choked out. "Many of the Serenite helped me learn the language."

Ventus released the boy. Dash coughed and rubbed his throat.

"You're telling me thirty-thousand Serenite helped teach you the language."

"No." Dash was careful about his chosen words. "Many of the twelve-thousand Serenite *left* helped me learn the language."

"What?" The truth of numbers was worse than the outright lie. "That's not right." Asmara counted on his fingers. Eighteen thousand died over twenty years. Nine hundred Serenite a year. Too many. "Those numbers can't be right."

Dash stared at him, considering. His eyes shone with hard accusation. "After a certain mage was successful in retaining a demon to his aid, others tried as well. Most failed and died for trying. Those who actually succeeded . . . went insane."

Asmara hissed, his lip up in a snarl. "And you blame this mage."

Dash remained silent. His glare didn't become any friendlier, and the shadows behind his eyes hinted at dark thoughts.

The mage huffed, "Why did you save me from the warlock then?"

"The council wants you to come back."

Frost chilled the stone under their feet. "The council can go fuck themselves."

"Don't they have you for that?"

Asmara snarled. Ignatius, his father, was on the council. He might be a courtier, but he was not interested in incest. Dash's insipid baiting would not lead to Asmara's self-introduction, which would make the mage vulnerable to the envoy, as was the Serenite custom. "How would you know?"

"You're right. I don't. For all I know, you're one of the successful ones in retaining a demon."

"Didn't Platt tell you who I was?"

"Ah." Dash's eyes transformed from red to a rainbow iridescent. "Is that her name?"

Puppis, Asmara cursed. *She is more careful than I thought.*

"Honestly." Dash spread his hands. "I had to practically tell her my life story before she'd give me the honor of carrying you home. She's more protective of you than I am."

Asmara scoffed, "You are dangerous."

"I am performing my designation." Dash cleared his throat. "Why are you so far from home?"

"I could ask you the same." Asmara winced at his admission to Dash's claim as the envoy.

"Courtier, you are needed." By the stars, Dash sounded so much like Asmara's own father.

"No." Asmara pointed a dangerous finger.

"I cannot, would not, cover for you." Dash looked passed the offending digit. "Not this. Not to the council." The envoy continued, "I might be born human, but it was a great honor when the Serenite approached my people and asked me to be raised as a Serenite and their first diplomat."

"Oh, so you can grow a tree?" Asmara stepped back, giving Dash an incredulous once-over glare.

Dash's cheeks colored. "I can nurture a tree." The envoy straightened taller. "She's not hollow on the inside, but she's mine. She has outside levels." Dash puffed his chest.

Another Serenite would laugh at the admission. Asmara didn't. He'd been trained in the subtle art of discreetness. The mage also had gained a robust amount of humility over the years. He admitted, begrudgingly that Dash exuded all the mannerisms of a Serenite.

"I didn't see this type of tree in your memory." The nightmare the warlock had placed in Dash's mind had recreated the mage's homeland perfectly. "Why did Nidra place you there?"

Dash's Adam's apple bobbed. "It's every Serenite's nightmare."

Asmara turned away from Dash. He couldn't believe what he was hearing. Dash thought of himself as Serenite. It had to be his truth. Dash was riddled. Ventus had proven demons didn't lie.

But they don't tell whole truths, Marcus said.

The mage turned back, looking into Dash's dark eyes. "You thought I was Ignatius?" Saying the name brought a mixture of admiration and loathing with a whisper of longing.

"Ignatius wouldn't need my help against a warlock, riddled or not," Dash said. "And you don't look riddled."

Asmara was, yet he wasn't. He'd not given his name to Dash yet, but the envoy knew. If his title suggested anything, Asmara's introduction of himself was the last formality before Dash tried to take him home. He remained silent.

"To answer your non-question"—Dash paused—"yes. Ignatius is still alive."

Asmara's upper right cheek tightened with his grim amusement. Serenite this human was not, but Dash knew the culture and the subtleties.

"What are you doing here, Envoy?"

"Since I was nine, I have taken my envoy mantle seriously. We all have commandments. Every Serenite must obey them if we are to survive. Even you."

"We?" Asmara scoffed. Sure, the boy lived with the Serenite, but he was not born one. "If *we* are to survive?"

"I have proven myself." Dash's hands shook. "I do not need your personal approval."

"Because you're the envoy," Asmara said with disdain, his tone mocking of the title.

"Yes. And we need you back home."

"I'm not going home," Asmara snarled. He couldn't. Not until he had Tiecus under control.

"You're the only one who survived a demon's riddle." Dash looked at him in earnest.

"This is not a cure for our . . . condition."

The envoy took a deep breath. "If I take you in front of the council and show them how you can separate the demon, perhaps you can train them how to control theirs, as you have."

But there was no control. Marcus is the control. The mage narrowed his eyes. "You said there were others that were successful."

"Successful, yes." Dash winced. "Coherent and sane? No."

Asmara's world came tumbling. "You killed them." He swayed on his feet, and when Dash came forward, Asmara held up a hand. "Of course, they'd need someone without the curse to destroy evidence of a Serenite presence." It was too dangerous for most humans, other than the peace-loving Frazzerians, to find out about them and their curse.

Dash stepped back, his face a mask.

"You killed them." Asmara reared back. "How could you? They were Serenite."

"I'm the only one that can free them." Dash drew his eyebrows in. "I had to. Those who didn't kill themselves were insane and dangerous."

He honestly believes that. "Monster!"

Dash's eyes widened, and he reeled backward, fists at his side. As the truth lashed out at Dash, his expression turned inward, exposed the pain, self-hate, and grief such a youngling shouldn't have endured. He closed his eyes, cutting off the light and exposing the demon inside. A layer of wetness clung to his long lashes. Dash nodded, admitting his sin.

No greater evil existed than destroying a creature that couldn't defend itself.

"Did you wait until the demon slept, approached the Serenite in their helpless state, only to *set them free*?"

"Stop," Dash whispered.

"Or did you fight the demon and send more pain to your *brethren*?"

"Shut up." Dash started shaking.

"Or maybe you used a demens to root the two out of each other. Digging into the minds of who you admire so much. To glean secrets. To use information against them and then watch as the Serenite died while the demon floated away to prey on someone else."

"I haven't been riddled that long!" Dash shouted.

"Which means you've had bloodlust even before this."

"No!"

"You were just doing your duty, isn't that right, murderer!"

The envoy spun on his heel, and in two shakes of a ram's tail, Dash was out of the room and setting off the warning ward on his way out.

Chapter 22

THE KNOCK AT the door sent Asmara flying to the armoire. If it were Cornelius . . . he couldn't be seen. He'd surely tell the king, and his servitude would begin. Now that Dash roamed the world telling everyone about the Serenite, about magical *elves* that couldn't protect themselves, Asmara had to stay hidden all the more.

He stripped and brought Marcus to the forefront faster than one could utter secret identity.

"Asmara?" Platt's hushed voice floated through the door.

Gathering his soggy boots, Marcus slipped them on his feet hopping across the room.

When he slid the door open, Platt stepped back.

"Cornelius?" he asked.

She shook her head. "He went after Dash."

Marcus pulled the door further and waved her in.

"Are you all right?" She wrapped her right wrist around the other and intertwined her fingers, latching her palms together.

Her worry touched him. She was beautiful. Maddening. Unpredictable. A fantasy like a unicorn. "I haven't been right since our first encounter." But not in a bad way. He brought his hands up to touch her face. Marcus wanted to study the facets of her emotions as one spins a jewel in sunlight.

She was going to allow this show of weakness. But no matter how he adjusted his fingers, his claws got in the way. He compromised and set his hands on her shoulders, aching to set them around her hips. The perfect curve that fit his hands and didn't hurt her. *If I were a demon, I'd riddle her and keep her in the background forever.*

Tiecus grunted in agreement.

"Dash ran out so fast I wanted to make sure he didn't hurt you—Asmara—whatever." She moved a stray hair aside.

"Asmara is unharmed." His stomach flipped. Dash was out there. He should follow him and rip out his tongue. "I must go . . ."

Questions flitted along Platt's face, and she reached a hand up in the air. Marcus froze. She was going to touch him. He held his breath and waited, rooted, waiting on her whim. All thoughts of the world drained from his mind.

She brushed his long black hair behind his shoulders. Without black strands to hide behind, Marcus feared exposing vulnerability in his face. Under the sparkling emotions that passed over her face, she swept his barriers aside. Every muscle in his body went slack. Her touch was the quiet of morning. A warm breeze in winter. Light. Softness. His head cleared of all thought.

"I am not human." Marcus searched for words, but none could hold his joy. Words meant nothing when the truth could be known with a demens. He wasn't going to taint this moment, but he wanted to sink into the peace of her soul. Action was the only way he could tell her.

"We are alone." Marcus rested his forehead on the crown of hers. "Is it the right time to claim your promise?" The promise of a kiss.

Her head tilted back letting him cradle the back of her head. Platt's lips invited him closer, but he resisted.

"Give me your answer." Marcus softened his tone. "Please."

She moistened her lips. "Claim your promise."

Whispers of need drifted to his nose. His arms dropped around her waist. The perfect curvature for his claws. If only one physical part of him could be inside her, it would satisfy him.

Marcus smiled holding off their lips from touching, watching her breathe in expectant drawls. His own breath dragged harshly across his throat.

The weight of her lips drew him closer, and her eyes tortured him with desire. Committing the sight to memory, he wanted to cradle this moment as long as possible.

She held halfway, waiting.

Pressing his lips to hers, his tongue stroked tentatively over hers. She met him with her own tongue and went further. Her fevered exploration drove him to match her pace.

Soft, she was so soft. Yearning stretched in an endless road. His token of appreciation wasn't large enough. His body started taking control, guiding him to seal the commitment he had started in the town square.

The demon fought his logical, restraining half for control. He wanted her closer, wanted to press against her. Marcus remained stock-still, but it took all his effort. It was a battle against all the elements of taste, smell, touch, and sight. One kiss was not consent for more. Determined to fight, he ground his teeth and pulled away.

Platt pulled his head back down to her. Instinct bent every last ounce of his reserve. He was failing to control his body, and worse, he wanted to fail. Quiet furtive voices guided his hands along her curves.

Let go, the voice suggested.

He was desperate to fight and desperate to do as the voice said. But he didn't want to hurt her. His claws had proved damaging enough. What if he lost control? What if he sliced her into pieces?

Need bent his logic.

You won't hurt her, the voice whispered. *She'll enjoy it.*

Marcus wanted to believe that more than anything. He wanted any clue from her that he could go further.

Platt exposed her neck in desperate surrender, and the barrier to hold back snapped as easily as a twig. Nipping her neck drove him mindless. He was kissing her, stroking her tongue with his, and pressing her against him as if he could riddle her by merging their bodies.

His hands were wildly gathering up her dress. Fingers touched bare thigh.

Platt gasped, turned her head, and pushed against his chest.

The slight rejection gave him the power to let her go. Relief washed away the tension. He could trust her to not let him go too far. Not take her where she didn't want to go. She held the power to stop him with a weak push.

Platt walked to the window slits and looked out into the night. Marcus was left throbbing, his chest heaving. Provoked by her proud shoulders, Marcus chased her. Pressing his hardened body against her soft backside, he trusted her to tell him when his affections were enough. She didn't deny him, but she didn't encourage him. Still, he wanted more. Marcus enjoyed the contact and scooped away her moonlit hair to one side. He wrapped a possessive arm around her and leaned his lips to an exposed ear.

"Look at her." He pointed up to the moon. "Sing to her while I take you. Each time you look up at night you can remember me."

Platt sipped in a breath, and he took in the delicious scent of her want.

"Please don't," she pleaded.

Her words skewered his heart over the fiery pit of humility. Whatever pride he retained slid down his throat. "I need you."

"Please understand—"

"Understand?" His hands gripped her shoulders. His lips tingled when they brushed against the tip of her ear. "Oh, I understand that your body conflicts with what you say. I understand your senses delight in my touch. I *understand* that you would deny what you've promised to me."

She stiffened and went to pull away.

He pulled her back to him and nipped at the base of her neck.

Platt whipped around. Her small hands clasped down on his nether regions bringing more pain than pleasure. "Even a peasant girl would figure out what the marks mean down there." Platt ratcheted her grip harder. "So, before you try to intimidate me with empty threats, you should know that I am not giving my consent."

She held his bluff, literally, in the palm of her hand.

Only by willing consent would he couple with her. Not because the thirteenth agreement demanded it. No doubt the embossed tattooed writing around his manhood would burn if he forced anyone for sex. That was deterrent enough, but her consent was the aphrodisiac allowing his mind to follow his body's desire.

An apology would be trite. Instead, he twisted his face in pain, letting her find satisfaction in seeing his agony. He owed her that. Yet the physical pain was not what hurt most.

"Your blood tastes of want." His voice came out raw and strained. "Your desire elicits a response. Your eyes draw me to be inside. Why do you deny the chance to relieve our need?"

Alongside Marcus, Tiecus writhed. The demon was getting a firsthand experience of what "no" meant.

Asmara aimed a chuckle to Tiecus. This little pain was nothing for the Serenite. *Not such an inconsequential agreement now, is it?*

She let go and turned back to the window. Her voice as meek as her body, she said, "Isn't it obvious?"

"You don't have to explain." He bent at the waist, waiting for the residual throbbing to abate.

She flashed him a Rehan death glare, but she looked away when she said, "I have nothing to give to a suitor. My promise is the only gift I have to give any man who will have me."

Marcus snarled, "You think I would allow any *man* near you?"

Platt lowered her head, and her body shrank in defeat.

Marcus took her shoulders and spun her around, needing to see her eyes. "Are you still expecting your gallant knight to save you? Is that what you're waiting for? For Riley to save you from your monster!"

Platt turned her head. She would not look at him. The agony on Platt's face was apparent behind the calm. "I'm sorry. I . . ."

In angry haste, Marcus let go, rushed to the door, and swung it open. Over his shoulder, he shouted, "No other will mate with you either."

Marcus slammed the door to meet with Cornelius's powerful gaze. Standing next to the seneschal was like standing next to a redwood trunk.

A red eyebrow cocked over the seneschal's iridescent eyes. He almost looked amused. "You need to be put out of your misery."

Marcus snarled, "Dash has been restored. Go back to Benicar."

Cornelius expertly hid his Tier Naug accent with chosen words. "My king asked me to restore Regin'art's keep."

"It's already fortified."

"By foliage?" Cornelius gritted his teeth. "You consider plants fortifying a keep?"

"Do you think you would have been able to enter this place without my approval?"

Cornelius looked beyond the oak as if the barrier wasn't there and returned his glare to Marcus. His eyes were orange shading to red. Death etched lines in Cornelius's face.

"Laddie," Cornelius said in insult and self-loathing. He bared his teeth and clenched his jaw like a riddled host trying to prevent words from escaping.

"Humans." Marcus spoke the words like a foreign disease. "They always lie. They never say what they want. They never are aligned with themselves."

Cornelius blinked and pulled back. His eyes shaded iridescent. The seneschal stared as if Marcus were a stranger, an alien. "You've never been, have you?" The statement was more a self-answered question.

"Never been what?" Marcus spat.

"Human."

Marcus's stomach dropped. He'd said too much, let Cornelius know too much. Recognition spread across the seneschal's face replacing the never-ending disapproval.

He wouldn't know, Asmara said. *He couldn't know about the Serenite.*

Dash, Marcus answered the unspoken question. *What exactly is the envoy's mission?*

Tiecus jabbed at the mage with a vision.

Iridescent eyes peered out from a forest in a moonless sky. One by one, pairs of light shimmered and peeked through bushes, tree trunks, from far and near. Hundreds of them. A throng of riddled humans edged the trees coming closer. But this wasn't just any forest. This was the great woods of the Serenite. The enormous trees the mage's people called home.

The riddled humans growled and snarled. Then they lunged into the enclave. The Serenite were caught off guard. Asmara's people were ambushed by riddled humans, were cut down, slashed, torn through. There was nothing any of them could do.

Asmara gagged as an automatic reflex.

Tiecus! Marcus dropped a shield between the mage and demon before he'd have to fight another war within.

"Marcus?" Cornelius eyed him suspiciously.

Marcus sneered at the seneschal, making a point of not answering right away. He stepped forward and put his face uncomfortably close to the riddled human. "Go away."

"I can't get through to Ardin."

"I do not understand the context in which you speak." Marcus used a low tone in contrast to Cornelius's rumblings.

"What have you done to the mirrors?" Cornelius stood threatening with his words and body language.

"Perhaps he's using his mirror to scry to someone else."

"He was expecting me to contact him at this time." It was a wonder how Cornelius was in control at all. His anger fed right into the demon's power.

Marcus smiled. "Then keep trying."

Cornelius's face turned ruddy. "I have been for the past quarter of an hour."

"This is none of my concern." Marcus waved a dismissal.

"I know how to scry." The seneschal was becoming uncorked. "Ardin is never late."

Marcus couldn't care less.

Stillwood coasted up the stairs as fluid as a rolling fog. "I think you should listen to what he has to say."

"None of my concern." Marcus returned to this mantra.

"That's true." Stillwood's watery irises bounced in unnerving jolts. "But you might want to consider something before you refuse your help."

Marcus faced the soothsayer and crossed his arms.

Looking old enough, Stillwood commanded a fatherly presence. "Nidra knows Benicarian, but the other language . . . does he know it too? Maybe. Maybe not." Stillwood let the words teeter in the air. Doubt worked for Stillwood, letting imagination take over.

Puppis, Asmara said. *Don't let him get to you. The Serenite did not teach their language to humans.*

"Dash," Marcus said.

"One thing Nidra is good at . . ." Stillwood said, "is languages."

Cornelius snorted, "Told ya t'at boy wasn't rambling. He knows every language t'ere is to 'ave."

Oh, by the bright star, Asmara buzzed inside.

"He's also seen you half naked." Stillwood waved a bony hand to include all of Marcus and furrowed his brows with an odd sort of pity. The same look Old Man George had given him. What the soothsayer didn't say was louder than what he did. His agreements. They were all over his body. If Nidra could read Benicarian, he'd know Marcus couldn't leave Reginhart.

If Nidra knew that Marcus was trapped, then he and however many riddled Tier Naug he commanded could go straight to Benicar minus a skirmish with Marcus. Or keep assaulting him until the warlock had what he wanted.

Why haven't they attacked already? Asmara retorted.

A faint tingle across his shoulders jolted Marcus into knowing he had to warn Valder. It was his duty as a *friend* to do so according to one of his agreements. But he couldn't go back. Not unless Valder commanded it. He needed a mirror.

Stillwood nodded, and then in his disinterested way said, "Perhaps it wouldn't hurt to check in with Benicar. If I'm wrong, then it's none of your concern."

"All right!" Marcus saw through the apathy to Stillwood's motivation. He wanted something. "I'll scry Ardin."

He turned and walked down the rest of the stairs and under the well. The most perfect mirror he'd ever seen hung under the keep's stairwell.

Marcus prepared for the crash of light and whispered, "Ardere."

The torch caught fire and lit the small cubby hole with brilliant force.

Cornelius tried to look around the bend and gave out a yelp. Stillwood, standing back and away, shook his head in distaste.

Blinding light shielded reflections of Asmara and Tiecus from Stillwood's and Cornelius's prying eyes. Three clockwise circles later, Marcus scryed for Ardin's laboratory.

Black haze flickered, absorbed the reflection, and quickly reverted back to reflecting the light again. Again, Marcus tried as Cornelius and Stillwood allowed him privacy. Light intense enough to be a second sun, or another "eye in the sky" as Tiecus put it, blasted the small underwell.

"Ardin must be enthralled with another scryer." Marcus stepped from under the mirror.

Cornelius squinted against the indoor sun. "I have to talk to him. Aren't you a mage? Can't you do something?"

"None of my concern." Marcus practiced his newfound excuse for all that was wrong with his predicament.

"Don't you think it's odd that Ardin would hold a conversation for this long?" Stillwood mused. "He doesn't even take this much time explaining things to his students."

Marcus shrugged. "Perhaps Valder is speaking with the scryer."

"Perhaps a Tier Naug army is being transported through Ardin's mirror," Stillwood countered.

Marcus slid his thumb claw down the length of the other four talons making the *shhhiiink* sound. His shoulders burned with more intensity. He imagined the words "act accordingly as a friend to King Valder" burning his shoulders.

"Stand over there." Marcus pointed to the far corner opposite the mirrored underwell. Not only was interrupting another's scry rude, but also he didn't want everyone to know about the procedure. Mainly, he didn't want them to see Asmara.

"Do you need assistance?" Stillwood whispered.

Marcus narrowed his eyes. "What assistance do you think you could be?"

Half-lidded eyes appraised him. "I can help turn the scry."

"No." Marcus folded his arms and waited until Stillwood went to the corner. He wasn't sure if he was perturbed or relieved that the soothsayer knew what he was going to attempt.

Under the heat and light, he practiced what he needed to do.

Breaking a scry is a matter of timing, Asmara said. *Mirrors have two sides. One reflective, one portal. Understand?*

"Yes." Marcus sighed. "We've been over this."

Asmara, in mage mode, didn't scoff at the tort. *The reflective properties disrupt the connection off the current scry. You must turn the reflective side to face the portal you want while connecting the two portals together. Make sense?*

"So, disrupt, turn, and connect," Marcus said.

"Or you could disrupt, drop the scry, and try to reconnect," Stillwood said.

Marcus growled at his peanut gallery.

You could, Asmara admitted. *It's safer, but if you do, then you can be disrupted. This way will actually shatter the mirror you want to disrupt.*

"Be careful," Stillwood said. "You could break your mirror. You could kill everyone around it. Disrupting is bad enough, but a flip gone wrong has infinite consequences."

In slow insolence, Marcus turned toward Stillwood who was slowly showing he was more than a soothsayer.

Stillwood raised his hands in defense. "I'm just a poor old wanderer. I know things."

Marcus returned to the mirror.

He's right, Asmara said. *Also, if you don't flip fast enough, you could connect to the wrong mirror.*

"So, you're trusting me to do this?" Used to the brightness, Marcus stared into the mirror.

Asmara nodded in the reflection.

Thinking of the mage tower, Marcus scryed.

He waited until the hairline timing was right for the other end. Then, in a split second, he saw a flash of white.

In the opposite mirror, Nidra howled at him.

Marcus flipped the reflection, connected to the other side, and Ardin's lab filled the under-well. He'd done it. He'd shattered the other mirror—which apparently belonged to Nidra and connected to Ardin's tower.

"It is done." Marcus waved the curious onlookers forward.

Order and tidiness were not Ardin's strong points. Still, the laboratory looked more disheveled than normal. A closer look in the dark interior and even in the limited times Marcus had been in the tower, it seemed the room had been tossed.

His indisputable clue was a five-tiered shelf spilling books like guts from a disembowelment. Any worthwhile mage, warlock, or a mere magician would never keep books in such a fashion. Not that Ardin was worthwhile, but even he knew the value of the written word.

Floating embers of parchment tumbled down from the high ceiling. Broken vials oozed liquid on the floor. Some of it mixed and couldn't be identified as liquid anymore. Ink puddled and soaked its way into groves of the stone ground. Pieces of a shredded table jutted every which way. Dark splatters from the high walls painted smears leeching destruction.

The books! Asmara yelped.

Marcus winced, fighting to get his clothes off in favor of leaving them intact. His whole body was on fire under the burn of several agreements. No question Tiecus would carry through the scry, and saving his only pair of clothes was no question either.

A faint tinkling of metal on metal, the sound of armor rubbing against armor, brought his attention to a gasping form underneath the bookshelf. One of Ardin's guards shifted below the books.

"Angus!" The seneschal pushed Marcus aside. "W'at 'appened? W'ere's Roger?"

The guard who helped stand watch over Ardin was no ordinary palace soldier. Angus looked like a smaller Bolden as was typical of the Blackened Elite. For the three months Marcus had stayed in Benicar, Angus and Roger had been the shroud protecting the magician.

Angus sat up on his elbows and peered up with the unmistakable iridescent eyes of a demon.

Cornelius swore.

"Sir Van Hoepen," Angus rasped. "Marcus." The Blackened Elite nodded. "There were three. Came right through the mirror. Ugly sons-o-bitches." The riddled Benicarian spat. "One distracted me, killed Roger." Angus lowered his head and gave out a scream something worthy of Tiecus's victims.

Cornelius got close to the portal and put a hand on the barrier. Ripples spread through the invisible surface distorting the light as a pebble would disturb a still pond.

The scream subsided to heavy pants, and Angus raised his head again. "Ardin went to protect the king." Angus turned on his side and grunted while reaching for his belt. The shine of metal shimmered.

Dagger in hand, Angus leaned heavy on his elbows and directed his face to Cornelius. Though his iridescent eyes had no pupil, Angus expressed admiration more than any words could and lifted the blade to his own neck.

Marcus pounded the barrier, making ripples along the surface. "Stop!" He turned to Cornelius. "Order him to stop."

Cornelius shook his head in grave disappointment.

He turned back to Angus. Marcus shouted at the Blackened Elite. "This is why I sparred for three months with you, getting you ready for this. You can't just give up. All my efforts were for nothing if this is the result!"

Claiming I told you so is a bit moot now. The voice belonged to Angus. Marcus hadn't felt a demens, but there Angus was in his mind speaking.

Shaken, Marcus turned away feeling a presence older than Asmara, older than the stars, fade from his mind. The demon inside Angus was ancient.

"It was an honor to serve." Angus shuffled and pointed the tip of the blade up.

"May the wind be at your back, laddie." Cornelius nodded.

Angus conveyed without words, sorrow, forgiveness, peace, and at the end, when he drove the dagger into his throat, triumph.

Marcus had never seen a suicide. The courage and conviction with which Angus performed in the line of duty shot an arrow through Marcus. Humans had honor, that's what Angus taught him. His mantra of "not my problem" now tasted sour on his tongue.

Stillwood leaned back against the wall, head bowed. Cornelius pressed his head onto the barrier and patted the window under the stairs. He whispered two words Marcus couldn't make out. They did not sound like words in the Benicarian language.

Marcus stood stunned, realizing he was too late to help the riddled human. "What was it all for?" Helping to train the Blackened Elite fight demons had failed. "What was all that work for?" he said again.

It was one thing to watch strangers die for your benefit. Watching someone whom he knew and in whom he had invested effort in sacrifice themselves was something entirely different. "Are they all just going to die?"

Stillwood backed away giving him a wide birth.

Iridescent mist poured out of Angus confirming the Blackened Elite's death.

Tiecus careened into the forefront. Numb, ripped aside, and shoved to the background, Marcus let the demon overtake him.

Coiled horns, front paws, hind hooves, stubby tail, jutted-out chest, barrel of a wolf, and hind quarters that could kick the stars from the sky lunged forward with the might of a battering ram.

Wide-eyed, Stillwood scrambled. "Find Ardin's journal. It will tell you everything you need to know."

Cornelius was pushed out from under the stairwell by Tiecus's large body. Tiecus's horns dipped into the mirror and the silver enveloped him.

Cornelius pushed to the mirror and roared, "Take me wit' you."

His request came too late. The silver took Tiecus, and the demon let go of Reginhart.

Chapter 23

I WADE THROUGH a white expanse of quicksand. This is opposite of Atra Solumn.

It is 'no' Atra Solumn? I ask.

Yes. The Enforcer hurts inside, but I need him now. Action is best when pain strikes its claws.

Correct. The mage gives me concession.

I have learned big today. *No is big enemy*, I say. *Even Atra Solumn has sky and rock.*

The mage snorts, *He'll never get it.*

Claws of thought cling to old ways, and my understanding fails. I fight the white expanse of quicksand. I thrash, twisting to get away from this white quicksand.

Next time you're asleep, the Enforcer says to the mage, *I'm going to turn a blind eye to anything of yours he wants to play with.*

The Enforcer speaks the words, but his effort remains impotent.

Go ahead. The mage tries "not" to care, but I know better. *There's nothing left to play with.*

Tiecus, listen to me. The Enforcer radiates well-being at me. He's the one who needs well-being. *You are safe.*

Doe eyes float to the surface of my mind. Those eyes help me focus. I stop thrashing.

Tower. I say where I want to go, and I am there. The white expanse quicksand spits me out. I must taste bad. My claws, hooves, and horns help me gain my bearings. They also help me shatter the white expanse. Shards of mirror pelt my hide.

Oh grand! The mage could give lessons to harpies. *Now how are we going to return?*

The wake of the three other demons' path is the blood and bodies of dead.

The great hall, the Enforcer says. *Go east.*

Dead lie scattered leading a path to where I need to go.

The mage sleeps now. He knows a battle is coming. This is why I riddled him. I thought he would be easy to control. But meek is no measure of compliance.

Stone gives way under my horns. I am inside a large human den.

Sixteen Dark Elite surround one riddled human in the middle of the human den. Oddities surround the humans. As if I have four sets of eyes like a spider. Four King Friend stand at the north, west, south, and east points of the room. Four Magician Hacks stand next to King Friend in each corner. My eyes focus on four sets of the same people like a phantasmagoria. Four identical King Friend. Four identical Magician Hacks. This room is a kaleidoscope of humans. The mage had a toy of glass once.

Oddity is only one riddled human. There are four of all else.

The smell of burning flesh wafts up to my nose. It is the Enforcer that burns. His right forearm smolders where King Friend's agreement sears through. I roar my intentions.

The riddled takes advantage of my honorable challenge. He fakes left, swings his sword right, dodges Dark Elite, and frees Dark Elite's blood along the jugular.

Four Dark Elite go down, but it is the same man. Another four-that-is-one fills the gaps. Others close ranks. The mirage is meticulous, all the four-that-is-one look the same. Magician Hack, master of sparks and light, does this trick of four-that-is-one.

My challenge goes ignored. I leap for the riddled. He wears armor and broad sword. I have elements at my command. Ferocity and horns harder than steel. He will quickly be dispatched.

You must be careful, the Enforcer says. *Keep the humans alive.*

The Enforcer thinks his agreements are my agreements. They are not. I understand what "no" means now, but *I* never agreed not to kill Benicarians.

Riddled's sword tip is caught in the coils of my horns. He steps on my face and yanks his sword out of bondage. Black flame rises inside me. The Enforcer calls humans rude. I agree. This riddled will be food. His demon will feel my fang.

"Don't move, not until I say." All four Magician Hacks speak.

One Dark Elite holds King Friend's belt. That Dark Elite is smart. He knows where his charge is always. Good. Riddled will die now.

My challenger is before me. The fight is bliss and too short. My claws rake the riddled. My fun is dead. Demon-cloud-pretty-mist pours out dead man's mouth and ears. The demon-cloud rises and thinks it safe from me. But I am Tiecus. Pillars tell me I am soul-burner.

"Fool!" Magician Hack's four voices echo. "You were not to kill him!"

I see Magician Hack throw sand. Images blur. All four groups of King Friend walk in one row like weeling ducks following their Maymay. Dark Elite dragging King Friend stops. Another riddled smelling of meat and guts holds a thin metal square blocking King Friend.

That thin metal square is a cleaver and very sharp, the Enforcer says.

The demon-cloud floats above men, spears, and my horns. Only Magician Hack and I see.

"We have to move," Magician Hack says.

Spearman and his three other selves step toward Cleaver Riddled. Four spears thrust. Cleaver Riddled swings his weapon in a wide arc. Four spears miss. Cleaver Riddled catches the real spear. One blow, and the spear is broken. I know Magician Hack's trick.

King Friend's throng surrounds me. I lower my head. I and my pointy ram horns lurch forward. My neck turns. I parry a strike and lash at Dark Elite riddled one. They fight well.

I didn't teach them all we know, the Enforcer says.

He taught them, but I am a demon.

Four-that-is-one Dark Elite riddled fake lunges, slashing his sword down. I deflect with point-end ram horns. My eye sees the real Dark Elite riddled. Fear smell grows. He knows I see.

The demon-cloud waits. If I were he, I would riddle the pack leader. King Friend is in danger.

Tiecus, play later, the Enforcer says.

I imagine the demon-cloud is a cougar demon. Hate rises from heart to throat. Dark Elite will die, but so will the demon-cloud. Hate mixes with air. I breathe in. I breathe out. Atra Solumn flame accompanies my roar. It is the soul-fire. Black flame reaches for souls.

The demon-cloud, now charred goo, bubbles on stone floor. Dark Elite lies dead beside my enemy. Neither were throng, but loss of King Friend's protectors is regrettable.

King Friend saved Marcus. I will save King Friend. We will be even.

If only it worked that way.

All sets of King Friend's four-that-is-one start running toward Cleaver Riddled. Cleaver Riddled swings his weapon because he is stupid. Only second set of four-that-is-one is real.

Real Dark Elite dragging King Friend smashes Cleaver Riddled. I like this Dark Elite. He hits Cleaver Riddled where he deserves. In the face, with butt-end sword handle. Another demon-cloud pours out of Cleaver Dead Host.

I think the Blackened Elite meant not to kill him, the Enforcer says.

The word "not" is still new, but I know what the Enforcer means.

Magician Hack yells and waves his cloak at the demon-cloud. Magician Hack knows what to do.

The four-that-is-one disappears. There is only one of each now. Dark Elite with King Friend and Magician Hack flee.

The demon-cloud chases, and I chase the demon-cloud. The opening is narrow. Stone breaks at my point-end horns' will.

Elemental Ignis roars—at me! The sound is laughing fire. Angry orange fire claws and sharp weapons attack. Sharp metal points hurl at me! Sharp points burrow into my left side. They slide between my ribs, my flank, my shoulder, many places. Surprise, hate, and air mix and Atra Solumn flame pours out of my mouth in my agony.

If demon-clouds could laugh, this one would.

Frigidus, the Enforcer casts. He fights Ignis while I chase the demon-cloud.

Point-end horns hit and widen another too small opening.

A sound of thunder, a flash of light, and I'm blind. Magician Hack is stupid. He thinks red spots dancing in my eyes will help him. I can smell Magician Hack's hate.

My hate and air mix. Atra Solumn flame bursts. Breathing becomes effort. Ribs hurt, shoulder hurts, flank hurts and slows me, but I must chase.

Dark Elite dragging King Friend and Magician Hack run into another man den. I follow.

Another boom, another flash of light, but I am prepared. This is my chance. I reach the demon-cloud. I roar. Tendrils of Atra Solumn flame pour out. My hate is tired. Burnt pile of soot goo bubbles on the ground.

Magician Hack faces me. He is afraid of me. He should be. I see why Dark Elite dragging King Friend stops.

A cougar demon blocks them. The last one.

Hate floods my heart. I will kill cougar demon. The demens starts.

My head aches at first blow. This cougar demon widens the pain in my side. Metal bits twist. My focus directs there. Sharp spasms rack my body. Pain fuels my hate.

The Enforcer burns inside. His agreements that are "not" mine affect him. If he doesn't know what he is, he may learn today.

I am the agreements, the Enforcer says. *I am Marcus.*

His anger is strong. I use it.

The cougar demon rips into my knowledge. He knows his last mistake. The cougar demon leaps for me. He is stupid. Dark Elite dragging King Friend is smart. He pulls them all away.

I meet the cougar demon, claw for claw. Hate and air mix. My breath becomes Atra Solumn flame. My breath is a weapon of Ignis. But the flame is ice to my tongue.

That is not fire you breathe, the Enforcer says.

He is correct.

The cougar demon looks the same. Golden fur, small ears, obsidian teeth and claws. His eyes *don't* glow. His eyes are pits of Atra Solumn. Inside, cougar demon is charred. Molten goo mess remains inside. *No thing* to demense there. The cougar demon is dead.

My hooves give way. Metal of pain stick out my left side. Blood mats fur. Still, vindictive pride spreads across my chest. I killed all.

We need to go back to Reginhart, the Enforcer says.

I want to sleep.

"Let go of me," King Friend says. The Dark Elite holds back King Friend from me.

"You're not safe yet," Dark Elite sneers at me.

I sneer back.

"Olof, that is Marcus, and he will not harm me." King Friend points at me.

"How do you know that's Marcus?" Magician Hack says.

Soldiers burst into the man den like tides of Glacias. They run slowly. A wonder King Friend lives this long under their protection. Then I remember, King Friend is pack leader. I have it wrong. They are under King Friend's protection.

"Stand down!" King Friend is angry.

Olof Elite grits his teeth. "I'll tell them to stand down when I deem you're safe."

"When you deem it safe?" King Friend makes his face stone and ice. "I am King Eric Valder, son of King Cedric Valder and Queen Cassandra Bellingham. As highest lord of Benicar, your exalted ruler, you will let go of me."

Olof Elite and King Friend play blinking game.

"Do not underestimate me, Olof. Let me go, or I will crush you."

King Friend wins blink game.

The Enforcer refuses to come up. He pushes me in front. If I remain up, I will sleep here until I wake.

I'll keep you awake until you remove the knives. The Enforcer speaks like a female sometimes.

He worries the knives will hurt. I will tell true. They will. When he comes up, they will move into him. But he can remove the knives better than I. I endured. So can he.

King Friend steps closer. Olof Elite threatens me with sword and glares.

I raise my upper lip in offense. I keep King Friend safe better than he.

I spread my claws for inspection. King Friend approves. He appraises my damage like any pack leader. I snarl telling him I am strong. I can fight.

Blackened Elite does not understand. He raises his sword.

King Friend is amused. He chuckles at my expense and waves away the Blackened Elite.

"Do you really want these in your side?" King Friend steps to my wounds. He grabs a cleaver and pulls.

I make no sound. I remain quiet. I make no move, I remain still. Even when a rod long as my foreleg is removed. Each piece clanks on the floor. The metal pile grows. I can breathe, and pain is less.

"Kindly, if you would, Marcus," King Friend says. "Revert to your more human form. You're grieving my constituents."

Chapter 24

TIECUS ENFOLDED TO the recesses while Marcus emerged with an audience witnessing his transformation.

Crouched down, hiding his body behind sheets of black hair, Marcus tried to ignore the embarrassing display. Over the past few days, his modesty had become moot. Still, danger lay in exposing dozens of agreements in the midst of strangers. One of which burned now that he was in Benicar.

Go to Reginhart and *Leave now* had appeared prominently among the numerous agreements made with King Valder soon after Tiecus had killed the other demons. The smoldering words were etched in Marcus's body and mind forever.

Valder's guards, too cautious to believe that the demon before them was an ally, pointed spears and swords at his hunched form. He didn't blame them. Changing from demon to something they recognized relaxed their disparaging faces but not their metal points.

Squatting before the king, Marcus brushed his long black hair from his face. His mussed locks were frazzles of snarled ends. They crackled with static as his natural comb of claws cut through unkempt mane. Fire-embossed lettering became less intelligible and more like smoldering embers singeing his arm.

"Better?" Marcus said in mock subservience.

He was painfully aware of all twenty-two scrutinizers. Marcus stood, hands at his sides, forcing them from covering his body. Showing modesty was a weakness in which he would not luxuriate.

Valder smiled. "Well, that does answer two questions."

The king was the only one who didn't blatantly stare at his body, yet Valder was the one in which he felt most vulnerable.

"I need to get to a mirror." Pain was a major influence on his decisions. In the back of his mind, he remembered Tiecus destroying the one in Ardin's tower.

"Of course." Valder wrinkled his nose.

Twirling smoke trails lifted from Marcus's arm. The agreements burned, forcing Marcus to go back to Reginhart.

Respect in his eyes, Valder said in a low apologetic voice, "I see what you mean by compulsion."

Valder waved a hand and gave a sharp command to his guard. "Stand down."

The soldiers eased their weapons. The squad's control impressed Marcus with their faith in Valder. They all smelled of fear from one varying degree or another.

His arm sizzled claiming his attention. Wanting anything to ease the pain, Marcus grabbed his forearm with his opposite hand. Before he could call on Glacias to soothe his arm, the burning spread to his palm.

Surprised, he hissed and jerked away. Imprinted was a partial copy of Valder's agreement: "Go to Reginhart . . . Leave now." The words felt like flesh held over a lit candle.

"Ardin," Valder said. "Please lend Marcus your cloak."

The magician hesitated.

Valder waited expecting his command to be carried out.

Ardin's silence and non-movement seemed less like defiance and more of a question. A question more than *why?* or *what for?*

Marcus couldn't articulate what Ardin asked through his inaction. His patience was growing thin. But Valder wasn't going to repeat his command. Any leader worth his element never repeated a command.

Olof rested his hand on the pommel of his sword. "Magician, your king gave you an order."

Ardin stepped forward stripping off his hooded top layer.

The magician revealed a black tunic and pants with long, unmistakably red hair pulled back with a thong.

Murky-blue eyes, which had always been hidden behind a hood, shone with river-deep hate. His complexion was complete with red freckles across his cheeks, forehead, and chin. But what made Marcus flinch was the man's face. Nidra.

"You!" Thunder cracked inside the dome when Marcus grabbed the magician by the throat.

Give Nidra a squeeze for pulling my ear, Asmara said, gagged, and then receded.

Twenty-two guards readied their weapons, aimed for Marcus, and prepared to charge.

Valder raised a fist. "Halt! Marcus is only following orders."

The black cloak fluttered to the marble ground staining the white floor.

Satisfaction spread across Marcus's face. His gleeful chuckle penetrated the otherwise silent room. Relief spread across his arm as the burning ceased.

Marcus squeezed the Tier Naug's throat and lifted him off the ground. Nidra, Ardin, or whoever he was lent a form of modesty by blocking his naked body from everyone.

"Sire?" Ardin rasped, but not for help, for direction.

Marcus squeezed. "You have plagued me for the last time."

"Intriguing." Valder seemed oblivious to his magician's plight and circled around Marcus and Ardin with deliberate heel-to-toe steps.

Caution prevented Marcus from demensing the Tier Naug. Ardin didn't have the telltale signs of being riddled. His eyes were clear and bright. A clear blue like his people. But a demens was too risky. The warlock wanted control over him, and Marcus didn't like pushing into minds in the first place. How Ardin didn't have iridescent eyes was beyond him. It was enough to sink a seed of doubt to neither kill the magician nor demense him.

But he could be like the mage, Tiecus scoffed at the Serenite. Asmara had once had eyes that shimmered like a demon's, but that feature was transferred to Marcus upon his birth.

Valder ran his eyes along the searing words on Marcus's left arm.

The magician choked and writhed as his fingers dove into the pockets of his pants. Ardin's sleight of hand wasn't fast or subtle enough to go unnoticed. Marcus shook his captive.

"I'm not fool enough to fall for your misdirection techniques." Marcus grabbed the magician's wrist and squeezed harder on Ardin's throat.

The magician's resistance bled away.

Marcus suspected something different about this Tier Naug. Whoever this was, magician or warlock, it wasn't Nidra. If it were, Marcus would be fighting a demens.

This made no sense. He had seen Nidra scream when he had flipped the mirror to return to Benicar. This couldn't be Nidra. Nidra might be dead.

Small wisps of smoke drifted up from his arm. Valder's agreement challenged his motive. Even if this was Ardin, Marcus enjoyed prolonging the magician's long-deserved pain. If it was Nidra, he felt the same.

"This is for treating me as a human's servant." Palpitating his hand, Marcus allowed Ardin small gasps of air.

Valder wasn't outright gaping at the agreements, but the king wasn't entirely subtle while studying the tattoos. Valder swept glances over Marcus's body with more than scholarly interest.

Without air, Ardin's face turned shades of red and purple. The magician squirmed under the claws digging into his flesh. Droplets of blood leaked down Ardin's neck.

As if in sudden realization that his magician was in danger, Valder waved a hand and said, "Marcus, if you could be so generous, could you please allow him to breathe. I have questions to ask of my magician."

Marcus forced Ardin to his knees and loomed over the Tier Naug and said, "You mean your warlock."

He was all too glad for any reason to extend Ardin's suffering even if it meant contending with his own.

Ardin gasped out in a whisper. "You mistake me . . ." Ardin looked at Valder in a sudden panic.

"Not smiling now are you?" Marcus lightened his grip. He still wasn't convinced whether he held Nidra or Ardin.

Nidra would have been attacking his mind with full force.

Ardin was trying to use tricks to get away.

Warlocks were oath-breakers, tricking or forcing elements together and creating abominations.

Magicians worked with divine properties, light, mirrors, and illusion to convince others they were using some innate force.

Warlocks twisted the elements.

Magicians twisted points of view.

A magician's artificial illusions were not equivalent to a warlock's power. The two were not compatible. Much like fire and ice.

Valder waved a hand at Marcus's tattooed right forearm. "Out of curiosity, Marcus, do you have the same reaction when you're near Cornelius?"

Marcus cut off Ardin's air a little more. "No."

Valder turned an icy glare to the magician. "Why is that, Ardin?"

The smell of anger hit. Marcus dared a glance to the king. Valder's face was a mask. His body, however, told of building fury.

Ardin gasped breaths and tried to speak. "Sire—I'm loyal—to you."

From his peripheral vision, Marcus watched Valder covertly contemplate the thirteenth agreement. His cheeks grew warm. Rushing blood and excitement expanded the lettering's surface amplifying the words legible. That is if the king was literate in the Serenite language.

Valder pursed his lips and turned to Ardin. "Why do you insist on keeping that mirror despite my requests to destroy it?"

The magician looked at the king, and his eyes pleaded. "I—can—ex—plain."

In the way a lover would caress a partner before separating for a long journey, Valder stroked Ardin's cheek with the back of his index finger. "Oh yes, love, you will."

Ardin leaned into the contact. "Eric."

"Shhhhh." Valder leaned in close and kissed Ardin on the forehead.

Marcus shuddered. He didn't understand how or why, but fear laced his inside chilling his blood. "Lay claim to him all you want. I'll still kill him."

The magician no longer resisted in either his body or his face. With bloodshot eyes, Ardin pleaded without words inviting Marcus to reach inside. Whether it was a trick or to dissolve Valder's doubt, he didn't trust the magician—warlock or whatever Ardin was—Marcus refrained from a demens. Partially, he didn't want to relive the grotesque experience of fighting the riddled humans played before him again.

Valder looked at Marcus's burning forearm. "You aren't going to let him go, are you?"

"No." Marcus squeezed harder, and Ardin's air was completely cut off. Killing the magician might be a mercy by the cold, impassive way his beloved king treated him.

"We are at an impasse then." Valder was an intelligent man and neither wasted time nor rushed a predicament. "I need my magician alive, and you need to keep your agreements."

Marcus smelled compromise. Through intense burning he clawed for clarity. Negotiation was the king's most formidable weapon, and he didn't want to rush into another one.

"Friend." The king sounded sincere in the double-edged meaning. "Would you please release my magician?"

Olof unsheathed his sword. "I can cure them both."

"Cooperation is not always found at the end of a point." The king gave the same faceted smile as if he had the upper hand. "You're too much like your predecessor."

"And I'm damn proud of being like Seneschal Cornelius Van Hoepen."

Marcus hissed. Did Olof know of his precious seneschal's predicament? Probably not. He relaxed as much as he could with a smoldering arm. As much opportunity as this was, he needed the burning to stop.

Wait. Asmara choked. *We have a tower. Don't pull anything foolish.*

At the cliff of pain and nostalgic wanting, Marcus could only think of one thing—stopping the pain. The only thing that would stop the chunks of his flesh from sloughing off his arm was a compromise. His agreements never conceded, and his mind clouded with pain. Searing burns smoked his arm. The *Go to Reginhart* deal with Valder etched a scar on his skin as his mind swirled in agony. Near insanity, Marcus said the first thing he could think of to quench the burning.

"Recall me," Marcus said, "before I snap his neck and leave."

Valder's tone was light and suspicious. "Nothing more?"

At the cliff of pain and nostalgic wanting, Marcus nodded.

Lacking all harshness when he made their last agreement, Valder said, "Marcus, I bid you to return to Benicar."

Instant relief. Marcus released his grip on Ardin.

The magician gasped for air and hung his head with his arms holding himself up.

Marcus assessed the enormity of victory. He had thought he'd feel vindicated. Benicar was the place he'd learn control. The city he wanted to return to and find peace.

Instead, the weight of his other agreements pressed in his mind. Platt wanted him to protect Reginhart. Stillwood told him to find Ardin's journal. Valder might have recalled him but what about disposing of the Tier Naug? Did Valder's "bid to return" wipe out the entirety of the agreement?

The words "*I bid you return to Benicar*" covered burnt scars of Valder's previous agreement of "*Go to Reginhart.*"

Valder's recall was just another agreement layered over the original.

He wanted to scream. He wanted to shred Ardin. He wanted to shake Valder and make him take it back. If the demon were awake, he'd make Tiecus fill the building with black flame.

"What does this new agreement mean?" *How could he be so stupid?*

That is the result of unspecified terms. Asmara crackled with indignation.

The king's smiling gratitude reminded Marcus of a certain smilodon, and a shiver shot up his spine.

"He's still a Tier Naug," Marcus said.

"No." Valder sniffed. "He took his vows to me and to Benicar the same as Cornelius. But he . . . hesitated."

"You wanted to test his loyalty," Marcus sneered at the king.

And yours, Asmara interjected.

Valder said nothing, gave away nothing, and stared Marcus in the eye as if daring him for an intrusion of the mind.

"I suppose he's still useful even if he didn't pass." Marcus sneered down at Ardin.

Ardin struggled for air.

"Oh, he passed." Valder lifted his nose in authority. "As true as day."

Confounded, Marcus contorted his face. "How so?"

Valder's mischievous smile shone bright matching the twinkle in his eyes. "I asked him not to kill you, and he didn't."

Marcus scoffed. Like Ardin could kill him.

Blood shot eyes stared up in merciless calculation. The magician shook all over and smelled of desperation. Not desperation for life but of knowledge.

Valder's smile was too nonchalant, his eyes too knowing, making Marcus feel as though the king had placed more faith in Ardin winning a match between them. Seeing the expression on others, Marcus now understood that smile. The thin toothless lip curl was not smugness, but a king's pity.

White scars behind embossed lettering formed its inky hold. The words were a testament to Valder's cunning and ruthlessness. Or how careless Marcus had been.

This is what happens when making deals with humans. Marcus kept the words inside but couldn't hide his expression.

More like promising to keep a secret before knowing the secret. Asmara would not let this mistake drop for a while.

Even though the burning faded, Marcus wasn't free of Valder's agreement, not in the least. Angrier more with himself than with the king, Marcus palpitated his hand imagining the grip around Ardin's neck.

Of course, Valder would recall you after seeing Platt's agreement. Asmara sagged. *You all but bound yourself to her and Reginhart.*

Marcus snorted, "Now you're angry because we need to go back?"

Valder eyed him in interest.

I'm angry, Asmara hissed, *because King Big Britches can call you to him any time he wants.*

Then you should have thought of that during the chess game. Marcus remembered to keep the conversation inside.

We had everything. Asmara's shrill cry nearly made his mind bleed. *Chasing Tier Naug, defending Reginhart, you had a duty, a reason, a purpose, and you couldn't let go of the ideal.*

Marcus narrowed his eyes. *When the ideal is obtainable, one should take it.*

You think if Platt's taken away from Riley and brought here, her feelings for the youngling will wane?

Marcus held his breath. He didn't dare confirm his hope at Asmara's thought aloud. It felt like a lie. He wanted to bring Platt to Benicar. He wanted to leave Reginhart behind and bring the only part of that place worth a damn here.

Wheezing, Ardin covered his mouth. All the magician could do was cough, gag, and gasp for air.

Valder stepped forward and offered a hand to his suffering magician.

Olof intercepted the king. "Cornelius spoilt you. No menial tasks befit a king I serve." Shoving his armored body in front of Valder, Olof offered Ardin a gauntlet-sized hand.

Valder stiffened, sighed disappointment, and backed away.

For one moment, Marcus lost his modesty and leaned over Valder. "Do menial tasks include wiping your arse?"

To his credit, Valder covered his grin by stroking his trim-cut beard. "Don't give Olof any ideas."

Marcus shuddered.

Accepting the Blackened Elite's hand, Ardin clawed his way up. The magician or whatever he was, dabbed at his cut neck, shot a nasty glance at Marcus, then addressed Valder. "You knew."

Ardin accepted a clean cloth from his king, the only assistance Olof allowed. "You wanted Marcus to attack me. Your deal with him proves it." Ardin dabbed at his neck and coughed into the white linen while managing to glare at Marcus's arm—the same arm that had Valder's agreement.

"Cornelius is still alive." Valder might have well slapped Ardin in the face and said *Of course, I planned it that way.*

Ardin used Olof as a crutch, but the Blackened Elite clasped the magician as one would hold a prisoner. Ardin's impaired equilibrium didn't impede his piercing anger. "Maybe it's because the fool got riddled. Your favorite may no longer be a man at all."

Olof stiffened. News of Cornelius hadn't reached all of Valder's throng. Stone-cold eyes sought Marcus for confirmation or denial. But he could give neither insight nor advice.

"Or maybe"—Valder said coolly—"Marcus mistook you for Nidra."

Ardin froze. The air grew stifling.

"Sire." Ardin's word was an apology.

"No," Valder said. "There is no excuse."

"Your options were unacceptable." Ardin pushed himself from Olof.

"I gave you a choice." The king tapped his lip with an index finger. The only nervous weakness Valder exposed. "You took a third option to which I specifically told you not to."

"But I can merge wit' 'im now." Desperate, Ardin wasn't as choosey with his words.

Merge? What in the Atra Solumn were they talking about . . . merge? But it was not an impossible thing. Marcus himself had merged with Asmara and Tiecus. *Can a person split in half?*

Asmara answered, *That's not the right question.*

Marcus thought and then asked, *Can a soul split in half.*

The uncanny way in which Ardin and Nidra were look-alike twins also had Marcus comparing Nidra's and Ardin's mannerisms. Both contained self-assuredness and cocky pride. But Nidra's rage implemented bold risks. Ardin held the command of a henpecker clucking at her mate. Ardin and Nidra might look the same, but they didn't act the same.

"Combined, we would be an asset." Ardin stepped forward as if in plea.

What does he mean? Marcus turned inward to the mage. *Does he think Nidra will join them?*

Asmara didn't answer.

"We'll discuss why you defied me later." Valder turned his gaze from Ardin and smiled to Marcus. "We have a guest." The king then swept his gaze over the destruction and chaos of the room and narrowed his gaze to the head of his guard.

Olof sprang into action as if the king's last words were a personal affront to the Blackened Elite and pointed to the nearest spearman. "You, start cleaning the main hall." He pointed to another man. "You, secure the room." The king's personal bodyguard began ordering the men. To Marcus's relief, they in turn stopped gaping at his naked form.

A woman in a jewel-toned blue dress glided alongside a Blackened Elite escort. Her blonde hair pulled back was pinned up with tight curls flowing down at her crown.

Her green eyes evaluated Valder as soon as she stepped into the room. Relief flowed over her like the ruffles around her thin wrists. Her evaluation continued, scanning Ardin, Olof, Marcus, and then the rest of the room.

By the judgment in her stance, she concluded the scene safe to continue forward with her queen's guard, one of the Silver Elite—the counterparts of the king's Blackened Elite.

She stopped before Ardin's black cloak and pointed to it. "Uros, will you retrieve that for me?"

Wordlessly, the Silver Elite escort she called Uros squatted down and handed her the rumpled guise Ardin wore.

The woman's languid movements projected her every intention deliberately transmitting exactly where and when she was going to touch or move.

She passed everyone, approaching Ardin, and flung the cloak expertly to settle on the magician's shoulders while saying, "Really, Ardin, this is dyed silk. Not something I come across every day. And *I* made it, not my handmaiden, not my assistant. Me. I would hope you'd treat it with more respect."

Ardin let her fasten the buckle without a sneer or ill word and bowed when she was done.

Valder turned a smile at Marcus. "I'm not willing to let you roam the palace . . . indecent. You can borrow a mirror as soon as my Lady Jessica gets attire situated for you."

At the mention of her name, Jessica whirled around, spinning her dress. Her eyes matched the mischievous smile she flashed. Jessica curtsied to Valder and then scanned Marcus head to toe. Her slow smile came through matching the mischievousness in her eyes. "He seems perfectly comfortable the way he is."

Immediately, Marcus felt uneasy. Not that he thought she was dangerous in a physical sense, but she had a visceral quality making her as persuasive as Asmara, the mage who had convinced a demon to combine their magical essence together.

Valder matched her guileful smile. "Dress him in a full."

Lady Jessica couldn't have looked more pleased. Her eyes widened. She leaned over to Valder and planted three slender fingers at the cuff of the king's sleeve. "I think ivory would wash his complexion out too much. Red would be perfect, but I'm running low and may not have enough for him." She scanned him again making a point of his vertical size. "I could use the rest of the blue—"

Valder shot an eyebrow up and gave her a pointed stare. "Give him the purple."

Jessica touched her chest and let out a gasp. "But, sire—"

"My Lady, he saved my life at great cost and pain to himself. Color him in the nobles."

The king turned to Marcus. "This is *my* Lady Jessica." He gestured to her and flashed a smile. "She is the queen of Benicar and doubles as my seamstress. Please treat her *in-kind*."

Marcus smirked at the words in Platt's agreement. The nuance did not pass by his social sensibilities, but her title of queen did.

No human ever explained the importance of their titles as if he should know what a duke or a knight or a queen was other than pieces on a chess board. He did understand Lady Jessica's blood was off limits, and she was not to be hurt. Especially if her position were parallel to the chess piece.

"After she fits you, come back to me." Valder's eyes flicked over to the magician. "We'll talk, and if you still want a mirror, I'll find you one." He then looked to Jessica. "My Lady." The king took her hand and placed a kiss to her gloved fingers. "Please take Marcus and fit him."

Jessica curtsied and turned.

Marcus had never seen Valder acquiesce to anyone. Deciding on caution, he appraised Lady Jessica's threat. It was always the female demons that were the more dangerous.

Chapter 25

JESSICA'S CURLED HAIR was tied neatly up with pins to expose her swanlike neck.

Platt had offered her throat like a submissive weeling once, unlike Jessica who seemed to wave it like a taunt. Saliva dripped down his waiting canines, but it wasn't guilt or orders stopping him from sinking his jaws along her spine. It was survival. Total control over every action saved him from being dispatched like the three cougar demons being cleaned up. Avoiding temptation, he stayed five steps away.

Uros followed behind Marcus.

Jessica led him down a guard-lined hall until she came toward two bookcases. She turned toward him, and her green eyes traveled up and down his long body. "We're not going to take the main hallways. Think you can manage?"

Marcus smirked. He'd known about the camouflaged doors and hidden passageways. He'd needed them to do "chores" for Valder.

Past the guards and between two bookcases, they faced a non-textured wall. She led him through its hidden opening disguised by a clever trick of the eye.

The thin corridor zigzagged, and he followed with Uros at his back.

Jessica kept her fingers trailing on the smooth wall. She stopped and then pushed against a rough part, and an angled doorway snapped open.

"Uros, take the long hall. You know you don't fit in these tunnels." Jessica turned to Marcus. "Tragic, really. All these hidden pathways and most of the guard are too wide and tall to fit." Her eyes glanced over him. "You'll barely make it as it is."

Uros hadn't said a word, nor had he left. The Silver Elite glared at Marcus.

Jessica gave a *tsk*. "I'll be fine, Uros. Who else to better protect me than a demon?" Lady Jessica flashed her brilliant teeth. Then she stepped into a dark hallway.

Without a word, Uros stepped in front of him. He made sure Marcus saw his unsheathed dagger the length of a smilodon's canine. Uros held it to his own throat, scraping stubble on his neck. Small black dots of hair clung to the blade, and Uros angled the flat part displaying the handiwork.

Incensed, Marcus pulled on Asmara's persuasion and said, "With the way you were staring at my naked body, I could have sworn you knew how to read. For if you did, you'd know I am unable to harm this human. Now I see your gaze must be for something else."

The Silver Elite turned a deep shade of red but held his tongue.

Marcus turned and followed Jessica through an opening. Being six foot five, he ducked as the passageway ceiling was just six feet high and four feet wide. His eyes illuminated the hall until Jessica came back with a torch.

The tunnel, like the one at Reginhart's keep, was one-person wide with a continuous stone floor and walls. But where his traveled down fading into dirt, Benicar's hidden tunnels were stone from floor to ceiling. The dank smell of mildew crashed into his senses, unlike the vanilla scent of *his* passageway in *his* keep. A startling thought came to him.

"Valder could have escaped using these passages," he said. "Why didn't he?"

"*King* Valder." Jessica gave him an admonishing look over her shoulder. "His trust in others is going to get him killed one day. He's always looking for the good in people. He probably thought he could convince Roger and Roan to join him. Like you."

"Roger and Roan?" Their opinions of Valder differed. His description of the king came down to one word, specious: seemingly just and right, but deceptive.

"The two that were demon-possessed. The two you killed." Jessica stopped and turned around. Green highlights in her eyes shone in the torch light. She either wasn't afraid to look him in the eye or didn't know what demons could do. He was getting used to fools who thought they could control him. "Thank you. Thank you for saving my Eric." She glanced at his right arm. "I can't imagine how much pain you endured just to come here."

Marcus pulled back. A hint of fear wafted to his nose that proved Jessica was not entirely stupid to the dangers of being alone with him. But there was arousal intertwined with her musk. A sense of dread crawled cold fingers up his body, warning him to be careful.

Despite her worries or admiration, she smiled. "So, you're the new lord of Reginhart." She shook her head in mirth. "Have they erected a statue of your likeness in the middle of town yet?"

Marcus sighed. "I am not a lord or a sir or a master. Our names are our titles. Mine is Marcus."

"Yes. The direct translation is shining hammer, meaning righteous mallet." Lips pressed together curving at the ends, seeming to suppress a laugh. Jessica turned around and started walking again.

Oh, I like this one. Asmara pushed at Marcus like a child straining for attention. *Tell her you're rhythmic too.*

"I'm not saying *that*," Marcus whispered, irked at the comment, figuring there was innuendo in there somewhere.

"Well, Demon of War, what's it like?" she said. "Being riddled?"

They walked for what seemed the length of the castle. After three turns and a flight of stairs, he answered, "I don't really know of any other way."

She cast a green eye back toward him. "Is it painful? Lonely?"

He was starting to understand that she was different from other Benicarians just by the wistful way she asked these questions. Sure Valder, Platt, and the villagers of Reginhart did not scream in fear of him, but Jessica was something more twisted.

"Where are we going?" He was getting tired of walking and answering her questions.

She gave a closed-mouth giggle. "My workroom, of course."

The twinkle in her eye did not reassure him.

She turned to the wall and pushed her weight against it. When she slammed against it, he heard the grating of stone against stone.

Jessica pushed her weight on the wall again, and it gave way a little more. Stepping behind her, Marcus pushed on the wall with one arm where Jessica was trying to throw her thin body.

An opening of about three feet swung back with little labor, for him anyway.

"What strong claws you have." She heaved breaths.

He felt a light touch on his thigh and looked down. Jessica stared into him with a fire in her green eyes.

"Please come in," she said but didn't move.

Marcus held his breath. He started to tingle all over. He could feel Asmara take a more active role in directing him.

Oh, I think we're somewhere in the Cetus constellation.

Marcus huffed at Asmara. *I have no idea what you're talking about. Constellation of what?* The mage's comment befuddled Marcus, but he understood this woman had powers beyond that of both the Atra Solumn and Brightside.

It means you're out of your depth.

Finally, after giving him a lustful stare, she exited through the hole in the wall and beckoned for him to follow.

Every hair on his arms told him *No, run!*

Before he walked in, Marcus looked for traps.

Plush maroon drapes with gold trimming hung from the top of the room down to the floor, just like Valder's private chambers. Bolts of brightly colored silk in every shade Jessica had mentioned to the king, and even some others she hadn't, lined every available space on the walls. Spools of thread covered long tables. A wooden contraption consisting of a wheel next to a bench sat beside the window in one of the room's corners.

The four-poster bed in another corner seemed almost misplaced amidst the work environment. It was the only piece of furniture that wasn't in organized chaos. Maroon sheets as plush and ornate as the curtains lay flat and neat beckoning for touch.

Uros and one other Silver Elite stood guard by the conventional door.

"Ava?" Jessica called gathering a bolt of a deep-purple material set separate from the myriads of colors.

After convincing himself it was safe, Marcus stepped inside and stood upright under a vaulted ceiling. A cool draft reminded Marcus to close the stone opening. With the light from Jessica's room, he noticed a lever inside the hidden tunnel making the stone door easy to push open.

He could feel Asmara's smile. *Oh, you fallen star, and you don't even know what to do with her.*

The door was easily sealed without a trace of its secret passage.

A petite youngling no older than Platt with brown hair and eyes parted a curtain opening. Ava made a shy curtsy to Jessica, took one look at Marcus, and screeched. She backed into a wall and cried out, "I don't want to die."

Ava's fear made him awkwardly comfortable. She was the first one to act like a human in the face of a demon for some time. Fear in others always made Tiecus react, but Marcus swallowed the automatic response to attack and locked himself in place.

The youngling's meek manner reminded him of his little doe. Ava crouched in terror. Her eyes reminded him of a frightened hare. Platt must have wanted to sprint away from him when they had first met. His blood doll was brave to stand up to him and suppress her terror at the sight of his bestial claws and shimmering eyes.

"Stop it!" Jessica shoved bolts of purple fabric into Ava's arms. "He is a guest, and you are embarrassing me. Start cutting. We need to get him dressed."

Ava, eyes streaming with tears, took the cloth with trembling hands and ran back through the curtains.

Jessica turned to Marcus and smiled. "Sorry."

He shrugged still very aware of the two guards and the queen staring at his bareness. "No matter."

All his adrenaline washed down to his feet where it sat and weighed him down. Being congenial was the last thing he wanted to do. Anxiety washed over him. He wanted to get to a mirror and go home to Reginhart.

Home was Reginhart now, not Benicar. His desire to go back to his commitments and to his blood doll felt right. He'd wanted to come back to Benicar so badly, but now that he was here, he just wanted to go back home.

No, Marcus thought. *I'm feeling what Asmara feels.*

A twinge of worry for Platt cut across his internal battle. He'd left her with Cornelius and Stillwood.

Jessica lifted a solid wooden box by its handles and carried it over. She set it down before his feet, stepped up on the box, and stretched her arms up to his neck with a piece of thin cloth that could have been a noose or a blindfold.

He jerked back. "What are you doing?"

Uros and the other Elite Guard were on top of him knocking Jessica off her stool. Two swords were stopped short by the steel of his claws, inches away from his neck.

"The both of you are as bad as my sniveling maid in waiting." Jessica recovered from being shoved aside. "Out!"

Marcus stood his ground displaying his agitation with grinding molars.

No one moved until Jessica raised her voice again. "I said, out!"

Reluctant to sheath his sword, Uros followed his companion not out of the room, but back to their posts.

Eyes closed, standing erect, Jessica breathed in slow long breaths. She raised her eyebrows and smiled with a tight lip. "I'll need to measure what size you are. Please, if you don't mind." Jessica stepped up on the box and held up the cloth tape. Nothing seemed out of the ordinary about the flat thin cloth except it had evenly spaced embroidered lines and was long enough to choke him.

Wary of the strip fit to hang someone, he inched toward her.

"Right." Jessica's confidence, and wandering eyes, made him both nervous and compelled. "No tying you to the bed posts."

Asmara melted inside, seemingly to curl at the ends. *If only . . .*

Jessica acted as if she was perfectly safe with any demon, not just him. Her eyes intermittently stayed on the measuring cloth, and she would often glance down or into his eyes.

Marcus was thankful Asmara did not include images in his snickering. He was embarrassed enough as it stood.

When she wasn't looking at him, he had the chance to assess her character and status. Clothed in silk, she must be someone of wealth, but she had the hands of a worker. A Benicarian was usually one soaked in leisure or trade. Nobles wore silk or fine linen. Traders, known as the commons, wore wool or rough tanned leather. Jessica's exotic dress combined with her calloused hands made her an enigma.

Chin up with an air of defiance, she glanced his way and smiled every so often, returning her focus to the measuring cloth.

"I must confess." She pulled the measure down his relaxed arm. "I'm pleased to know you're built like a man."

Asmara stirred inside and took this chance to slip further to the fore. *Allow me to assist you since you haven't a clue.*

"It's good to know there are beautiful seamstresses with a gentle touch." The words came from Marcus, but the inflection and tone belonged to Asmara.

Jessica held her hands steady and flicked that mischievous glint to him. Wrapping the measure around his biceps, she said, "I heard a rumor that Cornelius and his squad were attacked on their way to Reginhart. Do you know anything about that?"

"Perhaps." He smiled knowing very well the tit-for-tat game.

She looked like she was trying to repress a smile. "Do you know how many survived?" Her light touch set upon his hip. "I'd be *grateful* to know anything."

Concluding the information did not jeopardize his obligation of friendship to Valder, he said, "The seneschal and one other survived."

Her smile dropped as fast as her hands. The color in her cheeks faded. She blinked and took a step backward beyond where the stool ended.

Marcus caught her before she swooned off the box and before her guards could react. This time it was clear she was not manipulating her circumstance to touch him. She really was taken aback.

"Th—Thank you," she said, regaining herself. "Thank you for telling me."

"Are you all right to stand?" The queen was thin and wispy like Platt but weighed more than double his little doe.

She nodded and pushed herself away from his chest. "Who survived?"

"One named Dash."

Her head snapped up. "He's alive?"

Marcus scratched his chin with the tip of his index claw. Jessica held her breath. He was afraid she'd fall again but, dainty as she was, she was a woman who wanted the truth just like his little doe.

"I wouldn't call him alive," he said. "There is a place I've heard humans talk about. It's a place of fear, death, and torment. Humans say they will go to this place upon termination of their life if they've done bad deeds. I think he is somewhere between there and someplace worse."

Jessica shivered and held herself. "Well, if he's riddled, then I have a lot of questions for you."

His intrigue and respect for her increased. She'd seen the meaning behind his words.

Deliberately stepping off the box this time, Jessica went back to measuring his thigh to knee with a broad grin and the most mischievous twinkle in her eye.

He inhaled deeply when her cool fingers landed on his thigh. "I have a question for you."

She didn't look up and said nothing but kept measuring body parts.

"Did Valder know Ardin was a Tier Naug before today?"

She measured the length of his feet. "Yes, of course."

Interesting, Asmara thought.

"Do demons believe in love?" She lightly touched the outside of his hip and knee with the measuring rope in between.

Goose bumps lifted everywhere her fingertips landed. The light touch was seductive, and warm arousal spread through his body. Skin on skin had always been Asmara's favorite sensation, and Marcus now understood why.

"Demons choose a mate, if that's what you mean." An image of Platt's face materialized in his mind.

Serenite do not, Asmara sneered. *And you had best remember it.*

Jessica measured the other lower half of his body. Thigh to knee, knee to ankle, she measured him, pressing her cool hands against his skin.

"Why did Valder have me let Ardin go?" He didn't know if he should say anything about Nidra and decided against it. "Aren't Tier Naug the enemy?"

She stood up and faced him. "That is a complicated story and a question you should ask the source."

"Is Ardin a warlock?"

Jessica thought for a moment. "You don't know your own kind?"

"I'm not an oath-breaker." Marcus gritted his teeth.

She leaned over and laid the rope in places she'd measured before. "It was said he was talented and could have been any kind of magic wielder. Just the same as for a warlock, once a magician reaches a certain point, he can't go back."

Unless they are riddled.

"Do you have a mate?" Her eyes flicked upward.

At each new touch, Marcus sipped the air through his mouth. "I've chosen one."

From the smirk on her face, he didn't have to tell her that his chosen one hadn't chosen him. Color returned in her face, and she stepped up on the box to measure his chest and arms again.

"Do you use claws and teeth when you mate?" she said, intent on her measuring. The scent drifting off her was intoxicating.

Asmara came through for this question, and he smiled with wicked conviction. "Would you like to find out?"

Marcus growled at the implication. His chosen mate was not Jessica. *How dare you!* He pushed the mage down.

Jessica stepped down from the box. Lips parted, she looked up at him with half-lidded eyes. "Pardon me, I need your inseam."

Marcus gasped at soft strokes against his inner thigh. She'd wrapped the measure around his leg and then stretched the rope across from hip to hip while cradling the part of him that was, in her terms, "built like a man."

He brought his index finger under her chin and lifted Jessica to her full height. "One shouldn't tease a demon."

She focused on his lips. "Who's teasing?"

Asmara plastered a smile on Marcus's face. *Your first lesson in the art of pleasure. Feel and learn, young one.*

Chapter 26

EVERYWHERE JESSICA TOUCHED caused explosions. Decade-old tensions were released, overwhelming his mind. Marcus caught a mess of blonde hair to steady himself. His sole craving pretended her caresses were Platt's.

"Oh, a sensitive one." She giggled. "Do all demons react like this?"

Marcus pushed himself up trying to shake the fog climbing into his mind that dislodged rational thought. She wasn't his little doe, and Platt was who he wanted.

"Your chosen one, what's her name?"

His heart crashed against his throat. Was he so pitiful and transparent? Marcus let out a shuddering sigh. "Platt."

"Platt Ottern? How delightful!"

He didn't know why he was prolonging his frustration. If he could get this poison out, perhaps he'd treat Platt better.

Let go. Let it fill you. The small bit of retained resistance grew.

Doe eyes and white-blonde hair broke through the swirling of his mind. One of Asmara's tricks permeated the air with vanilla musk or perhaps his own wishful thinking produced the euphoria. Marcus kept his eyes closed, bringing up Platt's smiling face, allowing a lapse in reality.

Jessica squeezed his arm with tenderness. "You all right?"

He nodded, but the empty hole in his heart ached. He didn't deserve mercy. But hers wouldn't go to waste. Stripped, more exposed now than any other time in his life, he learned "naked" meant more than a bare body.

"Jessica?"

"Yes, darling?"

He lifted his chest and gave his full attention to any nuance in her expression. "What is a wife?"

For the first time, she was gripped by seriousness. Her somber silence didn't last. Understanding adorned her smile. "A wife is the female of a marriage."

"What is marriage?"

"Marriage is a contract between two beings. A union."

It sounded like what Asmara and Tiecus had. "What does it entail?"

A lazy hand stroked along his back. Marcus settled into its calming effect. "It's a set of standard agreements. They are fairly typical across any society."

She was talking his language. Straight answers. It made him think of the queen piece of a chess set. "What are humans' standards of agreement?"

An unsettling look of incredulity flashed across her face. "Be true to your mate. Take care of them. Protect them. Provide for them. Defend their honor." Jessica paused and gave a wicked smile. "Try to have as many children as often as either is willing."

Marcus nodded to himself. Minus the impregnating, he was already providing these things for Platt. "Can more than two entities join this contract?"

For a moment, Jessica was speechless. Her face had the shock of someone trying to hide a secret. Then her poise returned. "You mean, can there be a contract between you, your demon, and Platt?" Her eyebrows rose and fell with the mention of another woman's name.

He nodded.

Jessica laughed. "You're a demon. You can do anything you want."

He sighed as she stepped away from the stool.

A finger glided along the tattooed agreement across his back.

"Sit," she said. "I have a compliment of clothes to make for you."

Marcus did sleep for a time, recovering until darkness fell and temptation called his name. Lurking somewhere in Ardin's tower was a journal. Even if he didn't need an arquebus any longer, he was curious as to what Stillwood would claim as valuable. The bonus of taking an object of power away from the magician was just as alluring.

Scanning the empty room, he remembered he didn't in fact have clothes.

Jessica's commanding voice drifted from another room, and he assumed Uros and the other Silver Elite remained with her. Finding no obvious levers to the hidden passageway, Marcus took leave out the window.

The cool night air invigorated his bare skin. If he could get over his modesty, Marcus wouldn't mind going about unencumbered by clothes. Tonight, was also a good night to slink around without restriction.

The new moon or what Tiecus called the "no-eye-night" camouflaged Marcus's pale skin in darkness. No underground passages would sneak him into the mage tower, so he bypassed patrols using his demon stealth.

He kept his eyes downcast, and light splotched his path. Careful where he aimed his attention, he crouched low, his back pressed against the cool jagged palace walls.

How Ardin receives special treatment to have his own personal retreat and lookout is beyond me. Asmara mumbled his indignity. *It's a mage tower, not a mage-that-can't tower.*

Elite guards patrolled outside Ardin's residence. Two walked the base, and two maintained vigil at the second-story entryway.

Asmara held on to his previous witticism. *Magician. Magi-can. Magi-that-can't. Magi-can't.* Asmara laughed. The cadence echoed in the hollow of Marcus's mind.

The tower's first floor was solid wall. The bottom level was said to be a dungeon. It made sense, with no windows or doors encumbering the ground level.

Stairs lead to the second story and the official entrance. One window faced opposite the door and was his usual method contacting Ardin when he was in Benicar. The magician's private chambers resided on the top floor.

The building proved itself a mage tower because of the four windows that faced each elemental direction. Ardin claiming the room as his personal quarters never gave Marcus incentive to investigate the top floor.

Watching the patrols, Marcus doubted he'd be greeted and allowed entry at the second-level door. He could demense them, but these were men he had helped train against such methods. Taking over their minds meant surprising all four of them, and time he didn't have. The option to hurt these men was immediately discarded.

That itself was a revelation. He'd never thought of the well-being of humans, not in the sense other than his own survival. Not before Platt. An odd dichotomy that some humans were only good for draining dry and others were worthy companions shifted his mindset. Valder and now Jessica had a hand in solidifying his newfound epiphany, but his little doe had shown the way.

During a gap in rotation, Marcus bolted and darted to the tower. Like so many times visiting Ardin before, he dug his claws leaving scratches in the mortar binding. Cautious of anyone inside, Marcus peered through the second-story window before stepping on the landing.

The lab remained the same mess as Marcus remembered. A gold oval that once framed a reflective portal hung on the wall, empty and now framing brick. Not even shards of the mirror were left. Small glittering pieces of sand clung to bookshelves, vials, and the floor.

Marcus stepped on the ledge, and before he could slide into the room, a wall of air threw him back. The force of the blast made him cartwheel down to the grass below. Marcus crawled on his belly through itchy stubble and scratchy weeds. His slow journey gave him enough time to catch his breath. When he got to the wall of the tower, he stood and pressed his back against stone.

He hadn't thought beyond this moment. It only seemed imperative to slip by the guards—who were now rounding the bend.

The stone at his back pulled him inside the wall. Marcus panicked, his mind wild.

Easy. Easy! Asmara clutched at the elemental force of Terra. *Don't fight it. Meld with the stone.*

Trusting Asmara, he regained his composure and allowed himself to slide into a different expanse—a different world. Like the trees in Reginhart, or scrying through a mirror, his consciousness blended with a smooth, dense element.

"I can't breathe." The stone absorbed the sound of his voice.

You don't need to, Asmara responded.

"I can't see." He waded in dense cold spheres.

Again, you don't need to, Asmara thought back. *We must find the other end.*

"What happened?" Marcus fought through marble. "Where are we?"

Inside the wall, Asmara snapped. *Stop turning in circles; go straight.*

"I am going straight."

No, you think you're going straight; veer left.

Marcus did as he was told, but the effort weighed him down. In fact, his whole body felt sluggish, and his strength only responded under force of will.

Keep going! Asmara urged. *Don't stop.*

"I can't rest for—"

No!

Comfortable weight like the security of a warm quilt on a cold night enveloped his strained muscles.

If you stop, you will never see Platt or Valder or Jessica, Asmara cried in panic. *Now get through to the other side.*

Marcus felt a solid barrier, flat and separate from the inside. Communing with the wall, Marcus felt marbles against his back push him forward. Wading through the wall might have been like trying to swim in quicksand. Thick tar might have been easier to punch through.

"Why did we . . . ?"

That fallen star of a magician put a blocking spell so nobody could get into his tower through the window. Then guards were coming. You would have been caught. I had to do something.

It started with his nose. Air touched his face once more. His body felt stretched as if two opposing forces were using him as the means of a tug-of-war. He gasped for breath. His vision blurred. Coming out was just as much work as a full day of schlepping boulders and chasing Tier Naug, but he was out of the stone wall.

Now you can rest, Asmara said once they were inside the floor-to-ceiling marble room. Marcus was in the basement. Somehow, he'd sunk down a level.

"Did we just go through stone?" He collapsed to the floor, and his hair draped around his bare knees.

Yes. You did very well.

"The stars must have burned out," Marcus uttered, "for you to tell me good job."

I give compliments when earned, Asmara huffed.

The room was filled with junk. Heaps upon heaps of a roving gypsy trove spread across the floor. Books, statues, figurines, globes, scattered jewels, precious stones, a table dedicated to a row of vials, yarn, and several metal contraptions that looked like torture devices sat at the far end.

But the most intriguing item sat in the corner of the room.

A spirit tree from the Atra Solumn faintly glowed in a beautiful green hue and waved lazy seaweed-like leaves in the air.

Marcus was speechless. Tiecus had never told him of the beautiful trees, but he knew this plant was from the Dark Land. There was nothing like it on Brightside. Its long-calloused leaves waved in the current of air catching drifts upward, outward, across itself, and down to the floor in a dance of light and mystery.

The haunting tree reminded Marcus of what he really was and what he could do.

Platt had effectively tied his hands so that he wouldn't do anything to the villagers. He had to treat them in kind. In fact, when he thought about it, he owed someone a basket of fruit—and a pie. Which in the end, he was pissed he never got.

He'd been suppressing Tiecus so much in Reginhart that he'd forgotten a vital part of who he was. Marcus was a demon. Control was his power.

The tiniest creak of a door alerted him someone had entered the room above, and he thought to hide in a rubble pile.

Marcus groaned inside. "Asmara," he mouthed the name. "Do something."

I'd rather you be caught than expose myself to humans.

"You fallen star." Marcus clenched his fists hard enough to draw blood. "You exposed yourself to everyone in Reginhart."

Different circumstance.

"So, exposing yourself to Dash, Nidra, and Platt is okay—"

We were under attack. It's not my fault you can't take a punch.

"There were spears *inside* me."

He stepped under the stone stairwell, closed his eyes to keep their demon's glow from giving him away, and listened. The Blackened Elite was so quiet Marcus couldn't hear the footfalls until the man was halfway down the stairs. Waiting until the right moment, when the soldier was all the way down, he would spring into action. All of Cornelius's trained soldiers were physically and mentally strong, but when surprised, they were as susceptible to a demens as anyone.

The human held a torch in his off-hand and a hammer axe in the other.

Good boy. A surge of pride for the guard swept Marcus. *A sword here is useless.*

Marcus front kicked the Blackened Elite on the hip and sent the man into a barrage of junk. Quick to recover, the soldier looked for his assailant, and Marcus caught the man's eye.

He focused on the demens and barreled through the confused brain. "Halt."

The Blackened Elite stood facing the spirit tree.

Marcus zipped back under the stairs and waited. Like any cautious human investigating a noise, the Blackened Elite's counterpart stepped light as a mouse down the first stair.

Marcus waited. His mentally imprisoned captive stood listless in the middle of the room holding a torch upright in one hand and the handle of his hammer axe in the other. Marcus waited for any sound from the stairs. Nothing. The Blackened Elite were a silent group.

So slight he could have missed it, a creak of leather gave a location.

Marcus waited. If he moved too soon, he could very well get his head chopped off. Too late, and he'd definitely get his head chopped off. Marcus waited. The stairs were made of solid stone. There would be no creak in the floorboards to help him ascertain the man's location.

Inside the mind of the axe-hammer-wielding soldier, Marcus gleaned the Elite guard's orders to keep everyone out of Ardin's tower, especially the black fire–breathing demon, Marcus.

Pulling on Asmara's magic, Marcus turned his captive's head. Marcus's victim, whom he'd nicknamed Stub, fought with every ounce of will. He wasn't going to give his companion's location easily.

Two more Blackened Elite stood on the stairs. Illuminated by torch light, the first soldier looked with curled-back lips and eyes filled with disgust directly at Stub.

Marcus leaped from under the stairs. He latched on to an ankle and flung the body. Stub and the other Blackened Elite went down in a tangle of limbs. Leaping after the Blackened Elite entangled with Stub, he flipped the man over.

"Sleep." It wasn't hard to get inside a jostled mind.

The third Elite guard was fast on his feet, and Marcus raised his claws. He narrowed his eyes at the Blackened Elite's claymore.

"A two-handed weapon in a small room? Did you expect this underground tower to become an open field?"

The youngling—by the bright star, this *was* a youngling—blushed in a bright-red hue.

"Answer me, boy, or I will tell Cornelius to strip you of service for more training."

Marcus blocked a swinging blade with his claws.

"Poor response." Marcus threw a right cross. The blow landed square on the youngling's chin. The third Blackened Elite was out.

Ardin's lowest floor was now a compiled mess just as bad as the second story. Marcus sighed, glad the three were mollified and alive. But the fourth would bring reinforcements.

"Your turn, mage," Marcus said to Asmara. "Where's the journal?"

Third floor, locked case, corner of the room opposite the bed, Asmara said.

Marcus quirked his head. "How long have you known that?"

Oh, did I avoid you raping me of my privacy?

Marcus gritted his teeth.

Asmara lowered the pitch of his voice an octave in a mock tone like Marcus's. *Asmara, I don't know how to throw a firebolt—you do it. Asmara, where's that memory of that circle spell. I can't find it. Oh, wait, I'll just pluck it right out of your brain, never mind that you're deep in concentration and I've just scattered your thoughts across the stratosphere.*

"I don't complain when you take me over like a marionette." Marcus wheeled to the three Blackened Elite. "I don't recall complaining when the mood suits you to bend my body to your will."

You didn't seem to mind when I guided you through . . .

"Don't!" Marcus threw up a hand. "You said you'd never speak of it."

My point is still valid, Asmara grumbled.

"So is mine."

Asmara said nothing more, and Marcus ripped into the minds of the three guards to produce a different story than what had just happened. He was familiar with Stub and started with him.

Marcus reached inside to the core of the Blackened Elite's mind sending tiny lightning sparks to different areas of brain tissue. Memories weren't located in one place. The mind stored information in chaotic streams of association. Finding the lines of memory he wanted, Marcus sent several overlaid sparks and burned the parts of the brain that contained events of the last ten minutes.

A wave of lightning jumped from one area to another in response to the pain. Avoiding the strikes, Marcus smoothed over the burnt tissue adding his version of the past events.

Through separate demens, each Elite guided him to the last place they'd seen him. Each was instructed to wait five minutes then re-enact their search. That would help overlay their memory posing the scene as fear-based instead of an actuality.

After five minutes, Marcus shuffled up the stairs. He wished he'd given himself an extra five minutes to rest, but it was too much to ask. Through the west window he saw twelve human shadows descending upon the tower. These Blackened Elite were older, more experienced. The fourth patroller brought backup possessing the wisdom not to raise alarm and approach with the cautious grace of stags. In minutes, Blackened Elites were going to invade the tower.

Marcus flurried to the top story. A book inside a case lay on an illuminated pedestal in the corner. He was no metallurgist, and he had no power over that element to overcome this obstacle. Marcus raised a fist to smash the cabinet.

Don't, Asmara warned. *They'll hear you. You'll lead them right to us.*

"What then?"

Just wait. Asmara rifled through memory.

Sticking a claw in the keyhole, Marcus played with the latch. The contraption seemed simple enough. The lock might be more of a deterrent than anything.

"Lorem dolor." Marcus spoke aloud by Asmara's will.

Nothing happened.

Asmara squeaked. The mage was affronted that his spell hadn't worked.

One claw inside the keyhole, Marcus turned his hand widdershins. The lock clanked, and the double doors of the case opened outward.

"Finally, something gone right." Marcus reached for the tome.

His hand went through the book to the bottom of the case. The journal was a mirage.

Below, the front door wailed a short creak. He was out of time.

Frustration got the better of him, and Marcus lifted his claws and gave a silent howl to the ceiling. He knew that somewhere Ardin cackled at him. The candle giving off the only light cowered to a flicker at his intense soundless rage.

Leather boots squeaked. Air pressure shifted claiming the Blackened Elite's ascent. He'd lost his chance. Choosing the east window as his escape route, Marcus strode over, then stopped.

Magician, he thought. *Master of light and disorientation. Magi-can't.*

Magicians were soothsayers, starreaders, future predictors, esoteric interpreters, and—to save their own skin—tricksters. *The book is here.*

Still cowering, the flame high on the wall danced in avoidance. It produced a shadow of a recessed rectangle. Three beams of faint light streamed down the ceiling, shedding a soft glow over the case and the illusionary book.

The air pressure in the room shifted out the windows. Soundlessly, the Blackened Elite threat loomed. One long stride brought Marcus back to the pedestal. He leaped up, clasping the candle's recess. His other hand groped inside the rectangular hole.

The Blackened Elite must have heard his claws strike stone for the air pressure whooshed out.

Ardin's journal was a heavy tome and scraped in protest. With a heavy yank, the book was his.

The Blackened Elite were too late. He took leave through a third-floor window.

The journal seemed to cling to him during the flight down. Landing on two feet and one palm, Marcus ran. Not to get away, but from exhilaration of getting away with something.

Who's laughing now, Magi-can't?

Two different forms of power had pitted against each other, and he'd won. Like a father puffing his chest out with pride in his son, Asmara's praise heightened the reward.

Chapter 27

ELATED, MARCUS STREAKED toward Jessica's quarters. He'd taken every precaution to avoid people while going to Ardin's tower, but now he loped past the great hall in his defiant glee. He'd keep out of sight of course. He did not share Asmara's desire to show off his "accoutrements." But passing by the congregation with his prize unnoticed was too great a temptation.

How childish. Asmara reproached Marcus's actions but could not diminish his glory. *Normally, you're so stoic.*

Conversation, a sound as horrid as honking geese, drifted out the windows. Rows of tables sat under the windows topped with plates. Some were filled with fruit or meat while other tables piled plates holding no more than leftover crumbs.

Marcus leaned over the window and confiscated a handful of grapes and hid under brush cover. He sat in perfect vantage point of the grand hall. Valder's constituents presented their woes to the king among marble pillars, high ceilings, and other men of various fortunes.

The crowd on the floor must have been fifty strong—none of whom were quiet. Volleys of conversation melted into incoherent gibberish.

The king sat in his live tree throne above everyone. Calling Valder's seat of power a chair was a liberal interpretation. Chairs didn't grow after they were made and typically were fashioned from wood.

Valder lounged on a basket weave of tightly woven branches supported by an intricate root system. Bolden could have been mistaken as a dwarf sitting in the "chair," yet Valder's smaller frame and body seemed a perfect fit for the high-backed perch. From the right angle, the king and the throne could be mistaken as one creature.

Valder glorified arrogant piousness entwining with boyish antics. The twisted combination resulted in unmatched self-confidence. Among green leaves and small white flowers, the king looked equivalent to an imprisoned marble sculpture. One twitch would crumble his flawless poise. His statuesque manner dared nature and man to come forward and erode his unyielding presence of mind.

The one crack he saw in Valder's command lay in who wasn't there.

Ardin's usual menacing presence behind Valder's chair was absent. Instead, the magician crouched in a tucked away corner, hidden by his cloak, head bowed, hands encased in iron balls.

Fierce satisfaction spread like poison through Marcus. Seeing the magician cowed almost redeemed insults Marcus had sustained whenever they spoke.

He didn't trust Ardin or Nidra, nor what they seemed to be. Magician. Warlock. One person. Two entities. He didn't care. Neither deserved trust.

Two Blackened Elite paired off behind Valder's chair where Ardin usually loomed. Another two Blackened Elite crossed polearms in front of their king, admitting no one near. Even Valder's chair defended the king, rising to a height six feet taller than normal—which told Marcus all he needed to know. The king was being threatened.

Marcus caught the words of conversation between two nobles returning their empty plates to the table below the window.

"There certainly is blood in the water tonight," the first noble said.

"What would you expect?" The second noble set down his plate full of crumbs and went for a clean dish. "Betrayed by his closest confidant."

"Just because he's suspect does not make him guilty."

"Who else can call forth demons?"

The two men retreated to the table piled with food, their conversation mingling with the others becoming unintelligible.

The hackles on Marcus's back rose. Yes, Valder was a deceitful, conniving, specious human. But Valder had also spared Marcus. The king's single command had stood in the way of certain death. If Valder wasn't a leader that believed in fighting at the front of the line, Marcus might never have been offered a truce. He admitted full acknowledgement. Valder had saved his life in the middle of a decimated town. A king's word held back a squad of Blackened Elite and a battalion of soldiers calling for demon blood.

This time it seemed their roles were reversed. Eric Valder was in danger, and the time had come for Marcus to pay back the debt.

Young one, Asmara soothed. *This isn't a time you can just use claws and heat to get your way. He's in trouble, real trouble. Defending his life would be easy, but this situation requires subtle sociability.* Asmara didn't need to add "my specialty" to the end of his flourish. Marcus felt the sentiment dripping from the words.

"He needs help now," Marcus growled.

No, Marcus. This is a trial. Listen. They're calling him unfit to rule. They want to strip him of power.

"The only way to strip a demon of power is to kill him."

Marcus had been listening, but the debating men puffed their chests out like roosters, waved their hands in grand gestures, and lowered and raised their voices as if in theatrical performance.

Marcus . . .

"*Fine*," Marcus snarled, slinking away in true canine style, clinging to Ardin's journal. He picked the most expedient path back to Jessica's workshop. Subtle sociability required clothes.

The window was the only exit and entrance to Jessica's backroom. He needed to leave the impression he'd been there the whole time and keep Jessica as his alibi.

Patrols had just passed. All was clear. But he wasn't sure if he wanted to bring the book into Jessica's room. He could be caught red-handed. And it felt wrong to bury it in the dirt. Still . . . Marcus clawed at the ground and received an image of a grave.

"Where did that come from?" Marcus set the book down in the hole, but his hands wouldn't let go of the book.

No, that wasn't exactly right.

He opened his hand flat. It was the book that wouldn't let *him* go.

Marcus grasped the book with his right hand leaving his left hand free. He opened his right hand, but the book spread open and wrapped pages around his fingers and palm like an octopus with tentacles of parchment. He shoved the book into the dirt and used his foot to pin it down. His hands were free, but now he wore a book as a shoe.

"I will come back for you," he growled.

The book would have none of it.

"Oh, why in the name of the Atra Solumn did Stillwood tell me to get this thing?"

The guard patrol crossed this section once every minute, and fifteen seconds remained before the next pass. Journal in hand, he climbed into the frame of the window.

The dividing curtain swooshed aside, and Jessica stepped in with purpose. Marcus swung the tome behind his back conjuring his best innocent impersonation. With a demon and a sex-starved mage as examples, Marcus did his best innocent expression. It had never seemed convincing before, and with his backside to the window, he stood there feeling caught and foolish.

Jessica whirled on him with relief on her face and a sharp tongue. "Where have you been?"

He smiled showing teeth in answer.

"Oh, never mind. You look atrocious." She threw her hands up in disgust. "You were halfway clean before I left."

Standing unnaturally stiff, he fumbled with a tome that, for all he knew, felt big enough to contain the history of all the worldly species.

Apprehension settled creases along her forehead. "What do you have behind your back?"

His blood froze. Holding the same ridiculous smile on his face, he backed toward the window. He could jump out as soon as the patrol went by. The gleam of a helmet flashed down the aisle. The guard bent down to the half grave he'd started on. Marcus shot forward not wanting the investigator to see him or the book.

Jessica assessed him with a serious gaze. He believed she was talented enough to know answers to questions without confirmation. "Please don't tell anyone I left."

She quirked an eyebrow and held out her hand. "Tell me what you have there, and I'll consider it."

The book gave him an answer to his predicament. It wasn't going to let go of him. It didn't need to stay in his hands. Pressing it along his spine, he swiped his hands off the cover and exposed his empty claws to her. The book clung just as tenaciously to his back as it had to his hands and foot.

The playfulness in her gaze returned. She gave a closed-lipped laugh and walked over to him.

Lifting an arm to touch his chest, he grabbed her wrist.

She withdrew with a smile. "Oh, if we're going to play, then I choose the game."

He let go of her wrist and stepped back into a cool breeze but far enough away from the window to not be seen.

"Is it a gift for Platt then?" Jessica waved a wistful hand. "You might want another woman's opinion."

Marcus swallowed. He chose the safety of silence.

"Is it a gift to let her know your intentions?"

It wasn't exactly a gift, but it was a relief to let her control the conversation.

Jessica challenged him with her gaze. "You would do anything for her?"

"Within my power."

Jessica gave a triumphant smile. "Is it within your power to speak to her? Because if this is how you communicate, I wonder if she even knows you're alive."

Marcus blanched at her in answer.

"You would fight for her?" Jessica set her hands to her hips. "You would lay a king's ransom at her feet? You would bed her and claim her above all others?"

He knew a word trap when he heard it. When it came to Platt, his best bet was to keep his mouth shut.

"You would do all that, but you wouldn't do the most difficult thing of all. No, you would leave that to her. All men leave the most frightening of terrors up to women."

Marcus growled at her implication of calling him a coward.

"Prove to her that you are brave then. Prove to her that you above all others can withstand what most men can't and won't."

"And what, pray tell, would that be?"

"Talk." Jessica's small frame trembled. "Hand her your heart at the risk of her destroying it. Lay yourself bare and tell her how you feel." She waved her hand for whatever was behind his back.

Horror surfaced, and the words made Marcus sweat.

She does not mean literally, Asmara said.

Jessica pointed at his nose. "That is what women give with no reserve and with everything we have. It's no less devastating when a man shows nothing in return."

"She refused," Marcus whispered.

"Did she refuse you or the temptation of your body?" Jessica scowled. "One does not always equal the other. If she feels as you do, then the pressure is on her to give you what you both want."

Marcus breathed hard contemplating Jessica's words. He remembered Platt turning away from him under a full moon. Platt's words were precise and guarded. He'd missed something, didn't understand her. There was something she needed from him, but the customs of humans were not like anything he knew.

Marcus gritted his teeth. "I've tried to show her."

"Oh, I know you'd show her a wonderful time under silk. But so many do and set off without a word." Jessica waved off the incident. "If that's how you plan to show your feelings for an unmarried maid, then no wonder she refused."

"She won't talk to me."

"Are you asking any questions?" Jessica placed a hand on her hip.

"Where is this coming from?" He had no defense, no training against a woman's scorn, and Asmara wasn't retorting. The mage actually listened.

"I'm sorry, darling." She massaged her temples and sighed. "I can see I've befuddled you."

Jessica relaxed, but Marcus thought rapidly about what cue he'd missed from Platt. What Platt said from his second-story window bore meaning, but he couldn't pin down what she alluded to in the unsaid. Platt's body told him one thing while the opposite convictions came out of her mouth. He was missing a key and didn't know where the lock *was*.

"Let's get you in the tub." She waved at his upper torso. "You're not wearing my masterpiece alongside—" Jessica wrinkled her nose. "Is that grass embedded in your chest?"

Heat spread at the tip of his nose and across his cheeks. Why was Jessica mad? He couldn't figure it out, and that very fact fueled his own anger. Jessica's assault was unwarranted. He wasn't going to let her walk all over him. She needed to understand what she was dealing with and whom in order to give proper respect.

Jessica swung back to the curtain and held it. She waved him into the next room calling out, "Ava, I need the tub filled."

Marcus stomped into the adjacent room, halting over the threshold of the opening. He crossed his arms and leaned against the wall. The leather-bound book pressed uncomfortably along his shoulder blades all the way down the small of his back. If he wasn't careful, it might weld into his skin.

This room had a tan porcelain tub, a window, and not much else. The tub's scooped back invited anyone to luxuriate in a deep soak. The square bottom took up one end of the narrow room.

Ava came through the opposite curtain divide with a bucket of water. At the sight of him, she came to such an abrupt halt that water escaped her bucket and splashed onto the floor. Ava was on the cusp of screaming for her life. Tired and distracted, Marcus couldn't tamp down his demon side instincts and seized this opportunity.

Demensing Ava took no effort. He'd captured her mind so completely he could see her whole life within a blink. Her fear wasn't being demensed. It wasn't being drained of blood. It had nothing to do with him or demons. Ava's worst fear was of her own kind and played out in her own memories.

She could almost slide her wrists out of the stocks. She tried to pull her hands out, but it didn't matter much if her arms were free except the feeling might come back in them if she could just let them down for a while. Her head was stuck in the torture device barely leaving space for her neck. Her back ached from bending over. She hadn't gotten relief in two days. If she tried to kneel, she choked against the wood.

If no one released her, she'd die from exhaustion. Suffocating in her sleep was better than what the crowd had in mind for her.

Her face itched where dried tomato juice splattered after the first wave of mockers unloaded rotten vegetables on her. Ava's neighbor Mary struck her in the eye with a particularly soft brown apple. But none of the expired fruit or vegetables matched the smell of Ingrid's chamber pot. Ava's hair reeked of pee and droppings.

Today someone brought river stones. Former neighbors, friends, and relatives stood behind a line drawn in dirt, perfecting their aim. She no longer tried to avoid the blows. It was the laughter that hurt the most.

Marcus recoiled from her mind. This was not what he had expected.

"Why?" he demanded. Now that he had wrangled his control back, he wasn't about to demense her again for the answer.

Ava crouched, hiding her face in her knees. Jessica encircled the girl with elegant arms, glaring up at him.

"You see," Ava said, rocking in Jessica's embrace. "Even he doesn't want me."

"Why?" His question was a search for logic.

Ava wiped away the streaks of water lining her cheeks. "Because I'm not pure."

"What do you mean?" Marcus insisted.

Jessica hissed, "She means she was taken by a man as an unwed maid."

The blank expression must have given him away because Jessica amended, "She bonded without being married."

Dumbfounded, Marcus stood there staring down. That made no sense.

Asmara heaved, recovering from brutalities of the memory. *Humans really would have been better off as slaves. We would have put an end to that custom.*

Tiecus summed up his opinion of humans in three words: *Rude honorless lowbrows.*

Marcus still didn't understand Ava's memory. Groping for a reason, he tried again for an explanation.

"Why?"

"Why what?" Jessica snapped.

"Why did they do that?"

Jessica pursed her lips and gave him a pointed stare. "I just told you."

He shook his head. "That is not a reason. Bond or no bond, pleasure shared between two is no reason for a group to inflict pain."

Jessica's intensity softened.

"Ava." Marcus reached to touch her, found no way to keep his claws from hurting her, and pulled back. "I can burn the memory if you wish."

"You're not here to punish me?" Ava wound her arms tight around Jessica.

"For what?"

"I thought demons preferred the untouched and that they burned the unpure."

At her words, Jessica murmured a closed-mouth laugh. "No, my dear. I've come to understand demons don't have a propensity for virgins."

Marcus frowned and cocked his head. He didn't recognize the meaning of Jessica's last word.

Those who haven't had sex yet—with another person. Like you, Asmara supplied.

Ava smiled and let out a breath. "I guess not."

He wasn't going to get more answers. From what he could tell, humans had misconceptions about intimacy, which might explain Platt's reluctance.

"My offer to erase that incident still stands."

"No." Ava wiped her eyes and broke free from Jessica's hold. "If you do, then I'll forget how my lady rescued me." Ava's tears flowed again, and the youngling leaped to Jessica, embracing her as an overboard sailor would a lifeline.

Marcus looked away, and nearly forgetting about the book, almost turned his back.

"Go home, Ava," Marcus said, daring Jessica to interfere with an emblazed stare.

Jessica glared right back. "And who exactly is going to get water for your bath?"

Ava rose. "I'll get it."

"No." Marcus peered at her from under his brows. "I can do this." Ava reminded him too much of Platt.

Jessica sighed while lifting herself up. "Go, darling. No need to upset our guest."

Ava turned on her heel and walked in a dazed calm out of the room.

Marcus waited for the girl to leave the chambers and then wielded his most severe face to the queen. "I am not a servant. I am not a pet. I am a demon. Next time, tell me what's on your mind. Don't bait me and then club me defenseless with words that have meaning under their context. Be wary of what it means to treat a demon in kind."

Jessica rolled her sleeves listening with the insolence of a weeling and said, "Someone has to train you. Otherwise, it won't be a man's sword, but a woman's bodice dagger rammed through your heart that kills you."

He took a good long moment before breaking eye contact with her. His anger wasn't depleted.

Jessica disdainfully eyed the bucket. "Now I have no one to carry water."

"You obviously need an example of a demon's power." If he couldn't command a queen's respect, how could he claim a tower or a mate?

Smiling, he knew a constructive distraction to waste angry energy and impress upon Jessica he was a force worthy of deference.

"No one need carry the water." Marcus bared his teeth in a smile too wide for comfort.

Concentrating on Asmara's favorite element, Marcus called forth Glacias.

Cold air drifted in through the open-air window ruffling the neckline of Jessica's silk chemise. The sound of crackling, that of someone walking on ice, shot spine needles up his back making him shiver.

Jessica gasped as Glacias poured itself over the tiled window sill into the room, responding to Marcus's call.

Ice freezing, then melting, pushing itself in miniature ocean tides dripped down to the marble wall spilling in a puddle. Glacias found the path of least resistance, collecting the water dropped by Ava, and snaked a gliding path to the tub.

While Jessica watched in open-mouthed amazement, Marcus climbed inside the basin, transferring the book off his back to his left hand. Holding the tome in the space between the porcelain edge and the wall, the tank effectively hid his prize from view. The trick was holding it out of water and looking relaxed.

Ice formed around the square base of the tub. Water scaled the cliff by forming into ice, melting halfway, then breaking and twisting its own path up. Climbing, Glacias spread icy claws that cracked and reformed up the porcelain tub. The agonizing ascent intimidated the speech out of Jessica. Ice melted and liquid poured inside the tub.

The water was not as cold as he thought it might be. The energy expended to freeze, and thaw made the water tepid.

He marveled at the acquired power Glacias employed for a trivial power play. Elemental water proved his point to Jessica *and* hid a book the element would never touch. Marcus was not unmoved by Glacias indulging him. Elemental water had no sense of humor like Ignis or Ventus, but Glacias understood power. The element knew how to impress with grace, style, and force.

He closed his eyes and inwardly expressed his humble thanks. Leaning against the high scoop, he acclimated to the water's temperature. Silence prevailed in the room. It wasn't until he was comfortable with the water's temperature that Jessica approached lacking her too familiar candor.

Dipping a rag in the water and wringing it out, she respectfully scrubbed his arm. Her courage and silence instilled a fondness Marcus hadn't known before. It was an acceptance different from affections he felt for Platt. Valder was wise to keep Jessica as a cohort. She eased truths and information using a body and mind of which she wasn't ashamed.

"How can you stand it? This water is winter cold." She scrubbed his chest free of grass.

"It's just water." Marcus relaxed, enjoying the contact. A woman's touch was dangerous. He could forget about anger, duty, and agreements. About a king holding court.

Jessica pursed her lips. "King Valder sent word to you." She scrubbed harder.

His legs rested against the porcelain sides waiting for her to continue either with words or hands.

Jessica reached for the arm hiding the journal. "It's good they don't know you're here with me."

Using the lip of the tub he tried to scrape the book off his hand until he realized the sound of a ten-pound mass of leather and parchment would lend her attention. Taking the rag out of her hand he washed his own limb down to the claws. "They?"

He finished quickly and handed the cloth back to her. Keeping a symmetrical appearance, Marcus laid his right hand outside the tub. *Nothing* was in his left hand. Nothing at all. At least, that was what he hoped it looked like. The journal was still grabbing on to his left hand, hidden between the wall and the tub.

"They as in the faction that does not approve King Valder for making a deal with you." She focused on her task of removing the grime off his body.

He sighed and turned to face her. "What did I say about words within words?"

"I'm trying." Jessica held his eyes.

Yes, you are. Asmara made a sniffing noise even though he kept to the background.

Marcus smirked.

As if she could hear the mage, Jessica *tsked* and splashed water on his chest. Then she became somber.

"They think it was you. They claim you sent the three demons after him."

"They think I attacked him in the hall?"

He watched her struggle with the next words. There was more on the tip of her tongue, but all she said was "Yes."

"I see."

"Some think Ardin controls you."

Roiling deceit ate the edges off his sanity. Marcus growled, "I see."

As much as ripping the magi-can't apart would please me, it's still not too late to return to Reginhart, Asmara said.

Jessica sat watching him.

Marcus remembered something about the last chess game he had played. Valder had used every piece as an expenditure. Even the queen piece that could move anywhere on the board. Queen. Jessica's title was queen. A piece that moved anywhere.

She was goading him. Trying to point him in a direction and send him off.

"What was the message Valder sent me?"

"King." Jessica emphasized in cautious undertone. "King Valder said he sent this message to you acting as a friend. He said you'd understand."

"I do." Marcus smiled wryly. Valder was calling one of their agreements. "What did he say?"

Jessica rocked back on her heels in deliverance of a blow. "Go back to Reginhart."

Marcus gripped the sides of the porcelain. The tub screeched a dreadful protest at his claws. All pretense of hiding the journal would have been lost if the book didn't pin his hand under the lip of the basin. It clearly told him "no" in the convincing way one would use a wrist lock.

"Run?" Marcus sneered. A ball of anger swirled in his core, and he began to recognize the black fire writhing inside Tiecus. "He wants me to run?"

He might have obeyed if it didn't sound like an order. But, he knew the situation and knew Valder needed all the support he could get. Why didn't he want all his allies behind him?

Jessica sat staring at him. She had no answer.

"Is he *trying* to provoke me?" He would have gotten up but for Ardin's damn journal.

"They'll kill you." Jessica stood and unfolded a towel before him.

Marcus rolled his eyes and iridescent highlights scattered a rainbow of colors across the room. "Those pompous puff pants? They'd try."

The tub squeaked and complained at the scrape of claws against its side. Marcus sat on the edge to face Jessica and keep his prize of a book hidden.

"You're no use to him dead." Jessica waved the towel for him to get out.

Marcus took the towel with his right hand and with his left, plastered the book against his back. "Yet if I leave, I can't help him." And if Valder lost power, who would stand between Marcus and a mob army?

Jessica pursed her lips. "There might be a time when he needs to flee."

Little parts of the picture puzzle fit together revealing a bigger image.

And what better place to run than a broken stronghold to an inept demon, Asmara said.

Tiecus growled, *We kill King Friend's threats. Killing makes fewer enemies.*

Marcus wasn't so sure that killing Valder's opposition made fewer enemies as Tiecus put it. He mused it could be the opposite.

"Why deny our agreement?" Marcus looked at Jessica but wasn't really speaking to her. "What could Valder gain?"

The seamstress stood clasping her hands at her waist.

"I saw." Marcus narrowed his eyes indicating he spoke to her now. "The throne raises him from reach. It knows what I know. Why not call out every ally to stand with him? No one would go against his Blackened Elite and a demon guard. Not without an army."

The journal clutched at his back. He didn't know how the tome was hanging on to him. It almost felt like a part of him. Wrapping the towel over his shoulders, Marcus stared back at Jessica waiting for an answer.

She shook her head and beckoned him to the front room. "I cannot say."

Unlike her private quarters, the receiving room was prestigious and clean. Maroon drapes shadowed the windows from ceiling to floor. Plush chairs invited visitors to stay. A wool rug emphasized a redwood table standing at the proper height to rest drinks or feet.

A painting of a stag calling for his mate hung over a hearth. Not much else furnished the alcove. Valder's emblem of an entwined oak tree took up the middle of the door. Embossed branches coiled around the frame in a flowing pattern, which resembled not an oak, but the flow and ebbing branches of the Atra Solumn tree in the mage tower. The door claimed allegiance as clear to Marcus as if Valder had peed on the wood.

Jessica held a pair of purple-and-brown tweed pants, roaming her eyes up and down his length. Her mischievous smile reflected the sparkle in her glance.

"Will you return to Reginhart?" Jessica knelt holding the trews open.

Marcus chose to ignore her imperious tone. "Yes." *Eventually.*

Jessica snugged the trews up his waist.

"When you get to unbuttoning these, get help since those claws of yours are so indicative of shredding." She slipped a hand in the crotch and adjusted him forward.

Marcus snapped his breath in. She'd given no warning, but her fingers didn't linger. The touch of a seamstress instead of a lover. Then her words registered. He'd need someone to take his pants off. "The only help I'll have is—"

"Platt." She left the trews unbuttoned and fetched a deep-purple chemise. "Treat her well. The material chafes if not fitted properly."

Meaning—Asmara translated—*Platt will have your comfort in her hands.*

Marcus looked down in contemplation. This situation screamed "potential" for good and ill.

Letting out a breathy shudder, he said, "I'll remember."

The journal pressed into his back as if to merge with him, and Marcus reached behind adjusting its corners when Jessica turned around.

He balled his fists to keep his talons from ripping the material, and she assisted with pulling the sleeves through from his front side. The ends ruffled down to his knuckles, and he rolled his wrists playing with the extra material.

"What is the function of this other than annoyance?"

Jessica's laughing eyes underscored sly planning, but she didn't answer. Starting at his stomach, Jessica smoothed out wrinkles down his shirt giving him time to prepare for yet more intrusive handling.

The pants were tight but moved with him and showed every muscle and bulge he owned. It was worse than being naked. His whole body was on display accentuating parts he'd rather leave unfondled by sneaking glances.

Next, Jessica brought a leather doublet with alternating vertical panels of deep purple and dark brown.

For one reason or another, the complimentary colors reminded him of Valder and Ardin. The pattern was simple and fitting. The dark brown offset the bold purple.

He slipped his arms into the sleeves. "Do you think Ardin called the demons?"

Jessica pulled the front of the doublet and let out an exasperated gasp. "No."

"You seem very sure of your assumption." He teetered as Jessica strained to lace his doublet. Since her last measuring, Marcus had widened two inches. The excruciating pressure of the journal along his shoulder blades and the small of his back became uncomfortable.

"I am very sure that Ardin had nothing to do with the attack," Jessica seethed, making his cheeks flush. "What have you done?" Jessica pulled at the laces of his new shirt in haste. "Did you grow in the past two hours or did you eat someone?" She eyed him with unspoken emphasis when the two parts didn't come perfectly together. The queen extracted payment for this travesty with pain. Seamstresses, he discovered, had strong, dexterous fingers.

Leather cord in hand, she strung the doublet nearly all the way closed. The material didn't stretch, grinding the book deeper into his back.

Marcus accepted the treatment with gritting teeth and a smile letting out slow controlled breaths. "Does Ardin have a twin?"

"He's never said anything about a twin."

He took note of Jessica's curt tone within her answer. Her expression was not open, but not closed. Much like his doublet.

A brown and brass belt tightened around his hips. The torture strip of thong cut off any extra air he might have wanted.

She whirled around and shouldered his weight while slipping on the longest pair of boots he'd ever seen. They came to his thigh and matched the brown in the theme of his outfit.

"When you ride, pull them up as they are." She strapped a cord under his knee for each boot. "But whenever you're able to exhibit my work, please do." She rolled the riding boots down over at the knee and displayed remarkable tooling of Valder's connected tree emblem.

Demons held no need of clothing, but the material and Jessica's sense of pride for each piece made him feel as if he was placing armor around his body. It was a welcome change. Being naked was exhilarating while simultaneously bringing bone-stripping humiliation. When she went back for yet another piece, he groaned. "Is all of this necessary."

"Oh, it's necessary," Jessica bemused.

When she brought out the final piece, he knew she was right. Everything he wore was a work of tailoring art and comfort, despite the tight fit. He'd never felt cloth so soft or tailored. Each piece was beautiful and precise. But the long coat she brought out completed the ensemble.

The coat's lapel sloped up to his chin and fell to his shoulders. The sleeves were tight but amazingly flexible. He bent his elbow, and the material formed with him without resistance. The coat reached down to the back of his knees and flowed behind him like a dangerous shadow protecting his back and capable of warding off an impending knife strike.

The trim was a continuous flow of Valder's oak tree crest. He smirked at Jessica's sly detail. Being seen with the emblem of intertwining branches effectively claimed Marcus's allegiance.

She entangled her fingers together and pressed her knuckles against her lips not successfully hiding that mischievous smile.

"You look delicious. King Valder wouldn't be able to resist you." Her smile fell with her hands. "Too bad he may never see it."

Marcus stepped forward and lifted her chin with the blunt back side of his talon. "Who says he won't?"

He left the opposite way he had entered—through the front door. The time had come to create a tide of fear in Valder's constituents and deal out the consequences of betrayal.

Chapter 28

MARCUS STEPPED UNDER the high curved ceiling. The final hall leading to Valder's throne room echoed his footfalls announcing his approach. Guards emerged from their camouflage, not blatant in their warning but close enough to hear his one-way musings. They didn't prevent him from walking the halls, but they did let him know they were watching.

It's not too late to do as Valder asked. Asmara's mental shield blocked the mage's inner thoughts from escape. This wasn't unusual, still Marcus grew suspicious.

"Demons fight." His twitching claws scraped like knives sharpening against one another. "I'm asking why don't we kill them all? Why this . . . ?" Calling it a game was admitting he was a pawn. It was not comforting.

Oh, but a lethal game it is. Asmara brushed mental fingers over Marcus's crown. *In this game, death is for the lucky ones. The unlucky don't come away with their soul.*

Marcus shuddered remembering the black ooze coming out of the cougar demon's ears, nose, and mouth. But Asmara hinted about something more foreign than Tiecus's soul-burning power.

"He did tell me, as a friend, to return to Reginhart." Marcus turned around testing the first agreement he had struck with the king. If he had betrayed Valder as a friend, wouldn't his shoulders burn?

Nothing.

But moving away from the main hall felt wrong.

"He didn't tell me when to return." Smug in his clever play of words, Marcus turned around. This direction was the right decision.

Ahhh. You're learning.

"So, your idea of keeping my oath to Valder is to sacrifice me." Marcus clenched his fists.

We are one, but we are three, Tiecus said.

Asmara shut the demon's voice out with a thunderous command. *Don't listen to him!*

Tiecus roared over the mental barrier. *I want . . .*

Marcus halted. One hand drove his knuckles into the bridge of his nose, the other squashed his claws into the meaty part of his palm. "Stop yelling, both of you."

Tiecus lowered the volume of his thoughts. *The mage and I take different vows than you.*

"We're going with deception then." A bitter smile played across Marcus's lips.

What demons are good for, Tiecus added.

"You're sure?" Marcus continued walking.

No, Asmara answered.

"What does it matter to you?" Marcus snapped, his expression hard enough to crack ice.

You want this because you want to stay in Benicar, Asmara hissed in his brain. *And you think this will bring It peace of mind. But, Marcus, think. If we stay here, you won't be in control.*

Here is food. Here, little doe is safe, Tiecus whispered circumventing Asmara's speech.

Marcus was not completely agreeable to the "food part" of what the demon had in mind. But the double-doors of the great hall stationed the final physical barriers from Valder. Decision time.

Two Blackened Elite sentinels, a father and son duo, stood by the doors. They did not motion to give him access to the room, and didn't acknowledge him, but he knew they recognized him. They'd trained with him, and none who had fought with Marcus ever forgot him. Because palace doors could only be opened by a guard's key, they were denying him admittance by ignoring him.

"Have you ever hunted with your king?"

Their intent gaze remained forward with no verbal answer. The Blackened Elite observed a rule of silence. Cornelius and Olof were the only clear exceptions.

How are they to know you're speaking to them? Asmara asked. *You speak out loud and snap at anyone apart from us that answer.*

Marcus sighed. At this point, any confirmation from Valder's throng that would tip him off as to how to proceed was welcomed.

"The two of you are the last advisors I will consult." Marcus pointedly looked at the father, then the son. "You won't be able to stop me if I so choose to rip those doors from their hinges and slice the heads off every single one of those who oppose Valder." He looked for any sign of their acknowledgement. He found none but continued. "If that is the route you think I should take then by all means stand there as statues or try and fight to send me back."

He waited.

They remained stoic.

"Your king stands against his enemies. He never runs. He always faces challengers. Valder is the wall between what he values, his people, and their destruction. But he does not need to stand alone. Open the door so that I may claim allegiance to him."

The older Elite guard twitched, and a glimmer of recognition passed over his face. The two guards shared a look, and Marcus had his answer. The guard's key was inserted, and the double doors opened simultaneously.

After Marcus cleared the threshold, the doors closed with a quiet *cha-thunk*. He stood and observed the dynamics of the room.

No one but Valder gave notice of him. Even from fifty feet away Marcus could see the king's reaction. Valder closed his eyes and shook his head side to side almost unperceivably.

His heart sank, but it was no time to second-guess his decision.

The nobleman who spoke circled the floor in front of Valder. "I trust your grace implicitly, but you must admit the circumstances point in one direction." He wore clothing lined with green jewels the size of buttons. Pearls in the shape of spoons dripped down the front of his doublet. The rest of his clothes gave an impression a cougar demon had swiped him at the sleeves and thighs, but the slashes were uniform and precise with bloodred cloth spilling neatly from the cut fabric. Marcus thought the fine, controlled rips a testament of the noble's battle skills or lack thereof.

Puffy sleeves spilled matching red cloth guts. Marcus would have suggested Jessica help repair his worn clothing, yet the pattern of the fabric's open wounds was too symmetrical, too evenly spaced to be an accident.

Human's style is way too puffy and dramatic, Asmara commented.

Eighteen constituents that Marcus knew were loyal to Valder separated themselves on the right side and glared at the not-so-pleased-with-the-king– looking side of twenty-three. Nine nobles who apparently weren't choosing sides, milled around the outskirts. In sixty minutes, this trial had changed from hostile to murderous.

This is the way. Tiecus stirred irritably.

I agree that results are not always found at the end of a claw. Asmara echoed Valder's words with his own flare of mixed metaphor. *But there is another way.*

"How?" The entire situation smelled of ambush. Marcus was being funneled in, and he knew it.

To his right, Marcus heard someone clear his throat. "Sir."

Marcus faced a door server in white overcoat and pants. The man froze, and Marcus pressed his index claw against his lips, signaling the universal "be quiet" command.

"What is that one called?" Marcus glanced at the ostentatious noble parading in front of Valder.

"The current lord Reginhart here to petition the king for more troops to attend his township against the Tier Naug attack." Believing he was fulfilling his designation, the servant babbled. "He's cousin to King Valder. Next heir to the throne. Master of Reginhart."

Marcus growled, "Master of Reginhart?"

The presumed lord Reginhart paced in greater agitation. "Battalions are moving to the west, and you're trying to tell me we are not at war? Three hundred men deployed, more Elite around us than ever, Ardin accused of treason, Van Hoepen no longer reporting back, and demons running around the palace grounds trying to kill you, and we're not at war?"

Valder stared at the ostentatious noble. "There has been no declaration against us." The king's boyish air conflicted with his responsible posture. "Ardin is only suspect. He is under questioning."

"Only suspect?" Lord Reginhart pointed at two guards hovering over a dark lump. "Our best magical defense is in bells, Cousin."

Valder waved off the significance. "Your concerns are independent occurrences."

"I just want to know how I can help." Lord Reginhart flourished a grand gesture with his arms.

Marcus slid the thumb claw down each of his fingered talons, ringing echoes off the pillars and walls. The screech halted all conversation. If he thought serendipitous glances from Blackened Elite were uncomfortable, he knew better now. Eyes of judgment, horror, and suspicion were now directed his way. Everyone froze. That's when Marcus realized why Valder had told him to go home.

People were more likely to scream and run from demons—not debate with them.

A little late now . . . Asmara said.

Marcus lifted his chin and straightened his back. He had to take hold of the situation before these men formed a mob and came after him.

"He doesn't need your help, *Lord Reginhart*." Marcus sauntered down the stairs with a swagger he'd seen other noble's possess.

Their sneers, horror, and disquiet bounced off his armored ensemble of boots, trews, and overcoat. Even Valder's sardonic darkness flew over him.

Marcus led a direct path to the tree throne. He paid no heed to the humans parting in his forward wake.

I already have agreements with him, so how is this to work? Marcus stalked in leisurely dire wolf fashion giving him time to think and Asmara to answer.

The hidden soldiers along the side of the room stepped forward. The rest of the crowd began to back further away.

I will proclaim King Friend alpha. Tiecus disguised his command as sage advice. *Let me out.*

Oh yes, that'd be smart. Asmara's tongue turned to the demon. *He won't let you eat his throng if you're part of it.*

Marcus hoped his hesitation was seen as leisurely confidence. *What would you have me do, mage?*

Oh no. Not this time. I'm going to keep my mouth shut, since you don't listen to me anyway. All the while watching you continually mar your body with script.

The king's brooding expression changed to a come-hither glint. Valder licked his lips, straightened his short hair with dexterous fingers, and pulled at his emerald green doublet.

Jessica's right. You must seem intimidating. By the stars, where is a mirror? I must have a look.

Stay focused. Marcus noted the Blackened Elite beside the king readied themselves in a fighting stance.

You don't see how claiming him your king could be a huge mistake? Asmara huffed.

Marcus stood in front of the steps that led to Valder's throne. Asmara's words were harsh but true. Yielding to Valder in any way was not going to be easy. He took courage in Platt's strength. Her power wasn't skill with swords or even words but a self-sustaining confidence.

When she had stood before her uncle, Riley, and all those villagers exposing the rare gift she had as a blood doll, she'd sealed her fate with him to protect the entire town of Reginhart. Without complaint or denying her weakness and in full knowledge that he could take advantage of her, Platt had displayed her backward gift as an offering in full view of everyone.

Her fortitude was the secret of being vulnerable. Standing before her enemy, friends, and family and showing everyone her weak side, making no excuses for it, not hiding it, proved she was the strongest person he knew. Hiding a weakness was easy. But claiming weakness in full view, unwilling to keep it as a scar to hide, was undoubtedly brave.

It was also frightening. Someone that acknowledged themselves as fully as she had had no real vulnerabilities. To claim her as his, Marcus would have to rise to her stature. This was the most difficult thing in his life he'd ever had to achieve.

Ardin growled in possessive warning. The bells clamped around his hands clanked on the floor.

Marcus realized he'd been staring at Valder without any indication of his intentions. The vine chair still raised Valder to its full height. He paid Ardin no mind and climbed the steps halfway to the throne.

Murmuring broke out across the pond of humans. The smell of apprehension with a mixture of excited anticipation clogged his nose. He couldn't pinpoint who, but the cloud of immobilized fear mulled together with the kind of resentment that created angry mobs.

Olof and one other Blackened Elite crossed their spears protectively over Valder's path.

The king sat as inanimate as stone. But his eyes dictated an order for Marcus to come closer. Valder didn't blink or breathe. Behind those eyes was requited lust.

Marcus turned inward for guidance.

Yielding to a superior is not cowardice. Tiecus emphasized his new conceptual knowledge of what "no" meant.

Marcus wanted to turn and run. Giving fealty to the king could backfire. Forcing Valder to claim him an ally was a risk. Running back to Reginhart was easy. With a book-straight back, Marcus dropped to one knee.

"My king." Marcus near sighed the words.

An explosion of chaos erupted. Marcus had thought this action would protect him; instead, it brought the exact opposite. He couldn't see them, but he knew the crowd was scrambling. Angry shouts reverberated in the great hall.

Over the squabbles of skin-prickling cries, the king's voice slithered a path to Marcus's ears. "Clever. But we both know that's not how a demon shows allegiance, and you've never claimed to be human."

I see you chose life over your soul. Asmara was more amused at the human's reaction than the pseudo-allegiance claim. *Not how I would do it, but effective.*

"You have sided with demons going against man and nature . . ." One nobleman pointed a finger at Valder.

"That is no demon," Lord Reginhart chided. "Demons don't bow or . . ."

"What have we come to . . . ?" wailed another voice in the crowd.

Tiecus winced at the honks and blares of the flustered humans. *Allegiance claimed. Eat them.*

The noise volume became incomprehensible. They sounded as coherent as goats. Marcus shook in defiance of his need to turn around and devour the screaming prey.

"Silence!" Olof pounded his pole arm against the marble floor.

Marcus gritted his teeth from the loud vibrations.

When the room was quiet again, the tree throne lowered the king to floor level. In the slow draw of an apology or great loss, Valder said, "Rise, Lord Marcus."

Chapter 29

VALDER DIDN'T LOOK happy to see him, yet the king didn't seem to be able to look away. Libraries of unread emotion delivered sadness, excitement, and desire within Valder's eyes.

The temptation to know what the king was thinking itched at the back of Marcus's mind. The only problem was—if he demensed Valder—then he'd know what was behind the dark gaze.

You don't want to know, Asmara warned. *Stay naïve as long as you can.*

Valder flashed that boyish grin before he dropped all emotion behind a curtain of calm.

Still shaky about his proclamation and its implied consequences, Marcus draped himself across the stairs like a languid tiger ready for petting. It was not a comfortable stance, but the effect on Valder's would-be throng and attackers was enough. A deep, throaty rumble from Marcus pushed away the crowd inching toward the king.

Well done, Tiecus growled. *Now eat them.*

Marcus stretched a grin expressing the control he had over Tiecus's bloodlust, exposing knife-sharp teeth. Gasps emanated from the crowd.

"Lord Grimmoore," Valder started off. "I rather think Marcus has joined me." He then turned to the pompous man holding the center attention. "Lord Reginhart, I would think you of all people would know what a demon looks like." The king waved to Marcus and said, "Sir Tallie, this is the kind of peace I have achieved. To the rest of you, I introduce you to Marcus. It would be wise to treat him with respect."

A noble dressed all in black stepped forward pointing his finger at Marcus in agitation. "No matter what, in the end this creature will destroy us."

"He is the creature that has saved me," Valder snapped. "Your king. The one person that holds Benicar together, united."

Behind him, Marcus heard a heavy footstep land. He guessed Olof was giving Lord Grimmoore a Blackened Elite–perfected scowl.

"Marcus," Valder hissed out a whisper. "Should I bring in a chair for you to sit in?"

Lord Reginhart strutted over. "So, this is the not-such-a-rumor demon."

Marcus balanced on his legs and rose like a marionette on strings. Humans tended to get unnerved by the agility of demons, and Lord Reginhart was no different. His eyes widened, and the lord held his breath.

"Lord James Reginhart," Valder said. "Extend your gratitude to Marcus, our new proxy defending the town of Reginhart."

"You won't need him long." Lord Reginhart returned to his smooth, ostentatious manner. "I plan on going back the first of spring. I will protect Reginhart, as I always have. As my family always has."

Ardin murmured, "Coward," under his breath so low Marcus thought he was the only one that heard him.

"There's no need for you to go back." Valder lifted his words as easily as a hawk soared. He knew the signs of Valder's agitation. Lord Reginhart was an irritant. "Marcus has been keeping the town free from vermin quite well. There is a place for you here, in Benicar. Indulge me and stay with us a while longer." Valder smiled like this was all a game and he'd put Lord Reginhart in checkmate.

I see we're playing the keep-your-enemies-close strategy, Asmara chirped inside.

Marcus stepped forward to Lord Reginhart and said, "You are the descendant of the Dark Stag?" He recalled Platt's story about the demon named Reginhart and wondered if the stories of the demon-human offspring were true.

Lord Reginhart challenged him by making eye contact, and Marcus smiled with a preening satisfaction. Before Lord Reginhart could react, Marcus pushed through the boundary of the man's mind.

He whipped past memories to the smallest roots of ancestry. In that single cell, Marcus ripped backward through time. Lord Reginhart's descendants, from mother to great-grandmother, whisked by until he saw a demon within the ancestral memory.

The black stag sporting antlers, intertwined like tree branches, bayed out his possession across a familiar hill— the same hill the tower now stood upon. His iridescent eyes flooded light over the cliffside where the stronghold of Reginhart now stood.

Upon closer inspection, the antlers didn't just intertwine, they moved. They swayed as boneless as the Atra Solumn tree in Ardin's basement.

The stag was huge—his back coming to seven feet, his noble head and neck rising to nine feet, and his antlers could reach a second-story window without effort. Knowing how far and wide demon stags jumped, this one could scale Reginhart's three-story wall with no reservation. The vision was only ancestral memory, but the dark stag stared at Marcus as if he were there in Reginhart with him.

Far off in the distance, bells rang through the air.

The stag turned to Marcus and stomped one cleft hoof. "I see you, wolf-ram of the devourer clan, keeper of black flame."

Marcus stepped back but was held in place by an invisible wall. "You are Reginhart?"

The stag bore his icy stare and flicked his ears forward, but Marcus looked to the town. The bells were ringing. Did that mean Platt was in trouble?

"You hear the bells." The demon Reginhart spoke, his words clear and precise unlike Tiecus's choppy speech. "The keep claims you master, yet you prefer to stay away." The stag faced him, antlers flowing in air, but Marcus knew a touch from those waving extensions would kill him. Every single body part Marcus owned wanted to vacate the demens.

"You would abandon my children." The stag demon's eyes glowed red at this statement—the color of death. "You would abandon my daughter kin pledged to you."

"No!" Tiecus lent strength in the response, leaving Marcus breathless—finally, Tiecus had understood a concept incredibly difficult for demons.

"Good." Demon Reginhart turned to the trees where the bells rang and bounded into the woods like a rabbit on fire.

Marcus pulled his mental tendrils back and dropped the demens.

Lord Reginhart stumbled back and fell on his ass. People around him backed up, afraid to touch him. The man looked up and in palpable fear said, "What are you?"

The derogatory statement brought Marcus back to reality. He was in Benicar. Surrounded by betrayers, opportunists, and a handful of loyal men dedicated to Valder. Anger grabbed on to him, and Marcus rode it through. No matter what he was, how many entities were inside him, or what allegiance he gave, he was his own being.

"It would not be wise for you to return," Marcus hissed. "The villagers know the difference between a real demon and a supplanter now."

Valder quickly turned his head and made to cover his mouth in an act of stroking his chin.

From the corner, Ardin chuckled. "Your most noble cousin needs to be more careful." The magician stood faceless with his cloak covering everything but hands and feet. Still, Marcus knew the magician's gaze was upon him. "Now for me."

Olof stepped forward and pressed his polearm against the magician's chest. "You will wait until called."

"He is the one that can prove my innocence," Ardin hissed.

"The king decides your fate." Olof stomped the blunt end of his spear on the ground.

Valder ignored Ardin, kept his eyes on Marcus, and waved a casual hand in Lord Reginhart's direction. "What did you see?"

Alphas have two rules, Tiecus cut in, distracting his epiphany. *First rule, always follow the alpha.*

Marcus tensed but answered in his own truth. "I saw that the original demon of Reginhart tainted his seed if this *lord* is the result."

A flutter of gasps filled the room. Then the incessant whispering began.

That was pushing a bit too far, Asmara whispered while shaking his head.

Cold calculation flittered under Valder's eyes, and his face radiated ice and darkness as he leaned back in his chair.

You are no good at politics, Asmara said. *I think you just insulted them both. They are related.*

"Did you receive my message?" Valder mumbled knowing Marcus could hear him over the commotion.

Marcus might not be good at politics, but he understood the art of secrets in full view. He lowered his voice and said, "I did."

The curve of Valder's lips turned up but not in a smile. It had a feeling of gratification as if Marcus had proven him right. As if he'd passed some test.

Valder shifted himself toward his magician. "Will you look into Ardin as you did Lord Reginhart?"

Rule two, Tiecus said. *Always challenge the alpha.*

Oh, how surprising, Asmara huffed. *Demons have conflicting rules.*

Marcus blanched. *You would see the two rules as conflicting, but they aren't.*

How so?

Rule one is for safety. Rule two keeps the throng strong by keeping the strongest leader in power.

"No." Marcus stood firm. "I will not demense Ardin."

Murmurs continued to flow and echo in the room. But the audience remained in the background.

Valder's smile retained its cold properties as if he had expected the answer. "May I ask why?"

He wasn't sure how to answer and lifted an eyebrow at Valder. The king stared at him waiting for an answer.

Marcus sighed. "I have seen him bleed another warlock's eyes from the feat. I don't want the same."

"Worthless demon." Olof spoke in a low pitch. "Cornelius should have killed him."

Marcus growled a deep resonant threat.

"If he had," Valder snapped, "then I could very well have been dead. Ardin could be celebrating my demise with Nidra right now."

"You!" Ardin spat, pulling his chains and pressing against Olof's polearm. "You believe you've known all of it? You don't know Nidra like I do."

Valder seemed to consider this while scrutinizing Ardin. Their eyes locked together until the magician's anger drained away.

Ardin closed his eyes and shook his head. "I've failed. We failed. All we taught you was bitterness and revenge." Ardin remained poised, but his voice cracked. He sank to his knees with the iron balls clanging on the ground. The magician's spine, always perfect in posture, folded. The ever-looming dark, hooded presence that warned of death to any who so much as touched Valder withered and dispersed. It was like watching the demise of magic within a being.

The impenetrable fortress that was King Valder watched the magician break in half as if it meant nothing. A chill ran down the middle of Marcus's spine.

Valder turned back to Marcus. "Tell me of Sir Van Hoepen. Is he well?"

"Sir Van Hoepen"—Marcus mused to himself at Cornelius's state—"is riddled."

Olof's surprise matched Lord Reginhart's outrage.

"What?" Olof said.

"Madness!" Lord Reginhart flapped his puffy sleeves in the air. "This is what you get for employing a demon!"

Valder snapped his torso upright in his seat. "James, be still and listen. You'll learn something that way." Valder directed himself once more to Marcus. "Is there any way that can be remedied?"

"I could take off his head," Marcus said with a hopeful lilt. There would be about as much love-loss for Cornelius as there was for Ardin.

"I'd rather you did not." Despite Valder's thin shaped eyebrows and the shallow ridge of his nose, the king could give a menacing browbeating when he wanted. "What of the Tier Naug?"

"What of the Tier Naug?" Marcus snapped. "Be more specific."

Olof puffed up and leaned toward Marcus, threatening pain for any disrespect to his king.

"Last we spoke, Cornelius said he couldn't tell what had attacked him." Valder leaned forward. "Whoever converted him to be riddled either made a very poor calculation or had a genius of a plan."

He's looking for a confession, Asmara said. *Or confirmation.*

All the muscles in Marcus's face drew inward.

He doesn't know what you are, Asmara reminded him. *He thinks you are a warlock.*

Valder tilted his head over to his magician and smiled back at Marcus. "Can you riddle more?"

The mere thought of it pushed air into Marcus's lungs. *He wants to riddle Ardin?*

Ardin raged, "You're asking for madness!"

"What choice do I have now?" Valder snapped back.

"I've been loyal to you to a fault. I've used my talent to split myself into two for your benefit. I've done all you ask, and yet you doubt me." Ardin's voice strained from under his hood.

"We will see how loyal you are after you've been in shackles for a while," Valder quipped and waved at the magician. Two Elite guards picked Ardin off the ground.

"If it's all the same, I'd rather return to Reginhart." Marcus felt a tingling sensation rise from his feet as if a vine grew up his legs and bound him to the floor. Light-headed, Marcus swayed. He wanted no more of Valder's tricks and secrets. He didn't want to be manipulated by demons, humans, Serenite, or anyone else.

With great effort, Marcus stayed upright. He felt so heavy he wanted to sit on the floor.

"Marcus!" Valder didn't hide the concern on his face. "What's happening to you? What is that?"

Vines rose from the floor, winding themselves around Marcus's legs. Two ivy appendages encased Marcus's wrists. They forced him down on his back. He twisted, panicked as more wrapped around his torso. Marcus flexed his fingers, snapping taut creepers, yet the plants didn't relent, pulling him further into the floor. The journal cut into his flesh. Its edges drove into his shoulder blades.

Ardin's insane cackle hit Marcus like a physical blow. "You've been careless, demon. Someone knows your names."

"Stop what you're doing magician." Valder stood from his chair.

Ardin lifted his arms to insinuate his iron bonds and hissed, "It isn't me."

Marcus struggled to free his arm, flexing his hand, using his claws to cut the lianas in half. Many of the vines snapped, but more came, driving him further down, pushing him through the floor.

Valder raised his voice to panic. "Ardin keep him here."

"What do you want me to do?" The magician clanked the bells on his hands.

There was a commotion, and then Valder was kneeling over him.

Marcus broke several of the ropes driving him down, but more came.

"Damn you, demon." Wild determination broke the mask Valder clung to. The king clasped a hand over Marcus's throat nearly choking him. "I command you to stay here."

Power surged in his body. The force of the command near ripped him in half. Part of Marcus sank further. The other part was losing the struggle to stay—Valder's eyes told him that much.

The king joined in his scramble to throw off the ivy, but it was too late.

Voices muffled into vibrations, and the floor devoured him.

Chapter 30

THIS TIME WHEN Marcus seeped into the stone, he didn't panic. As before with the mage tower, his essence raked through heavy boulders. Dirt enfolded him. The root of a tree snagged his essence and pulled Marcus through its gnarled arms. Preventing the unconscious act of breathing was odd. Friction burned him.

Marcus tumbled underground—he understood it instinctively, yet the concept caused a whirlwind of confusion. He was being whipped around faster than the speed of thought. His limbs folded back over themselves twisting and rolling as if his body were not made of flesh and bone but of rope. He could scarcely hold on to his own name being thrown from one sharp angle, spiraling down, then careening into knotted fingers tossing him like a hot stone.

Asmara screamed in his mind. Coherent thought wasn't possible. Protectively, Marcus wrapped his essence around the other two entities.

The mage screamed out again barely registering in this underground hurricane.

Marcus barely made out one word, ". . . background . . ."

His skin burned as his soul began to grate against a tunnel too small for him but being forced to fit through.

Hands within him pulled him back, inside himself. Asmara shouted again, *Background! Now!*

Folding himself into Asmara, letting the mage come to the forefront, Marcus found himself on his hands and knees inside a stable bubble.

"You know," Asmara's voice rang clear. "I am a mage. I have traveled roots systems before."

There, sitting on a bench with Ardin's journal in his lap, Asmara stared at him with an indulgent smile. This was the first time Marcus had seen the mage directly without a mirror, without a memory, plain as he could see before him.

"Although"—Asmara waved a hand—"it was very chivalrous of you to try and protect us."

It was strange seeing Asmara's mouth move. The Serenite was stunning. Beautiful, androgynous but leaning toward a male influence. Tight curls framed his angular face, mimicking the pigtail tips of his ears. Spirals curled the ends of Asmara's long lobes, a mark of age for a Serenite, and wisps of crow's feet proved his extensive life. Blue eyes, neither the color of sky nor sea, sparkled sharply with a mind full of mischievous wit. Eyebrows slightly slanted and a generous mouth, that matched his love of hearing himself speak, completed his image.

Marcus got to his feet. The bubble jostled but being inside the translucent dome was steadier than being on the outside of it. This was nowhere near the torture of spinning ass over teakettle.

Tiecus growled next to him, leaning his head down as if to relieve the pressure from his horns. The demon was breathing heavily in exhaustion.

For all of Asmara's beauty, Tiecus was the exact opposite. Teeth only meant to rend and tear, puncture and wound were prominent features of his face. His long snout wrinkled in agitation. His red eyes glared with so much pain and hate that Marcus felt as much sorrow as fear for the creature. Horns curled angrily around his ears like a ram, but his body was shadow and mist.

Marcus had seen a myriad of odd sights, but none were as unsettling as seeing Asmara and Tiecus as separate beings before him. It was far more familiar seeing all three of them standing in the same place, like ghosts in front of a mirror.

"So." Asmara used the word like a threat. "Where are we going?"

Marcus threw up his hands. "I don't even know what's happening."

"We've been summoned." Asmara pointed to Tiecus. "I've told no one his name, so whom have you told?"

Exasperated, Marcus pulled his hair at the scalp to relieve stress. Surprised at the shortened length of his fingers, he pulled his hands away. His claws were gone.

"What . . ." Rolling his hand around, Marcus was more interested in this change in him than the answer. "What is happening? Why are we not together?"

"It's the trees." Asmara stood up holding the book against his side. "They see us like this. It's just an illusion. Now answer me. Who knows our names?"

Marcus glanced over at Tiecus. "Platt."

Asmara set the book aside and walked to the demon. "I should shove you out of here and watch your essence burn."

Marcus stared down mesmerized at his human hands. "Dash knows your full name."

"It doesn't work that way. If it did, we'd be in Ziodonia." Asmara placed a hand on his hip and narrowed his eyes at the demon. "To summon us, they have to know all of our names. Knowing just one of us doesn't work."

"Don't make this solely his fault." Marcus swayed as the bubble jostled. "Besides, false threats don't become you. You'd never part with Tiecus."

Asmara straightened from looming over the demon and turned his sharp eyes to Marcus. "Why in the stars would I not want to be rid of that thing?" The mage threw a hand to Tiecus.

The bubble they rode in shattered, and the mage lost his balance, catching himself on Marcus. Asmara adjusted Marcus's new coat, swept the Enforcer's black hair forward, and parted the silk mane to rest in front of the purple coat.

"If we die," Marcus stated in a monotone voice that gave away his anger, "you'd die."

"Maybe I'd find peace then." The smile on Asmara's face mirrored pure hate.

Marcus let coils of venom out. "You want power with no regard to the cost. You think you can control a demon and twist him to throw off some ancient curse that you and your people deserve."

"You've been listening to Dash too much." Asmara's eyes twinkled in amusement. "Throw off a curse? You think that's all I want?"

"You need me to control him." Marcus glanced at Tiecus.

The demon snorted.

"Oh." Asmara tsked. "You think I was having a problem controlling a demon?"

"Isn't that why you made me?"

Asmara reached up and cupped Marcus's face. The chaos in the Serenite's eyes filled with the depths of a galaxy. "No."

Suddenly, Marcus's safety sphere shattered. Once more, Marcus was the combined essence of Asmara and Tiecus. After being siphoned through marble, the floor presented the only pliable but dense exit. Air hit his skin, and every nerve blazed like fire. Marcus shattered. He no longer had a body or voice to scream, only memory, knowledge, thought and essence, all the elements every demon and mage possessed to rebuild themselves after being summoned.

Marcus reconstructed his physical form starting from the inside. Dust particles colliding with unprotected nerves scrambled his senses. He couldn't reshape bone and muscle fast enough to avoid feeling every stretched cell, every organ, his heart, stomach, and brain. It hurt.

Asmara snarled at him, forcing him to recreate his own organs before Marcus could convince himself he didn't need any to avoid the pain of it all.

Overlaying the insides with skin and stretching it over his body set his mind on fire. Before losing his nerve, he rebuilt the clothes made for him to the finest detail.

His coat, boots, pants, everything was separate but grated against his sensitive skin. He was *inside* the sun, what Tiecus called the "bright eye" as far as he was concerned. Depleted of his reserves, Marcus collapsed face-first on Asmara's sleep chair, the angle bending his spine backward, but he didn't care.

Well done, Asmara complimented in mock appreciation. *You even managed to reconstruct Jessica's masterpiece for you.*

"Fuck you to Atra Solumn." Marcus rose from his uncomfortable position in a drunken slavishness. He was going to kill the person that summoned him here as soon as his eyesight fully recovered. Being able to see past an arm's length would lend him a direction.

If you knew she had our names, Asmara sniffed, *you should have taught her the proper way to summon you.*

Stillwood's pine-and-soap root scent permeated the room along with traces of Platt's forest vanilla perfume. At the quiet snap of a closing door, Marcus maneuvered a way to his feet. There was no one in his room.

Unbalanced and uncoordinated, Marcus took fumbling steps out the room and halfway down the stairs when he halted at the sound of Platt's sobs. Hearing her cry wrenched his heart and abated his anger.

"Lassie," Cornelius's voice rasped. "I fear I won't be around to assist you wit' your plan."

Marcus crouched down enough to see Platt kneel beside a bloody lump of a body propped up against the staircase wall. This mutilated figure was the torn and shredded body of her stepfather.

Dash crouched with Platt, wiping blood off the body with a wet towel. Opposite them, Stillwood crouched in deep concentration. No one noticed Marcus on the landing.

"He'll come." Platt's hand seemed dainty inside one of the lump's bloodied paws. "I know he will, and when he does, he will know how to heal you."

The lump of flesh barked a laugh, harsh and determined, then drowned to a murmur. "You've done your best." The lump's voice was gravel and ice and belonged to Cornelius, but the body was somewhat mutilated.

Dizzy and fumbling over his own feet, Marcus did not make the ideal fighter. He didn't care. Someone was going to answer for dragging him through roots.

Good sense was never your strong point even when clear minded, Asmara said.

Platt gasped and hopped up. Her eyes sought Marcus out and ran to him. She clutched the lapel of his new coat. He could no longer avoid her tear-streaked face and crackling desperation. "Please help my father."

"It's too late for me, and my demon knows it." Cornelius was surprisingly triumphant. In fact, he sounded elated.

Marcus found his equilibrium and took tentative steps toward Cornelius. "What happened here?"

Dash greeted him with a firm nod.

The seneschal's wounds were deep, but they should have been healing. Cornelius should have been lusting for blood, and his demon should have been helping him with the pain. But Cornelius was mending as fast, or rather as slow, as a human.

"Who did this?" Marcus inspected the damage with grave comprehension.

"Get lassie away." Cornelius lulled his head. "I want no temptations."

Cool hands took ahold of Marcus's face, and with resigned determination, Platt said, "I'll give you what you want if you help him live."

Marcus blinked at her. His shoulders dropped down. Claws impeded his fingers once more, preventing full contact with her cheek. "What I want you can't give, and I wouldn't take it from you even if I could."

Her soft eyes were the quintessential of innocence. "Then I will find a way, but you must help him."

Platt held on to him. With every fiber of her body, she seemed to will him to do her bidding.

Marcus searched her pleading eyes. "Can you forget Riley?" His breath caught. "Forget whatever wrong he's done to you? Can you leave the world of men and enter the lair of a demon?"

Platt's eager willingness burned out. She didn't need to speak. Her face told him she would never be able to discard the memory of the rude youngling.

Marcus would mourn the death of his soul later. Right now, his little doe needed him.

The dregs of pain from the summoning had drained his will. Marcus stripped off his overcoat. Dash stepped in front of Cornelius with caution.

Platt rushed the stairs with purpose.

"Where are you going?" Marcus asked her.

She didn't answer and kept climbing the stairs.

Marcus sighed and let her go. His attention turned to Dash. "Well, are you going to let me see if I can help or not?"

Dash stepped back and Marcus knelt by the seneschal's side ready to give condolences. There was nothing he could do for Platt's father. Marcus would abide by Cornelius's wishes and leave him to die.

"Who did this?" Marcus whispered.

Cornelius rolled the unmarred eye to him. He was a mass of blood and ripped skin. Loose flaps of meat dangled from arms and legs. His stomach was held fast by five belts.

"Pity is a 'uman trait." Cornelius smiled with torn lips.

Wrecked or not, Marcus was going to punch him in the face if he flung insults.

Platt dropped beside Cornelius holding one of Asmara's books on alchemy. She opened to a random page and held the book in front of her father's face.

"Read it to me." She flipped to another section. "Look for what can heal you."

Another book lay next to Dash. The mage recognized it as one written before the Serenite reached the secluded forests of Ziodonia.

Is that the book on the Atra Solumn? On the floor? Asmara was appalled at the casual treatment of the revered book on demons—only respected by the mage because it was a book.

Cornelius squinted for a moment and then leaned his head back on the wall and closed his eyes. "Daug'ter." The word was a plea.

"No!" Fire couldn't have burned worse than her command. "If you die now, I will become the whore you think I am."

Cornelius chuckled. "I versed you well. And I was wrong. It's *him* I blame. And me."

"Little doe." Marcus tried to cajole her away from Cornelius. The seneschal was in a dangerous state.

Platt swung up and dropped the book by her father's bleeding leg in one motion directing her angry fire to Marcus. "You will heal him."

Marcus straightened and gave back his own elemental force. "He is dead already."

"No! There's still time. If you leave him to die, I will not stay here with you." Platt's breathless threat echoed up the high stone walls.

He pulled back and looked at her anew. She was the daughter of Rehan Ottern and Cornelius Van Hoepen. She was threating him. If he'd been bound to stay in Reginhart as she probably still suspected he was, it would be a death sentence. Tiecus would run out of food. They'd starve to death.

Marcus pointed his chin over at Dash. "Cornelius may die anyway."

The envoy too was riddled now. Marcus could control Tiecus with the enticing smell of loosened blood, but Dash was new to demon's cravings and their power.

"What?" Dash widened his eyes. "No. I would never hurt him."

Marcus took in the mixture of fear and admiration from Dash. "If your demon didn't do this . . . tell me what happened."

"I won, that's what 'appened." Cornelius held up an eating knife and struggled to speak. It was Bernard, the last guard within Ardin's tower, sacrificed himself all over again. "It won't 'ave a'old of me anymore."

Marcus snapped in a breath. "You fought with your own demon?"

Tiecus had done the same to Marcus. The demon had challenged him, and Marcus had ripped their one body to shredded pieces before the demon had relented. "You did this to yourself."

Cornelius chuckled. It seemed he was too weak to take his own life. "Tore us up well and good. This thing won't be a problem anymore."

Indeed.

Marcus put a hand on Platt's. "If he lives, I want one wish."

"Platt." Cornelius pushed the word out.

She looked up at him with pleading eyes. "Anything."

"No." Marcus kept his focus on Platt. "Not anything." He raised his index finger to exaggerate the point. "One wish."

"Yes."

He dropped before Cornelius and took the cutlery from the seneschal's flimsy grip.

"I'd die before you make my lassie an unwed strumpet."

Cornelius was prepared for a fight, but the seneschal had little physical or mental resistance left.

"Speaking" directly to the demon was effortless. He pushed inside Cornelius's mind like he had an invitation and found images as gruesome as the injuries. Marcus became a voyeur in the memories of the seneschal and the demon.

His daughter sat next to him in a chair across from the fire. The overwhelming pain in his heart was that of it being crushed. Not by her, but by his own words. Regret overshadowed failure. Failure as a father. Failure to protect a daughter.

Now his daughter was telling him how she was going to get out of the mess he'd failed to protect her from. A spark of pride kept his heart from collapsing and from queer thoughts turning into compulsion. Thoughts of getting closer to her, putting his nose at the crook of her neck, and licking her skin. He pushed them aside before they went further, trying to shake off his projections as odd happenstance.

"Father." Platt turned in her seat, happy at their reconciliation. "Are you well?"

Her movement caught his eye and compulsion turned to want. Frozen to the seat, he didn't dare move. If he did, he would kill her. It would be Morgan all over again. Except this was his daughter.

Platt knelt to the ground as graceful as flowing water and lifted her chin the picture of innocence gleaming in her eyes. His little girl, grown up and asking for his permission to marry a demon. His heart could not say no to her wishes. He softened to her request, allowing the demon called Redolence within a foothold. It grumbled in hunger. Cornelius shuddered in revulsion. Pale-blue eyes, distant and resigned, elated the demon and sent the seneschal to the lowest part of hell. Gripping the arms of the chair, Cornelius made his decision known.

"No," he growled. Not to Platt but to the demon, Redolence.

Marcus pulled out of the memory but remained inside Cornelius's mind, shaking with madness that another had nearly fed from Platt. He knew Redolence would not understand the word "no," and his only condolence was that Cornelius was willing to die before he fed from his own daughter. Both the seneschal and his demon had escalated the issue over Platt's blood. Marcus had no need to watch Cornelius tearing himself and Redolence apart, and no need to extract revenge. The end result was the riddled man slumped against the vine-covered wall.

"He wants you to die." Marcus translated Tiecus's thoughts to Redolence.

"Let 'em float to some ot'er victim." Cornelius coughed spraying flecks of blood in his beard.

"So, you die, and his essence will occupy the first unriddled candidate." Marcus glanced to Platt. His anger not as violent as it had been a moment ago.

Between the two demons, Tiecus did not use words to convey the consequences of Redolence allowing Cornelius to die. Their conversation was a flow of thoughts back and forth. Marcus found it hard to follow. Yellow fire and black flame tangled together. One lashed out in fear, the other in protective ownership.

Reconstruction of memories played, from both demons, surrounded by death, in Marcus's mind. Redolence felt like hurt pride, hazy logic, and slow starvation. Tiecus held understanding but firm urgency.

"You humiliated him." Marcus felt the push then pull of someone entering the stronghold grounds and growled. It would take a few minutes for the caller to enter, but he stared at the door expectantly.

"Good," Cornelius chuckled.

"How noble," Marcus snarled. "How proud you must be, beating up on a weak opponent who is starved and crazed. You must feed him."

"Ta Atra Solumn I will."

The front door opened with the force of Ventus, and Rehan bristled at the entryway.

"This gives him a choice." Marcus tightened the muscles around his eyes and gave a wry smile to the seneschal.

"I'm here." Rehan's steps echoed up the pillar and stopped when she dropped next to Cornelius.

The seneschal turned his good eye to her, and they stared at each other.

Rehan bore the scowl she reserved for life upon the seneschal. She did not turn away from the mass of flapping skin or the oozing blood but remained fixed on to Cornelius's face.

The seneschal wasn't demensing her. Marcus would feel it if he was.

"Timothy misses you." Rehan's face softened. "He wants you to come home."

A sliver of weakness, a small crack, divided Cornelius's resolve to die. "And you?"

Rehan said nothing. She assessed the damage to his body.

"He needs blood," Marcus said.

If Cornelius would feed his demon, Redolence would agree to the terms Tiecus had set. What those terms were, only Tiecus knew.

Platt came forward toward her father, and Rehan held a hand to her daughter. "No."

For the first time since she had entered the stronghold, Rehan spared her daughter a glance. Then she wrapped her hand around the blade Cornelius carelessly perched to his neck and slid her hand down the weapon's length. Blood pooled in her palm, and she held the wounded hand up to Cornelius's face.

Cornelius pushed her hand away. "I didn't win my battle to lose its principle."

"You need this now to live." Rehan pressed her palm up against Cornelius's mouth. "You can't *serve* Valder otherwise." Rehan spoke the last with as much spite as pain. He flashed approval toward her, but she never saw his glance.

Betrayed iridescent eyes shot to Rehan, but Cornelius took hold of the offered blood and drank.

Marcus stifled his sigh of relief and pulled completely out of the seneschal's mind. Now that Cornelius was accepting blood, Redolence would heal the wounds.

Dash sat against the wall. He tucked his knees around him and brought a flask up to his mouth. It held the pungent smell of copper. After he swallowed, his teeth were coated in red. "Will the seneschal be all right?"

"Yes." The air sliced apart at Rehan's fierce words. "He's going to be fine now."

Marcus glanced at all the scattered books on the floor and picked up one of the tomes. Bloodied fingerprints smudged the page matching Platt's small hands.

"You summoned me." Marcus gritted his teeth and slid suspicious eyes to Platt. Knowing she was responsible for calling him settled his alarm to bitterness. She knew his names and had used them without remorse. Without apology. But at least it was she who had called him.

"With Dash's help." She avoided eye contact and started picking up the books.

He understood why she'd done it. He reasoned she couldn't possibly know the pain of traveling through roots. She was inexperienced. She didn't know to make a protective circle at the end of his journey, so he'd return intact. He gave note that she had done most of the calling ceremony correctly. Yet every reason to excuse her left him angrier than before. His outrage was irrational, and he needed time to cool down alone.

Snatching books from the floor, Marcus went upstairs to his room, guessing Platt would stay downstairs. He wasn't worried for Platt's safety. Rehan was there.

Upon opening the door, he saw Asmara's small bookcase in a state of distress. Platt must have scattered the books looking for Cornelius's cure and to summon them. He'd been too incoherent to notice before.

Books were spread out everywhere. Those in the selves leaned caddy-corner on their side or disturbed and in the wrong section. The mess irked him. This was the first time he thought about Ardin's journal and glanced over at the recliner.

The book wasn't there.

He got an image of Asmara holding a tome about the right size with the same type of leather as the magician's diary. Marcus found it more suspicious the mage hadn't said anything about the unkempt state of his prized possessions. He reached behind but knew the book was not clinging to his skin.

I should have you converge with all my books, Asmara said. *That way I could reference you instead of wrenching them out of Alene.*

Marcus clawed his scalp. "What in the Atra Solumn . . . ?"

Absorbed in new knowledge, Asmara flipped another page of the journal.

The book had become a part of Marcus. Inside him. He could recall any page he desired.

"Of course," Marcus snarled. "Because I'm just parchment."

When Marcus was reconstructing himself during Platt's summon, the book had become part of him. It was forever lodged in his mind. Unless he wanted to be called to another circle-less place, where his essence could be scattered in the wind, there was nothing Marcus could do.

Marcus sighed and picked up a book that lay face-first on its pages. He smoothed over the crinkled paper and wondered when Asmara had pulled this volume from his tree. The cover didn't look familiar. Opening to the first page, it was dated two days ago in the Serenite calendar. A message from a vaguely intimate hand wrote:

Asmara—
I know you're alive. Contact me.
—Ignatius

The blood drained out of Marcus's face just as Asmara snapped Ardin's journal closed. Marcus stood for a long moment not thinking of anything.

"Dash," Marcus hissed. "He reported back."

I'll kill him, Asmara said.

"No," Marcus breathed, seeking out each preordained position for the mess of books. "We think, then react."

I'll trap him in an air bubble and watch him suffocate.

"We knew he was sent." Marcus replaced another book.

I'll leave a hook trap and let him hang while he is being eaten by bears.

"We knew he'd report in."

I'll flood the place and watch him drown.

"We will ignore Ignatius."

Asmara laughed with a desperate, high-pitched tone of a madman. *He'll come after me. After us.*

The door opened. Dash entered the room as if he owned the stronghold, closed the door, and leaned against the entryway.

"Just the man I wanted to see." Marcus continued to push books back to their respective places dropping his conversation with Asmara.

Marcus waited for Dash to explain his presence with seething patience. The dark room cast shadows of intimacy over the two chairs, the armoire, the sleeping chair, and his library.

"You've seen Jessica." Agony twisted Dash's lips. He was the pure aspect of a battle-worn soldier tormented with strife.

Bewilderment and an odd fond warmth rose in his chest.

Dash marched across the room, leaned over, and inhaled at the coat Jessica had made. The Frazzerian closed his eyes and in languid breaths said, "She made this for you." Dash sniffed at Marcus's sleeves, and his face collapsed in ecstasy. "I can still smell the bone of her needle on it."

Unsettled at the familiar demeanor, Marcus stepped back.

Dash reverted to the hard, reserved soldier. "You didn't hurt her, did you?"

Curiosity over Dash's control won over prudence. Marcus gave a sly grin in taunt. "She is good."

Dash's face remained placid, standing as if he were the only pillar holding the room. Dash schooled his emotions well.

Marcus's grin turned to a half-twisted smile. "She spoke of you." Curiosity abated, Marcus dropped the childish test and returned to his monotone. "I'm positive she thought of you during my visit."

The bravado Dash had extended remained. "You told her."

"That you've been riddled? Yes."

"What else?" Dash held motionless.

"That demons should be handled with caution."

Dash turned and grasped the back of a fireside chair. "And what did she say to that?"

That little shit, Asmara seethed. *Tell him to address you as a Serenite, not as a human.*

Marcus ignored the mage and said, "She said she would be careful."

Dash stared into the fire. "Marcus, you'd better make that wish from Ms. Ottern wisely."

"Wise?" Marcus dropped his charade. He grabbed the new book with the message from Ignatius. "I don't think you have any right to tell me what's wise."

Dash's eyes widened. "Is that . . . ?"

"My father's grimoire, yes."

The envoy eyed Marcus. "I thought I recognized it."

Without a word, Marcus opened the book to the first page. Dash took it and read the inscription and slammed the book closed, putting it back on the shelf.

"What? Are you afraid he can see you?" Marcus huffed.

"You never know." Dash regarded him with suspicion.

"What did you expect? You told him Asmara was here."

Dash shook his head. "I told him I found you, never where. He shouldn't have been able to send the book to you."

"The trees," Asmara whispered through Marcus. "He could feel me through the trees."

When the forest had helped Asmara escape Nidra, they knew of him. Any mage searching could find him through the trees.

"You have to answer him." Dash gave him a pointed glare.

"No, we don't." Marcus raked claws through his hair.

"Right." Dash gritted his teeth. "Because I'm supposed to bring you back." He closed his eyes and shook his head.

"You're afraid what your demon might do if you go back." Not a question, a fact.

Dash straightened and looked at the exit. He walked with silent steps and then wrenched the doorknob and flung the entrance wide.

Rehan stood, head high, eyes piercing.

"Well, well, well," Dash said. "Quite the little sneak, you are."

Indignant, Rehan rose to her full height, which was not impressive, but she was boulder shaped and sturdy like her brother.

"I might have to employ you in the name of Benicar." Dash stepped aside like a gentleman, and Rehan glared into the room.

She'd been relatively quiet during the exchange downstairs, but her threats and protective instinct as a mother had never been dismissed. The spirit of Ignis was with Rehan this evening, and she managed to keep her inner fire to herself while walking up to Marcus until they stood toe to toe.

He waited, watching the rage in her expression writhe, demanding release. Energy lifted from her core through her heart, filled her lungs, and then she demanded, "What must you take from my daughter now?"

"I haven't taken anything without her permission," Marcus snapped.

Dash leaned against the far wall, observing as if this was his form of entertainment.

"What more can you take from her?" Spittle flew from Rehan's lips.

Marcus bared his teeth.

"Mother." Platt stood at the doorway. "Our agreement has nothing to do with you."

Dash looked over at the door with interest at this new development and perhaps understood the doe's quiet strength.

"You are my daughter—that's enough." Rehan turned her death glare back to Marcus. "So, I want to hear it."

"What are you blathering about?" Marcus waved his claws in the air.

"One wish. You made her promise one wish. What is it?" Rehan clasped her hands together drawing her shoulders in a stiff pose.

He hadn't thought of how to word what he wanted.

Placid as ever, his little doe gave him no eager sign to what she'd have him do. Her eyes were a magnet, but they held in waiting. He searched for guidance, for a clue, for words, but none came. Then Jessica's voice rang in his memory. *You would fight for her? Lay a king's ransom at her feet? Bed her and claim her above all others?*

Marcus gulped. "I wish . . ." *Lay yourself bare and tell her how you feel.*

"No." Rehan growled out the word.

"Mother." Platt stepped forward.

"You are to marry Riley." Platt's mother whirled around.

"Marcus hasn't asked for anything yet." Platt's voice filtered through her mother's glare. "How do you know that's what he was going to ask for?"

All eyes were on Marcus now.

He cleared his throat preparing his words. "This ritual of marriage humans have—it will make you more pliable to me?"

He could swear actual fire burned in Rehan's eyes.

Dash hid his face behind a hand massaging his temples, shaking his head, and letting a suffering sigh escape his lips. "Prince Charming."

Platt walked around her mother ignoring the scathing contempt from Rehan. "It's your right to have everything you've asked of me. Everything you're doing wouldn't change. But it's the way we do things here." She brought up her arm and laid her fingers on his chest. The weight of her touch held light and steady. "I cannot promise to forget Riley. But we can make memories that don't include him."

"And . . ." Dash raised his head and commented to Platt's mother. "Riley would have no contention over her."

"So, you would make her yours?" Rehan scowled. "Defend her honor? Ask for her hand in marriage."

Marcus pressed his palm over Platt's fingers. "Her hands need to remain on her person."

Platt laughed and Marcus nearly came to his knees at the sound. Her smile brought a surge of excitement warming his heart. "Little doe."

She smiled at him, but the worry on her face stirred his core. How he could be angry, elated, anxious, and content all at once in her presence drove him mad. But he loved the feeling of hope and life she presented. His emotions were as varied as the colors of a rainbow when it came to Platt.

Searching for anything to say, he took this chance to find out more about strange human customs. "Why do you refuse my gifts?"

A knot formed in the middle of her brows, and she shook her head. "What do you mean?"

"How is it you would rather revoke an agreement than take gold from me?"

"Oh." Her face relaxed. "When a man gives a woman money, it's a significant form of ownership."

He nodded for her to continue.

"You giving me that bag meant that I had . . . earned it." She cast her eyes away and blushed.

Marcus bunched his eyebrows at his perplexed frame of mind. "Earned it?"

"It means," Dash said, "that you'd slept with an unmarried woman. For humans, that's a sign of an undesirable mate and worthy of death by stoning."

Ah, yes. That appalling fate Ava underwent, Asmara said. *If we took humans in as slaves, that practice would cease.*

"Ahhh." Marcus hummed.

The more he thought about it, the more he liked the idea of giving Platt a down payment on *earning* his gold. He reached inside his coat and retrieved the purple velvet bag of

Valder's reserve coin. With a smile wide enough to hurt, he took her hand and placed the bag in her palm.

"I'd rather you feel obligated and give this to you now." He peered shyly at her face.

She gawked at the bag and looked toward her parent. "Is this acceptable dowry?"

There was still much to learn about Platt, her customs, and her language. But he'd learned that Platt asked for things instead of taking them, and this situation was no different.

Dash kicked off the wall and stood before Rehan. "As his representative, I stand on ceremony to ask that Marcus have Platt in marriage. Do you accept?"

Rehan brought her chin up. "No."

Dash's brooding eyes narrowed down on Rehan. "Thankfully, you are not the deciding party of this union." The envoy set off down the stairs and waved them to follow. "Come. The true decider is downstairs."

Marcus followed, pulling Platt with him. Rehan pushed Marcus aside before he went through the door and ran down the flight of stairs yelling, "Lee . . . I won't have it!"

They found the seneschal in a chair near the hearth fire amid dancing pitchers and bubbling stew. His skin had knitted together and the scars across his chest were but deep wounds. Cornelius stared at the hearth like a man lost in a past which he couldn't reconcile.

Rehan rattled on a mile a minute. "He won't have my daughter. He's no lord. This isn't the way it's supposed to be."

Platt set down the velvet pouch next to her father gently but enough for the coins inside to rattle, making her own quiet statement.

Cornelius looked at the pouch, looked at his daughter, and then shook his head. "I won't marry the lassie to Riley. He's no good. Laud-less. Degenerate of a boy."

"He is the one she's promised to," Rehan countered not listening, uncaring of the father's wishes.

"Marcus can protect her." Cornelius grabbed a mug from the table and sipped water.

Rehan grew desperate. "Marcus will wind up killing her. Have you seen her neck?"

Marcus and Dash stood by and watched the argument until Platt's calm demeanor turned on Rehan. "Mother. This is what I want. I choose Marcus."

His heart dipped and then soared. She claimed him. Platt wanted him.

Rehan's face swept through shocked white to the purple of rage within seconds. The scent of disregarded sanity radiated through her—the kind of musk from irrational humans sacrificing themselves for loved ones.

"You want to marry my daughter?" Rehan's lip quivered. Her steel eyes penetrating Marcus.

"I am not a mockingbird that repeats words." Marcus crossed his arms in front of his chest.

Dash elbowed him in the ribs, and Marcus returned it with a biting snarl. Dash bared his own teeth and without moving his head, shot his eyes to Platt and then to Rehan.

Marcus breathed and cursed for patience. "Yes. Yes, I want to marry your daughter, Platt Ottern."

Rehan lifted her chin in superiority. "I'll allow it on one condition."

Of course. He nodded to hear Rehan's terms.

"Teach my son to kill demons."

Cornelius stared into the hearth fire, uncaring. No word, no protest, staring at the fire and drinking from his mug.

The question was not whether Platt was worth it. She was. The question was how he could get out of Rehan manipulating him into a corner. The heat in his blood turned to ice. A wave of cold vengeance settled to his feet.

Frost crusted under his boots and spread through the floor coating the stone with a white sheen of ice. He imagined his satisfaction of raking his claws over Rehan's face, four bleeding claw marks across her features, but he would not strike her. No, what he had in mind was more vindictive than anything he could do to Rehan.

No, no, no, no, no—Marcus! Asmara clamored inside.

Pulling his upper lip in a snarl, he gave his answer. "I accept."

Chapter 31

"AND NOW YOU'VE condemned Tim as well," Cornelius snarled in demon fashion.

"Well, you weren't doing anything to stop this." Rehan swept her arm to encompass the whole of the tower.

Neither retorted. They both stared at each other in a tense game of *blink*. Dash came around to the seneschal's side to silently voice his allegiance.

"Platt?" Stillwood's soft voice interrupted the mute war between Cornelius and Rehan.

Cornelius turned his furious gaze upon the interrupter, but Stillwood remained stoic, reserved, regal, yet respectful. "King Valder requests your presence."

Platt jerked toward Stillwood. "What?"

Cornelius shot forward. "W'ere?"

Stillwood raised a thin eyebrow at Platt. "The king of Benicar, Eric Valder, your liege, has scryed. I answered the summons."

Platt looked up to Cornelius. "Me? Why me?"

Cornelius offered his daughter the crook of his arm. She wrapped her hand around his bicep shyly, and the two walked side by side out of the room. It seemed they would stand united despite whatever hurts they'd inflicted on each other earlier.

Marcus and Dash followed, leaving Rehan alone in the kitchen.

Underneath the stairwell, the mirror reflected King Valder, Olof, and his other Blackened Elite counterpart. Behind the three men, glints of iron bars shone. Valder and company seemed to be in a dungeon. Not Ardin's, but a real torture dungeon. The mold was oppressive enough Marcus could smell the stench through the mirror.

Everyone on this side of the scry bowed to their knees except Marcus. Valder was a king, but Marcus was not human and didn't feel the need to observe human customs.

"Rise, dear ones." Valder made a hand-lifting gesture.

Marcus was addressed by the king first. "I see you are well."

"So we are." Marcus crinkled his brow remembering how he'd left Benicar. Valder had seemed genuinely concerned—frantic even—at the time.

"Good." Valder's outline professed that of a man unimpressed with past events. "You have the most remarkable timing, Marcus. I couldn't have planned a better strategic coup."

He couldn't tell if the remark was facetious or not but wasn't surprised the king used his exit as a military move. It stung that his pain was thought of as adventitious. If he could be sarcastic and not have Ventus wrap around his throat and choke him, he'd have made a remark.

"Have you thought about my request?" Valder asked lightly. The request of riddling humans.

How ... political of him, Asmara whispered in Marcus's mind. *He won't ask to make more demons in front of his subjects.*

Marcus found the king's "request" disturbing. He glanced over to Cornelius standing in eager anticipation.

"I haven't." He rounded a glance to Dash. "You can't expect to control them. They won't be like your trained soldiers."

Valder prompted like a teacher to a promising student. "So, demons don't march in position taking orders from a commander?"

Nidra. He had the Tier Naug marching in line, doing as commanded, and staying in formation amid panicked villagers. Tiecus wouldn't be as reserved, but the warlock seemed to have a hold on his riddled men.

Marcus didn't answer. He didn't want to think about the implications of a strike team of demons leading an attack. Valder seemed to think fighting demons with demons was the best way to win against his enemies.

"Well?" Valder demanded an answer. His ever-present patience seemed thin.

"You fail to realize that demons aren't rational." Marcus scowled at Cornelius, then Dash, and finally Stillwood. He wished Valder wasn't so adept at gathering information.

"Nonsense." Valder waved a hand. "You, Cornelius, and his two men are prime examples they can be mastered."

He was talking to a mad man. A mad man he'd pledged to. Marcus wanted to pull out every strand of hair on his head. "I'm not speaking about this any longer." Marcus turned and made for the door.

"Come back here." Valder's commanding voice was filled with anger.

Marcus halted and swore. *Always follow the alpha.* He had to convince Valder not to riddle Benicarians as Nidra had the Tier Naug. With reluctant steps, he returned to the mirror hoping reason would prevail. "I won't condone the riddling of humans."

"You don't have to condone it." Valder's eyes twinkled in that knowing sparkle. "But enough of that. I have another matter to discuss with you."

Valder acted as a feared monarch, and his predatory smile reigned its wrath down on Marcus. "Recently there's been a theft. It seems something was taken from the mage tower."

Marcus fought to keep steady. He couldn't lie. His only alternative was not to answer.

"Do you know anything about that?" Valder leaned forward.

Marcus didn't smile. He didn't nod. He didn't blink.

Breathe, Asmara reminded.

Don't swallow, don't swallow, Marcus repeated his mantra, knowing any physical sign would give his secret away.

The soft red tinge reflecting the color of Marcus's eyes off Valder's face turned yellow.

Valder chuckled.

A throaty groan outside the scrying circle on the king's side rose to a threatening growl.

Valder flicked a sharp look of warning to the side at someone beyond the mirror's boundaries.

Ardin was there, listening.

The king waved his hand to Platt and said, "I hear congratulations are in order for you, my dear. Congratulations"—Valder smiled and looked to Marcus—"to both of you."

His skin crawled, and Marcus bared his sharp teeth to Stillwood—the only one who'd been able to hear what happened not ten minutes ago and report back to the king. Marcus sent as much disgust as he could at the soothsayer.

Platt curtsied and wrapped her wrists around each other and entwined her fingers, palms together. She was nervous but didn't seem surprised Valder knew. "Thank you."

"When shall you be married?" Valder grinned.

Platt looked up at Marcus questioningly.

He gave his idea of a reasonable amount of time. "Tomorrow."

Platt stuttered, "I need a few days to prepare."

Marcus narrowed his eyes, curled his lip up, and growled at her with the force of a demon.

Doe lips pouted and almost brought him into submission.

"Unless you plan on carrying me through the scry or if Ms. Ottern plans on . . ." Valder seemed at a loss for words and tapped his forehead. "What was it you did . . . calling you . . . ?" The king looked at Platt. "Summoned him, is it?"

Marcus scoffed. Valder never had trouble retaining words in any fashion.

Platt brightened and nodded. "Yes, he has an extensive library on the subject."

Marcus raised his head to the ceiling and sighed. Lovely as she was, Platt had no sense of privacy.

Wonderful, Asmara said. *And clever of him. Not that she all but answered where Ardin's journal is now.*

Don't blame her. Valder rigs all kinds of information from unsuspecting victims.

Learn from alpha, Tiecus said.

"Interesting." Valder smiled at her. "I'd love to see it when I get there. I don't mean to be presumptuous, but when the daughter of my closest seneschal marries a dear friend, I would hope that I would be invited."

"No." Cornelius pushed to the front. "It is not wise to come."

"Pishposh." Valder waved a hand. "I wouldn't miss a demon wedding for all of Benicar."

Marcus choked. He understood what Valder planned and why looking weak in front of his constituents was a strategic move. Valder was playing an old-demon trick. Elder demons used this strategy to the dismay of the foolish. Looking defenseless, when you weren't, flushed out enemies disguising themselves as friends. It had been an ambush. An alpha testing his throng's devotion would fake injury and limp or lie down as if defeated. Thinking the alpha vulnerable, the less loyal would attack. To their surprise, when the attacker went up against an alpha at full strength, they usually lost.

Platt curtsied. "Of course, you're invited." She threw a panicked look to her father.

Cornelius turned to Olof.

Olof shook his head.

"I wouldn't advise coming," Cornelius said with the air of a bored parent knowing his words wouldn't be heeded.

"Wonderful." Valder ignored his seneschal. "Ardin can perform the ceremony."

"What?" both Marcus and Ardin near shouted in defiance.

"That's not disturbing," Marcus grumbled.

Ignoring both, Platt said, "Then seven days is enough time?"

Another week, Marcus groaned in frustration.

"Yes," Valder said. "I'll make it work."

Plans were being made for Marcus, and everything had spiraled out of his hands. He was too old to mewl and too inexperienced to ask intelligent questions. Before he could regain clarity on the subject, the king bid them farewell and the connection to the mirror was disengaged.

For once, Marcus feared for the habitants of Benicar, not because he would lose his mind and eat them, but because Valder might demand he create an army of riddled humans out of them. Cornelius and Dash were the exception, not the rule. A demon riddling a human successfully was on par with the mortality rate of newborn humans. Everyone had a fifty-fifty chance of surviving it.

He looked at Platt and vowed she wouldn't become a feeding line for anyone, not even himself. In seven days, she would be his and only his.

Chapter 32

TIM THRUST HIS sword. Marcus made a dance out of sidesteps and twirled, avoiding the sharp point. For a youngling, Platt's brother knew more about sparing than expected. Still, Rehan's son was not going to kill a demon any time soon, not on purpose anyway.

Tim, panting like a horse running from a cougar, shoved the stringy brown hair from his eyes and turned to parry Marcus every step of the way.

Marcus dominated the center of the circle. "When I actually feel threatened, I'll feel the need to parry or take my coat off for that matter." Jessica's clothes had proven more formidable than just covering his nakedness. Particularly, his coat protected him from pointed objects more than plain cotton.

Tim growled, flashing with teeth from the edge of the sparring circle. "How's your hand? I bet it hurt when you made this deal with my mom." His soon-to-be brother-in-law resorted to taunts, a sure sign the boy was exhausted.

Marcus adorned his best wry smile, held his left hand up, and wriggled his ring finger. The tattoo that formed after Marcus agreed to Rehan's ultimatum spanned the length between his knuckles. As he understood it, a band of gold was worn to show the claim after a ceremony. Thus, he truly wore his commitment and was proud of it. "You have to do better with your insults, youngling."

Platt's younger brother dug his brown boots in the dirt near the worn groove of the twenty-foot circumference Marcus had clawed to mark the space for their training. Every other piece of ground was occupied by stakes, ropes, tents, and soldiers. All had arrived in anticipation of their king.

Ventus pushed and pulled on his raw skin signaling yet more men passing over the threshold of his home boundaries. Three days after Valder's scry, squads of Benicarian military units came tromping into his courtyard.

Marcus snarled at the wind taking his eyes off Tim.

The boy thrust his sword, and this time Marcus had to parry. His claws met steel with a dull scrape. One eye never left the boy, but the other watched men struggle at the wheel that opened the main gates. Live vines fixed the entrance closed by draping thick roots through the grate and planting themselves in the ground.

"Marcus!" Cornelius packed the entire conversation in one word. The seneschal's *you-will- allow-these-men-safe-passage-through-the-portcullis-or-I-will-gut-you-in-your-sleep* conversation occurred several times a day.

"I don't know where they'll be stationed," Marcus groused as he kept Tim at bay. "There isn't any more dirt to stake a tent inside these walls." Tiny prickles lifted every hair on his body notifying him of each individual traveling up the road to the keep.

"Nonsense. I can fit twenty men at your feet."

"Fine." Marcus thought he could feel Ventus smirking at his arms going numb. He broke away from Tim and gritted his teeth. "Ventus, Terra, let them in, please."

At his words, the vines uprooted, and the portcullis gates rose. He kept his main attention on Tim, but scrutinized the soldiers entering for any new face revealing telltale signs of a demon's riddling.

"Why don't you act like a demon?" Swinging his sword, Tim lunged.

Marcus sidestepped the blow without bothering to block. "I am a demon; therefore, I do act like a demon."

Tim caught himself before he stumbled out of the circle and into a captain's tent. He scrambled back out and huffed. "How are you doing that? It's like you're a phantom."

Marcus laughed. The boy had been his half-amusement, half-interruption, but he admired Tim's dedication.

"Why don't you be in your demon form?" Tim twirled his sword. "We all know your two-legged self is a lie."

"Demons usually refrain from lying."

"Then why don't you go around in your ugly, scary form?"

At that, Marcus lifted a brow. "Did Reginhart go around in his ugly, scary form?"

Tim stopped and thought.

Marcus moved in and swiped at Tim's shoulder.

"Ow!" Tim grasped his new wound and shot a defensive look.

Cornelius shouted from the gates, "Don't lower your guard, boy."

Tim scoffed and raised his sword. "The real Reginhart, the first one, I don't think he had a second body."

"And no knights came to challenge him?" Marcus stepped forward assuming the power position in the circle. "No one called him a monster? No one felt uncomfortable around him?"

Tim opened his mouth as if to say something and then attacked with a thrust.

Marcus turned his body allowing the strike to pass in the air, and then grabbed Tim's extended wrist and threw him across the fighting circle.

Cornelius groaned in frustration, shook his head, and pretended to pay attention to his men.

Tim quickly got up and faced Marcus.

Marcus expected the youngling to strike him in anger. Red-faced and eyes burning, Tim lowered his gaze and took deep breaths. The sound of the weeling's heartbeat slowed.

"He was our kin, our founder," Tim said.

"Your founder?" *How many children did Reginhart produce?*

Tim bowed his head.

Marcus didn't fall for the ruse.

"Our founder married Isabel. Some say she rode on his back into the woods and never came back. But they had to of come back. We're all here."

Remembering demon Reginhart sent a chill down his spine. Marcus felt spiny tingles along the outer rims of his body. His hands went numb. He held his breath, and heat traveled up from his neck to his head. *You would abandon my children?* Marcus remembered the voice of the demon through the human lord at the court.

"Tim!" Cornelius pointed at a main pavilion where the seneschal stayed most nights. "Bring my spyglass."

Tim rolled his eyes. "Da! How am I supposed to learn to kill Marcus if you keep interrupting me?"

Snorting, Marcus turned hiding his amusement under the brim of his hat. One thing he hadn't expected out of Rehan's agreement was his growing fondness for Platt's brother.

"It's been long enough." Marcus waved his hand. "You can go."

Tim looked back. "You aren't going to take my sister away, are you?"

The worry on the youngling's face made him want to reassure him. "If I did, I'd have to take you with us in line with my agreement."

The boy looked pleased with that answer, and Marcus smiled in return.

As Tim charged to his father's tent, Marcus locked his knees in place, closed his eyes, and stifled the instinct to chase. With Tim around, he was getting better at conditioning himself to think before reacting.

"Chief." Dash appeared at the top of the catwalk above the gates. "Valder's carriage has almost passed into the clearing."

A string of non-Benicarian curses tumbled across the stronghold's courtyard. "Damn 'im. 'es a day early."

Cornelius bellowed at his son, "Tim! Get cleaned up. You'll be proper for our king."

The youngling burst in the opposite direction in a perfect rabbit imitation and leaped between ropes navigating a canvas sea to the east tower.

"Don't run!" Cornelius stood like a taunt bowstring.

Behind the seneschal, Dash honed in on Tim like he was prey.

"Sorry!" Tim slowed to a fast-paced walk.

Dash closed his eyes and balled his hands into fists. The Frazzerian slowly melted from hunter to human and controlled his demon's urges. His expression remained subtle and dangerous. The transfer of power was intangible, but Marcus felt the demon pressing along Dash's skin.

The envoy opened his eyes to Marcus's warning glare. Dash nodded and turned away.

Selkie whinnied from his stone cavern in calling.

Faint in the distant, from the four chargers pulling King Valder's carriage, hearty shrieks returned the demon horse's cry.

Marcus charged into the east tower, eager to tell Platt the king had arrived, and have an excuse to talk with her.

He climbed the second set of stairs and ignored the ball of worms wiggling in his stomach with more intensity as he approached Platt's door. His awe of her quiet strength overcame his pride to claim her and make her his. But her dispassionate, aloof demeanor as of late sent an ache in his heart, dislodging him further.

Without knocking, he barged into her room and stopped dead.

Across the way stood Riley. The rude youngling was holding Platt in his arms.

Marcus wanted to shred his finely tailored cloths, allow Tiecus the forefront, pull the youngling's heart out, and eat it in front of Platt.

The two culprits froze. No one moved. Riley clung to Platt with desperation. Worse, Platt returned the embrace with gentle acceptance. The room dropped from focus. A sharp tunnel of death pinpointed Riley in his mind's eye. Marcus bared his teeth in a silent growl.

The youngling reeled back and slipped out the window leading to the portcullis catwalk.

Following Riley, Marcus rushed the exit.

"You can't kill him." Platt blocked the way with her arms extended.

"And you would stop me?" Marcus pushed her aside and stepped up to the sill.

An explosion of red spots in his vision and a mind-numbing disorientation made him forget how to climb.

Woozy, he felt wetness on his backside and reached for the back of his head. The wetness was water. Pieces of clay littered the ground. The handle to Platt's water pitcher lay as a broken piece. Pain registered across his hindbrain.

"Don't go after him." She held her stomach and leaned over like she was going to puke.

He lunged for her and pinned her down on the bed by her shoulders. "Is this how you make memories without him?"

"Please." She clutched at her stomach. "All will be explained in one more day."

Understand then react. Marcus stared at her. "Why do you protect Riley?"

She sighed, looked up at him and motioned to his agreement with her. "How long will you burn if you slaughter a villager?"

His eyes widened. *Could it be she thinks to protect me?* "But you had your arms around him."

She shook her head and her entire body shivered. "To say goodbye."

Teaching Tim, enduring seven days before he could bond with her, being summoned back to Reginhart in the most painful way possible, Platt's body conflicting with her words, doing everything she asked, his gifts of appreciation, none of it seemed to matter.

She was staring into him reminding him of their first agreement. He could never demense her without pain. He could never know what she desired without corrupting his own mind.

The problem with knowing was that once he knew, he wouldn't be able to do anything but give what she wanted to her. His hope teetered on compromise. Pressure of what he wanted, everything he desired, finding the calm between Asmara, Tiecus, and himself weighed on one word. *Tomorrow.*

His senses drifted back, but not back to normal. The blood in his veins remained hot, turning to a different base emotion. Marcus scanned her body and then tightened his face. But another rejection would undo him. He would wait for her.

"Promise me he won't interfere with our arrangement."

Her eyes started to well up. "After tomorrow, you won't ever have to worry about him."

"Tomorrow?"

"Yes." Her voice broke under emotion.

"So that he can have you tonight," Marcus growled.

A tear dropped off the side of her face.

Marcus pulled away, hurt, heart breaking and feeling betrayed. "Do you even want me?"

"That's just it." She crawled toward him and grabbed his outer coat. "Whose wife will I become tomorrow?"

He blinked at her. "I don't understand. You are mine."

Clutching his coat, her question rose to a shrill. "Am I *your* mate? Do I belong to Tiecus? Will Asmara be my husband? Do I marry you or all three of you? Who—" Her face turned red.

Marcus stared back at her. He thought each had in turn made clear their intentions. "Whom do you want?" After her stunt of blocking him from chasing the youngling, he was sure she'd answer Riley.

She let go of his coat and slumped to her knees. Dumbfounded, she stared up at him.

Flaring his nostrils, he breathed in vanilla musk. He pressed a lock of her hair between his clawed fingers, brought in the scent of Platt, tasted the coarse strands, and rubbed her hair over his neck like soap.

She took the lock back from him. Her lips parted, and a shuddered breath escaped. A thought was under her tongue.

He could see it, and then Platt lowered her face and shook her head.

Air pushed and pulled on his skin. Marcus growled at the warning ward wondering how much amusement the element derived from annoying him.

You can take the warning ward down, Asmara said. *If you can't even tell when that whelp is around, might as well.*

From the vantage point of the second-story window, Marcus glimpsed four dark draft horses pulling a cherry wood carriage on the road leading to the stronghold. Eight Blackened Elite rode separately on mounts and guarded the king's transportation.

Dejected and hollow, Marcus whispered, "Valder is here."

Wiping her eyes, Platt jumped up and over to her window. A squeak escaped her lips, and she ran across the room. Smoothing down her skirts, Platt opened the door like a king arriving at her home was an everyday occurrence.

Chapter 33

AN INFESTATION OF guards patrolled the stronghold grounds. The Benicarians were in a flurry causing Marcus agitation on top of his heartache. The soldiers ran in a flurry of chaos reminding him of the busy streets of Benicar where mongers roamed, shouting about their wares. The bustling people crawling around each other like ants made him pause at the tower's entrance.

Beside him, his soon-to-be-mate didn't help his frame of mind either. Seeing Platt in Riley's arms had shattered his confidence and brought out a possessive anger. He was tempted to snatch one of the passing soldiers to hear the satisfying snap of bones.

He refrained for two reasons.

First, Marcus didn't want the burden of consequence if one of them turned out to be a villager. Second, Valder might have the poor sod riddled and have the gall of calling it mercy. Bringing a demon inside a human to heal the person from a fatal wound was death by insanity.

Platt stepped out of the entryway, and Marcus slid up behind her.

"We need to have a chat," he said in her ear.

"Later," she whispered.

"You've been avoiding me all week."

She turned with eyes expressing guilt. "I know."

Stop! Tiecus thundered, preventing Marcus from pressing further.

Tiecus showed him a true-life experience of an angry female demon being courted by her would-be suitors. She thrashed her hind hooves, snarling, and ripping their skin off for their "coaxing" attempts of mating.

Marcus shifted in his pants. He wouldn't burden Platt. Not yet. Prodding or forcing a female for anything caused bruising. He'd learned his lesson about that firsthand. Remaining quiet kept his underside safe from Platt's grasp. However, his heart didn't escape the blow of her actions or her words.

The wide chests of four black mounts flexed, and the horses used their energy to defy the last feet of slope up to the keep. The team charged with high spirits overcoming the challenge of a difficult goal. Marcus felt the pang of distant homesickness watching the steeds working together as a throng with the reward of accomplishment.

That was what he wanted. Marcus wanted Platt on his side. He wanted the goal, for good or ill, to fail or win, as a team, not alone. Technically, he wasn't alone, but in many ways, he was.

Platt's passive eyes watched as the carriage rolled through the portcullis. Soldiers scrambled to make way for the chargers and lined up as a barricade against any who'd try to cross the coach's path.

As the team pranced, sweating and breathing hard, ten Blackened Elite on wide-backed steeds sanctified a moving circle around Valder's transportation. Their armor, a black matte, soaked up the sun's rays.

Cornelius stayed behind the Blackened Elite and out of sight of the rolling carriage. The seneschal could not become inconsequential even if he tried. Platt's father did not accomplish subtle well.

Dash was nowhere in sight, but Marcus got a sense he was somewhere on the stronghold grounds.

The carriage door lined up to the tower entryway, and the spoke wheels came to a stop. Five Blackened Elite guards dismounted. The other five stayed on top of their horses. Olof, one of the Elite off his horse, waved for the portcullis gate to close and scanned the courtyard until the stronghold had the semblance of confinement. Olof skimmed the grounds before opening the door of the carriage.

Small, thin fingers took hold of Olof's gloved hand, and Jessica stepped down the ladder with dainty precision.

Marcus cast a look to Platt. The doe's eyes were wide in awe at the finely dressed seamstress queen. Movement in the background of the portcullis archway caught his eye. Nothing a human would notice, just the flick of hair in the shadows.

Crammed inside a murder hole big enough to toss down boulders, Dash tracked Jessica's every move with wild longing. The seneschal's second had chosen the best vantage point to admire the brown travel dress, the curl at the end of Jessica's pulled-back hair, the citrine gems fastened to her cloak that drew attention to her bosom, and her infectious smile.

"Cousin!" Jessica floated to Platt and embraced her like long-lost family. The little doe smiled and graciously returned the queen's affections. "Why are you in this drab?" Jessica pulled away and looked Platt up and down. "No cousin of mine should ever suffer anything but the finest."

Ardin, not so dainty, stepped out and tried to maneuver the bottom of his hooded cloak.

Marcus curled his lip and growled. "How did he get free from the iron confinements of Valder's wrath?"

Temporary ostracizing, Tiecus said. *Throngs do it for the good of the whole. Sometimes underlings take the brunt of everyone's frustrations. Especially in hard times.*

Marcus rejected Ardin as that brave member enduring tensions and allowing his bludgeoning to unite the throng. The magician wouldn't sacrifice his ego for the whole. Ardin wasn't interested in keeping his pack healthy or limiting injuries to only one member. Throng mentality was brutal. Ardin wouldn't understand the justification of bringing the rest of the throng together. Nor would he care that one hurt member was better than many unable to hunt.

Ardin avoided the stairs altogether and landed on fresh grass. The magician swept a circle around the carriage without a word. Ardin's hood bobbed up and down to Olof who then walked a circle around the carriage while Ardin stood guard at the front. After the Blackened Elite had made a full pass, he tapped on the window.

"Piss-poor security sweep if you ask me," Cornelius roared out at Olof. "Did you cast a look beyond your nose? I believe not."

Jessica whirled and gave Cornelius a dazzling smile. Ardin backed up against the carriage and seemed to melt into a shadow. The guards didn't react to Cornelius.

Olof gave Cornelius a perfunctory glance. "I saw you in the recess, sir."

"Sir?" Cornelius bellowed out. "I still work for a living, cretin. Careful of your jaw."

Olof gripped his pole arm. "You're nothing I can't handle, Tier Naug."

Marcus stepped in front of Platt. Blood rushed through his veins. The hopeful prospect of having an outlet to his frustrations sent his blood rushing.

Then the sergeant-at-arms did something Marcus had never seen any of the Blackened Elite do. Olof smiled.

The seneschal threw his head up and roared a thunderous laugh.

Valder popped his head out of the carriage and scanned the area. Everyone, except Marcus, bowed when the king fully emerged and stepped down.

"Rise." Valder seemed bored with the reverence of the crowd and fluttered a hand. There was something different about Valder. The king looked younger, more like a boy and less manicured. His movement was not as precise or calculated. Valder seemed, of all things, free of burden.

Cornelius was the first to recover. The seneschal looked at the king then at Ardin and muttered, "Fool boys."

Valder raised an eyebrow. "I've followed your instructions to the letter. Are you saying I've taken the advice of a fool?"

Cornelius challenged his king, or at least that was how it looked to Marcus, by the intense glare the seneschal bore into Valder. *Demon's rule number two. Always challenge the leader.*

The king looked around in curious fascination. Everywhere except his seneschal. Marcus took that as Valder refusing the challenge.

"Is but a pillow residing on your seat in Benicar?" Cornelius stepped closer.

"A pillow has always been on my throne." Valder lifted his chin, and his smile was full of insolence. "Would you like to fluff it for me?"

If the seneschal could bury a man with his eyes, the king would have been ground to dust. "Name your delegate running Benicar during your visit away."

Impervious to the seneschal's murderous glare, Valder wrapped his hands behind his back and smiled with blinding-white teeth. "That delegate would be King Eric Valder."

Does he mean he's two places at once? Asmara flipped a few pages of Ardin's journal and shoved his nose in another page. The answer didn't seem as important as the tome.

Cornelius's iridescent eyes turned to a red-hot glow. "You didn't." He turned to Ardin and bared his teeth. "Tell me you didn't."

The magician straightened and stepped forward. "It's perfectly fine."

What were they talking about?

In the corner of his eye, Marcus saw Jessica inch Platt into the tower.

"Fool." Cornelius's eyes were sharp as shovels consigning Ardin to his grave. "As if splitting yourself wasn't enough."

"He's fine," Ardin snapped, and the opening of his hood cast toward Marcus. "I've perfected the procedure. Even without my notes, I know it by heart."

Well, Asmara quipped. *He's not going to get his notes back. This is preposterous. The nightmare spell he has reminds me of Nidra's demens on Dash.*

Cornelius growled, "Dangerous tricks you play."

Ardin stepped into Valder's shadow. "Trust me; it's not his first time doing this."

"What isn't the first time?" Marcus asked.

Ardin and Cornelius peered at him in distaste. Valder spun, looking at the tower, the courtyard, and the portcullis as if his attention span were no more than a dog's.

The seneschal spun around and barked over his shoulder, "Inside. Now."

Valder flashed a smile at his two hosts. "Ah, Marcus, Platt. Wonderful to see you both again."

Platt bowed a second time.

"Move." Cornelius grumbled the command, crowding Valder as if herding the king. "Make your greetings indoors."

Valder kept his smile. "Still the same seneschal I know. The demon hasn't tamed you a bit."

Marcus let Jessica, Ardin, Valder, Platt, Cornelius, and the four Blackened Elite enter the tower before taking one long look around. Dash was gone. The soldiers remained motionless. Nothing else seemed out of place, and he closed the door.

Cornelius snapped his finger and rolled his wrist, and Olof and his men spread out, inspecting the tower.

Once inside, the king took Platt's hands in his. "Ms. Ottern, you remember my wife, Jessica."

Marcus leaned toward Cornelius and mumbled, "What is wrong with him?"

"Nothing," the seneschal snapped.

Platt squeezed the king's hands, pulled away, and bowed in front of Jessica near to the floor. "My Queen, I thank you for coming."

"Nonsense, Cousin. After what Eric told me, I had to come." Jessica meticulously laid a hand to the pearls on her necklace. "Who would burn a dress? Honestly, I don't care whom you marry, but don't destroy an heirloom."

Platt rose and wrung her hands together.

A growl behind his teeth, Cornelius swung his eyes to his daughter. "W'at?"

Platt's quiet grace turned to still terror. "It's nothing."

"It's not not'ing," her father rumbled.

"The loss is just an inconvenience," Platt uttered.

Valder slid an icy gaze over the two and raked a hand through his scalp, straightening any out-of-place hairs. After preening, Valder extended a palm to his wife. "Jessica is a talented seamstress, my dear." The king glanced to Platt. "She'll make you a new wedding dress to your specifications."

The queen lifted a delicate hand to Platt. "Come, show us to our rooms."

Platt obliged, and the two women went upstairs, with the men trailing behind.

Blooming vines grew over the walls like spider webs to the top of the east tower. Purple morning glories displayed their vibrancy and reached up to the ceiling making the tower an atrium of sunlight and wild splendor. Small birds chirped from nests and darted from one vine to the other.

The stronghold was vastly different from the smooth walls of the palace in Benicar. Terra permeated every room with her green crawlers. Vines reinforced the stone and covered every inch of wall with its protection. The stronghold remained camouflaged, guarded by an element older than demons.

"It's very"—Valder tapped his forehead with his two dominant fingers—"captivating. Mayhap, you were swayed to the druid teachings."

He's fishing, Asmara said.

Marcus burst out laughing. "Only if I learned through osmosis."

At least, he didn't call you an elf.

Marcus laughed harder at Asmara's expense.

Valder's face drew in like he was confused, and then the king dropped a mask over his expression.

A chill crawled up Marcus's spine. The king seemed odd, not himself. Like he had an intangible loss of continuity. The king was . . . missing something about his own being.

Platt climbed the stairs leading the procession along the floral-covered banister. Wandering vine coiled around her fingers and wrists for the brief moment wherever she held on to the organic railing. Marcus wasn't the only one yearning to touch his little doe.

Gentle as the strings of greenery were, no one else ventured to hold the vine support.

They'd decided that Platt would give her second-story room to the king and queen and stay with her mother for the nights they were there, until she wed Marcus.

Her room was bare of furniture except essentials. Roots twisted around the feet of two plush chairs. Strands of morning glory surrounded the burning fireplace, waving on the thermals from the hearth. The bed, delivered by Old Man George, took up a third of the room, and ivy hung neatly tied streamers from ceiling to floor over the latest bunk addition. Thick roots created a nightstand entwining tight enough and flat at the top to hold a pitcher—the one she'd cracked over Marcus's head.

"That is the largest mattress I've ever seen." Valder appraised the work of Reginhart's resident bed maker.

Platt rushed over to the other side of the bed where pieces of clay had littered the floor.

Marcus knew she'd find nothing amiss. No trace of their earlier fight, not even water, remained.

His little doe gave him an expression of gratefulness.

He smirked and gave her his best "thank me later" bedroom eyes.

Sucker. Asmara prodded. *Cleaning up the very pitcher she tossed at your head.*

Marcus loosened a silent growl only meant for the mage.

The king walked up to the bed, faced his companions with a wicked grin, lifted his arms, tilted back, and fell onto the comforter.

"I bet all three of us can sleep in it." The monarch rolled side to side on the bed.

Jessica gasped as if she'd been scandalized. "Eric!"

Ardin groaned, and his brown hood wavered as if the man inside were shaking his head.

Cornelius waved a hand to the king and turned to Ardin. "This is your perfected process?"

Platt giggled behind a shy reserve.

Marcus held Tiecus back from pouncing on the bed and rolling around with Valder. To him it looked like fun. This was a side of the king he'd never seen. It was disturbing, and he couldn't pinpoint why, but he felt this version of Valder was closer to the real person behind the crown.

In playful candor, Marcus pressed against his mate's back and whispered, "Won't you reconsider sharing my covers tonight?"

She stiffened and replied, "I'll be staying at my mother's."

He didn't like the sound of that, and his smile dissipated. "Will Riley be there, too?"

"How can I forget him if you keep reminding me?" she whispered back.

"Tell me, Ardin." Cornelius kept his voice low but not quite enough to keep Marcus from listening in. "You *and* Olof for a decoy? Bernard remains in Benicar, pray tell?"

"Thank you, Cornelius." Valder sat up. "You've always had a knack for making me feel so significant."

"At least, you still retain command of your faculties for banter." The seneschal could have been a beam to hold up the building with his stockiness. "So, which aspects did Ardin separate and put into you?"

Asmara lurched, the mage's mind working a mile a second.

Unbelievable thoughts rushed Marcus, and he couldn't help but voice them. "Ardin can separate people?"

Everyone's eyes turned to Marcus. No one said a word. He couldn't see Ardin's face, but Jessica looked away as soon as he met her eyes. Cornelius squinted at him, suspicious, dangerous, as if Marcus were now marked by knowing a secret.

"That is . . . how?"

Valder hopped up like a child remembering there were sweets in the kitchen. "Do you have a library?"

The question broke the odd tension of the room, and Platt grabbed his question as if eager to change a forbidden subject. "Oh yes. Let me show you!"

Asmara panicked. *No-no-no, Marcus!*

"Perhaps you'd rather have refreshments?" Marcus hastened to the king. "It was a long way to travel."

"Sure." Valder's eyes sparkled in mischief. "Bring them to us in the library."

"No!" Flustered and unprepared, Marcus scrambled to calm his voice. "I don't want tea staining the books."

"Then later." Valder waved. "A drink after I see the library."

In the corner, Ardin, Jessica, and Cornelius, caught whispering to each other, stopped and stared at the king.

Platt smiled and gestured for Valder to follow.

Do something! Asmara said.

Marcus did the only thing that came to mind. He ran.

His scramble to get out the door first left the two women gasping and the Blackened Elite guards in a flurry. While the humans were squawking about disappearing demons, Marcus grabbed the syllabus he used to teach Platt to read, a spell book, and Asmara's grimoire. Searching for a hiding place for them, he decided on an empty drawer and shoved the three books inside. He shoved one of Asmara's gowns in the closet, folded and draped a fur over the sleeping seat and went to inspect the bookshelf that Platt called a library for any books that might leave incriminating evidence.

Cornelius rushed into the room ready for an attack. When his gaze swept over Marcus, he paused. His suspicious gaze then wandered. No one entered until he gave a signal, and three Blackened Elite, including Olof, marched in. When Platt entered, the hearth fire blazed alive in greeting.

Valder followed on her heels.

Ha! He won't find Ardin's journal in here. Asmara flipped another page of said book inside Marcus's mind.

After inspecting the room for assassins, Cornelius leaned against the wall.

The rest of the king's entourage filed in. Ardin took a seat next to the hearth fire. The magician's back, usually tall and straight, hunched over in exhaustion. Jessica eyed the décor no doubt cataloging what tapestries she could hang from the vine covered walls or what furniture could replace the empty room. When her searching stopped at a certain place, Marcus looked over to see what caught her eye.

Marcus didn't know where Dash got the Silver Elite garb. The suit fit perfectly. Dash stood flush against the vine mimicking the other king's guard. No one paid him any mind. All spectra of light shimmered in the riddled human's eyes.

Valder's wife blushed and threw a glance to her husband. The king either didn't notice or pretended not to pay his wife any mind and watched Platt shift through the perfectly alphabetized books.

Platt pulled out a tome with a wooden cover. "It's been a while since the last time you read to me." Platt handed Valder the book.

Asmara snorted in Marcus's mind, confident the secrets inside the book were safe. *She's not so far along she can read that.*

"And a difficult one you've given to me." Valder swiped a hand across the cover. "Dear one, you were so little when I left that I can hardly believe you remember me."

That begged the question of whether Platt had lived in Benicar or if Valder used to live in Reginhart.

"Oh, this is divine." Jessica held out a white leather and gold trim-fitted robe. She'd gotten into the armoire and was presenting Asmara's clothes to everyone in the room. "I dare say it might fit you, Ardin."

"Look who's being rude now," Valder smirked.

"You must tell me who made this." Jessica admired the pliable garment in her hands. "How did they get the leather so soft?"

Marcus stomped across the room, took the robe out of Jessica's hands, shoved it back in the closet, and closed the door. Roots grew across the armoire locking Asmara's clothes away.

"Well, it certainly wouldn't fit you." Jessica slid a forefinger across his chin. "You're much bigger than that."

Platt's gaze fell to the queen's back, and he'd be surprised if Jessica hadn't felt the hot possessive stare-down his little doe cast over at her.

Marcus ground his teeth and sent a menacing growl meant for only the seamstress to hear.

Flashing one of her most disarming smiles, Jessica winked and went to sit next to Ardin in the accompanying chair.

Valder opened the book and touched the handwritten scrawl, moving his fingers from left to right.

Marcus snorted, *The Serenite written word was read from right to left.*

Valder lovingly shifted the book, opened to the pages so the cover opened to the right, cleared his throat, and read. "It is of my belief that the elements were once a single being split into four from the aftereffects of our reality separating into three dimensions. This is my dissertation of such hypothesis. Asmara Grey." Valder quoted the words from the book exactly.

Marcus scrambled, ripping the book out of Valder's hands faster than the Blackened Elite could react. "Where did you learn that?"

Valder's command of the Serenite language was choppy, but the inflection of the accent was flawless. Marcus swayed were he stood as if he had lost the anchor that held him grounded. He turned to Dash and ground out, "Envoy!"

Glancing at the book, then at the king, Dash gathered his muster and stood his ground.

Marcus dropped the book onto the recliner and then switched his speech to the Serenite language. "What have you done?"

"We are tired of running." Dash too spoke in the Serenite language.

"What do you mean *we*, abomination." Marcus winced. The comment was Asmara's.

By the expression that washed over his face, Dash no doubt was used to being called such names. Mercy was not a word in the Serenite language.

"Integration will be slow, but it will happen." Dash reverted to the cool stance of an envoy befitting the Serenite. "Certain successes have revitalized their hope."

"Humans are dangerous. How do they think they are going to integrate?" Marcus waved at himself. "They think this is an acceptable form of adaptation?"

"You are another one of the Serenite's experiments?" Valder sat in the polished wood recliner. "Like Master Dash McGrady?"

The king spoke in Benicarian, but Marcus needed no other proof that he'd understood their conversation. Horror in a sweeping tide spread from his head seeping down to his toes and keeping Marcus fastened in position.

"As I understand it"—Valder stood up—"the Serenite are a very shy people." He waved to Dash. "Master McGrady was teaching me the language to be the first to consort with them."

At no other point in his life had the mage and Marcus conspired together with such attunement that they could have truly been one person, but both were in unison now. "Shy?" Marcus lifted his face to the ceiling and laughed. "What you mean to say is that you've never met one."

"Aside from Dash"—Valder's gaze went flat and his lips thinned—"no."

"Dash is not a Serenite," Marcus fumed.

Dash turned and faced him. The full force of a demens attempting to barge its way into his mind bounced off Tiecus's natural defense. Marcus ignored Dash and kept his eyes focused on Valder. "So, you know the language," Marcus said. "Do you know the history?"

The mischievous gleam in the king's eye was enough to make him believe Valder was ready for any game Marcus wanted to play.

Platt clung to the book she'd been handed, but it was her motionless stare at the floor that caught Marcus's attention. Her face grew pale, and she didn't look like she was breathing.

"As I understand it, they are somewhat of a nomadic race." Valder changed to a defensive stance that looked unconscious. "Something of a band of druids."

Dash tried a demens again. When it didn't work, the envoy resorted to another distraction. "Serenite . . ." Dash hissed.

Marcus stepped forward, and two Blackened Elite guard, including Cornelius, came to the king's side.

"You think you can negotiate with them?" The wave of hate Marcus injected in his voice made his opinion clear.

"Things have changed." Dash faced the king. "We want a mutual and beneficial alliance."

"Only for as long as they can be fed from." Marcus watched Valder's reaction.

But Valder gave no disclosure to his thoughts.

"Why are you doing this?" Dash asked Marcus.

"So, they are like demons then." Valder appraised Dash. "Do they have the same affinity for demons as the Tier Naug?"

"Don't . . ." Marcus didn't want Valder assessing the Serenite to be used for his benefit. He needed to scare him away from ever wanting to meet them. Or force the Serenite to stay hidden. But to protect them, he'd have to expose them.

Do it, Asmara hissed. The mage also had ulterior motives to expose the truth. If his people had to stay hidden, Ignatius would be forced to stay in Ziodonia.

"They would use demons to rid themselves of the curse, but they would make sure the demons would have something to eat." Marcus gave Valder what he hoped was a meaningful glance. "A blood doll would suffice."

Valder froze. The king paled, fear replacing his mask.

Another piece of the bigger picture clicked in Marcus's mind. He looked at Platt and remembered what Tim had said—*Reginhart was our founder.*

Reginhart was the father, the protector. Descendants— that's what the demon had called the villagers.

"The whole town." Marcus locked his knees. "The whole town. Everyone in Reginhart is a blood doll."

The subtle hints. The lord cousin. The relations. Platt knowing Valder as an uncle. The king was born in Reginhart, which meant . . . "You're a blood doll." Marcus smiled wide, with sharp threatening teeth.

Cornelius rumbled a growl and placed a hand on the pommel of his sword.

"Why are you really here?" Marcus ignored the seneschal and focused on Valder.

Sharpened senses turned his eye to Ardin's sudden movement.

"No!" Dash rushed forward.

Marcus extended his claws and flew himself at Ardin. The magician threw a coin-sack-sized pouch. Marcus's chest exploded with light and heat. The concussion temporarily blinded him. His nose filled with the smell of burnt grass and powder.

"Give me my book, you interloper," Ardin said.

Marcus snarled and launched himself toward Ardin's voice. This time he tackled someone to the ground, but he didn't know whom as he couldn't see.

Climbing on top of the male form, Marcus didn't care if it was Ardin or not. He balled his hands into fists and started whaling away at different points of the body underneath him.

Rough hands threw him off and shoved him to the wall. His sight was coming back. Dash curled around himself, clutching his stomach. A pool of blood and puke settled into the stone floor beside him.

"Enough!" Valder squatted down next to Dash and tried to brush hair out of the envoy's face.

Platt! Marcus looked around. But she was hiding her eyes behind the book clutched against her chest and safe on the chair. Her eyes glazed over and fixed to a point on the floor as she rocked back and forth in shallow slow swings.

"Ardin!" Marcus swung his head but couldn't locate the magician. "Where is he?"

The magician was gone, no longer in the room.

Dash wheezed out. The sound was sand against stone, and his eyes were cold hard marbles staring at Marcus.

Shouts from the soldiers in the courtyard brought Marcus's attention out the window. A flaming stone boulder arced from a distance and catapulted toward the east tower.

Chapter 34

MARCUS RUSHED THE window, aggravated by the burning agreement on his right arm. He thrust his arms out, palms facing the projectile as if he could catch the fiery blaze. Asmara rushed as close as he could get to the forefront, and their voices mingled together in unison. "Nocte muros Terra!"

A boulder, as big as a horse, tore from the ground below his window and launched into an arc, meeting the opposite stone just above the keep's wall.

The stones' collision thundered. Rock pelleted the ground. The explosion created a crushing shock wave scattering pebbles like arrows to the troops below.

Soldiers shouted. Their chaos and pain jolted Marcus into further action. He leaped through the window into the air, using Ventus to cushion his fall. The lapels of his jacket smacked him in the face as the rest of his coat whipped around his body. The ends of his hat equally thrashed at his eyes while gravity pulled him down. Marcus planted two feet on the grass with a thud.

A sea of people parted in his wake. Soldiers ran, fortifying the outward wall, climbing the ladders to the wall walk, and hiding behind crenellations. Blackened Elite still on horseback formed a half circle at the tower door.

Weapons of war trounced in the courtyard as men rolled trebuchets in position. Metal clanked beside him. Soldiers shouted, and their words rushed over him: "Man the gate!" and "Incoming!"

Olof had followed him through the window, landing harder than Marcus had and rolling forward from the impact. The Blackened Elite didn't miss a step, stood, and began commanding soldiers to action.

From the stable, Selkie cried, but there was no helping it. The horse had to stay inside despite the risk of being crushed under another blazing rock. In this pandemonium, Marcus couldn't trust Selkie's hunger or rather the horse demon's lack of discrimination for blood. He wouldn't add a flesh-eating horse to the scene. Selkie wouldn't know the difference between a Benicarian and a Tier Naug. Or at least, he assumed it was the Tier Naug who had attacked.

Bounding across the courtyard, dodging swords, men and contraptions, Marcus scaled the stone steps near the portcullis leading up to the wall's pathway. Soldiers peeked from behind the stone crenellations and looked out over Reginhart.

The land was in twilight. The hill led down to a sizable clearing breaking up the forest from his vantage point. But in the dim light, he made out a moving barricade of humanoid figures from the forest like a group of meerkats closing in on a snake.

They came from the trees, the village, and beyond the road leading to Benicar. They came too uncoordinated to be men and too slow to be riddled. The inhuman lumber in their gait combined with the wails of death sent a chill down Marcus's spine. It was a horde. Not a small pack-sized family, but an army so large they couldn't hold a battle formation. By Atra Solumn, the way the front lines edged their way toward the keep, they were packed together not only because of lack of space but because they needed to hold each other up to keep moving. The stench of decay and magic sent his nose recoiling.

By the bright star. Asmara flipped open Ardin's journal. *If there was a time to go, it's now.*

"You know, we can't leave." Marcus set his hands down on the stone embrasure watching the lumbering dead.

Asmara stopped at a page and let Marcus see through his eyes.

It revealed a cascade of drawings, depictions of clay humanoids rising from the earth, blocky creatures made of mud or stone, monstrosities leaving puddles where they went. Marcus zoned in on skeletons wrapped in a thin layer of mud walking away from their own grave site.

Asmara started reciting a journal entry: *Golems are made from earth, clay mostly, but also rock. They need a skeletal structure to wrap around, but once infused, they can move at will. You can chop their heads off, break them in pieces, burn them, smash them, crush them, drown them, but they will regenerate. They cannot be stopped in any way. They will keep coming. And, according to Ardin, whomever they are set upon will not survive.*

"I don't think I'd like to be anywhere near anything like that," Marcus unceremoniously mused.

Whoever these creatures are after is completely screwed. They are unstoppable. We call them death wardens.

"You've dealt with them."

I've used them. Asmara peered out from Marcus's eyes. *They smell like death, and the wails coming from them is . . . disturbing. No doubt this is Nidra's work. We should leave.*

"So, running is your answer."

Why not?

"We agreed to protect the villagers and the king. Both are here. Nidra is a Tier Naug; I agreed not to just let him pass."

Asmara snorted, *So . . . watching them rip that king limb from limb is a no?* Asmara said "king" with a fierce slur.

Marcus sighed. "Your indifference is understandable."

Is it? Asmara closed the book and stood in Marcus's mind's eye. *Do you really understand? That conniving human . . . he sent you here to use you as his shield while he captures Nidra.*

"You think that's what this is? A trap for the warlock?"

Valder won't even put himself in jeopardy. What you see is his double, a doppelganger, bait.

"So here we are, fighting a tidal wave of death wardens. All because you wanted more freedom."

Asmara remained silent. Typical. But it wasn't Valder they were angry with. It was this entire mess throwing his plans to marry Platt into chaos. The mage fantasized about the first night with his new bride. Those daydreams slipped through Asmara's usual tight mind shields and affected Marcus more than he'd thought it might. This would postpone taking their vows.

Marcus jumped down from the wall. Hoping he wasn't making another mistake, but not really having much of a choice, he strode to the cluster of Blackened Elite hustling Valder toward the carriage.

Cornelius was in the lead, guiding the small circumference of black-armored guards protecting the king. The seneschal tossed soldiers in his path without remorse or care. The queen and Platt held each other tightly surrounded by their own set of guards, Acting in his Silver Elite capacity, Dash led the women. But everyone halted before Marcus.

"They are golems," Marcus said.

The seneschal eyed him with suspicion.

Marcus scoffed at Cornelius's mistrust. He, Marcus, was the one who had been betrayed. Used. Told half-truths and strong-armed into agreements he never wanted. Sent ahead as a sentinel to fight Nidra and his band of demons without so much as a warning. Oh sure, he'd been told about the Tier Naug, but not that he'd be battling a warlock, a being specialized in dealing with demons.

Valder stood courageous, but his expression was that of a man resigned to die. "Golems? You're sure?"

Marcus nodded. "Death wardens, I believe they are specifically called."

Valder swore. "Of course. Ardin hates golems."

"Will we be safe inside these walls?" Cornelius asked.

Marcus lifted an eyebrow to the riddled human. "No."

Cornelius narrowed his eyes. "And why should I trust your word?"

"Golems don't feel pain," Marcus growled. "Golems don't stop. One is enough to wipe us all out."

Valder smirked, finding his ill humor even through a death sentence. "Even a demon?"

Through his question, the king confirmed his reason for sending Marcus to Reginhart. "You knew Nidra would send golems and thought a demon could protect you?"

It wasn't a real question. The answer lay in Valder's faltering smile. Marcus huffed in mock amusement.

Olof ordered his men to steady. Vines around the walls grew thicker as if understanding a threat came to crush their inhabitants. The first shot of a trebuchet whooshed. Archers prepared their bows. Boiling oil bubbled in vats over murder holes. The Blackened Elite on horseback surrounded the small group of the king and queen and remained vigilant to their safety.

Marcus hissed at Valder, "Golems are not disposable. Arrows don't stop them; fire doesn't stop them. Behead them, and you have two angry golems once they grow back. If you plan on pouring oil over the walls, they will absorb it."

"There must be a way to defeat them," Cornelius said.

"You can outrun them." Marcus sniffed. "But you'll be running forever."

Kill the one that called them, Asmara whispered. *Or get Nidra to return the golems to their original state.*

Presumably, Nidra was the one that had called them. They could run, but that option never sat well with Marcus. He would fight.

"Run we will." Cornelius grabbed Valder by his baldric. "Until I can find a way to kill 'em."

"No." Valder ripped away from his king's guard.

"No?" Cornelius scowled. "No giving up on me."

"Lee." Valder's voice was calm. "I'm just the duplicate, remember? This is why I'm here. This is why I was sent. I'm not afraid to die."

"If t'is part of you dies, t'at one in Benicar will be less tolerable." A moment passed as Cornelius and Valder stared at each other. The king stood, determined. Cornelius lingered menacingly.

"I'm not giving up." Valder preened his hair.

"T'en running is the only answer." Cornelius grabbed for Valder's arm and pulled him forward.

"The only way is to let Ardin reintegrate with Nidra. Then he will put an end to the golems." The king fought against Cornelius, but the seneschal would have none of it. Valder, for all his regal stature, was still a scrawny human up against a boulder of a soldier.

"We'll find 'em t'en." Cornelius pointed to the east tower. "We can travel Regin'art's tunnel."

A familiar voice boomed. "A wonderful prospect. I'm so glad it was available."

No! The bottom of Marcus's stomach dropped out.

How is he in here? cried Asmara.

Nidra stood within the walls of the keep. Five riddled Tier Naug stood behind the warlock in front of the tower door. The queen and Platt couldn't turn back, and Dash turned, pulled his sword, and lowered to a fighting stance.

Riley stood firm, expression cold, next to Nidra. A desperate man, using desperate measures to get what he wanted.

"You!" Marcus growled. Riley had sold them out. He'd shown Nidra the way through the hidden tunnels. For what?

Didn't matter.

He'd sunder the warlock in half regardless. He clenched his hands and leaned forward, ready for the fight.

"Marcus," Valder hissed. "Let Ardin deal with him."

He remained, like one of the king's subjects, listening to Selkie bay in the distance. Another swoosh of the trebuchet sent one more boulder sailing over the wall. Soldiers cheered drowning out Olof's orders. A little earthquake rattled the ground and a wet boom sounded over the wall. The men celebrated as they watched the horrors outside the keep, thinking they were doing well, not knowing the warlock was within the courtyard.

Nidra looked to Riley with a smile and waved to Platt. "Collect your price."

Riley stared nervously between Platt and Marcus. "Come here, Platt."

She separated from the queen but clung to the regent's hand. "Riley, what are you doing?"

"I told you." Riley reached a hand to Platt. "I'm not abandoning you."

Of course. Riley was here for Platt. Fingers extended, the youngling waited for the little doe to come to him as if she knew this was all in his plan.

The little doe scanned Marcus's face. Fear the only expression on her pale complexion.

All would be explained tomorrow night, she'd said. Platt had promised, but she'd been stalling. Her plan was to be gone before she had to explain her betrayal. It made sense. Who could blame her? Riley would betray them, come for her, and Marcus, at the very least, wouldn't be able to follow. They'd sent enough death wardens to kill him and everyone else in the keep. Had she planned that? If she wanted to get away from him that badly, she should have just asked. Now that he knew the townsfolk were blood dolls, they could take turns feeding him. There was no need for this ruse. No need for an agreement.

Wide-eyed and pale, Platt didn't move. She stood gaping at him.

"Well?" Marcus spat. "Why are you hesitating? Weren't you waiting for your knight to save you? Has he not come through for you?"

Horror clasped her mouth in a snarl. "He's not my knight."

Marcus laughed. "Oh, are you waiting for him to slay me, slay your *monster*. My death as payment for all the wrongs I've inflicted upon you." Not that he didn't deserve her vengeance. There were plenty of crimes Marcus had committed against her. None for which he'd atoned.

"I don't want him!" Platt's eyes glistened.

"Stop lying!" Marcus spread his claws. "Don't pretend your ruse was not for revenge."

Betrayals collided in his mind.

Dash revealing Serenite secrets to humans based on Asmara's *success*.

Valder using him, for what? Getting a part of Ardin's soul back?

Platt and Riley plotting her escape.

It all came down to one thing.

Marcus was mere parchment. A tool. A thing. Something to use. Trash to discard. A monster to get away from.

Protect the villagers? So that he couldn't eat them. Go to Reginhart? So that he could die for someone deemed more important. Becoming the wall between mage and demon? So that they could rip *him* to shreds instead of each other.

And the worst of it was Platt pretending to want to make this work. Join them together. Become his bride. Become theirs.

If Marcus was suffering, Asmara was devastated. The mage's emotions ran strong as the tide with the depth of oceans. Loyalty was somewhat of a sticking point for him. But Marcus was sent the distraction of fighting a tidal wave of death wardens while everyone else ran.

Everything she had said, everything she had done, her touches, the looks, Platt's gazing awe had been an act. All to keep him from wondering what she was up to. To keep him satisfied. Unsuspecting.

The seething hate, the betrayal that Marcus felt right now, with these golems here to destroy the entire village, Marcus was tempted to help them if he could. But he couldn't. All because he was an enforcer with no other will. Parchment waiting for more words to be scrawled on his skin. Etched tattoo agreements that would sunder him alive if not followed.

And there was his answer. He just wouldn't follow the rules. Marcus would burn to ash and that would be that. Everyone would be happy except Tiecus and Asmara. It would be enough.

A voice deep as thunder inside his head scattered his newfound plan.

Enough treachery. Tiecus's power was something intangible but undeniable, like trying to look into the bright eye. *Little doe is ours. She would not betray us.*

She admitted betrayal! Asmara's emotions swept across his mind and crashed over Marcus as cold as the depths of the ocean.

Little doe admitted no such thing! Tiecus defended.

I warned you—I warned you this very thing would happen. Asmara frothed. *Now we are bound. This is your fault. This is both your fault!*

A battlefield of fire and ice raged within Marcus. He was pinned between both sides—furious heat on one, glacial cold from the other. Volcanic lava spewed forth, and a devastating tsunami met the challenge. Marcus clutched at the two sides of his brain unable to fight both the mage and the demon. Holes, both frigid and scalding at once, burned through his brain.

A different type of burning seared through Marcus. His muscles screamed as if ripping apart. The first agreement blazed at the front of his consciousness. He held on to it like a physical barrier and slammed both Asmara and Tiecus with its force.

No killing Serenite. Marcus forced the mage and demon alike to their respective corners of his mind. *Not from suicide or murder.*

"Marcus?" Platt was there, by his side.

Blackened Elite both on foot and cavalry joined the king's fight against riddled Tier Naug. Dash guarded Jessica with his body as she threw thin bladed knives at the riddled Tier Naug. Riley squatted to the side unnoticed by the others, apparently waiting for his chance to grab Platt and run.

Marcus hovered over the little doe holding his arms out in the physical attempt to separate the mage and the demon in his mind.

"You don't get to look at me with pity," He snarled at Platt. "Your summons to bring me back from Benicar was fruitless." He ran the back of his foreclaw along the altered agreement on his left arm. "See, I don't have to stay in Reginhart. I can go anywhere. Go away from here. I can protect your precious villagers simply by leaving! But you chose . . . you chose not only to chop my heart into pieces but also rip out my soul as well." Marcus felt a smile creep on his face, a smile seemingly belonging to someone else. "Well done, little doe." Marcus mused about his insanity despite his heart throbbing, his entire body burning, and his mind tormented in madness. "I am broken."

Breathless, Platt remained squatted next to Marcus's feet. "I didn't—"

"Go with Riley." He let the youngling's name come out with a snarl.

"No—" Platt scrambled to her feet.

"It's what you want." Marcus wrapped a hand around her waist. "Have a happy life together."

Riley bolted toward them. Marcus tossed Platt the ten feet into Riley's waiting arms.

Platt screamed as Riley caught her. "Noooo!"

Nidra bellowed out in laughter.

More soldiers surrounded Valder, and the archers on the walls started firing arrows toward the oncoming horde beyond the keep. Riley pulled the little doe into the tower, and they were gone.

"Nidra!" Ardin stood at the top of the portcullis wall walk. The magician looked bigger, his cloak darker, his voice more menacing. "It's time you returned."

Nidra laughed. "I'll return, but not with you."

"Come here, little copy." Ardin held out his hand palm up.

Nidra's iridescent eyes burned towards the magician. "I've promised my demon he can have my other half. That would be you."

A disgusted snarl marred Ardin's lips.

Physically, Ardin and Nidra were identical. Nidra held the same straight stiffness of pride, and his posture reached to an unimpressive height. The warlock's hair, face, and even expressions were the same as his twin. Marcus wouldn't be able to tell the difference between the two save for the iridescent eyes of Nidra.

The warlock snarled like a demon, stepped back, and crouched like he was going to scale the wall and attack.

Ardin dissolved, and it was like he'd never been there. The magician reappeared holding a knife to the warlock's throat. "You will come back into me."

"Ardin!" Valder shouted. He, Cornelius, and the others were engaged with the handful of Tier Naug.

The magician hesitated and Nidra chortled, sending a hand signal to his compatriots. One of the Tier Naug howled. The door of the tower burst open. Riddled humans poured out, pouncing on the soldiers. The men protecting the king tightened as one of them went down. Marcus lost sight of Valder and Jessica, but pieces of their clothing peeked through a wall of gleaming metal. Olof bellowed, and Benicarian soldiers rushed to meet the Tier Naug inside the walls. Cornelius shouted orders. Dash was nowhere to be found.

"You've forgotten yourself," said Nidra's, his voice strained. "And my capabilities."

Nidra blocked Ardin's wrist keeping the dagger from digging in. Then Nidra reached back with his other hand groping for the magician's eyes.

Ardin's mouth moved as he turned his head to avoid his face getting clawed. The magician disappeared and reappeared in front of the barricade of soldiers protecting Valder. He threw his hands up and four of the Blackened Elite became eight. It was the same trick as the night Marcus went to the king's aid.

"Pitiful," Nidra said. "You chose tricks and divination over real power."

"I decided wisdom was greater over arrogance," Ardin said.

Ha! Ardin had enough arrogance for both his halves, but Marcus focused on the warlock. Nidra had to be handled.

"There is nowhere for you to go!" Nidra yelled at Ardin. The warlock's obsidian sharp claws glinted in the sunset as he raised his arms. Dirt lifted in a solid clump in unison with his raised hands. "And I will kill you!"

"Careful you don't bite your own tongue off." Marcus raised his hands. "Nocte muros terra!" His own clump of dirt rose and hurled toward Nidra. The warlock turned and countered Marcus, sending the earth in pieces across the courtyard.

"Don't worry." Nidra pointed to Marcus. "My little golem pets are coming for you."

Marcus could feel his blood drop to his feet. He snapped his head over to Valder and then scanned the soldiers. It was clear Tiecus would not let him die from self-immolation which left Marcus one choice. Not because he wanted to, but because his new hate for life gave him an immense amount of energy. He wanted to rip and tear. He wanted to kill. And because he didn't care if he burned to death, he set Selkie free with two words, allowing the horse to eat whomever he wanted. "Glaciem desolati."

"This *discussion* is over." Ardin started to fade, his body swirling like grains of sand. "You are done."

"I'll make you listen. And when you die, you'll understand why I never returned." Nidra stomped his foot. A shock wave scattered the sand that became Ardin shot back against the crowd of soldiers. Everyone in front of Nidra fell flat on the ground. Tier Naug, soldiers, everyone, even Marcus found himself on his ass.

The warlock smiled at Marcus. "You like that? I learned it from your elf friend."

"Serenite!" Marcus clutched his hands and gritted his teeth. "They are called Serenite!"

But the effect of a bark blast stunned Marcus the same as everyone else. He fought against the ringing in his ears and the sluggish movement of his limbs.

Ardin reformed, unaffected, helping Benicarian soldiers stand up.

Nidra grew furious. "After all this time, you want to reunite now?" Nidra shook his head. "It's too late. We are too different."

"And yet here you are!" Ardin taunted.

"Because you have something I need," Nidra shouted back.

"Yes!" The magician disappeared and reappeared before the warlock. "We need to be reintegrated."

Nidra howled, "You believed you could ball your anger, your wrongs, your mistakes, your fears, and"—Nidra looked at Valder—"all your sins."

"Nidra." Ardin held his hands up in supplication. "I was wrong to push those things into another self—into you. I wasn't even prepared for my success."

Marcus stood with his mouth agape. Ardin claiming fault? That was new.

"For a first attempt, you did very well." Nidra opened his arms. He sneered at Valder, just starting to rise from the shock wave. "But then you thought you could kill me and get rid of your discomforts as if you could write 'em down, crumble 'em up, and toss 'em to be rid of 'em."

The warlock's words hit Marcus in the heart. It was almost the same thing he wanted to say to Asmara and Tiecus for a long time. Marcus was a pit to place their despair and pain. They had used him to deal with their incompatibilities instead of dealing with it themselves. Because of their lack of cooperation, none of the three had found peace.

He bayed in chortles at the moon unable to stop. He understood why Nidra had hunted them down. Why he was here for Ardin. It wasn't all that different from what Marcus wanted. To be whole without needing the other parts of himself. Marcus laughed with an intensity of years of frustration.

Both Tier Naug and fighting soldiers near Marcus took incremental steps away. Valder assessed him with a concerned eye, which made Marcus laugh all the more.

With an expression as sour as cheese on a hot day, Nidra lunged for Ardin. This time the magician eddied into a small whirlwind of sand and floated over the keep's walls. The warlock followed him over, and they were both gone.

There was only one way Nidra and Ardin would find their unity.

"Let's find out if warlocks have souls." Marcus loosened Tiecus and let him come to the forefront.

Chapter 35

THE ENFORCER CLIMBS the wall, but I descend with my horns and claws. Glacias begs her freedom from the death wardens. She wishes me to help. The moving waters that fire-horse-friend longs to join crash into the rocks. It is angry that all it can do to help is pound at the cliffs.

Terra has the worst of all. She screams against the death that holds her. Death and decay are her right, but these bodies hold her hostage instead. The sisters screech as they are torn asunder. I am their brother. I will free them. None torment my throng but me.

"I can help." Mostly-Serenite named Dash looks over at the death that holds my sisters. He stays outside the gates. At least he is courageous.

I huff. What great power does Mostly-Serenite have? Will he puke them to freedom?

"No." I understand the word now. Fully. My sisters need my black flame, not pointed ear tricks.

Dash's skin ripples as bones crack and adjust. His five fingers merge into four-digit claws. The fourth digit grows thick and long like the branch of a tree. Skin, muscle, and tissue stretch to their limits. Wings 35 feet long spread out. His neck pops and grows. A thin membrane of skin widens, connecting his arms down to his ankles much like a bat.

More snaps of bone and cartilage pop. A toothy jaw extends out like a flesh saw. His long tail wraps around his short legs and feet. Furry hairlike fibers cover his body and parts of the wings. Mostly-Serenite is not a bird nor a bat but a very large flying reptile.

"Wing Finger." I give respect to the very old demon, one of the elders, that has taken Dash. He can ride Ventus. He can be four paws on Terra. He can be the shiny silvers that swim in Glacias. His demon can go where others shy away. But does he have breath of black fire? No. "It is an honor."

Wing Finger screams the high-pitched screech reminiscent of an old one as his form becomes prominent. The beak is long and straight. Four claw fingers at the ends of each flesh wing twitch. He is possibly uglier than me. But I am scariest. I am also impatient.

"Follow." I flatten out and lengthen my stride. My hind hooves catch up with my front paws. Strong weight sits upon my crown, my death-point horns aim toward these golems.

They're dead Benicarian soldiers, the mage says. *At least for their sake, I hope they're dead.*

"They are Nidra's army." I charge forth toward the walking mud and bones.

Silt drips down their empty eyes to open mouths. My sisters, Glacias and Terra, scream trying to escape their bonds. Splotches fall from the golems, but Glacias and Terra are pulled back to the walking bones.

Rotted flesh lumbers. Elements are unaccustomed to legs or arms. Sweet meat scent, ocean rank of dead shiny silver swimys, and musk of a bog rolls off my pursuers. Life and death together in one being is a curse of agony. Death, chewing their insides forever, rides them.

Their sickening cadence, their mud droppings from every hole enrage me. My sisters are twisted and forced to bond with death. My breath of anger will send them back.

Cornelius.

One word brings understanding. These are the men alpha king sent. They died feeding the flame heads. They were part of our throng. These golems will feel my wrath.

I breathe in, and air meets the reservoir of hate in our core. My roar explodes. Fire rakes through my lungs. Darkness before me, from me, lets no light or life escape. The Atra Solumn is my breath, and it wraps around these golems. The air around us flees. Shadows climb away in terror. Even the light from the Twinkling Eyes in the sky above dim from the pull of my black flame. Before it consumes me, I stop to tally the claimed.

None. All are impervious. These golems have no souls, and the rank, shuffling, soulless ones advance. My footing slips. My claws and fangs will spread their bones. I am enraged by my sister's wails, and talons flash. The first is struck.

Ventus slaps me as diaphanous wings beat but make no sound. Wing Finger comes and takes away one. Hundreds still trudge forward.

I strike. Limbs drop, mud ooze slides, my sisters' tormented song continues. Shards of bone pass by, limbs fall to the ground but reconstruct as they meet with the body of ooze. How long my rage lasts I am unsure, but I tire. They keep coming.

These golems bleed mud that floats back to them. Ignis urges me to rush in, to consume. This is the backward way of escape. Ignis reasons if we reach the other side, the danger is behind. It is fire's way. My way.

Death-point horns lower to plow my way through. Powerful hind quarters lurch forward into these golems. I toss mud-men right then left, over my shoulder. I force them away. I drive further into their numbers. But they use mass as their weapon. They cling to my fur by the dozens.

These droves don't use swords to cut or fists to hit. They hold on with hands of mud. Silt weighs me down as effective as boulders on my back. Clumps and clods of clay thicken under my step. They want me immobile, to crush me.

I keep moving.

A wall forces me down. I lurch forward, but these golems grow heavier. Claws and hooves slip. Crushing weight will be my death.

More pile on. Terra will swallow us whole. Air grows thick. I sneeze as mud oozes its way into my nose. The curdling sound of slime crawling down my ears muffles my sisters' anguished lament. Silt coats my tongue and gags my breath.

The Enforcer wraps his presence around me. He will bear witness of my death. I am in my body, my form, and have no host to protect me. I expect nothing from the mage. He chants his annoying phrases in the way mages do.

The weight on my back shifts. The ground below feels dry. I can make purchase with my paws and hooves.

Wait, the Enforcer says.

My tether to this world, the rope that will prevent me from sinking into the depths of the dead, pulls me back into life's fight. Water flows away from the golems. The mage, he has done this. Without water, the golems are dirt and rotted flesh. My sisters are temporarily removed from these golems making them immobile and lighter.

"Lighter" is a relative term. All my effort goes to scratching, clawing, and reaching for Ventus. Scratching and clawing rips flesh into pieces. Coughing releases the dirt air blockage in my lungs. I have no chance for more.

Ventus drifts inside the cave of golems. I greet the darkness of night discarding the stagnation of death. The crumbling flesh of these golems encourages me to fight.

Hurry! The mage can keep my sisters away for only so long.

Glacias and Terra are forcing their way back to these golems. My sisters fight their impulsion, but I feel the cost is their sanity. Loose earth and dead flesh pile under my chest like stairs. A paw strikes air, and I climb out of my grave. Bodies with eyeless sockets look up at their current master of the bone pile.

That would be me.

Oozing clods begin to fill the golem's holes. This time I run for the forest and call on Ignis to boil the water inside these golems. Steam burns my paws. I run, but heat cooks the golems. An ear-piercing cry from above shoots out. Wing Finger flies past, shaking his feet and flying in erratic bursts. I wince. My chest fills with sympathy.

Oh, perfect timing, fur ball. The mage makes situations worse.

"Go, sleep." I send an image of the mage underneath the den of golems.

These golems lumber faster after me. Steam rises in a cloud, swirls, cools, and seeps back into their hosts.

Tiecus! The mage speaks my name for the first time since the Enforcer's birth. *You are a stupid kur!*

Asmara, the Enforcer booms as if he shouts over a wide space, not within the confines of my mind. *Freeze the water.*

I noticed, the mage retorts, sending me condescension as if I knew heating their water would help these golems move faster.

Asmara! the Enforcer shouts again. *There's no way to defeat these things? Can't you conjure up some help?*

The mage chants, but it is sound he hides behind.

Asmara! There is force behind the Enforcer's thought. *What do you know!*

A word. The mage relents. *Only the conjurer knows the word.*

Tiecus! the Enforcer roars at me. *Go back! Turn around!*

That's exactly what he wants, the mage snarls.

So, he'll demense us if we're dead or alive. The Enforcer agrees with me.

If we die, Tiecus must promise not to return, the mage says. *He is not allowed to reveal anything about the Serenite.*

Why are you retaining that train of thought? The Enforcer pulls himself to the surface. I push him back. *Dash has already done the damage.*

And if Nidra enslaves us?

Would you rather run for all eternity?

A wave of power splutters through my body. Frost coats my fur. I stumble over the thicket as the mage pulls on his element. He calls the wild water.

I run faster. I must outrun Glacias. I toss my horns in fury. Bark columns fly past. The sound comes first; angry water sweeps everything in apathy.

The first layer is nothing, a small wave, a discreet warning that comes too late. A second layer of water blankets over the first. This new layer washes over my hocks. A tide pushes me away from the golems. Ground melts, and golems dissolve. Bone alone does not keep creatures upright. These golems tumble. The tide sweeps them in front of me.

Another wave crashes. This one sweeps me under. I am overturned and slam horns first into Terra. Flailing, I try to right myself. My horns wedge under a wood column. I shake my head to get free. Saltwater fills my nostrils. Twisting my head, I snort, forcing Ventus and Glacias out. At least, it is only salt water.

The sound of a thousand voices whisper in my mind. These voices are not my sisters.

Soul Burner. The living columns speak.

Cold numbs my mind, my body. My paws thrash in the underwater silence.

The mage pushes to get out.

No. I force the mage back. *They talk to me.*

We cannot save you, Soul Burner. The living pillars say what I know. *But we can help you.*

The root I am pinned under releases me. For this I have no words. More than grateful is all I can give. I am free. I swim to air.

Crunching noises of wood on wood, I see living pillars fall. I know what the living pillars sacrifice. They are many. I am one.

Glacias is angry. Wild water claims everything. Golems grow on each other combining to the height of the living columns.

Cold burns. Weakness numbs my mind. But my sisters call.

Let me up! the mage screams. *I can get us out of here.*

"My sisters," I snarl. How dare he want to abandon my kin. "You call. I help."

My hooves try to gain hold in grooves of the floating wood. I rest against the ones that dare stay upright against the wild water. The dead float by. Not the living dead golems, the living now dead. Parts of human-made dens, they call houses, ride Glacias.

The living pillar that saves me starts to lean. It has given up Terra's hold to release me. I jump to the closest living pillar as the one goes down.

My refuge wood living pillar catches its sinking throng member by the tips of its pine needle arms. Its companion, my friend, hangs precariously. Rocking against waves of uneven dips and ascents, I descend.

Strain and cold shake my hind quarters, but I am no mage. I do not leave. Four claws dig into the uprooted wanderer. With all my Ignis, all my strength, I pull.

I feel them. A thousand voices speak of resignation. A thousand voices fight the sadness and dig further to remain. One thousand voices are silent watching me. They show me this living pillar was one of many wave riders. Many are lost.

Why save one when more have fallen? I feel their despair.

This is reason why Ignis is the great brother. When all seems lost and when loss turns into hopelessness, Ignis turns away the lethargy. Fire burns hotter before it grows cold.

I am Tiecus. My name means great hope. I pull on the energy that hope produces and lift the uprooted living pillar horizontal.

"Why save one?" the mage says.

"Because, to save many, you begin with one," I say.

My perch holds its companion, and I hang in exhaustion. I feel the living pillars sway, grabbing on to other lost throng members. They will save their kind and the creatures that cling to them.

I hear the *kersplunk* behind me. One huge, muddy golem, as tall as the living pillars, lifts a stump leg out of the wild water. Another *kersplunk* with the same lumbered cadence.

My reserves are spent. My sisters sing that I will join them, and we will be joyful. They must be mad. Gravity takes me.

I hear the sound of Glacias being broken, and Ventus shifts so cold it burns. I land on jutted ice. The wild water freezes in place. Waves harden. Forever cresting peaks jab my body. As sleeping grounds, I would claim for wanting.

Yet, I underestimate the mage. He has yet to expose this extent of his power.

The ability to make wild water stay in place makes me wonder what Serenite were before the curse. Stillness prevails. The living pillars, the wild water, the golem, the moving tide of presence the mage calls time, all of it remains still. Efforts to remain in the forefront dissipates my energy. I would let the black consume me if not for the burn in my tail.

Stay awake! the Enforcer says.

Slow abyss will have to wait for one more final act.

Talons pierce my shoulders. Defiant, I roar.

"Heavy," Wing Finger hisses, throwing Ventus in all directions with his flapping wings.

We rise, and I know why my tail nub burns. The frozen wild water has captured the only scrawny part of me. I am held between the frozen wild waters and Wing Finger's talons.

Cut it off! The mage is frantic to the point of unreasonable.

I illustrate the suggestion's equivalent by showing my claws swiping off his ears.

The Enforcer laughs, and it quiets both mage and me. His laugh is the want of death. His laugh is the sound of mindless destruction. I've heard stories of hosts descending to madness. It was not a fate I wished for any. The Enforcer travels beyond madness. Essence of my essence is broken.

Tiecus, the mage whispers under the sound of madness. *Don't let him up.*

Enough. The Enforcer pushes me down. His strength comes from wrath.

Marcus, perhaps we should let him handle this, the mage says.

The Enforcer pulls the mage. Where he takes him, I am unable to say. I only feel a hole where the mage usually resides.

Wing Finger strains against my weight. His vicious wings pump harder.

The golem separates into single entities. The one golem crumbles into many shards of frozen wild water and ooze. If I stay here, the silt ooze will pull me down, and I will join my sisters.

The Enforcer rips me from the forefront. I hear a crack like thunder, and then I am alone, cut off from the mage, from the Enforcer, in blackness where sleep resides.

Chapter 36

DASH'S DEMON COMMANDED Ventus as a true warrior of wind. Bursts of air swirled from the beating of his wings. The muted flaps were felt more than heard. Claws retained their hold on Marcus when he metamorphosed to the forefront. Talons sank into his shoulders like swords and sent burning pain. Marcus didn't have time to notice. The golems were recovering.

Just as Tiecus's tail was stuck in the ice, so was Marcus's last vertebra. He pulled Dash with him, the old one flapping his wings as Marcus shrank to size. Neither his tail bone nor the ice gave way. Still, Wing Finger used both wings to pull harder and screeched.

"You." Marcus spat the word. "Why didn't you go back to Ziodonia?"

Iridescent eyes flickered red and scowled. Wings flapped unyielding to their task.

A golem half-crawled, half-oozed its way toward Marcus. Its undead hand stretched out to grab him with an open mouth in a silent moan.

"Pull, now!" Marcus pushed against the frozen water with his feet as wings beat and slapped his arms.

Ice dust scattered and threw stinging shards of frozen miniature peaks. His long black hair whipped like saw grass across his bare chest. The crack of ice, a burst of lift, and Marcus was free.

They rose with the aid of Ventus—Marcus dangling by the winged demon's talons. Without Asmara holding the tsunami back, the ice began melting. Soon, the hardened blocks would become rivulets of water. Those puddles would become streams, and rivers would flow on land. The golems would escape their prison soon. Then they'd be after him again. Thank the Atra Solumn mud couldn't fly.

The pain didn't come immediately. He was too numb. Through gasps, Marcus said, "We have to find Nidra."

Nothing. Dash's demon didn't acknowledge him.

Marcus's shock faded, and pain ripped the wind out of him preventing Marcus from screaming. As he gulped for air, the throb in his tail bone climbed like spindly legs up his spine and planted a sack of agony at the base of his skull. His backbone reverberated like he'd fallen and smacked, arse first, from the height of the portcullis. Small gasps defied tears taken away by the wind.

His shoulders ached with a dull sensation of sharp cutting slashes along his shoulders and back. Three sharp talons gouged holes through the soft part under his collar bone. He wished he could fall back into his mind, but that meant he'd have to let one of *them* out. Tiecus was shaking off sleep, and Asmara's presence felt small and exhausted.

Ice shards must have molded to his tailbone because he was so cold. Forcing air in and out of his lungs, Marcus remained a passenger while Dash's demon coasted over a treetop landscape. Pushing aside the throb in his shoulders and the stunned vibration in his spine, Marcus, wanting any distraction to shield him from the pain, looked down.

The moon emphasized every crevice, every low dip, and all the rough leaves on a superficial ground. The treetops spanned forever. He focused on the landscape to the west where the line of forest stopped and the ocean took over and continued. The watery expanse glittered and reflected the moon. Platt's hair shimmered like the ocean waves sparkling along the surface. He could see her along the coastline slumped over Riley's shoulder.

Dash's demon flew so high Marcus could almost see the entire forest. The chill of the wind splashed over his naked chest, and Tiecus doused them in warmth. His fire could provide a fight from the cold better than clothes.

Pain gave way to a groggy dizziness. His head light and his body heavy, Marcus saw the exotic surface of foliage as a bed.

"They search for light. Ignis could help them." Marcus lolled his head to the side. "But Terra needs Glacias and Ventus to help grow trees." Marcus chuckled, wishing Platt could see this.

But Platt was gone.

She'd left with Riley, and Marcus was never going to see her again. Stab wounds to the heart plunged cutting out the remaining kindness left within.

You're losing too much blood. Tiecus can't keep healing you, Asmara whispered in his ear. *My magic will help, but you don't have long before you faint from acute anemia. Try to focus.*

Asmara's help was a spell to slow his heart rate so the blood he was losing would slow. It wasn't much, but Marcus felt a tickle and his awareness snapped into place—and he screamed in pain. "Why the ever-loving fuck did you have to poke holes through my shoulders!"

Wing Finger continued traveling south, away from Reginhart toward Ziodonia, the Serenite enclave.

A voice chimed like a bell in his mind. It was not Asmara's voice, nor did it belong to Tiecus. Dash's demon was an old one. The older the demon, the less a demens became a fight against wills and more about a telepathic link to anyone close by. *There was only the soul-burner's mass to grab.* The voice within his head reverberated in his mind, and its presence was as vast as the sky. Then it was gone. Wing Finger had spoken to Marcus in his mind without fighting through his mental defenses.

Marcus's body burned all over. It wasn't just one or two agreements on fire—all of them blazed.

"Dash." Marcus hedged his words in warning. "We need to go back to the stronghold. We need to find Nidra."

A concept flitted the edges of his mind. Asmara came across an interesting journal entry. One the mage was reluctant to share. Marcus suspected the edges of this idea came only because they were in dire need.

"Tell me what you know, mage," Marcus growled.

Asmara hesitated then said, *Everything has a name. A true name. The designation assigned to them—at the beginning. At their beginning.*

"The beginning of what?" Wind lashed at his limbs draining heat and feeling from his hands. Marcus could no longer feel the scales of Dash's legs.

The beginning of their existence. Everything started as nothing, but then with a designation, a name, they became something. If I can find out the name of the golems, the name Nidra gave them, then we can stop them.

"I thought you said all we have to do is kill him and the golems would stop."

Yes . . . I did . . .

"What are you not telling me?" The riddled envoy kept a firm grip on Marcus and continued to fly south.

There's a chance that won't work. We could kill Nidra, but that might not stop the golems. The only way to really know is . . .

"To demense Nidra." Marcus felt a cold brick settle at the bottom of his stomach—and the brick's name was acceptance. "Dash, if you take me to Ziodonia, the golems will follow."

Dash stopped flapping and soared. He didn't turn to Marcus or look at him. His beak faced south and didn't waver.

"The only way they will stop is if I get their name. You know what that means, don't you, old one?"

The rocking motion of wings sent ripples of pain across his shoulders. Marcus gasped and gritted his teeth.

"If you don't turn north right now, I'll make you drop me."

Dash closed his own talons, and Marcus cried out. The quiet and flapping of wings continued south.

"Fine," Marcus raged. "When they come to the enclave, I will lead them through every part of the clutch. They will cut down every tree, trample every root, and dislodge every shrub to get to me." Marcus twisted to get free and shouted as his muscles ripped further. "And when you find out you can't stop them, I will help them destroy your precious little inside-out piece of bark."

Insulting Dash's tree in Ziodonia worked. The flying demon opened his claws and let Marcus go.

A flash of shock, the lurch of his stomach, and panic twisted new urgency in his elemental training.

Marcus spread out his claws desperately calling to any element. The treetops came closer at top velocity. He willed forth all the elements using the terror of the free fall as his conduit of power.

But the elements didn't respect emotion nor could they relate to it. Just as demons didn't understand the concept of "no," the elements didn't understand fear.

Get yourself together, Asmara hissed. *This is what I've been training you for. Call them. Call to the elements.*

His stomach equalized to the fall, and Marcus spread his numb body out and opened his eyes.

Plummeting to his death, naked—no less—gained him clarity. Every bump and rise of the exotic false ground came into focus. The ocean, the trees, the air he fell through, and the light of his shining eyes cast a beam in the darkness and converged.

Instead of fear, Marcus felt the powerful force of all the elements. Not as singular pieces coming together, but as a whole to create a different type of power. A different type of element. What Asmara had told him about his abilities, about all the elements not as four but as one, came to focus.

Glacias nourished Terra. Earth in turn gave fuel for Ignis. Fire had the power to create Ventus. Wind could sway Glacias, shape Terra, and move Ignis. Ventus, the most intangible element, had sway over the rest. Air connected each of its sisters and brother to the other—or separated them just as Marcus separated Tiecus and Asmara. They all were powerful.

Marcus saw the cycle of the elements not as a circle but as four points coming together and weaving apart in a dance of balance.

He knew what Asmara meant by letting the power grow and setting it free. Trusting his preferred element, he called forth Ventus, not expecting a miracle, but believing in wind's control.

Marcus asked to fly. At the very least, stop falling, and preferably not because he had reached the ground.

Ventus responded. Wind pushed against his body. The force of a hurricane splashed air and leaves in his face. His body slowed its descent. Marcus asked, and Ventus responded. The forest top was closer now, but he just might manage to claw his way down safely.

Marcus held his breath and hoped not to break bones in the process. If he lived through this, he was going to kill Dash—even if it meant going back to Ziodonia.

And then his head became light and thoughts were too hard to hold on to. His blood loss was too great a burden to stay awake, and the affects of anemia took hold. Marcus couldn't focus, or think, and could barely breathe.

A reptilian foot wrapped around his ankle and yanked him sideways. Silent wings beat. The force of air from Dash's effort to snag him slapped Marcus in the face. Blood and wind rushed to his ears.

Dash's demon righted Marcus and set him on the ground. Without the talons in his shoulders, the wounds healed, but the damage would take days to mend.

The elder demon landed and eyed Marcus. A set of clothes, boots, and a waterskin dropped in front of him. It was not water inside the waterskin. There was blood and Marcus drank it all. It was enough to clear his head and stop the sharp pain in his shoulders.

Without a word, Dash's demon nodded his round head and took for flight, again heading south.

"Thanks so much for the help," Marcus yelled out. But he understood how complicated a human–demon power struggle could get. It was not Dash in control, yet the Frazzerian and the demon seemed to share many of the same goals.

He won't hurt them, you think? Asmara asked, "them" as in Serenite.

"I don't think Dash would allow it." Marcus put on his pants, shirt, and boots finally having relief from his burning agreements.

Hmmm . . . The mage hummed noncommittally.

Across a field, he saw streams of light chasing a sleek yellow cougar demon.

"Selkie!" Seeing the demon steed pulled Marcus out of his thoughts.

The streaks of light slowed, and a whinny pierced the night.

Marcus laughed, and the fire burning from Selkie's mane, tail, eyes, and hoofs flashed on a course to the fleeing cougar demon.

Nidra!

He ran alongside Selkie until the horse put in speed after the cougar demon, leaving Marcus behind. An eerie silence disoriented Marcus, and then he was completely turned around when the tree line broke and the cliffs of Reginhart prevented Nidra's cougar demon from escaping Selkie.

The fire horse pranced in agitation stepping from side to side as the cougar spat and backed up into a craggy circular patch that dropped down into the ocean. It was a lookout, a place where the wind could knock a person over the side to never be seen again.

No matter which way the cougar demon went, a fifteen-hundred-pound fiery horse was ready to pounce.

"He's mine." Out from the trees, Ardin walked in front of the king.

It was Valder, but his hair was peppered with silver, and his shoulders framed the body of a fit warrior the likes of Cornelius. His eyes were cold, harder than Marcus had ever seen in him. His handsome face weathered by sun. This was not the young king who'd sent Marcus to Reginhart after winning at chess. This was the adult Valder would become. This was King Eric Valder's other half. A part of his soul.

Marcus eyed the king who turned his battle-hardened expression to him. *Is this the real king or an illusion?* Marcus stepped forward, thinking very unfriendly thoughts untoward the man before him. A twinge of heat flared across Marcus's shoulders, right where the first agreement with Valder spanned across his back. This was the king.

Wind whirled a sand shield around the cougar demon and then dropped, leaving Nidra in his robes.

Marcus scoffed in disgust. "Why can't I have my clothes on after a change?"

Illusionist, Asmara said. *Remember?*

Nidra ignored Marcus and cast his attention to the older Valder. "I knew you weren't far behind."

Ardin stood before the king, but his body was too thin to block Valder's wide chest. "Enough of this . . ." Ardin motioned to step forward.

The king set a hand on Ardin's shoulder. "Nidra, time to come home. You have fulfilled your mission."

"No!" Nidra snarled. "I am not stupid to the games you play." The warlock snapped his eyes to Marcus and waved at the triad. "You don't think I know why he's here."

Killing Tier Naug was the definition of the reason Marcus came. Nidra had all the hallmarks of a Tier Naug, and yet . . .

"None of my agreements burned when it came to you." Marcus stared at Nidra. Just as they'd never burned for Cornelius either. And there'd never be a more perfect specimen of Tier Naug than the seneschal.

Valder let out an audible sigh, filled with relief, saying more than words.

"That's not proof!" Nidra screeched. He stepped back, stumbling at the very edge of the cliffside.

"Stop!" The king's voice boomed as his fingers clutched Ardin's shoulder.

Nidra looked back at the sea and turned back with a threatening smile on his face and balanced on the balls of his feet on the edge.

Valder growled in a deep baritone, "Nidra . . ."

"He's going to go over the edge," Marcus whispered.

Nidra is threatening suicide, Asmara said. *He knows he's too valuable for the king to lose.*

"He won't," Ardin said.

"How do you know what I wouldn't do," Nidra hissed. "You haven't had the experiences I've had."

Something moved from behind Marcus. Selkie swung around and went charging into the trees. The fire steed had been inching his way back to the forest. He could guess why. Golems weren't fast, but they were persistent. His time escaping them was up.

The three beside Marcus focused on each other and paid no mind to Selkie. Valder sidestepped Ardin, held out his hand to Nidra, and said in a voice so low that Marcus could barely make out the word "Please . . ."

Nidra crouched and narrowed his eyes. He stared at the offered hand and up into the king's face. Whatever the warlock saw made him hesitate and lick his lips.

"You always do this." Nidra scowled. "You say things will change, but they never do, and you lie. Look at him." Nidra motioned his chin to Ardin. "You're hurting him the most."

The king didn't look to Ardin and took another step toward the warlock. "You could stop the pain for all of us, but you chose . . . this." Valder rolled his wrist to encompass all of Nidra.

Within, Asmara watched intently, and something clicked in the Serenite's mind. *Oh, for all the stars . . . this . . . is a love quarrel? A love quarrel!*

"Like me and Platt?" Marcus huffed under his breath.

A pang went through all three hearts. *Maybe.*

Tears welled up in Nidra's eyes, but the pain matched the expression of hate. "You put it all on me. I'm to blame?

Of course, you would. A king can do what he likes," Nidra spat. "You just push until you get what you want. And then I live with your decision. You . . . bastard!" Nidra lifted a hand and sent a fire ball toward Valder.

"No!" Marcus leaped for Nidra.

Ardin tackled Valder.

All four went down.

Marcus held the warlock as they both went over the side. Nidra froze in shock. Asmara rushed near the surface. He let out a concussion bark. The sound hitting the air was enough to send them back into the cliffs. Marcus threw his free arm out, cementing his claws into the cliff's edge. His shoulder muscles felt as if they were torn again, and he gritted his teeth and screeched.

This is it Marcus! Find the name!

Nidra's eyes were wide, and Marcus shoved into the warlock's mind. The initial push was easy. Nidra had been distracted, but then the real fight began.

The warlock's mind was an emotional mess. Silver lines were strung across a vast cavern with their ends tied to tangled messes of balled-up threads. They hung against the cavern walls like spider silk pouches holding eggs. A ball of light hit Marcus, pulling him in, twisting reality, and showing memories. Words would not form.

Nidra went straight for the part of Marcus's brain that controlled body mechanics—specifically, the part that reminded his lungs to breathe. Marcus choked. Air didn't go through his windpipe. The shield that protected Asmara and Tiecus remained, but once Marcus suffocated, the two wouldn't have his protection.

In a distant part of his awareness, Marcus felt someone grip his wrist on the outside world and pull him up from the ledge.

Valder.

Another presence attacked Nidra from another side. Ardin. He wasn't a warlock or a mage, so how?

"Ardin . . ." Valder's voice wavered. "Make it quick."

Out in the distance, Selkie let out a high-pitched bay, and the slick, sucking sounds of golems approached.

Nidra screamed, allowing Marcus to plunge into the warlock's mind once more. Marcus felt Nidra's separation between demon and host. Chains sank deep into the cavernous walls. The deep anchors of the cougar demon tore away from the warlock's mind, pulling chunks of flesh from the inside. The wall bled, and Nidra started disintegrating from the inside. More chains sprang from the blackness and sank into the wall, damaging Nidra's mind. Four-pronged anchors crashed into the silvery nests.

Keep his memories intact, demon! Ardin screamed from inside his mind. *I need him to remember!*

He's being attacked by five sides. Asmara cast his heated response back to the magician. *His constitution can't barricade against the different minds. Stop overwhelming him and converge already!*

Nidra twisted and screeched.

Every memory, every thought was laid bare for Marcus to watch—to know. Things they did for Valder, to him, and in his name came tumbling into his mind. Crushing shame. Self-defeating embarrassment. Pure elation. Innocence tainted with lust. The pain of a rendered soul. Thoughts came and went too fast to process. But one memory bound the two halves of Nidra and Ardin together and filtered through Marcus's mind clear as if it were that morning.

The journal that lay open to a page on the ground instructed Ardin how to summon a demon. Thick yellow mist the color of Nidra's cougar demon twirled in a slow spiral. A much younger version of the magician stood before the mist. His head had been shaved to show the shape of his skull, and still it was as if he wore a red-skin cap. His freckles were many over his face, and his murky-blue eyes sparkled in hope. Ardin wore a plain tunic and pants, no sign of a cowl, hood, or cape. The young Tier Naug couldn't be more than a fresh adultling. Not fully grown, but not a weeling.

"You can take this part away? I'll remain the same?" young Ardin said to the yellow mist.

Inside, Marcus groaned. That was not how you made an agreement with a demon. "Specific!" Marcus spat. "You must name specifics."

Neither entity heard him. The memory played without change.

Too fast to react, Ardin was on the ground, a mirror image of himself crouched opposite the magician.

He hadn't seen everything, but Marcus knew enough. In effect, Nidra and Ardin shared a broken soul over a person they could not rightfully have.

"Out!" Ardin blasted at Marcus. And with that, Marcus was allowed to breathe. Once again, his body flared hot and burning.

"We have to help Valder." Marcus gritted his teeth.

How? Tiecus was awake, and his strength added to distracting Nidra.

We work together, Asmara said.

Marcus remained inside Nidra's mind but also saw himself in the outside world holding the warlock.

On the inside, Ardin pulled half of Nidra inside himself, rejecting the demon, pushing the cougar demon out. The process was fascinating. He'd never seen anyone expel a demon from its host. Marcus held fast, breaking free of Nidra's hold now that the two mangled spirits from the same person quivered, one fighting the process, the other trying to fuse them both.

Ardin kept thwarting memories. The fact that the memories were technically his own was of no consequence.

Stop trying to choose which thoughts to keep and which to throw out, Marcus admonished.

But Ardin's rejected memories would not reinsert themselves into Nidra or his demon. They went straight for the magician. Horrified at the recollections trying to reinsert themselves, Ardin shoved years of tattered incidents at Marcus.

It was too much to process. Marcus shoved the thoughts right back at Ardin.

"I don't want them." Ardin's hood dropped back and exposed his tear-streaked face.

"You have to take them, good or bad. All of them or don't take Nidra back at all." Marcus didn't blame Ardin for wanting to cast out a part of himself he didn't like. But excluding these parts meant rejecting Nidra. And Nidra was being torn apart by Marcus, Ardin, Tiecus, and Nidra's demon.

Silt wrapped itself around Marcus. Mud golems slithered up his body and turned into hard stone, constricting his movement and his breathing.

Marcus scattered Nidra's mind searching for the word he needed. Through haze and a colossal headache, he couldn't find the name.

Mud seeped into his mouth. Gobs of sand and water choked him. The golem around him reached down to fill his lungs. Clay squeezed his insides. More sludge crawled its way inside.

I would rather die than go back, Nidra thought.

The admittance solidified Marcus's suspicion. *He doesn't have the word for the golems, does he?*

Kill them, Marcus! Asmara said. *That's the only way to live.*

Valder stood over them, eyes intense, hands threaded through his hair. A powerful man helpless to do anything about the situation.

If I kill them now, I kill them both, Marcus thought. *I may not be able to have the person I want, but it doesn't mean it's too late for others who want each other.*

Can you not feel the golems climbing in through your mouth! Asmara screamed. *They'll destroy you!*

Ardin! Marcus called out in thought. *Accept him for all he is.*

Marcus pushed into what was left of Nidra's consciousness. He fumbled with Nidra's split vocal chords. He made Nidra feel the burn of his lungs, his organs being crushed, of sludge seeping into his nose. He made the warlock believe the golems were after him.

Then they were all inside a bubble much the same as when Platt had summoned them from Benicar.

Ardin sat on a translucent curved bench. Tiecus lay on the ground avoiding the walls with his horns while Asmara shoved a book behind his back and sat across from Ardin. Marcus leaned a shoulder against the spherical wall still feeling the effects where his physical body was still entrapped by golems. Asmara was giving him a reprieve inside wherever this sphere happened to be.

"My journal," Ardin seethed. "Give it back."

"Is it really yours?" Asmara's voice reflected a cool, icy wave of indifference.

Ardin stared at his counterpart across the way. "You . . ." The magician glared at the mage's long, curled ears. "You're the people Dash has been talking about. You're a Serenite."

Asmara scoffed, "Of course, you'd be the only one to call me what I am."

And not an elf.

"Give me the name of the golems." Marcus placed a threatening step toward Ardin.

"Why should I?" Ardin shot back.

Tiecus lifted his head and growled. It seemed to be the first time Ardin acknowledged the demon and scrambled back away from him.

"Name," Marcus growled.

"He doesn't know." Asmara leaned forward. "Do you?"

"How do neither not know?" Marcus turned to the mage.

"The name is lost between them both." Asmara stared at Ardin. "The only way to stop the golems is for *this magician* to accept Nidra. All of him. You can't cut away the pieces you don't want."

"Give me the book, and I can call off the golems." Ardin straightened his robes trying to look at ease with a demon five feet away from him.

Asmara snarled. "See, this is why I don't like magicians. Deceivers. Tricksters. Charlatans. You can outright lie. As a true elementalist, I must tell you that I can hand over the book to you in here, but you won't be able to take it outside." The mage waved his hand toward the sphere.

Ardin looked from Marcus, to Tiecus, and then to Asmara. Marcus could tell when the magician put it all together. "You're the mage." Ardin pointed to Asmara. "He's the demon." Ardin pointed to Tiecus. "But why do you need him?" Ardin pointed to Marcus.

"You know that golems don't stop, right?" Asmara narrowed his eyes. "They will go after your king. Do you want your lover to die?"

"That isn't your business!" Ardin stood, fists clenched, teeth bared.

"And neither is your concern for Marcus." Asmara retained his cool demeanor. "But if you don't stop the golems, they won't stop at us."

"Nidra wouldn't . . . he wouldn't . . ." But the refute died in Ardin's unfinished sentence.

"You don't know *that*." Asmara's eyes drifted beyond the walls in an unseeing stare. "Because you refuse to know all of him."

Platt. Marcus would have refuted anyone questioning her loyalty too, before . . .

"I don't want him to poison my heart," Ardin whispered.

"The part of you that sees the king for who he really is can also love him anyway." Asmara continued to stare off. "And *you* can reconcile that."

Ardin shook his head.

"Nidra still loves him," Asmara said. "Despite the hate, it's very apparent. You have to show him how you stayed by his side for so long."

"That demon whispers in his head." Ardin shook his head again.

"So then walk away." Marcus shrugged. "Let them go." It's what Marcus did when he let Platt go with Riley—what the three decided. They could have given chase, but in the end, he knew that forcing someone to love a person was futile.

"What?" Ardin snapped his head up, incensed.

Asmara smiled and sent a sparkling glance to Marcus before turning to Ardin. "Don't like that idea, do you?" Asmara gave a sweep of his arm and cast a glance to Marcus. "Then fight. Love is worthy of any battle."

Tiecus snorted in agreement and caught and held the mage's eyes a moment before looking away.

Marcus snapped back to his body. Sparkles outlined his vision. Nidra's mind was still locked with his. His lungs burned, and no air could pass through. Dying took an eternity.

Then . . .

The silt sank away. The mud eased from his throat. Marcus heaved sand, water, and blood to the surf below. Waves crashed against the cliff and sprayed a cool mist over his heated face.

"Ardin!" Valder's outburst echoed desperation.

The magician slumped over on all fours breathing heavily. "No," Ardin said and held a hand up. "Not quite."

The king froze, his mask of ice shuttered down his cautiously hopeful expression.

Mud and bones lay across the cliffside in piles. The golems were gone, back to their original form and harmless. Dirt piles towered high making the terrain difficult to maneuver. Though Nidra was not gone, only the magician remained.

"I need a moment." Ardin showed his palm to Valder.

But the king pressed. "Nidra? Ardin?"

"Damnit, you . . . you arrogant, self-centered, pompous excuse of a man!" Ardin turned his murky-blue eyes to Valder and railed. "Yes! Yes, we are both here! I am trying to process fifteen years of memories into one cohesive life. Can you give me a handful of minutes to jumble the pieces together without you clamoring for attention!"

Valder lifted an eyebrow and thinned his lips trying to hide the curl at the ends of his mouth. "My apologies. Heaven forbid I concern myself with your welfare."

"Our welfare or yours?" Ardin snapped back.

This time the king did not look amused, but he remained quiet. The splashing waves presented the only sound between any of them.

Five minutes passed as the warlock magician stood, paced the small cliff alcove, muttering. When he wasn't holding his head in his hands, he was looking out beyond the sea.

"Nidra? Ardin?" Valder's low voice carried over the sound of crashing waves.

"What?" The warlock magician turned to the king.

"Please come home." He reached out his arm, offering his hand though Ardin was twenty feet away.

"Why?" Ardin spat. "What for?"

Valder blinked, and his arm slowly fell to his side. He said nothing as if he were a man whose voice had been taken from him. Marcus remembered what Valder had said the night he left for Reginhart.

For all the directions a king can go, he can't make a move without advisors clamoring for an audience before a decision is made. A king can't make a statement without his subjects taking every word to heart. A king is surrounded at all times, has precious little secrets, has secrets he doesn't even know he possesses.

"Because it's your home," a voice from behind them answered.

Marcus turned and gazed upon the young Valder, the spindly, youthful king he knew.

"You should be back at the stronghold." The older Valder's voice rasped.

"A good lot that would do." The younger king smiled at his older counterpart. "He won't come with us if I leave this up to you."

"He needs time."

"He *needs* words." Young Valder licked his lips. "One you won't give him, but I can."

The older Valder cast his glance around. "Boy . . ."

Young Valder snorted, "Never realized how much of my father I have in me."

"Father was a great man." Older Valder stood tall.

The two stared each other down until Ardin squeaked out, "Eric?"

The young king skirted his counterpart and climbed the dirt, rushing over to whichever ego had control of Ardin's body.

"Don't come close." Ardin waved at him. "I don't really know if I want to drive a dagger in your heart or if I . . ." Pain and hope collided in Ardin's eyes.

"I'll risk it." The young Valder took his hands and stood with his back to Marcus and the older Valder.

Words.

Marcus had never given Platt words. He'd tried but did he ever tell her the most important ones?

No.

The young Valder's voice sent waves of garbled high and low words yet sincere sentences. Marcus watched Ardin's expression melt to pleading hope. The warlock magician hung on every spoken word. The struggle of who they wanted to be to each other shone through painful, longing looks and slight touches. Knowing humans, Marcus realized Valder and Ardin probably had a tenuous arrangement that could get them stoned, just like Jessica's maid.

"Don't you have some Tier Naug to chase down?" The older Valder turned his cold countenance toward Marcus.

He took the king's expression for the want of privacy Valder likely wanted to have and nodded. "Yes. I think it's time to go chase down a traitor."

Chapter 37

THE SILENCE WAS maddening. Yet Marcus kept Asmara and Tiecus in their respective shells, the places in his mind they retreated to in order to protect them. They were the voices of reason, and at this moment, he held no value in consequence.

He followed Riley's trail and lost track of how long his arm had been burning. The embroidered lettering charred his flesh. But he welcomed the fire. The searing heat staved off the dizzying lunacy and drove him to seek the youngling.

The boy could run, but Riley didn't have the stamina of a demon, and soon, Marcus had the youngling pinned between the ground and his claws.

Riley cried a sweet painful noise, and laughter bubbled from Marcus's chest. In the back of his mind, Marcus knew the blood loss, the pain, and his hunger for revenge created a heady cocktail for insanity. But his compassion had disappeared with Platt back at the stronghold.

He hauled the youngling's ankle up. "Where's Platt?"

The boy held still, dangling from one leg but didn't answer.

Marcus pitched the youngling against a tree. A sickening crack echoed against the forest. "Where is she?"

"I'll never tell." Riley spat out a tooth.

Marcus flung Riley on to his back, and the youngling heaved breaths, sucking in air as a fish out of water. "Just the invitation I needed." Marcus grabbed Riley by the throat and shoved his mind into the youngling. Sharp needles dug into Marcus's brain. Without regard to his own sanity, Marcus clawed at the ward.

Everyone had natural mind barriers. The more secrets one had, the more likely they would keep those secrets close. The more secrets, the more barriers. Blocking off a part of one's mind with things they didn't want disclosed created a natural barrier. Riley's mind held his secrets tightly wound.

But the youngling's mind was as ordinary as any human's. Silver strings attached like spider's silk connected from wall to wall. Balls of light ran from line to line. Riley was the height of smug. Sparks converged to one particularly pristine web. A memory—one engaging all the senses and revealing the meticulous perfection and order of the silver lines.

Curiosity peaked, and Marcus followed the lights into the preserved secret Riley held.

Platt picked her favorite berries behind her mother's home. Her hair was braided behind her back. Fingers slipped in between thorns for berries. Riley poked his head from behind a tree and whispered to her. She smiled at him, a genuine warmth that belonged to a best friend or a betrothed that struck Marcus so hard it hurt. It hurt to know she could smile with sincerity and passion. It hurt to know Riley was the cause.

Riley took her by the hand and led her behind a thick redwood, thick enough to hide them both from view of her house. He set her basket down and pinned her against the tree. The feel of her warm skin. Her soft skin. The gaze she turned to him stirred his insides. Riley couldn't wait to make her his wife.

As he kissed her attentively along the chin and neck, she wrapped her arms around him. His kisses moved to her mouth. The thrill of her tongue electrified his body. His hands wandered, touching everything yet not being able to feel all of her at once sent frustrating moans in his mouth.

"The spell you have me under," Riley said.

Platt giggled, and it was a sound of light and air.

Marcus had never heard such a noise before, and it enflamed his skin.

Riley began to hike her skirts up, but Platt stopped him.

"What are you doing?"

Riley started to grind his hips into hers. "I won't tell."

Her eyes grew so wide the whites of them made her face look smaller than it was. "No. Three more months."

Marcus groaned with Riley.

"I can't wait that long," Riley whispered. He started to fumble with the buttons on his pants.

"I'm going to call for mother if you don't stop." The twinkle in her eye and playful tone wasn't all that convincing. But he did stop. He'd do anything for her.

Riley kissed her hard on the mouth, and Platt softened and returned his kiss. He resumed pawing, and she stopped resisting the upward climb of her skirts. The skin of her legs was so soft it ripped a moan from him.

Platt squeaked, "Riley, wait."

"Platt, I need you," Riley whispered in her ear. "Please, please, please."

He pried his pants open at the front and searched with his manhood until he found the lips of her promise to him. She was ready for him no matter what came out of her mouth.

"But—" Platt's voice gave away temptation.

Her cry was more motivation to convince her to say yes.

"I won't tell." Riley spoke fast. "I swear I won't tell. I can't wait. I need you. You're going to be my wife. It won't matter. Please. Say yes."

The pressure in his body pushed him forward. He gripped his manhood holding back his animal instinct that urged him forward.

"No one will know?" Her eyes adoring, trusting, and full of need.

"Oh, god's woman! I'll chop my right hand off if I do."

Platt pulled back, but her eyes shone in excitement. "Yes."

His civility ended, and Riley pushed inside her. He barked in surprise and fell into bliss. He was making too much noise. The house and Rehan were nearby. Pumping mindlessly, he was frightened of discovery and excited at the prospect. It was almost too much to enjoy his first time with Platt. Almost. A wave of pleasure crashed into him, and his strength left with the current's ebb.

The crash pulled Marcus out of the demens, and he sat there, gaining his bearings.

Riley smiled at Marcus like a man who has bested his superior.

"That was the most enjoyable demens." Marcus smiled in grateful admiration. "It didn't even hurt to meld with you."

Riley's face fell.

"Show me again." Marcus sat back and gave a long, satisfied sigh. "I want to experience all of it. You held back."

"No." Riley's cheeks flamed red.

Marcus chuckled and brushed his claws against Riley's face. "I know what you expected. You thought I'd be disappointed that she wasn't 'pure.' But demons don't stone each other for ridiculous expectations."

Grasping Riley's right arm, Marcus stood. "Did you expect me to uphold human customs?"

The thought that Riley showed him the memory expecting his mind to change about Platt disturbed Marcus. He loved Platt. That would never change. He didn't wish her destruction. He didn't like Riley's attempt at hurting her. It was wrong to want to hurt her. But was he hurting her now by hurting Riley? Using the youngling to get to her? But . . . Riley had promised. And now, he'd broken his word.

Marcus raised the youngling's right hand and pursed his lips. "You told."

"No." Riley pulled against his grip. "No, I didn't tell; I showed. There's a difference."

"You broke your word." He held Riley's right hand, examining it. "And I don't feel like showing mercy contingent on technicalities."

Marcus swiped his claws along Riley's wrist. The detachment was clean and swift.

The youngling didn't scream. He'd gone straight to shock. Riley stared at his missing hand, pumping blood with every heartbeat.

Marcus wrapped his lips over Riley's stump, lavishing the life water squirting into his mouth. His strength returned. The blood brought back some of his reason. Not enough to let the mage or Tiecus out, but enough to drag the blood doll with him in search of Selkie.

THE VILLAGERS SHIFTED through broken homes, shattered wood, and demolished possessions when Marcus walked in the washed-out streets. The body he hauled slid side to side in the mud. He looked up trying to follow the bright eye, but the thing kept moving. His body ached. The smell of smoldering flesh followed him everywhere. He looked around to get his bearings, but his head hurt, and he couldn't focus. He turned to his cargo. Riley's unconscious body chased him, and he couldn't get rid of it. His mind remained fuzzy, but he'd wanted to deliver his cargo to . . . something. Someone. Plenty of someones existed in the village.

People stopped and watched in grim resignation as if this was what they had expected to happen.

"Stop." A woman with long colorless hair, blue eyes, and a beautiful face spoke words that floated on a breeze. She was familiar, and a knot of disappointment, glee, pain, and a lightening of his heart made him comply. Her words were not a command or a plea but spoken wisdom. "You can't kill him."

"Because you say so?" Marcus let go of Riley's leg and realized if he'd opened his hand earlier, the body wouldn't have chased him. He was angry but didn't know why. The burning overruled reason. This was the price paid for a broken oath. He just wasn't sure if it was his own or someone else's.

"You can't kill him because it will hurt you." She kept moving forward toward him never looking at the lump of flesh.

A flash of insight struck him lighting fast. The meat bag he carried behind him was a gift. For whom he couldn't remember. Lightning was like that. Here and gone.

He stood, processing the words, and then laughed. It was a sound Nidra would make.

She touched him with two fingers at his sternum. "It will hurt you here."

The touch seared into him, and he swatted at her arm.

She didn't seem hurt or offended and raised her face in open invitation. "If you kill him, then that spark I see in you that tries to be decent will die."

"Decent left me on the hill." Marcus furrowed his brow and pointed to the stronghold.

He was a shell, a place of pain. Parchment to burn at the whim of scribbles. He couldn't make sense of the tattoos on his body. To him, that's all they were. Intelligible markings that glowed and burned.

"When we met"—Platt laid her light touch on strands of his fly-away hair—"I felt you. You wanted me, not for my blood, but for what I could bring you. I wasn't prepared or strong enough then to hold you in that place, but I am now."

Three spheres of light coiling together brought the little doe's face in focus. Platt. Love and pain together in one person.

"You're saying this to save him." Marcus reeled. He only half knew what he was saying. But her riddles made sense to him. He remembered the place she spoke of. The place he tried to protect. "You're trying to confuse me so you can have your precious knight."

Real anger flashed across Platt's eyes. She backed a step and turned to look at Riley. She made a pointed look at Riley's missing right hand. Decision flashed over her face, and then her expression calmed into something more deadly.

Platt pulled out a cleverly hidden misericord from her bodice. The blade, triangular in shape, was a foot in length. Platt kneeled to Riley, kissed his lips, and touched his forehead. Swift, merciless, she plunged the misericord into Riley's heart.

The youngling hadn't moved or shown any indication that he was still alive. But the burn in Marcus's arm ceased. The cloud of pain began to evaporate.

Doubled over, Platt crouched with her back to Marcus. He couldn't see, but he thought she was clutching her heart.

Marcus stared at the youngling. He kept looking from Platt to the now certainly dead Riley.

Clear-blue eyes that pierced as deftly as her misericord turned to him. Her expression was soft and tinged with a sadness that drew him forward.

Marcus saw what she'd done but didn't believe it. After all, she'd gone with Riley, wanted him.

"I *did* care for him." The pain in her face drained, and that soft smile ripe with secrets emerged. "But he took me away from you. Any other that tries to remove me from your side will receive the same welcome."

He gaped at her trying to comprehend what was happening. Hope cleared the fog of insanity. Highlights of white-blonde reflected her hair. He'd never seen such a color on another human or demon. It made him want to clasp that liquid silver and never let go.

"I told you that I'd deceived you." She pointed at Riley's missing right hand. "Now you know what I kept from you."

His hoarse voice came out a whisper. "I experienced it."

Platt was again that small girl nearly a woman in a cold forest pleading with him. "Do you remember, you said to me once, if I told you no lies that you wouldn't try to force your way in."

Did he remember? Oh yes, he knew. He rubbed his hand across the agreement situated on his scalp. "I remember."

She squared off to him. Her entire body stiffened in the way humans did when they weren't sure of the outcome.

Platt drew a large breath and with every syllable emphasized said, "I do not love you."

He did nothing but stare at her. He didn't know what to feel or do. He stood there numb. The grasp of insanity loomed.

Platt's expression distorted, and her eyes welled up. She wasn't breathing. *Three times a lie and then you die.*

Tears streamed down her face, and she clasped her hands between his face. She wasn't breathing, and the magic of Ventus spun around her throat. Platt's lips turned white, and she blinked several times.

Marcus tossed groggy instinct aside and stared at her.

Three times a lie . . .

Her lips turned from pale to blue. She stared, tears streaming, waiting.

Three times a lie . . .

He rushed into her mind expecting the pain, but in a span of seconds, he understood . . . She'd given him the choice of her death.

She was a blood doll. A human-born demon. Like everyone in the village, Platt was a creature with demonic heritage. An elemental unlike anything else. He could argue their aspect was water with the power of being able to recover from being drained of blood. Therefore, blood dolls were susceptible to elemental rules. Rules such as . . . three times a lie and then you die.

Platt's mind was a chaotic stream of thoughts. Light bounced off strings and the inner wall of her brain. One thought broke to another and another. He tried to grab one, but they were as slippery as fish that dissolved at his touch.

Come back to me, Marcus called to her cavern of reckless regret. An entire room filled her sorrows and feeling of wrongs she'd done to him. She was apologizing with her life. In her mind, she deserved to face the consequences of her actions.

But Marcus wasn't willing to let her go.

She told him, not in so many words, that she'd betrayed him a year ago. Before they had even met.

His mind screamed with what she could do with her human customs.

Their connection dimmed and hazed. He was in her mind, and she wasn't breathing. She shoved at his mind, pushing him out with the intent to save him from her last moment.

In the physical world, he held her in his arms. Her eyes fluttered, and her body fell limp.

"Platt." He shook her. "You have to tell the truth to breathe."

She didn't breathe. Marcus did not know for how long.

"Platt!" He shook her, this time harder.

She didn't respond.

He would make her tell the truth.

His second demens wasn't as seamless as the first. His scalp burned, threatening what little sanity he had left. Marcus had to try. He wouldn't let her throw away her life, not as an apology. He ground his teeth knowing this would hurt them equally.

He bore into her unconscious mind.

His scalp burned anew. Her mind was closed. Their agreement was a ratio of one-to-one. One lie, one demens. The burning he'd endured for days had a cost. He screamed at his own weakness and tried again. This time he could smell burnt hair when he tried to demense her. It was too late.

He snarled at Ventus, clawing the air around her neck. "Let her go."

The element didn't care.

Her lips were blue, and her skin was turning deathly pale. Her life was slipping away in his arms.

Marcus shook her, screaming, "Platt."

She looked at peace. The kind of peace he'd been trying to find. He realized she had with her last breath shown him peace didn't come in the guise of an overwhelming force like love. Peace was subtle, slow, and more often than not, it was found with oneself, and not aside from life.

Sad acceptance was overtaking him. His eyes burned from the sting of tears. Bitter ones earned from great cost.

Her arms fell to her side, and her head lolled. He squeezed her body to him tighter than he had ever dared. It didn't matter now if he cracked her bones—she was gone, and he was already feeling the loss.

The smallest wisp of air escaped her lips in his crushing embrace. In that faint exhalation, Platt whispered the oldest hymn of beloveds understood in any language or across any barrier: "I love you."

He'd imagined the words in his insanity of course. He could even imagine Ventus lifting its harsh condition upon Platt as she breathed again. Marcus loosened his iron grip to see her face once more. Her head tilted back, and a faint inhalation, a strained huff, and the smell of her sweet breath smacked him in the face.

She was breathing. She *had* spoken. She *had* told the truth. She *did* love him. It was not a trick of his tortured mind. Platt had spoken the words he hadn't known he longed to hear.

He buried his face in the cover of her hair and allowed the salt and water escape from his eyes in quiet relief.

People gathered around lowering their heads, showing respect.

Humiliating sobs left his insides exhausted.

He lifted Platt in his arms, and people gathered around them. Rehan forced her way through the crowd and covered Platt's nose and mouth with a hand.

Marcus heard his little doe's heartbeat just before her mother wailed, "She's alive!"

Chapter 38

THE GRAVEYARD HAD the usual number of demons circling below the humans burying their dead. It had taken weeks to delegate the Tier Naug bodies to the burn piles, the Benicarian soldiers to honored pyres, and bury the villagers.

The residue of smoke and flesh seeped into the air, the clothes, the remaining trees, and left a thick rain of ash that fell as soft as snow.

Despite the golems being made with the bones of disturbed graves, the people of Reginhart were certain their loved ones would not return to haunt them. One grave in particular was smaller than the others with freshly raised dirt thick with water. It was marked by a headstone, and it stood upright even if the others had fallen over or washed away. It read "Jacob Thatcher."

Marcus stood at the end of the two worlds between the Atra Solumn and Brightside. His sanity returned, and he could approach the barrier without Tiecus frantic to run from the area.

An oath tingled on his tongue, words swearing this much destruction would never happen again. He would never be responsible for the deaths of so many. Platt lived, so he might be able to keep the unspoken promise.

"The journal helped?" Stillwood leaned his gnarled back against a tree, arms crossed.

Marcus slid his eyes to the old man. "How did you know?"

"The question is"—Stillwood pushed off the tree holding out one of the Tier Naug's weapons—"what will you do with it now?"

In the background, Tiecus pinned his ears.

Marcus no less considered what was offered. "I no longer need an arquebus."

"And yet, Ardin still wants one." Stillwood casually tossed the arquebus forcing Marcus to catch it or be clubbed by it. The long stalk thrummed in his clawed hand. "Besides, he held his end of the bargain." Stillwood raised an eyebrow that some would call a misplaced caterpillar. "It's only responsible to hold up yours."

Marcus tightened his grip on the arquebus remembering it was Stillwood who had helped Platt summon him from Benicar. "I find it strange that a magician should keep such a book unless, of course, that magician was guarding it from a warlock." Marcus shot Stillwood an accusatory glare.

Stillwood scolded with one bony finger. "Be careful about what chasms you look unto, Terci Uniter."

The name triggered a shivering ripple through his body, and Marcus pulled back, holding down an illogical aggression. "Why do you call me that?"

"Terci Uniter?" Stillwood looked at the skies. He had the focus of an artist wanting to paint what he saw. "That's what you are. Three united. The elemental, the focus, and the essence. And now you have the knowledge."

The pit of his stomach flipped, and he tried to see Stillwood not as a human but as a villager. He saw traces of Valder, Bolden, Rehan, and even Platt within the old man's confirmation, the eyes, the face, his stance. Stillwood's whole being could be a map of history. Reginhart's history. *Firstborn.*

"You should go see him before he leaves." Stillwood jerked his chin to point behind Marcus.

He spared a glance, but the graveyard was empty. When he looked back, Stillwood was gone.

On the Atra Solumn side, the smallest fawn he'd ever seen pranced with legs and knees not yet grown. The upside-down world mirrored the one above it. The world that Marcus stood and peered down upon reflected new graves. Just as above, so below. The fawn stopped and walked with a newborn cadence, first over Jacob's headstone on his side of the Atra Solumn, which he nudged with his nose, and then stood under Marcus. He pressed his muzzle to the ground and looked up into his face.

Marcus could almost feel the youngling's hands on his cheeks, eyes pleading to save the town from Tier Naug.

The faun's eyes were iridescent but retained an innocence, ignorance, and delight in life.

Marcus said a word, "Jacob." The fawn turned his ears to the forest beyond and darted off. Marcus shook himself convinced he was seeing what he wanted to see in the baby demon. He took the arquebus and walked to the east tower.

A PARADE OF horses pranced in the stronghold's east tower. They were lined up, crowding around the king's carriage. Valder and Ardin, now whole, remained behind in Reginhart while the dregs of the king's army marched to

Benicar. The monarch was his usual young self with exception to a bit of gray at his temples. Apparently, splitting his soul had aged him a few years, and the two Valders had not exactly wanted to become one seeing the advantages of duplicity. In the end, they had decided not to repeat Ardin and Nidra's mistake.

"Hail, Master Reginhart." Valder lifted his hand in greeting.

Marcus furrowed his brow. "You are leaving?"

"Are you sure you won't come with us?" Valder countered.

Ardin, back in his concealing robes, turned his hood to the arquebus in Marcus's hand.

"No." Marcus cast his gaze to the second floor of the tower and held out the weapon to the magician with warlock tendencies. "Here, Ardin. Our agreement is void."

Ardin lifted his hood, and the faint impression of a scowl sat behind the darkness, likely in readiness to argue.

Valder lifted a brow, turned to Ardin, and thinned his lips. "We talked about secrets—"

"It was from before." Ardin took the arquebus, and it immediately disappeared into his robes. Then the magician gave Marcus a begrudging thank-you.

"Well." Valder squared off with Marcus. "If I can't convince you to come with us, then you'll have to remain as Master Marcus Reginhart, keeper of the eye over the eastern seaport."

Ardin cackled, "Your cousin will have a fit. He'll seek reprimands as soon as you return."

Marcus surveyed the stronghold and waved his hand. "What seaport?"

The sparkle in Valder's eye shone in mischief. "You've rid the town of Tier Naug. I can now build a seaport in the alcove of Nidra's Bluff."

Ardin groaned, "We are not calling it that."

Valder laughed, light and innocent. "Why not? It's appropriate."

"That means there will be more humans here?" Marcus asked.

"Yes." Valder stood a foot shorter but placed his hands on Marcus's shoulders. "And you will oversee them all."

This did not sound like the peace Marcus had in mind. "Why?"

Valder huffed with a smile. "Because there's always been a demon in Reginhart."

"No . . . that's not what I meant."

But the king paid no heed to his question and gathered on the steps of the carriage. "If you see Dash, tell him I wish to continue negotiations."

Absolutely not, Asmara scoffed.

Marcus said nothing.

Valder quirked a lopsided smile as if he'd heard the mage and then entered the carriage.

"Do take care of her." A soft, sweet voice pulled Marcus to the side.

Jessica stood in her finest gold gown fit for travel and elegant enough to wave out at subjects from the carriage window.

"I will." Marcus received her hug without complaint, though it was not with the woman he wanted.

Too soon, soldiers filed out as the carriage travelled beyond the portcullis with one seneschal trailing behind on foot.

Cornelius said nothing and stared at Marcus. His eyes burning not only from a demon's riddling, but from a father's overprotective nature. Marcus was responsible for his two children. The only saving grace was Platt. Her faith in Marcus, proving he would destroy himself for her sake, had told her father in no uncertain terms that she and Tim were safest under Marcus's protection.

As Cornelius marched through the gate, wandering vines pulled the portcullis down, and ivy twisted through the iron bars so thick there wasn't light to see through. No means remained to tell Cornelius that Ardin's agreement concerning the arquebus had disappeared. That the flesh smoothed over completely where the scrawl once reminded him he'd wanted to go back to Benicar—but Marcus's agreement with Rehan to teach Timothy to destroy demons had not.

Chapter 39

HE DIDN'T DARE disturb Platt tonight. She hadn't batted an eye for Riley. But her brethren from Reginhart had been a different story. He'd waited this long. Knowing how she felt about him helped calm his desperate carnal claim.

Climbing the stairs, he stopped at his door and gazed up at the staircase to Platt's room. Longing pulled on his heart to continue up, but he decided not to disturb her just yet. He rested his forehead on the door and set his hand on the latch.

Internally, he was already slipping beside her and holding her naked body to his. The thought of rejection stopped him from traveling further down that daydream. He couldn't take it if she weren't ready for him. All the pleas and cajoling, all the agreements and vows . . .

If she didn't bond with him now, it would unravel his tentative sanity.

He walked the stairs another floor, stepped into his room quietly and turned to sit fireside to rest, only to find someone else was in the room with him.

Platt sat waiting on the rug by the hearth. Wet hair covered her glorious golden body. When she saw him, she stood with the only suit with which she'd been born.

All thought vacated. Only Platt existed.

The curves of her hips rolled with her movement. Her breasts rippled with each step mesmerizing him. He felt the slow draw of all the blood in his face retreat down his throat, below his chest, and into the seat of lust.

Her submission was intoxicating. Platt's languid steps made him want to drop to his knees—to proclaim her as his demoness. To serve pleasure in a manner his body wanted to provide, but he did not do these things. He stood locked in place.

Claws caught his peripheral vision. His arms had acquired a mind of their own much like the rest of his body, and he watched himself close his hands then opened them, imagining how he could touch Platt without hurting her.

She walked to him like she would keep going, entering his body as a demon did a host. Soft arms and nimble fingers, the kind that worked hours collecting berries, wrapped him in an embrace that conveyed one who needed and forgave.

With as much will, Marcus held her, molding her naked body to his clothed one.

She pulled back and parted her lips. "Yes."

In the span of a heartbeat, her lips were on his, desperate for any part of him to be inside her. His tongue stroked along the length of hers. She was slow and explorative. He was wild and uncontrolled trying to be everywhere at once.

Being fully clothed with her naked body against him was exhilarating. For once he wasn't the one exposed under critical eyes. He was shielded and could bask in her pure form.

Still . . . there were too many clothes. His heavy coat fell to the floor. She untied the front of his tunic and another layer of his cloth shield was forgotten, tossed to the ground. Her eyes wandered his chest in hunger making him want the exposure and give what he had for her. His body was an instrument; its sole purpose was to bond with her.

The belt came off next and clanked as it hit the floor. The silk material of his shirt flowed up caressing the organ manifesting his desire. He moaned, breaking away from their contact. It was the only opening Platt had to take his shirt off. He wouldn't have separated from her otherwise.

She pulled back and stared at him. This time he could tell she was looking beyond the tattooed agreement on his chest. Embossed contracts had been added, but she didn't pay them any mind. She was looking at his body as a whole. Her eyes filled with awe.

Slowly, deliberately, Marcus straightened to his full height allowing the range of his muscles to flex. Somewhere down the line he'd stepped back into a stone wall, and his shoulders leaned against it, his breaths thick, his chest heaving his desire.

Platt looked from his face to his chest to his pants and shrank the tiniest bit. Intertwining her wrists one over the other and entangling her fingers together, she reverted to the submissive doe.

She did not look down as he expected, but she swallowed. The bold woman who took him in hand a moment ago deflated to the little doe that fought with her fear.

Immediately, Asmara rushed to the front of his mind. *Stay still. Don't frighten her.*

"Platt," Marcus sighed her name.

As if he'd barked the words, she flicked her eyes to him.

"I won't hurt you." It was as much eloquence as he could muster, even with Asmara's coaching.

Platt lowered her eyes. "I know."

From his hardening length, his trousers cut into his front and back. The trews didn't have room to expand with the added length.

"There's a part of me that wants to meet you." He smiled as best he could. Marcus hoped it didn't come out as a grimace.

Platt looked at his crotch as if she were calculating.

Her first time was probably not enjoyable, Asmara said. *She's worried about your size.*

Marcus drawled out the vowel in her name. "Platt, I won't hurt you."

She unfolded her hands, closed her eyes, and swallowed.

As she breathed, Marcus undid the straps wrapped around his lower knees and took his boots off. His claws were still a major deterrent to unhooking his pants. He thought about ripping the material off.

"Little doe, I need help." He looked down at his pants and flexed his fingers accentuating his clawed state. "It hurts."

Dexterous fingers came to his rescue. The tension eased after she unhooked the front of his pants and helped him peel off the trews. For a long moment, he stood there allowing her to stare at him. He didn't move, and he took this glorious moment to explore her, if only with his eyes.

Her breasts were a perfect melon shape with hard pebble-like nipples. She had no straight lines anywhere on her body. Even her neck was curved to suit a swan.

Slender fingers reached, exploring the air, as Platt extended her hand to touch him. If she wasn't so timid, he would have thrust his length into her palm. Marcus laid his claws against the wall behind him, gritted his teeth, and held his breath willing himself not to respond to her curiosities.

Marcus would have lost all control without Asmara's help. The one reason he didn't pin her down and charge his way to their delight was the reasoning that he might hurt her.

His heart raced. Platt went from tentative touching to long strokes. There was no thought, only sensation. No words, only now. His hips convulsed involuntarily. It was like dry heaving—just as painful but without the relief of expelling the pressure.

Platt kneeled, and his mind exploded in overwhelmed sensitivity when she took him in her mouth. Her tongue rolled around his shaft. His body was in control now, mostly, and his hips thrust. One clawed hand found the back of her neck, and Marcus let his moan be the last of his control giving in to his body.

"Mmmm, you've been holding out on me." Marcus said with the lilt of Asmara's voice. "How do you know so much about pleasure?"

Platt smiled as she continued and did not answer. Her secrets were hers, but it seemed Riley had not shown all of his encounters with her. To the Triad's delight, she had more knowledge about the art of sex.

He kept his back flush with the wall and tilted his pelvis in a rhythm set by her.

Breathing like he was being chased, he focused his eyes and saw the moon peeking from the open air slit across the way. The voyeur made him smile. It was he who was going to bay to the "closing eye." He would remember this every time that pale moon became visible. He wanted Platt to see it too and looked down.

Watching her take him in sent a jolt up his stomach and made him more ready than before to let the tension overflow to release.

"Platt," he panted.

She didn't stop and kept pumping while a hand wrapped around his girth. Meeting his eyes, she continued to swallow him again and again.

Energy, slow, sensual, and powerful, entered his eyes in a demens fashion. The energy caressed the insides of his brain, floated down his spine, spreading warmth, and then moved down through his cock back into Platt's mouth to her eyes in an endless cycle bringing him faster to a climax.

It wasn't a demens or any demens he knew about. There was no thought or inclusion of a foreign mind inside. It was energy, alive and vital, but not invasive.

Marcus climbed higher and higher, but his climax didn't come.

Asmara was chanting—not fevered in the way when he hid for cover from violence, but slow and erotic. He got the impression the mage was doing something in accordance to extending their pleasure.

"Get on the recliner." He pulled her away and plunged his tongue into her mouth.

Where his hands were inhibited by claws, his tongue could explore. He wanted to chart every inch of her.

Platt set herself on the chair as if she were going to read, parted her hair, and laid it over herself covering her breasts, belly, and waist.

He hovered over her enjoying the sight of his manhood and Platt in the same view.

"If you continue to hide one beauty with another"—Marcus scraped his thumb and foreclaw together—"I might find it imperative to shorten your hair to where you can't hide any of those pleasing attributes."

With a sour expression, Platt reached up and entwined his own hanging strands around her fingers. She toyed with his hair then made a fist and pulled down. "You have no room to talk."

Laughing, he lowered down and kissed her. Her hand went to the base of his scalp, and she pulled his chin up. Marcus exposed his throat. Submitting to her sent a new swell of arousal. He could let go. She had control. Platt giving orders lifted a weight off his mind. He didn't have to worry about what she wanted. She was giving her own needs to herself. His arms and legs were taut but comfortable waiting for her command.

"Don't even jest at removing my hair, understand?"

"Yes." He remained still, chin toward the ceiling, body at the ready.

She let go, and when he returned her gaze, she wasn't afraid. She was calm and silently triumphant. He swallowed and smiled. With a knee he parted her legs, and because the recliner was built for only one, Platt had to spread her legs and set her feet on the floor.

Pushing her hair back with a knuckle, Marcus admired her dipped waist, soft stomach, and lean legs. Palm hovering over her breast, he moved his hands to see how best he could grasp the curves of her body.

When he couldn't find a way to touch her that didn't involve claws, he dropped his hand away and gave out a frustrated sigh. Instead of touching her, he tasted. His lips covered the enticing pebble of her breast, swirling his tongue in lazy circles.

Platt jerked her body in an arch of bliss. A surge of erotic, ego-based pleasure sent its lightning strike down to his core. He switched to the pebble's twin and did the same, gaining the same reaction. Nuzzling the underside of her breast, he continued down.

Fingers combed his hair and splayed out his black sheen blanket over her legs. His tongue trailed down her belly, searching for her folds and what the mage called the "pleasure button."

Eyes closed and panting, Platt remained in her position like a good little doe. He tested for a reaction on the outside of her lips and ventured inward. She quivered, but when he reached near the top of her horizontal "smile," he found a nodule that made her buck so hard he swiped his tongue over his gums checking for all his teeth.

"Sorry." She looked down at him with wild abandon that made his ego soar.

He grinned and lowered his head searching for that particular fleshy yet hard place. This time when she bucked, he held on and rode her through it. She pumped, squiggled, gyrated, and thrust, but never told him to stop. He kept going until she was too slippery to keep up with.

"Marcus." Her eyes glazed over with a bit of crazy. "Yes."

He could feel the smugness over every bit of his face. Marcus climbed up wiping his face on the back of his hand. His tongue was cold and worn, but it didn't stop him from letting her taste herself from his vantage point.

Holding firm, Marcus let the tip of his cock glide up and down the wet area of her folds.

"Lie to me," he said.

"What?" Platt startled. "No."

Marcus cursed himself. All egotistical superiority he felt turned sour. "I apologize. That was stated poorly."

"I don't want to lie to you," Platt said in a rush. "I don't ever want to lie to you again."

Marcus grazed his nose along her cheek. "I want to feel what it's like for you when I"—Marcus dipped the tip of his manhood inside her—"enter you."

"No. It hurts you."

He raised a knuckle to her lips. "The demens will only take a moment. Tiecus will bond us as fast as he can, but we need to be united in body and mind to do it."

She held his face in her hands. "Isn't there another way? Can't we annul the agreement?"

Marcus pressed his face to her chest. "I was trying to protect you when I made that agreement."

"I know." She sounded sad and resigned.

Platt raised his face up and looked into his eyes. Her gaze was unfocused and beyond him. A faint glow around the rim of her pupil oscillated in the same manner as fire. Marcus was intent on the growing light. This time, when he looked into her eyes, he did feel the pressure of a demens.

The pressure grew and Marcus realized the impossibility of a human being able to reach inside another's awareness but cried in pleasure when Platt penetrated the natural defenses of his mind. Her demens was ink spreading its curls along the currents of his mind. Her thoughts clouded over him, inside him, and through him.

He could feel what she felt, and the sensation was overwhelming. He pushed his body, their body, inside. Intense pleasure and relief echoed in their minds sharing the same experience in different ways.

He started pulling out to push back in at her unspoken request. Frenzy and pure heat from desire guided their bodies. Marcus stopped directing his thrusts and descended into the pleasure. They found a pace of mutual enjoyment letting go of any resistance.

Marcus loved how he made her feel. Her sensations felt richer in her body. Where he climbed, she descended. He pushed forward, and she gave way for him to go deeper. Except . . .

Marcus stopped pumping and mentally reentered his own body, pushing her into hers. He was holding her in his lap. Shame filled her face, and he was holding his anger back determined to use it as an energy source. He pumped in and out of her again, this time faster than before.

They weren't bonding. The connection waved like string in a windstorm unable to attach to Platt's heart. Every time the string caught hold of her center, it was thrown off. Cramps down the back of his thighs didn't stop him. His body ached. Beads of sweat ran down his back, but Platt kept the demens open, and he continued. He was determined to pump his way into her heart.

If they didn't bond, if the string didn't connect, then the vows he took would essentially mean nothing to Tiecus. It wasn't a matter of wanting to bond with her—it was her heart rejecting the ties. It was not that she did not love him or trust him. But damage had been done that hadn't been repaired.

Sweaty, tired, and rolling solutions in his mind to this challenge, Marcus stopped.

"Don't quit." She pulled him close.

She felt his exhaustion. She was just as worn.

"We can try later." Attempting to hide his disappointment was futile.

Panic rose from her gut and spread to her heart, which only threw the tentative connection off with more vigor.

He didn't need to voice it. Platt could feel what he was thinking. Still, he had to get the poison out.

"Riley," he sneered.

They couldn't bond. She loved Marcus, but her heart had unresolved issues with the youngling. And he was dead.

Platt wrapped her arms around him. He reached inside, into his core, and lifted his intangible tribute to her. He poured out what he felt for her. Words couldn't express the warmth, the pride, how he needed to be worthy of her. She felt his heart in raw form.

Her tears came hot and fierce. Marcus saw through her memories the hope, the lost trust, the devastation of betrayal, shame, and helpless fear she bore for so long. This was what she'd held on to, and the emotions were attached to Riley.

Connected in mind and body, Marcus rocked them back and forth in a slow rhythm. Her tears of guilt poured.

He wanted to tell her they were making memories without the youngling, and as soon as he thought it, she knew his words.

She draped over him, letting him make love to her. Slow, gentle movements retained more than pleasure. Their connection went deeper than physical. He let her cry. At her request, he continued rocking them back and forth.

It was enough to be inside her. He wouldn't leave her because the demon's bond went unconnected. He didn't need to know what she was thinking or feeling every moment. He could ask, and she would tell him.

Water stopped flowing from her eyes. The weight of lies and secrets lifted from her chest. Her heart felt hollow. Hollow enough to fill with forgiveness. Forgiveness of herself. The string waiting to connect two hearts waved inside.

Her body opened, expelling doubt. She drew Marcus inside. Their tenuous connection, the elusive bond, clicked in place and held.

Her demens fell away, yet he could still feel her. His body shuddered in release. Her body responded contracting around him in several spasms. The closing eye was the only witness to their bonding, complete and final.

Epilog

THE SOFT PLIABLE cloth felt too delicate to hold in his hands. Thumbs inside his fists, Marcus scooped the leather into his forearms afraid to tear the ancient skin.

"Are you sure?" Marcus whispered to Asmara.

Platt was still asleep on the recliner. He didn't want to wake her. If he did, he might have to explain his actions, and she might tempt him against the decision. But it was not hers to make.

"Once he sees this, we'll never see him again."

I am sure. Asmara's resolve was final.

Marcus walked in the cadence befitting a funeral. It was in a way. Selkie's longing cries at the ocean clenched their decision to finally set the demon steed free. When Marcus opened the door, Selkie stood motionless near the remnants of the stable. With a clear view to the ocean, the demon steed stared into the distance and nickered at the crashing waves.

Marcus shuffled the skin in his hands. Selkie's skin. The demon steed's ocean skin. Two flukes and a dorsal fin dangled from one side. The blue-green scales shimmered from fish oil religiously applied to it for the past two decades. The upper half, from the waist up, was the shape of man. It too was treated but with a different oil. Asmara hadn't said what kind. The face adorned two eye holes, two nose holes, two ears, and a mouth that was wide open without muscle underneath to keep it closed. The middle was split open and could have been used as a cloak with a fish tail.

Marcus shuffled the nine-foot-long leather. He was trying to think of what to say.

Sorry, I didn't give this to you earlier seemed insincere. *Thank you for hauling my arse around with the hope that I'd give back your underwater form* also didn't seem appropriate.

When Asmara had stolen the half-man, half-fish skin when the Selkie had shed it to play on land, the demon steed had been gracious. Instead of running or threatening the mage to give back what was his, Selkie had chosen to serve Asmara.

The demon steed had befriended the Serenite by choice. Perhaps because he'd been bested. Perhaps he saw no other way to get his skin back. Whatever the reason, Selkie had been genial not bereft. When it came to losing, Marcus couldn't say the same.

But it had been a long service, and Selkie clearly missed the ocean. Animosity had a way of growing when one forced another to forego their desire. That Marcus knew.

Selkie's eye rolled to the long trail of leather draping end to end off Marcus's arms. The demon steed's tension shifted from longing to the death pounce of a cougar demon. Selkie had never looked more dangerous. Marcus considered putting the skin on the ground and backing away before Selkie leaped.

The skin and Selkie were gone before Marcus could react.

Marcus ran toward the ocean, over the wall of ivy and the vines that waved from the touch of Ventus. He scaled the bluff, and when he reached the sand, Marcus allowed the tide to careen around his boots while scanning the water. Selkie was gone.

His mainstay had left him as eagerly as if drinking blood. Marcus brought his hands to his face and closed his eyes.

Well, that's done. Asmara washed himself of the departure.

Harsh words, but Marcus understood the mage better than before. Apathy was a type of defense. A guard against the cruelties of life.

"Give a message from me to Asmara."

Marcus snapped his eyes open and put his hands down.

A half-man, half-fish "stood" on an arched tail covered in scales. Selkie reached two feet taller than Marcus in his ocean form.

The shell hadn't given justice to the creature before him. Calling this regal being proud was too humble a word. Scales glowed blue, green, gold, silver, and reflected like a mirror. His upper half was strong and wide, cart-horse wide, and his skin was a golden yellow. The eyes were a waterfall, the way water trickles down stone constantly running down. They were blue and cold.

Selkie slithered forward leaving a wide indentation on the beach.

Marcus bowed his head. "Asmara is listening."

Water engulfed Marcus's face. Marcus choked on a wave. How the ocean got to be at an odd angle he wasn't sure. The world was sideways. No. He was sideways. To be precise, he was lying in the sand on his left side, allowing the tide to roll over his body. He sat up before another wave could choke him, and he probed his jaw. His face was sore. His whole skull felt bruised. The sky spun. His former demon steed walloped quite a punch.

Selkie rose up on his flukes with crossed arms and weary, angry eyes. "If I hear from these sand bars of a selchie missing, I will be back."

Marcus got that he'd be back, unhappy, and not in the mood to talk.

"This wasn't easy." Marcus gestured to Selkie. The lower hinge of his mouth cracked.

Selkie relented and sighed. "Yes. I understand that." Then after a moment, the selchie dropped his arms to his side. "Was it Platt?"

"That let me give back your skin?" Marcus got to his knees. He was too dizzy to stand. "By the bright star, what did you hit me with?"

Selkie gave a champion's smile and splashed the rolling tide with one of his flukes. Scales bounced morning light into Marcus's face. Selkie looked back at the sea and returned his cold glare at Marcus. "Treat her well, old friend."

Marcus snorted and raised a brow at the tone of what *friend* meant to Selkie.

Selkie grinned. A genuine smile belonging to an adored cohort. "My hide is soft, my scales are moist, my skin you took care. That of I am grateful."

Marcus rose, half expecting to be tail slammed again, yet wanting to say more. He wanted to demense Selkie and give him the knowledge of the guilt Marcus had felt over keeping his skin hidden. But he wasn't going to intrude, and he didn't have the words.

Selkie chuckled in cold mocking that sounded much like a nicker. The tide rolled in, and Marcus stepped back from the sea water. The selchie melted into the swell as a double wave struggled to get to shore. When the tide stopped fighting the waves, and the water reached the beach in its exhausted collapse, Selkie's head slipped underwater and did not resurface.

Marcus felt oddly relieved. He hadn't known Selkie's captivity weighed on him as much as it had. But the sense of loss, when a friend is gone forever, ached more than his chin.

His bereavement was also his peace. He'd done something right, something just.

A stream of warmth spread through his heart. Platt was awake. She shared his contented sadness. And he finally grasped what Tiecus had meant. For so long, he had thought isolation would bring the demon under control, and estrangement would appease the mage. Nothing could be further from the truth.

After dusting off the sand, and returning to the tower, he found a book on the floor. Blank pages stared up at him except for one sentence that came and faded. *I will find you.*

It made Marcus smile and write back to Ignatius. *Then come.*

The threat could not disturb his peace, especially in the folds of an embrace. Contentment was lying with Platt and not needing words or thought. Happiness resided. Fulfillment came at the cost of protecting his town from invaders.

He gathered his mate in his arms letting gratefulness follow the bond to her heart. The string remained strong and lively. Marcus grinned at the wisdom of a demon. Tiecus was right. Peace doesn't mean alone.

The End

Acknowledgements

Penn Scripter would like to thank all those wonderful people who believe and supported us along our journey to create *The Demon of Reginhart* which took five years in the making!

First, thank you to our life partners, Donald Weller and Mark McKibben. You don't get mad when we yell, "I'm in the zone!" Or "Go away, I'm writing!" You both often make sure we eat something. That great because otherwise we might fall on our faces.

Next, thank you to Julia Rohwedder for our beautiful cover design and Ravi for his amazing editing skills.

A heartfelt thank you goes to the following people who believe in us enough to support our cause. We could not have published this book without your love and support!

Andrea Michaels
Franny Jaynes
Jane Plant
John Daly
Lauren Hicks
Lee Brown
Mark McKibben

Natalie Hicks
Rett Hicks
Shelly Scallan
Leftwich
Tracy LeBlanc

About Penn Scripter

Penn Scripter is the nom de plume for the writing team of S.N. and Carol McKibben. This mother-daughter combo writes unexpected paranormal romance. Separately, they each have a healthy list of novels.

The two authors have combined their talents and interests to produce unexpected paranormal romance that will include fantasy, mythology, paranormal, dogs and horses, relationships, unusual circumstances, and, of course, romance.

Unexpected Paranormal Romance